Restitution

Restitution

Susanne M. Beck

Renaissance Alliance Publishing, Inc.
Nederland, Texas

ISBN 1-930928-65-3

First Printing 2001

9 8 7 6 5 4 3 2 1

Cover art and design by Mary A. Sannis

Published by:

Renaissance Alliance Publishing, Inc.
PMB 238, 8691 9th Avenue
Port Arthur, Texas 77642-8025

Find us on the World Wide Web at
http://www.rapbooks.com

Printed in the United States of America

Thanks go out to too many to name, but I'll sure try my best! To Kricket, Pudderbear, Lynda, Sulli, Elizabeth B., Elizabeth and Mary (if they ever read this, I'll be shocked!), Carol, Judi, MaryD, Lunacy, Missy, the folks on the SnQ list, RAP for their wonderful support every step of the way, Mom, Dad, Paul, Steph, Julia, Alex, every person who ever wrote to me and enjoyed my attempt at entertainment, and a million and one other people who I'll be kicking myself later for forgetting to mention. Thanks, guys! It's been a blast.

For Sheri.

You know why.

Chapter 1

Time is the coin of your life. It is the only coin you have, and only you can determine how it will be spent. Be careful lest you let other people spend it for you.

My mother always loved Carl Sandburg. I don't know why. Reading one of his poems has always reminded me of the smell of chalk dust and mimeograph ink and the droning voice of Mrs. Davis, demanding I come forward and recite his works "by rote, Miss Moore, if you please."

I never liked Mrs. Davis.

I liked Sandburg even less.

And yet, without any conscious desire, I found that quote echoing through my brain as I sat on a high-backed wooden pew near the center of the very same courtroom where, seven years ago almost to the day, my life as I knew it came to an end.

Courtrooms are interesting animals. Like prisons, they turn a blind eye to the passage of time as the rest of society knows it. Fads mean nothing. The change of seasons is measured only by the amount of overclothes the visitors enter with. To the victim, the wheels are ponderous in their slowness. To the accused, only lightning moves more quickly.

Justice, that blindfolded woman with scales in one hand and a book in the other, simply grinds on, unseeing and uncaring, bound by laws which have stood for centuries, nearly unchanged from when they were first set down.

Time, rather than a coin, seemed a tunnel through which past and present sped to merge and meld in one finite space, affecting me with a queer sense of déjà vu. Though now I was sitting behind the gate that separated accused from victim instead of in front of it as I had seven years ago, my purpose was essentially the same.

I was fighting for my life.

And though the fight was very much a silent one, it was fought with more intensity and more desperation than I had ever fought for anything before.

And, as was the case seven years ago, I was losing.

Badly.

Come on, Ice. I know you know I'm here. I know you know I've been here since the trial started. Just turn around. Please. I need to see your face. I need to know that you're all right. I need to know that...you don't hate me.

If my eyes had been laser beams, they would have bored a hole straight through her skull, such was the intensity of my unconscious pleading. However, since God had seen fit to only bless me with optical light catching devices, my continual stare was about as effective as putting rain galoshes on chickens.

Which is to say not very effective at all.

A murmur through the spectator section, followed by the judge's pounding gavel, broke me from my musings and I looked around, startled.

"Order in the court! There will be silence in this courtroom!" As the gavel pounded again, the noise quieted and I turned to look at Corinne, who was seated to my left, my eyebrows raised in question.

"Donita just asked for a directed verdict," my friend whispered, her lips very close to my ear, the comforting smell of her sachet drowning out, for the moment at least, the pungent odor of too many people packed too closely together in an almost airless room.

"What's a directed verdict?" I asked, softly as I could so as not to bring the attention of the imposing female judge to bear on me.

"It basically means that the defense believes that the prosecution's case is so weak that it doesn't need to put on a case of its own and wants her to render a verdict right away."

"But that's crazy!" I said, a bit louder than I'd intended.

Quite a bit louder, I noticed, as the judge's dark eyes, magnified to the size of golf-balls behind her huge tortoise-shell glasses, aimed their angered gaze at me. "For those of you who have difficulty with simple comprehension," she said in a voice that simply oozed exaggerated patience, "I'll repeat myself one final time. If any of you even thinks about making another noise while this court is in session, I will personally have you escorted out of my courtroom and into a rather uncomfortable jail cell for the remainder of the day. Am I making myself perfectly clear?"

If a tornado had chosen that exact spot in which to cause a little mischief, I wouldn't have been at all adverse to just spinning away. When the sky chose instead to remain blue and sunny, I sunk down into my seat as low as I was able and tied my best not to notice as my neighbors moved quickly away, as if just learning that I was the reincarnation of Typhoid Mary herself.

When absolute, pin-dropping silence reigned in the courtroom once again, the judge nodded authoritatively and switched her gaze toward the front of the room. "Both counsels, approach the bench, please."

I watched as Donita stood and smoothed the skirt of her bright red power suit before approaching the bench, the prosecutor following closely behind. Then I turned back to Corinne, making sure to keep my voice at its lowest register. "That's crazy. Has she even been listening to the prosecution's case? I think they'll be putting this in the law dictionary next to the description of 'open and shut.'"

"One might think so, yes," she whispered back. "But then again, Donita's always been somewhat of a card shark. I'm sure she has an ace or two up her sleeve."

"God, I hope you're right." Turning, I once again faced the front of the courtroom, my gaze fixed upon the glossy black head of my lover who was staring, as she had from day one of the trial, straight ahead.

"She knows you're here, Angel," Corinne whispered, reading my thoughts.

"Then why won't she look at me? It's been three months, Corinne. Three *months*!" I bit the inside of my cheek to keep my voice down as I felt the sting of tears welling up in my eyes.

An entire season had passed since that fateful, horrid night in late summer when my world was shattered, seemingly beyond repair. A season of tears, of guilt, of hopelessness. A season of repeated trips to the Bog, only to be turned away at the door. A season of unanswered phone calls and returned letters. A season of not eating and not sleeping.

And now, after three full months spent dying an hour at a time, I was finally close enough to touch her and she wouldn't even look my way.

"I'm sure she has her reasons, Angel."

Only then did I take my eyes off my disinterested lover, pinning Corinne to her seat with my glare. "I just hope you never find out how heartily sick I am of that piss poor excuse for an explanation, Corinne."

A good deal less than injured by my withering words, Corinne calmly turned her head forward, appearing to watch the still-silent proceedings with intent interest and leaving me, once again, to fume alone.

A clack of heels against the highly varnished wooden floor brought my attention back to the front of the courtroom. Donita caught my eye and smiled faintly before turning and resuming her seat next to my lover. I felt an irrational flash of white-hot jealousy as their heads bowed together intimately, Ice nodding and responding to her beautiful lawyer in a way I'd only known her to do with me.

Enough of that, Angel, I said, barely able to keep from voicing my thoughts aloud. *She's on trial here and that woman up there just happens to be the best damn shot she has of getting out of this mess.*

Still, I couldn't help but breathe a sigh of relief when Ice nodded and they separated, both assuming identical postures of quiet confidence as they awaited the judge's next words.

"This court will be in recess indefinitely. I expect both counsels to meet in my chambers at noon tomorrow. Dismissed."

The gavel banged as the bailiff stepped forward. "All rise."

Feeling strangely part of an extremely Fundamentalist religious congregation—Pentecostals raised to the fiftieth power, perhaps—I rose in communion with my fellow attendees, and watched as the diminutive judge, who wouldn't see five feet if she stood on tiptoes on the New York City White Pages, gathered her robes and left the courtroom through a rear door situated just to the left of her bench.

Then the jury, composed of five white men and seven white women, left through yet another door, ushered out by the ever-helpful bailiff. Their faces were expressionless as they filed out one by one, obedient children exiting the classroom on the last day of school.

Only when the final juror had left the courtroom was yet a third door opened, this one admitting four large and well armed guards, two of whom were bearing, like cruel vestments to a fallen Queen, shackles and chains with which to keep society safe from the woman I loved.

Ice stood relaxed as they wound the belly chain around her narrow waist, holding her wrists easily out to be cuffed together by an officious guard as the rest stood by watching, hands on their holstered weapons. Even in flats, she towered over them all, looking elegant and refined and the very antithesis of a chained animal in her expensively tailored black suit.

Her wrists secured, another guard knelt, getting an up close and personal view of legs which went on forever—a view that I would have killed for at that point in time or any other—as he attached the leg shackles to her ankles and rose once again, an almost sheepish smile gracing his otherwise somber face.

It might have been funny, this elaborate and ritualistic chaining of a woman beautiful enough to have stepped fresh from the cover of a fashion magazine, if not for the always present air of danger which hovered around her like a tarnished halo which is almost—but not quite—visible.

I could feel my neighbors react to it as she stretched casually, the chains jangling with her easy movements, the long, muscular lines of her perfect body hardly hidden beneath the expensive cut of her suit.

All around me, the crowd of onlookers tensed, as if the courtroom was the Roman Coliseum and Ice, the hungry lion.

Would the beast leave in peace or would it feed?

I swore I could hear at least one exhale of disappointment as Ice obediently took up her position within the center of the phalanx of guards, never once looking at anything save for the space directly in front of her, now occupied by the balding head of a guard as he led the processional from the courtroom.

Quiet murmurs rose in the vacuum left behind and I felt the walls closing in on me once again. "I've got to get out of here," I said to Corinne, blindly shouldering my way through the milling crowd, my lungs heaving and my stomach lurching. Of my heart, there was no sound. It had already been broken and so lay quietly as the rest of my body rebelled.

I could feel Corinne following in my wake, but I spared her not so much as a passing thought, such was my need to be free from the room that held within its walls only the worst days of my life.

I went out through the open doors and didn't stop until I was standing outside on the steps, hands on my knees and gasping in great, sobbing lungfuls of air. My head was spinning as if I'd just stepped off a carnival ride and I found my vision reduced to a point of light at my feet.

I'm gonna faint! I thought in disbelief just as my knees started to buckle.

Fortunately, my soon-to-be intimate acquaintance with hard cement was mercifully halted by a pair of strong arms that wrapped themselves around me and pulled me back up to my feet.

When my vision finally broadened its scope, it was Donita's beautiful face I saw, her eyes narrowed in concern as she looked down at me. "Are you alright, Angel?"

I shook my head to clear it, which was a really bad idea as it almost served to start the whole process going all over again. Her arms tightened around me and I fell gratefully into her concerned embrace, using the safety and strength she offered to gather my own before somewhat reluctantly pulling away. "Yeah, I'm fine. I think."

She smiled a little. "You think?"

"Well, I've never almost fainted before, so I can't be too sure."

Her smile broadened as she fully released me, draping instead one long arm over my shoulder and guiding me away from the crowds and down the stairs. "Well, let's get you into the shade so you don't almost do it again, ok?"

"That sounds...really good right now."

Corinne attached herself to my other side, and together we walked onto the courthouse's winter-brown lawn and under a denuded oak that nevertheless provided at least a modicum of relief from the surprisingly powerful November sun.

Faux marble benches surrounded a round cement table, and I gratefully sat down on one, absorbing the stone's cool smoothness into my overheated and overstressed body. After a moment, feeling much more like my normal, albeit empty, self, I looked up at Donita, who was still standing, one elegant hand on the table's top. "Forgive me for sounding impertinent, but why are you here? Shouldn't you be with Ice?"

"She's on her way back to the Bog. I'll catch up to her later."

"The Bog? Why aren't they keeping her here for the trial?"

"She's an escape risk. The court doesn't think its little county jail can hold her."

I shook my head in disbelief. "Did they forget that she gave herself up to the police?" I didn't know how they possibly could. It was a scene that haunted every minute of my life.

Donita laughed softly. "That doesn't matter to them. She's a dangerous criminal, so they say. She escapes again and heads will roll."

"So then, why are you here?"

Sitting down across from me, she laid her briefcase on the table and crossed her hands over it. "Because you need to be in the judge's chambers with us tomorrow, Angel. It's very important that you're there."

A feeling curiously akin to dread rolled through me, but this time I was prepared and simply went with it. "You mind telling me why?"

"I can't. Not yet. You'll know tomorrow, though."

The not-good-enough answer paled, though, in comparison to the question I hesitated to ask.

"Yes," Donita said, answering it anyway. "She'll be there."

"Then so will I."

Reaching out, she gave my hands a squeeze before standing up and gathering her briefcase once again. "Thank you, Angel. I'll see you tomorrow then. Goodbye for now. Goodbye, Corinne."

She had gotten three steps away, maybe five, when I found myself bolting to my feet. "Donita!"

"Yes?" she asked, turning partway around.

"Tell her...would you tell her that I love her?"

Her smile was almost sad as she nodded. "I will."

"Thanks."

"Goodbye, Angel."

"Bye," I whispered as she turned away.

I looked up as Corinne's warm hand landed softly on my shoulder. "C'mon," she said, jerking her head to the left, "let's get out of this miserable waste of prime real estate before the birds start mistaking us for lawn ornaments needing to be decorated."

Smiling a little, I squeezed her hand. "If you don't mind, I think I'll stay here for a little while. You go on ahead. I'll grab a taxi and meet you back at the hotel."

"Are you sure? I could stay, if you like."

I nodded. "I'm sure. I'll be back in a little while."

"Alright then." Her sachet filled my senses again as she leaned down and gave me a gentle kiss on the cheek. "Stay strong, Angel. This is happening for a reason. Tomorrow, you'll find out what it is."

"I hope you're right, Corinne."

"I'm always right, Angel."

I watched her as she walked across the lawn and stepped into a waiting taxi. Only when the bright yellow car pulled away did I rest my head down on the cool table, closing my eyes and summoning up the image of my lover as I remembered her: free and beautiful, her eyes filled with love.

"God, Ice," I whispered, "I miss you."

The clock struck the quarter-hour as I was led into the chambers of one Judge Judith Allyson Baumgarten-Bernstein, a name longer than she was tall, and that by a long, tongue-twisting mile and a half.

Since my only previous exposure to judges' chambers came from the television show *Night Court*, I didn't know exactly what to expect as I stepped through the massive oaken door which guarded her inner sanctum sanctorum like a blind sphinx guarding the secrets of Egyptian tombs.

Night Court must have had some legal advisor, I thought as I took a quick, and not very subtle, look around after first assuring myself that I was the first to arrive. *Either that or a guy who spent way too much time in courtrooms. On the wrong side.*

Early Urban Decay it wasn't, but in all other aspects, all that was missing was a hulking seven-foot bailiff to make it seem as if I'd walked right onto a studio set somewhere. All the requisite and familiar trappings were there: framed law degrees, letters of commendation from one high ranking—and name-dropping, no doubt—citizen after another, leather bound books standing in staid rows upon scarred bookshelves, a coat rack behind the door, even a picture sitting atop a broad, varnished desk. Only instead of Mel Torme, the framed photograph showed a bespectacled young man in cap and gown looking so much like the good judge herself that he didn't have any hope of being anyone other than her son.

And, in the center of it all, the battleground; a large square table with chairs three to a side, it's highly polished top shining smugly in the recessed lighting, taunting me with the myriad of secrets it alone could tell.

As I stood fingering the chair-back furthest from the judge's desk, the door opened to admit a smiling Donita, dressed in another of her endless supply of knock-out power suits, this one a brilliant green. After giving me a warm and friendly hug, she pulled out a chair for me before seating herself to my immediate right and placing her briefcase atop the table.

"Is she here?" I asked, the first question always in my mind.

"Yes, she's here."

I nodded and then swallowed. "Does she know I'm here?"

"She does."

Before I could open my mouth to ask another question, the Prosecutor hurried in, giving us both a brief glance as he sat down and looked at his watch as if to remind us that his time was much too valuable to be wasted on the likes of us.

He was the epitome of every prosecutor, living, dead or fictional, that I've ever seen. *Keebler must stamp them out,* I thought, biting the inside of my cheek as I pictured the little elves working hard in their tree house making prosecutor after prosecutor after prosecutor and boxing them up for shipment to parts unknown.

Dark suit with regimental tie, straight brown hair cut by someone with very steady hands and not a creative bone in her body, and features so blandly handsome that you'd forget him the moment you passed him bleeding in the gutter.

Which, of course, is exactly where I imagined him.

Just as I was about to slip his tie knot up so high and so tight against his neck that the next sound he made would have been a wheezing gasp instead of an aggrieved sigh, the door opened and the judge sailed in, her black robes billowing out behind her like the sails on a very tiny pirate ship going full steam into an unfortunate harbor.

"I'm so glad you all could make it on time," she commented as she sat in a chair at the head of the table, looking at each of us in turn. The stare she gave me let me know in no uncertain terms that she remembered my little outburst in her courtroom, and that her offer of a cozy jail cell for the night was still very much open if I was so inclined to react in a similar fashion while in her presence.

I was tempted to tell her that jail cells held no fear for me, but somehow I think she already knew.

"Well, if we're ready to proceed, have the bailiff bring in the defendant."

Four pairs of eyes, none more anticipatory than mine, went toward the door opposite of the one through which I'd entered as it opened to admit two stone-faced guards followed close behind by the chained and shackled guest of honor. Resplendent in her bright orange prison jumpsuit, she looked exactly as she had the first time I'd laid eyes on her; cool, calm, collected, and fitting her name to an absolute "T."

As always, my heart sped and my mouth dried at the sight of her and it took every single bit of strength I had not to jump up and rush over to her; not to put my arms around her and bury my face in the sweet warmth of her flesh; not to grab one of the guard's holstered weapons and attempt a jailbreak, guns ablazing.

The look in her eyes as they met mine, however, stopped those notions unborn. Glittering and silver, her eyes were absolutely empty and absolutely dead, as if her soul had already departed for greener pastures, leaving only the shell of her body behind.

An involuntary shudder ran through my whole body and only the warmth of Donita's hand atop mine gave me the strength to stay where I was and return the look she gave me with one as warm and as loving as it was possible for me to give.

With a gentle jangling of chains, Ice gracefully sat down on the chair the guard had pulled out for her, her eyes finally leaving mine and turning instead to the judge, who stared back, her expression unreadable.

"Well," the judge began after a moment, her voice sounding just a shade less confident than before, "since we're all present and accounted for, shall we begin?"

Both lawyers opened their briefcases, pulling out thick manila envelopes stuffed full of papers. The prosecutor opened his folder first, pulled out a very thick document covered stem to stern with typed writing, and slid it over to the judge, who adjusted her glasses and began to read.

Completely lost and trying my best not to fidget, I chose to spend the quiet time waiting by looking at Ice and reading the tale of her capture in the gaunt, pale lines of her face. Lines which told me that the past three months had not been any kinder to her than they had to me.

And though to a stranger her posture appeared completely relaxed and completely confident, I could tell by the tense interplay of muscles across her broad back that she was wound tighter than a watch spring.

After some time had passed, the judge finally looked up from the document before her, her eyes slightly narrowed. "This is...rather irregular."

The prosecutor nodded, folding his long-fingered hands over the open folder. "I know it is, Your Honor, but it's within the bounds of the law."

"I realize that," she snapped back, pushing the document back across the table at him. "Or did you think these robes came as a prize at the bottom of a box of Cracker Jack?"

Donita snorted softly as the Prosecutor blushed and lanced a rather weak glare at her.

"And you agreed to this?" the Judge asked Donita, the tone of her voice conveying her disbelief.

"We did, Your Honor."

Shaking her head in amazement, the Judge turned back to the Prosecutor. "Read the agreement aloud, if you'd be so kind, so everyone here knows what's going on."

My look of infinite gratitude was disdainfully ignored.

Clearing his throat and adjusting his tie, the Prosecutor lifted the document and scanned it. "The People agree to drop all charges against the defendant, Morgan Steele, relating to her escape from the Rainwater Women's Correctional Facility and in addition agree to ask the Judge to commute her previous sentence to time served."

My immediate impulse to jump up and scream my joy—the Judge's order be damned—drained out of me the minute I realized he wasn't quite through.

"The defendant will be released on her own recognizance on the condition that she assist law enforcement in the apprehension and subsequent conviction of Joseph Cavallo. She will be under the constant scrutiny of said law enforcement officers and will have a period of time decided in advance by the State in which to affect a capture. If she fails in this duty, the plea agreement will become null and void, and she will be once again remanded back into the custody of the State and forced to serve her full sentence in addition to any further penalty the judge wishes to impose upon her for the escape. The People will, of course, ask for the maximum penalty to be added onto the end of her sentence."

"No," I whispered, before slamming my hands down on the desk and jumping to my feet. "No! This is ridiculous! Ice, you can't do this! Donita, tell her!"

"Sit down, Ms. Moore," the judge ordered, her eyes flashing neon warnings behind the thick glass of her spectacles.

"No! Not until somebody yells 'April Fool!' Donita, you can't let her do this! You can't just throw her back in the pit she's tried so hard to crawl out of! You can't!"

"Sit *down*, Ms. Moore! I won't tell you again!"

"Why are you doing this?" I demanded, ignoring her. "Donita, why? You can win this thing! Her conviction was a sham! You know that! Why don't you *fight*?"

"Bailiff!"

"Angel, sit down," Donita said finally, her dark eyes pleading. "Please."

Angrily shrugging off the meaty hand, which landed on my shoulder, I finally returned to my seat, hitting the leather padding so hard my teeth clacked together, almost severing my tongue.

A nod from the judge, and the bailiff returned to his place by the door.

"Continue," the judge ordered.

The prosecutor rattled his papers, sighed, and spoke again. "In addition, should the defendant satisfactorily fulfill the duties spelled out in this plea agreement, no legal action will be taken against one Tyler Moore for aiding and abetting the escape of a fugitive from justice, and further, no legal action will be taken against Ms. Moore for knowingly harboring a fugitive from justice. Should she fail, Ms. Moore will be prosecuted on these two charges, as well as any others the State deems appropriate, to the fullest extent of the law."

A jaw frozen in utter rage now hung slack as I realized that the Sword of Damocles, which had hung suspended over Ice's head had stopped being the Bog and had started being me.

"Son of a bitch," I whispered, turning to the prosecutor. "You god damned *son* of a *bitch*!" Reaching out quickly, I grabbed his necktie and yanked him halfway across the table with it, my heart thundering painfully in my ears and my vision washed red with my rage.

"Angel, no!" Donita's voice sounded far away as she grabbed me from behind and spun me to face her. "Don't do this, Angel."

"Why? Because they'll arrest me? Fine! Great! I *want* them to arrest me. In fact, I demand it!" I whirled back to the prosecutor who was staring at me as if he were the rabbit and I was the barreling semi. I held out my wrists to him. "Go ahead! Arrest me! I won't fight you! I'll make it easy for you! Put the cuffs on! Throw me in jail! I admit it! I'm guilty! I harbored a fugitive! I just assaulted someone! Arrest me, god damn it!"

"Angel, don't—"

"*Arrest me*!" I screamed before the sobs won out and I crumpled into Donita's warm embrace. I heard the sound of chains jangling, but I couldn't see my lover as the lawyer blocked my view.

"I know this isn't exactly protocol," I heard Donita say over my head, "but could you give us a moment, Your Honor? Please?"

After a long, silent, and tense moment, the judge's eyes softened just slightly and as I watched, she slowly nodded and rose from her position at the table's head. "A moment only, Ms. Bonnsuer, and the guards will remain inside."

"Thank you, Your Honor."

Without answering, the judge tapped the still frozen prosecutor on the shoulder, and together they made their way out of her chambers, closing the door softly behind them.

Gathering what remained of my strength, I pulled away from Donita's firm embrace, sidestepped her grab for me, and walked resolutely to where my partner was now standing, her bound hands clasped so tightly that the white of her knuckles stood out even against the prison-bleached pallor of her normally bronzed skin.

Though my mind ran riot with a million and one questions, my lips, I'm afraid, could articulate only one. "Why?"

Though her eyes were steel walls behind which her emotions were trapped, I could see things warring behind them, fighting their damnedest to come out. But, with the stubborn and determined strength of will which awed even me, who had been exposed to it on a daily basis for more years than I cared to count, her face maintained its expressionless cast—a granite mountain against which no water flowed to soften and change its blank and foreboding facade.

The only sign that the woman I loved was somewhere beneath all that careful blankness was the faint tremor which ran, almost unnoticed, over her tightly clenched fists.

Reaching out a trembling hand of my own, I almost—almost—touched the warm flesh bared to my eyes, but drew back at the last second and covered my mouth instead. "Please, Ice. Why? Please answer me. I deserve that, at least."

If I thought my pleas would fall on anything other than deaf ears, I was sorely mistaken. It was as if the sound of my voice raised the shutters in her ever-changing eyes, closing them off to me once again. And with them, I feared, her soul as well.

And that angered me. I had been through too much heart-ache, too much guilt, and too many tears to just give up without a fight. "Answer me, Ice."

Squaring her broad shoulders and lifting her chin, she tore her gaze away from mine, leaving a gaping hole where my heart used to lay.

All around me, the world seemed to grow faint and unimportant. I felt as if part of me had painlessly detached itself from the rest of my body and stood hovering somewhere above my head. "*Answer me, damnit!*"

Was that really my voice, sounding so small and so scared?

Was that really my arm, raising itself up into the periphery of my vision?

Was that really my hand, striking a brand across my lover's pale face with the speed of a striking viper?

The sound of the slap, ringing like a rifle shot through the room's still, stifled air, brought me back to myself much too quickly. As I watched, utterly horrified at what I had done, the blooming, bloody rose of my handprint appeared on her cheek, a death-writ outlined in stark, blinding white.

For the second time in as many days, I felt the world spin out of control as my legs buckled beneath me. This time, however, I welcomed the darkness I knew would follow.

Darkness which was staved off yet again as a pair of warm, living hands reached out at the last second and grabbed me by my shirt front, pulling me up and holding me steady.

Forcing the black spots from my vision, I looked up into eyes which had grown dark not with anger but with profound understanding, immense sorrow, and more than a little respect.

"Ice?" I whispered, not sure if what I was seeing was real.

"Angel." Her voice was rough and harsh and cracked, as if it hadn't seen use in a century, or maybe two.

Anything more that might have been said was lost as a large

guard came up from behind her and pulled his nightstick tight across her neck, jerking her backward. Her hands released their grip on mine quickly so as not to pull me along with her. Just as quickly, I was grabbed from behind and pulled away.

"No!" I yelled, trying to reach her with the very tips of my fingers as the distance between us grew.

Across from me, Ice mirrored my attempts, stretching her long, strong hands out to the limits of her chains. The very tips of our fingers brushed together for the tiniest of seconds before slipping away once again.

"No!" I screamed once again, trying every trick I knew to squirm out of the death grip my captor had imposed upon me. A low, rumbling grunt told me I was on the right track, and, encouraged, I redoubled my efforts, fighting for all I was worth to escape the guard's hold.

A nightstick found its way against my windpipe then, blocking my breathing for an agonizing moment. My panic reflex kicked in and I gasped for air that just wasn't there anymore. My arms came up quickly to try to pluck the club away long enough to gasp in a breath, but I might as well have been trying to pull a boulder from a mountain, for all the good the effort did me.

A roar that I first took for oxygen-starved blood pounding a desperate riff against my eardrums started out low, then gained strength and volume until the entire world seemed full of its primal, agonized rage.

Though I'm sure the guard's only thought at that moment was for my safety, as well as his own, he had managed to do the one thing that would guarantee him a death warrant as valid as if the governor himself had signed it.

He had touched me against my will.

And if my partner had anything to do with it, by the look in her eyes and the sound of her howl, it would be the last thing he *ever* touched.

Fighting against every instinctual response within me, I forced myself to go completely limp in his arms. No doubt surprised by this unexpected action, the guard let go.

It was the only thing that saved his life.

Blindly stepping forward while gasping for badly needed breath, I ran into Ice's onrushing form. Somehow, even in the state she was in, she must have recognized me because I felt her still-cuffed hands latch once again onto the front of my shirt and pull me close against her tightly coiled body. I threw my arms around her and hugged her for all I was worth, my lungs still heaving, and my sinuses filled with her wonderful, heady and desperately missed scent.

Four guards hit us a bare second later; the American justice system's version of a goal-line stand, with me as the football and Ice as the halfback.

This is getting to be a very bad habit, I thought as my legs buckled under me once again.

Her stance compromised by the manacles on her ankles, Ice couldn't stop me from falling this time, but she managed to cover me with her body as we were both borne to the ground under the weight of the guards. Her long form protected me completely, her bound hands landing in a place where, had this been anywhere other than a judge's chambers, I would have been enjoying myself immensely. A soft grunt of air was the only indication I had that the guards were doing more to Ice than just trying to pull her off me.

Which, of course, started me seeing red once again.

Before I could do anything with my anger, however, Ice's body was once again separated from mine and she was hauled back to her feet, the nightstick making an unwelcome reappearance against her throat. I scrambled back to my feet, a stream of invectives raunchy enough to make an entire whorehouse blush dancing on my tongue.

The door chose that moment to fly open and the judge ran in, followed closely behind by the prosecutor. At the sight of her, everyone froze as if she was the principle and we all had lit cigarettes in our hands.

"What's going on here?" the judge demanded, hands on her hips.

"Prisoner was attacking that woman," one of the guards supplied, jerking his nightstick against Ice's throat for good measure, though she obviously wasn't trying to get away.

"Do that again and you'll be standing on a street corner begging for quarters," Donita warned, pinning the guard with an angry glare.

Contrite, the guard loosened his hold. Which was a very good thing for him, because if he had maintained it just one second longer, he would have been wishing that Ice had killed him. I quickly turned to the judge. "That's not what happened."

One eyebrow appeared from behind the protective shield of

her glasses. "Then would you mind explaining just what *did* happen, Ms. Moore?"

"I...um...I slapped her."

I've never seen anyone's eyes go quite that large, my mind helpfully supplied as I watched the judge look from me, to Ice, and back to me again. "Ok, so I admit it wasn't the smartest thing to do."

The judge smiled slightly. "Has anyone ever told you you have the gift of understatement, Ms. Moore?"

"More than once, Your Honor."

"Mm. And then she attacked you?"

"She *didn't* attack me. After I realized what I'd done, I sort of...collapsed. She just kept me from falling. Then the guards tried to separate us and...well...you walked in on the end of what happened after that."

The judge eyed each of the guards in turn. "Is she speaking the truth?"

"Looked like she was bein' attacked to me," a guard mumbled.

"And the rest of you?"

The remaining guards seemed to be suddenly afflicted with cases of spontaneous laryngitis.

"I see. Do you wish to press charges?"

"She *didn't* attack me, Your Honor!!"

"I wasn't speaking to you, Ms. Moore."

"No." The answer came from Ice, and there was just a hint of humor coloring the low, liquid melody of her words. "I believe I'll live."

A gentle knock sounded, and a bailiff's head appeared through the opened doorway. "They're ready for you, Your Honor."

"I'll be right there, Mr. James." Walking back to the table, she hefted the thick plea agreement. "While you children were busy playing, the prosecutor filled me in on some of the background on this case. While highly irregular, he is correct in saying that it fits within the bounds of the law. That being the case, if there are no objections from either party, I'll sign off on this agreement and you can all be on your way."

"No objections, Your Honor," the prosecutor said.

"No objections," Donita added quickly, obviously afraid I might say something to squelch the deal at the twelfth hour.

Biting my tongue, I turned my head to look Ice square in the eyes. The dazzling blue threatened to swallow me whole. *Trust me, Angel,* her eyes said simply.

And though it killed me to do so, knowing exactly what that trust entailed, in the end, I simply had no choice. "No objections," I whispered.

The look in her eyes made everything I'd gone through in the past three months fade silently away as the strength and power of her undying love filled me once again, leaving me almost giddy with its return.

Donita's sigh of relief was audible as the judge bent over the table and, with a flourish of the President signing a détente between two warring third-world countries, inked her Jane Hancock on the document that would send my lover back down into darkness.

Though no more words passed between us, the look of utter and undying love remained in Ice's brilliant eyes as the guards, more gently this time, led her out of the room, closing the door behind them.

"What happens now?" I asked Donita after a few moments spent staring at the door in the hopes that it would reopen again and Ice would come back to me.

Closing her briefcase with an authoritative snap, Donita put her arm around my shoulders and gently led me from the room. "That's something we need to talk about."

"Why don't I think I'm going to like hearing what you have to say?"

"Most likely because you won't," she answered honestly.

Together, we walked down the hallway, out of the courthouse and back to the sheltered table out on the lawn, the silence growing pregnant between us.

After we both claimed seats, Donita reached out and grasped my hand. She smiled slightly. "As part of the plea agreement, the prosecution wanted you placed in the Witness Protection Program," she began.

"What? Why?"

"For starters, you're the only one who can identify Cavallo as Ice's shooter back in the Bog. And we're gonna need every shred of evidence we can dig up just to make sure he's convicted on charges that won't be overturned somewhere down the line."

"Surely you've got more than that one shooting to pin on him."

"Yes, but he's a snake, and he has an even bigger snake for a lawyer. That man could get Satan off if he wanted to." I thought I heard a grudging admiration in her tone, but when I looked up, her eyes were filled with nothing but revulsion.

"Well, I hope you and everyone else knows that I'm not going to go for that."

She smiled. "No, I know you won't. It took a bit of doing, but I managed to convince the prosecutor to release you, as it were, into my custody."

"Which means?"

"Which means that it's my responsibility to make sure you don't decide to take another midnight stroll over the border, Angel."

I could feel my back stiffen and my teeth clench at her words. "The last time I checked, Donita, I was still an American citizen," I began, my tone as frosty as my lover's name. "Has something changed that I'm not aware of?"

"No."

"Then why am I under house arrest?"

Donita sighed. "You're not under house arrest, Angel. If you recall, I'm trying to keep that from happening here."

"How, Donita? And more importantly, why? Since I seem to be the cornerstone upon which this entire house of cards is being built, don't you think I deserve to know?"

"Angel, I've told you about all I can tell you. I'm operating under some pretty severe constraints here. Lawyer-client privilege being the smallest among them."

"Then I guess there isn't anything else to talk about, is there?" I said, well aware that I was being churlish and not caring one little bit. Standing up, I looked down at her without smiling. "Thanks. I'll be going now. And don't worry about me leaving the country. Canada holds nothing for me now."

"Angel, wait," she called before I had gotten more than four steps away.

I stopped, but didn't turn around.

A bare moment later, her warm presence filled the space at my side. "I'm sorry. I know this hasn't been easy on you."

"You're right. It hasn't." After deliberating for a second, I turned to her. "Donita, I watched the woman I love more than I love anything in this world taken from our home in chains. I've spent three months realizing that I never knew what true Hell was until I found myself actually living in it. Every avenue I've tried has been a dead end. Every call for help I've made has resulted in yet another door being slammed in my face. And then, when I finally think I'm going to get some answers, I find out that not only isn't the journey going to end, it's only just beginning. I'm sure you'll forgive me if that makes me sound a little bitter. I just can't seem to help myself."

She laid a tentative hand on my shoulder, her eyes warm with compassion. "You have every reason to be bitter, Angel. In fact, I'm surprised that you aren't taking this worse than you are."

"Well, I'll admit that buying a gun and going down to the Bog to break Ice out has a certain appeal right now," I admitted.

She laughed softly. "I'm sure it does. Truth be known, it holds a certain amount of appeal for me as well. Even if it isn't a realistic solution."

"Then what is?"

Her shoulders slumped. "None of it, Angel. We're all between a rock and a hard place here. There's more going on with Cavallo than you know. Suffice it to say that he has some friends in some very high places and those friends have a vested interest in making sure he doesn't get caught."

I felt myself relaxing a little, knowing that she was trying her best to tell me things she shouldn't in the only way she could. "Why Ice, though? Her 'special skills' aside, she's one woman. What can she do that the police, or whoever, can't?"

"She can get the job done. She knows how he thinks, how he acts, what he'll do. She's been where he is and she knows his weaknesses. She's the best person for the job, to put it as simply as I can."

After thinking on her words for a moment, I nodded. "Can you answer me one more question, though?"

"If I can, Angel."

"Why didn't you fight it?" I held up a hand as she opened up her mouth to speak. "I know that, no matter how strong of a case you have, there's always a possibility that the verdict could come back against you. Believe me, no one knows that better. But...even if it did, and even if I was charged and convicted, as horrible as this may sound to you, I'd be happier in prison with her than free without her."

She smiled. "It doesn't sound horrible, Angel. But it just

wouldn't happen."

"What do you mean?"

Looking down at the ground, she looked to be preparing her words carefully. "Since Ice has been recaptured, Angel, she's spent twenty-three hours a day in the Hole. Not because she's done anything wrong, but because she's considered a huge escape risk."

"That's inhuman! They can't just keep her there forever!" I could feel my whole body go numb with the thought of what that would do to her, my mind going back to the last time she'd been kept in the Hole, and the shell of a woman she'd become because of it.

"No, they can't. If they tried, I'd have so many protestors outside the Bog the warden would think that what happened with Corinne was a little pep rally in comparison." She laid a hand on my arm. "He knows it, too. That's why, as soon as the trial is over, he wants her transferred out."

"So, even if I was convicted, we wouldn't be together." When the thought sunk in, I began to realize just why it was that Ice had agreed to the plea bargain. It also helped to explain the returned letters and the rest I'd been suffering through for the past three months.

"I'm afraid not."

"When will I get to see her?"

"I don't know. Probably not for quite some time." Though her words rang true to my ears, there was some sort of knowledge hidden deep within her eyes that, try as I might, I just couldn't decipher. And I also knew that she could tell I saw it there. Those same eyes begged me not to ask the question she couldn't answer.

With a sigh, I relented somewhat. "So, I'll ask again. What happens now?"

"The most important thing is for you to be kept safe during all this." Her smile was slightly lopsided. "The prosecution may have to answer to the people who want Cavallo's ass, but *I* have to answer to Ice. And personally, if something were to go wrong, I'd rather be them than me. *They* only run the risk of being fired...."

As her voice trailed off, I couldn't help laughing a little, knowing her words for truth though some small part of me resented the hell out of the implication that I couldn't keep myself safe. The rest of me, however, well remembered my last run in with Cavallo's men and wasn't too proud to accept help when it was offered.

"I have some friends who are very happy to give you a place to stay for the duration. They're good people, Angel, and they have a very safe, very secluded ranch south of Tucson in Arizona."

"Arizona? But that's...."

Grasping both of my shoulders, Donita looked me dead in the eye. "Cavallo isn't here, Angel."

"What? What does that have...?"

"He's not *here*." Once again, those deep chocolate eyes begged me to take what she was saying at face value and to please just have faith in her explanation, poor though it was.

Now, I might not always be the brightest bulb in the bunch, but on occasion, I *am* known for putting two and two together and coming up with the requisite four. "So, if Cavallo isn't *here*," I said, putting the same emphasis on the word, "he just might be somewhere, say, to the southwest of Pittsburgh?"

Her smile was quite knowing. "It's a big old world out there, Angel. Who knows what little part of it he's stinking up?"

Faith has always been somewhat of an elusive enemy to me. Just when I think I have it in my grasp, just when I think I've been rewarded for having it, it slips away yet again, leaving me damning myself for being foolish enough to believe in its existence in the first place.

And now I was being asked to grasp hold of it again.

Or maybe not. Faith is one animal. Belief, however, is another. And even if I didn't believe in Donita—which I did, my belief in Ice, even after everything that had happened since her capture, remained absolutely bedrock.

And I knew, with every fiber of my being, that while Donita might be saying the words to me, Ice was the one pulling the strings.

So, in the end, the choice was a simple one. The mountain was high, but I knew without doubt that there would be a safety net well able to cushion the fall should I choose to damn the height and take the leap. And with that knowledge, I did the only thing I could do. The only thing my heart and soul would allow me to.

I believed.

Donita must have seen it in my eyes, or in the set of my jaw, because she smiled and squeezed my hand. "You're a very special woman, Angel."

"Yeah, well, that's not always the gift people make it out to be. I have doubts, too, just like anyone else."

"I know, Angel," she replied. "And I know it's hard. If there was anything more I could do to make it easier on you, I would. I hope you know that."

"I do know that, Donita. Believe me, if I didn't, I wouldn't be here talking to you right now." After a beat of silence, I released her hand and looked up at her. "Arizona, huh?"

"Arizona."

The way she grinned at me, I got the feeling that a little time spent in warmth and perpetual sunshine just might not be such a bad idea after all.

"She's...big," I commented to my lawyer as we watched a woman the size of a small mountain make her way from the large sedan parked at the courthouse curb to the table we were currently occupying. Of obvious Native American ancestry, she had a long fall of deep black hair which ended below her waist, deep copper skin covered with intricate tattoos, intense almond eyes more black than a storm-tossed night, and the body of a female Arnold Schwarzenegger, pre-heart attack. Massive arms thick with muscle eased out from a sleeveless flannel, swinging easily with every step she took. Legs as solid and as huge as full-grown oaks strained the seams of well-worn jeans.

Staring at her as she approached, I was forced to admit the true inadequacy of my words. To call the woman simply "big" was akin to calling my lover "pretty." True? Yes. But hardly fitting the grandeur of the sight presented.

Before Donita could respond, if indeed she was even planning to, the woman stopped a foot or so in front of us both, all but filling up my vision with her sheer size. The two of us stood, Donita's smile warm and welcoming. "Angel, I'd like to introduce you to my friend, Rio. Rio, this is Angel."

Mirroring Donita's expression, I held out a hand. "Hello, Rio. It's nice to meet you."

The reverse, however, was quite obviously untrue.

It was almost as if I were meeting Mouse or Derby for the first time back in the Bog, such was the chill that wrapped itself around my body as she looked at me. Her flat, black eyes held not even the faintest flicker of warmth, and her expression told me in no uncertain terms that she had assessed me carefully and found me wanting.

The woman who exited the Bog, however, was so changed from the one who entered it as to be a different person entirely. And *that* woman had changed even more during the last year. Instead of looking down and away as I might have once upon a time, I met her stare, look for look, feeling nothing more than a vague disquiet as the seconds blended slowly into minutes.

It was Donita who finally halted the standoff by stepping in between the two of us and laying a hand on my arm while looking at Rio. "Are the bags packed?"

"They're in the trunk."

"Everything's ready, then?"

"Yeah."

"Thanks. We'll be along in a minute."

"Fine."

And with that, she turned on her heel and started back the way she had come.

"If that's a taste of things to come, Donita, I think I'll take my chances with Cavallo," I half-whispered as Rio took up a stance beside the car and stared out into the light traffic as if daring someone to hit her.

"I'm...not sure what's wrong with her, Angel. Normally, she's one of the sweetest people I know."

"Maybe she has something against green-eyed blondes."

"No. Not at all. She's a little reserved at times, yes, but—"

"*Reserved*? I don't know if you've noticed, Donita, but that woman makes Ice seem like a regular Chatty Kathy!"

With a somewhat rueful smile, she turned to face me. "Just give her a little time to get to know you, Angel. She really *is* a good person, and before you know it, she'll be joining your fan club just like everyone else who meets you."

"I don't need fans, Donita. What I need right now is someone who doesn't look at me as if I'm something they just stepped in on the sidewalk. Believe me, I have no desire to find myself being scraped off the bottom of her shoe somewhere."

"That'll never happen, Angel. I promise. Please, just give it a chance?"

After a moment, I shrugged. "Why not? Worse comes to worst, I still have Corinne and her magic teakettle on my side."

Laughing, Donita threw her arms around me and pulled me

close, kissing me on the cheek. "You're one in a million, Angel," she whispered into my ear. "And Ice is one hell of a lucky woman."

"You just remind her of that when you see her again," I said, only half-joking. Giving her a final hug, I pulled away. "Thanks, my friend. Although it might not seem like it right now, I really do appreciate everything you've done. I don't know where Ice or I would be without you."

"It's my pleasure," she replied, her dark eyes sparkling. "You just be careful and stay safe, alright?"

"Will do."

"Let's go then."

Side by side, we walked over to the huge silver sedan, a car that might have been all the rage prior to the oil crisis, but was now, in these days of streamlining, big enough to qualify for its own Congressman. Though I had no wish to be treated like a passenger in a taxi, Rio's body language spelled out explicitly that I was either going to ride in the back with Corinne, or be forced to brush up on my hitchhiking skills if I ever intended to see Arizona.

Never having hitchhiked, I wisely opted for the former and slid into the back of the gigantic car with alacrity, pulling my feet in quickly lest they be amputated by a swiftly slammed door. "Service with a snarl," I remarked softly to Corinne as I tried to adjust clothing rucked up into uncomfortable crevices by my abrupt entry into the car.

"So I noticed. This behavior is rather unlike her."

I turned round eyes to her. "You *know* her?"

"Indeed I do."

Which, of course, could mean only one thing. "The Bog, right?"

"It's not as if I've been making friends and influencing people anywhere else, Angel," Corrine replied, nudging me a bit. "Not for the past forty-some-odd years, at any rate."

"Please don't tell me I have another Derby on my hands," I moaned.

Corinne snorted. "As if Ice would allow someone like that within a hundred miles of you."

My reply was abruptly silenced as the driver's side door opened and Rio slid her massive bulk behind the wheel. Nary a word was passed between us as, with a roar of the engine and the squeal of rubber against road, I found myself moving forward into yet another unknown future. Only this time, the miles weren't leading me into a future ripe with almost limitless, wonderful possibilities. They, rather, were leading me away from the only possibility I wanted—needed—in my life.

Ice.

It took every single atom of waning strength I possessed not to jump across the seat and wrestle the wheel away from the behemoth babysitter I'd so recently—and reluctantly—acquired. Even the thought of what my face would look like after I failed miserably in the attempt didn't sway me.

The remembered look in Ice's eyes as she silently asked me to have faith did the trick, however, and with fists clenched and jaw set, I slumped back against the worn, soft leather of the back seat and watched through weary, saddened eyes as the miles sped by.

Somewhere about three hours later, by my inadequate reckoning, too many nights of too little sleep combined with the soothing sway of the big car had made my eyelids grow heavy and drooping, the way they used to when I was a young child riding in the back of my father's station wagon.

With that strange clairvoyance she always seemed to possess, Corinne read my mind like one of her precious library books and, giving me a warm grin, patted her lap. Well past the point of playing dentist to a gifted stallion, I took her up on her invitation without a second's passing. Letting the comforting scent of her fill my senses, I felt myself drifting off into what I hoped would be a peaceful slumber.

It was a warm summer's day.

The kind so perfect that it seemed to have been made just for me.

The sky, a brilliant, untouchable blue, seemed the perfect playground for the newly-born sun.

I found myself sitting beneath the welcoming shade of a towering pine, ostensibly writing in my journal. What I was really doing, however, was watching the splendor that was my lover as she laid out on the wooden raft which floated, buoyed up by empty oil drums, about fifty yards into the center of the lake.

Resting back on her elbows, her head tipped back so the wet, inky mass of her hair trailed along the weathered wood, eyes closed and lips parted just slightly, and both long, tanned legs stretched out to their fullest, she seemed the poster child for every boy's first solitary foray into nocturnal bliss.

I felt a surge of jealousy as I watched the sun make sweet love to her bronzed and beautiful form.

My journal dropping unnoticed to the fragrant nest of pine needles, I stood and shucked off the long T-shirt which was covering my bathing suit, tossing it thoughtlessly god knows where as I ran down over the narrow beach and into the tepid water, suddenly unable to stand one more second separated from her.

My arms warmed to their task quickly, pulling me easily along through the water. Having long ago memorized the exact number of strokes needed to get from shore to raft, I stuck my hand out blindly at number forty, pulling up in surprise when it encountered nothing but air.

Blinking droplets from my eyes, I tread water, trying to discover if what I thought I was seeing was really what I was, in fact, seeing.

The raft was exactly as far away as it had been when I started swimming.

If I hadn't known for absolute truth that the raft was anchored to the lakebed with a secure cement plug, I might have thought Ice was having me on.

"Ice?" I asked, well knowing she would hear me over the still waters of the lake. We were the only ones there, after all.

If she heard me, she chose to ignore my summons, seemingly content with the sun's relentless seduction of her body.

Shrugging mental shoulders, I struck out once again, carefully counting my strokes and willing myself nearer with each one to the woman who was my heart.

Something brushed against the bottom of my foot, but I took it for an inquisitive fish and continued on unafraid.

When the contact was repeated, I kicked out strongly, my foot landing against a soft, giving surface. A surface which was most definitely not a fish. Unless I'd missed the biology class that would have let me know that fish had suddenly developed the ability—not to mention appendages—needed to grasp a person's ankle and yank. Hard.

Just managing a startled breath before I was pulled under, I kicked for all I was worth, using every trick Ice had taught me in our years together, as well as a few panic induced ones that she hadn't.

Finally able to break free a split second before the need to take a breath would have resulted in a rather rapid drowning, I rose to the surface and filled my lungs with sweet, sweet air instead.

"Ice!" I screamed when I had the lungs for it, hearing the sheer panic in my voice as my lover's name echoed over the lake.

Any chance at seeing her response ended abruptly as the hand, joined now by others, found purchase on my flailing legs and again pulled me swiftly beneath the now frigid water.

Forcing my eyes to remain open, I looked down and almost screamed again as I saw the grinning, water-bloated corpses of Carmine and his minions gathering around me like sharks to a bleeding whale. Blood oozed out from the bullet holes each had suffered, turning the water murky and dark as their hands, slimy and rotting, wrapped themselves around my ankles, wrists, and waist.

Twisting with all of my strength, I was able to break away, using the bodies beneath me to push off and shoot to the surface.

My relief was short-lived, however, and after one quick gasp, I was pulled under yet again. And I knew without doubt that my first taste of freedom would also be my last.

Just when the lack of oxygen began to become a seductive Siren's call to death, another hand reached for me, from above this time, and I felt myself being yanked toward the lake's surface by a strength known and loved only too well.

"Ice!" my mind screamed with the last of its energy, my lungs already preparing for their first clean breath in what seemed eons of tortured waiting.

"I've gotcha, Angel," came the blessed contralto purr of my lover. "Hold onto me. I've gotcha."

Hold onto her I did, with both arms and legs, as I took in great, heaving breaths and tried to meld our bodies together.

"It's alright, my love. It's alright. I've gotcha. You're safe now."

Well and truly I believed, right up until the second that a death-frozen hand latched itself to the bottom of my bathing suit and once again pulled me beneath the water, this time dragging Ice down with me.

Though we both struggled with a might to rival the ancient Titans, we might as well have been fighting against the weight of the earth as we were pulled unceasingly down into the tenebrous, blood-filled depths of the lake.

Well knowing that I would never see air again, my soul did the only thing it could.

Unlocking my death-grip, I attempted to push my lover back toward the far-away surface, knowing that whatever Hell I found myself in would be made infinitely worse by having caused her death.

Baring her teeth in that fierce smile which scared as much as thrilled, she shook her head and grabbed onto me again.

This time, however, instead of struggling, she brought our lips together in what I thought was a final kiss. My eyes widened in shock as I felt the last of her air being blown into my starved lungs. They widened still further as, with a mighty wrench, she pulled me free and sent me rocketing back to the surface as if blasted from the world's largest cannon.

My head broke through into the day's warmth and I spent a moment instinctively gasping for air before I realized exactly what it was she had done.

The unmistakable sound of a gasoline nozzle slipping into the tank awakened me a split second before my scream would have shattered every window in the car.

"Are you alright, Angel?" Corinne asked from the darkness somewhere above my head.

"Yeah," I replied softly. "Just gimme a minute to collect myself."

"I still believe we should market these nightmares of yours, Angel. Apt to be a damn sight better than the current drivel filling the cracker-boxes calling themselves theaters these days."

"You don't wanna go there, Corinne," I said, pulling myself up and away from her and running still trembling fingers through my hair. "Believe me."

"It was just a thought," she replied primly before lapsing into silence once again.

Rubbing the sleep from my eyes, I gradually became aware of the yellowish light that filtered in through the windows. "Where are we, anyway?"

"Somewhere just outside of Knoxville, I believe."

"Knoxville? Tennessee? Isn't that just a little bit out of the way for where we're going?"

"There's an ice storm headed out over the plains. She's taking us via the southern route."

"You managed to get that much out of her, huh?" I tried hard not to sound as envious as I felt.

"But of course. *I'm* not the one she's ignoring, after all."

"Just what I need," I sighed. "Trapped in a car for three thousand miles with Smug and Silent. And I thought my *nightmares* were bad!"

Her gentle laugh filled the car, chasing away the remaining fragments of my dream.

Chapter 2

A few hours later, we pulled to a stop in front of a nationally known motel chain; a name you'd recognize easily if you'd ever been treated to the down-home earnestness of an announcer promising he'd keep the illumination burning for all and sundry.

Before I could even think to blink my eyes against the bright neon that cut through the car's interior gloom like the motel chain's promised beacon, the door beside me opened and a key, bearing the number 139, was thrust without comment into my hand.

"Thank...you," I finished to an empty space. "Corinne...."

"I'll talk to her, Angel. Tomorrow. This car seat is doing a great number of unpleasurable things to parts of my anatomy best left to the tender care of others. So, if you don't mind too terribly much...."

"Out it is."

"I knew you'd see it my way."

Though my legs lodged a formal protest with my spine over being suddenly asked to bear my weight after so many hours of inactivity, they were soon happy with the chance to stretch and so promptly withdrew their grievance and willingly carried me to the open trunk, before which was standing Rio who shot me a look that would have frozen erupting lava, had such a volcano been handy.

Responding to her look with a withering one of my own, I reached into the trunk and grabbed hold of my overnight bag, inside which lay nestled all the necessities for my life on the road. Pulling it out easily, I then reached for Corinne's bag, which was a great deal heavier than mine.

For a moment, I thought my "tougher than thou" act would be all for naught as my rebellious arms almost failed in their appointed task, but, wisely succumbing to the scathing invectives tossed downward from my brain, I grasped hold of the bag and hauled it out, giving my watcher a smirk that would have done my lover proud.

Corinne gave me a round of nearly silent applause as I reached the door bearing the same number as the room key. Taking said key from my outstretched finger, she jammed it home in the lock and flung open the door. A blast of frigid, disinfectant-scented air wafted out, causing my entire body to erupt into goose bumps the size of small boulders. "Jesus," I gasped. "Did somebody forget to tell them it was November?"

"Apparently, Tom Bodette doesn't get out much," Corinne muttered, striding to the air-conditioning unit and turning it off with a vicious twist of her wrist.

Shuffling forward, I managed to dump the bags on the bed before collapsing there myself. The bedsprings poked at my kidneys, reminding me of yet another task I needed to perform before I could try and relax the strain of the day away.

Getting up from the bed, I walked into a bathroom that made my cell in the Bog look positively mammoth. As I sat down on the commode, my knees brushed against the opposite wall. The image of Rio in a similar situation brought a nasty grin to my face and, though it embarrasses me to say so, I readily confess to hoping that the greasy burgers we'd eaten along the way decided to play absolute havoc with her digestive system.

Though little more than a closet with a nozzle, the shower beckoned me and I, in my utter exhaustion, couldn't help but respond. Repeatedly smashing my elbows and knees to bleeding against the faux stucco of the room's interior, I shrugged off my clothes, reached in and turned on the water as high and as hot as it could go (which was, unfortunately, no more than "gentle summer drizzle" and "slightly-less-than-tepid") and stepped inside, groaning with relief as the warm water hit my body.

My hands gliding over places which hadn't seen my lover's

touch in months, I was sorely tempted to do more than just get clean, but the thought of Ice locked down in a rat-infested and pitch-black cell froze the little square of soap in its tracks and my libido promptly followed the water down the drain.

Drying off was another exercise in futility, given the scratchy towel of a size more commonly seen on the upper right corners of envelopes.

That task completed to the absolute best of my somewhat limited ability, I realized I'd forgotten to bring a change of clothes in with me, and after debating for a brief moment over the wisdom of calling for aid, I shrugged my shoulders and wrapped as much of the pitiful excuse for a towel around my waist as I could; girding my loins, so to speak, against the comments I knew would follow once I stepped out of the bathroom.

And follow they did, though thankfully they were limited to a slight, almost inaudible intake of breath and the widening of dark eyes behind prim half-glasses.

Flashing Corinne my most rakish grin, I brushed airily by on my way to the bed and my suitcase thereon.

And almost lost what little composure I'd managed to maintain when Corinne, too busy staring at me to pay attention to where she was headed, missed the entrance to the bathroom entirely and became intimate acquaintances with the wall next to it. Nearly biting my tongue clear through in my attempt not to give vent to the laughter rolling silent through my body, I heard clearly Corinne's muttered invective which promised dire consequences of the arsenic kind should she ever have the great good fortune to meet up with a certain male member of the Bodette clan.

After she disappeared into the bathroom, I let my laughter run free as I fumbled in my bag for something with which to cover myself. I pulled out an overlarge T-shirt that I freely admit belonged to Ice. Unlaundered, her scent clung to the fabric. I breathed deeply of it as I pulled the shirt over my head, hugging it close to my body after it was fully on and crying just a little with missing her.

Knowing that tears at that point would quickly degenerate into a storm of mournful sobbing, I savagely brushed at my cheeks and slipped in between the cool sheets of one of the narrow beds, picking up the television remote and clicking listlessly through the dozens of channels available.

When nothing struck my fancy, I tossed the remote carelessly back onto the nightstand, punched my pillow a couple of times and, with a sigh, laid my body down on the bed. Though emotionally exhausted, the six-hour nap I'd taken in the car guaranteed a restless night.

Corinne exited the bathroom clad in a demure nightgown that I would never have expected her to own, much less wear. Bypassing her own bed, she came to sit down on mine, smiling kindly down at me. "Can't sleep?" she asked, stroking the bangs from my eyes.

"Not really, no," I replied softly, closing my eyes in response to the tender caress. "Do you think I'm doing the right thing, Corinne?" I asked after a long, silent moment.

"Do *you* think you are?"

I opened my eyes. "Would I be asking you if I knew?" Then I sighed. "I'm sorry. I shouldn't be taking it out on you." The tears welled once again, Corinne's sweet compassion breaking down any walls of resistance I might have had. "I'm...I just...I miss her."

She smiled tenderly. "It's quite alright, Angel. I miss her, too."

"Why does it always have to be like this? Every time I think we've earned a break, something happens to separate us. Why? Is our love such a sin that we're destined never to share it for more than a heartbeat at a time?"

"You don't need me to answer that for you, Angel."

"No. I guess I don't." Ice's past was something that would never leave us alone, unless and until she paid full restitution on it.

"And would you have made a different decision had you known, way back when, how this path would unveil for you?"

"No," I answered without hesitation, knowing it for absolute truth. "Not even for a second."

"Then I think you have your answer, don't you?"

I smiled a little at that. "Yes. I suppose I do."

Returning my smile, she gathered me close and laid a gentle kiss against the crown of my head. "Sleep well, sweet Angel," she whispered, releasing me. "Morning will no doubt come early."

"Goodnight, Corinne," I said, kissing her cheek. "Thanks."

Getting up, she sketched a bow and grinned, her eyes twinkling. "At your service, oh Angelic one."

Though I felt immeasurably better for our brief conversation, sleep was still a very long time in coming.

A savage pounding on the door harshly interrupted what little sleep I'd finally managed to get. Had I been a cat, I would have been hanging upside-down from the ceiling, my claws sunk full into the plaster as my body shook in uncontrollable fright.

As it was, I let out a breathless scream and hit my head hard enough against the wall to see stars floating through the blackness of the room.

My life being what it is, I fear I'll never respond to a knock upon a closed door with anything close to equanimity again.

Beside me, Corinne shot from her bed in a move faster than any I'd ever seen her make, her nightgown trailing behind her in a surprised blur as she strode across the small room and yanked open the door. Stepping through the space created, she slammed the door behind her, bathing the room in dark silence once again.

Silence which was fractured by the sound of Corinne's tightly controlled voice spewing epithets which would have peeled the wallpaper had she been enunciating them inside the room rather than outside the door.

While I might normally have either stayed nearby to listen or gone outside in an attempt to make peace, my heart was too busy trying to crawl out of my mouth for me to give more than a passing thought to either possibility. Instead, knowing my sleep was well and truly a thing of the past, I went into the bathroom and tried my best to prepare myself for the coming day.

By the time I came out, clean if not necessarily refreshed, Corinne was again sitting on her bed, looking completely composed, as if being jolted out of bed in the middle of the night was an everyday occurrence for her. She gave me one of those smiles that your pet cat might give you after he's eaten your prized canaries and made vast inroads on your goldfish as well.

Knowing better than to ask, I contented myself with running a quick brush through my hair and packing up my things in preparation for our no doubt imminent departure.

Still wearing that look of smug satisfaction, Corinne brushed by me on her way toward whatever morning rituals she had to perform.

A very short time later, we were both packed and ready. Opening the door, I winced as a frosty November wind sunk talons into my overwarmed body, the scent of snow in the air reminding me of things I was trying desperately to forget. Like long autumn nights spent curled up in front of a blazing fire, my body so entangled with that of my lover that I honestly didn't know where I ended and she began.

Enough of that, Angel, I told myself, looking up just in time to see the mother of all "hang-dog" looks being shot Corinne's way by an obviously still-embarrassed Rio. When her eyes came to rest on mine, however, the mask of cold indifference slipped smoothly over her face once again.

With a vast mental sigh, I walked over to the open trunk and stowed my belongings, preparing myself as best I could for spending yet another day in the company of someone who, for reasons beyond my knowing, detested the sight of me.

In some ways, it was even worse than being in the Bog. At least there, I had love to balance out the hate, friends to balance out the enemies, and a sense of belonging which made even the hardest day easier to bear for the family I'd been so wonderfully given.

Now, even with Corinne's loving, comforting presence never more than a breath away, I felt alone, adrift, lost in a way that frightened me no end. It left my defenses in such shambles that I didn't even mind that Corinne had fought my battle for me.

I knew that I was headed square into the mouth of a very deep depression, one whose slippery slopes would be very hard to navigate once I got down far enough, but frankly, I couldn't seem to dredge up enough energy to care.

Ignoring the deeply concerned look Corinne tossed my way, I slipped into the car and stared nowhere but forward, hoping that time and distance would be allies in a war I had no desire to fight.

The morning of the forth day of our journey found us headed down a nearly deserted highway as the panoramic vista of the New Mexico desert unfurled itself, like a carpet preparing for the tread of a king, before us.

Never having been to this area of the country, my interpretation of the word "desert" ran along the lines of a Lawrence of Arabia type; vast, empty, lifeless, with a cloudless sky and rolling sand dunes. A beach in search of an ocean, in other words.

What peered back at me through the car's lightly tinted windows was, however, as different and as foreign to me as a Martian landscape would have been. Where I had expected a vast, empty wasteland, the desert—a definite misnomer, in my opinion—was instead literally teeming with life. Strange, stunted plants dotted the landscape as far as the eye could see. Cacti stood like silent sentinels guarding all who lived in their domain. Hawks and other birds-of-prey circled endlessly in the vast expanse of deep blue sky while beneath them, all sorts of animals moved with quick assurance—hunter and hunted each fulfilling its destined role.

The wild, untamed beauty, untouched and untouchable, struck a chord deep within me. It was a land which promised, by its very nature, to give up its secrets reluctantly, if at all. Danger lurked everywhere, not in the least camouflaged by the true and undeniable beauty of the land.

Proud and remote, it seemed to issue a challenge I was helpless to ignore.

Come within. If you dare.

As I continued to stare out as the rising sun revealed more of the desert's treasures, a smile creased the plains of my face. A curious sense of coming home filled my soul, lightening the heavy burden there immeasurably.

"What?" Corinne asked, looking at me with eyebrows raised.

"Ice," was my simple reply.

Brown eyes narrowed as Corinne peered out my window. After a long moment, she looked at me the way one might look at a friend showing the first signs of absolute lunacy. "I don't think this is the right type of desert to support mirages, Angel."

I glared at her and then turned my attention to the window once again. "That's not what I'm talking about and you know it."

After a long moment, Corinne's voice came softly to my ear. "I believe I can understand the connection. Undeniably beautiful, mysteriously remote, and tangibly dangerous. An intoxicating combination."

I could see my broad smile reflected on the glass of the window. Though it wasn't a necessity, it felt good to know she understood.

A flash of light caught itself in the periphery of my vision, and when I turned to look forward through the windshield, I saw the sun sparking off the gleaming metal of a tanker truck still some distance away and chasing the sun as it rose to the east.

As I often did while on such journeys, I wondered where the driver was from, and where he was going. Was he heading for home, or was he leaving it? Where would the setting sun find him? Home with his family? Alone in a hotel room with only a television for company? In some nameless bar, searching for easy companionship for the price of a beer?

Beside me, Corinne stiffened; an action which quickly brought me out of my nonsensical musings. The truck was a good deal closer now, and barreling down upon a red Jeep trundling along the one eastbound lane. "Jesus," I breathed. "Is he drunk?"

"I don't think that's the greatest of our worries right now, Angel," Corinne replied, her voice beyond tight.

I turned slightly to look at her, then followed her frozen stare back to the view presented us through the somewhat dusty windshield just in time to see the onrushing truck try to pass the slow-moving jeep by pulling oncoming traffic—which, at the time, consisted of only one thing.

Our car.

"Rio!" I screamed, as if she couldn't see the three tons of polished death screaming toward us like some great white shark on an intercept course with a piece of plankton.

At the very last moment, she jerked the wheel sharply to the right, veering off the road and onto the desert hardpan beyond. The sedan fishtailed wildly, the tires smoking and spinning in a useless attempt to gain traction on the loose sandy gravel of the desert floor.

For a split second, I thought we were going to flip over when the backwash of air from the narrowly missed truck blasted against us with the strength of a passing tornado. It was probably the only time in my life I actually thanked God for Detroit's one-time propensity for making cars the size of small housing developments.

Somehow, Rio managed to keep us level, if not actually controlled. As she wrestled with the wheel clamped between white-knuckled hands, I heard a loud noise that heralded the explosive death of one of our tires just as Rio managed to get us off the desert and onto the road.

Once again unbalanced, the car did a slow looping skid onto the opposing lanes before stopping, with a sharp jolt, which pulled the seatbelt tight against my hips, against a low boulder lying partially exposed on the other side of the highway.

"Jesus," I whispered again when the air finally reentered my lungs, the quietly ticking engine the only other sound to be heard.

Looking to my left, I saw a Corinne who sat stiff and still as a marble statue, her face drained of all color, her eyes wide and staring behind glasses which sat askew on her face, her jaw slack.

In short, she looked like a corpse.

"Corinne? Are you alright?"

After a moment, the corpse came back to life as her head slowly turned to face me. "It's amazing how short one's life really is when it's flashing before one's eyes."

Barking out relieved laughter, I pulled her as close to me as our seatbelts would allow, hugging her tight against my chest, beyond joyful that she was still among the living.

A moan from the front seat cut short our reunion, and when I looked forward, I saw the windshield sprinkled with droplets of blood, looking as if a grisly rain had somehow fallen from the cloudless sky.

Reaching into one of Corinne's pockets, I pulled out one of her ever-present handkerchiefs and vaulted myself over the front seat like I used to do when I was a child. Of course, since there was a good deal more of me as an adult, the "vaulting" didn't go as smoothly, or as easily, as I'd planned.

Flopping gracelessly into the front seat, I rearranged my limbs into their proper places and then took a long, assessing look at Rio. Her face was literally painted in blood from the combined forces of a gash over her left eyebrow and an obviously broken nose.

"I'll need another handkerchief, Corinne," I said, pressing the one already in my hand against Rio's forehead in an attempt to staunch the heavy bleeding.

As another square of cloth was handed over, I tilted Rio's head back against the headrest and brought one of her own hands up. "Hold this," I ordered, clamping the second handkerchief over her nose and melding her hand to it.

A mumbled phrase sounding suspiciously like "fuck you" floated out from beneath the cloth.

"Not on your best day, sweetheart," I replied, grinning fiercely into her blazing, pain-shiny eyes. "Now just hold that cloth tight and keep quiet. I've got some other business to attend to."

Grabbing the keys from the ignition and unlocking the passenger's side door, I stepped out onto the road and walked around to the rear of the car. The rear driver's side tire was a shredded mess well beyond even the faintest hope of redemption.

Sighing, I went over to the trunk and popped it open, reaching in and hauling out all the baggage stored there. The bright, warm, and unrelenting sunshine provided ample light as I fumbled around in the compartment for the jack and spare tire.

I heard one of the doors open and close as I set about dragging the items I needed from the trunk and setting them down on the hard-packed sand on the side of the road. As I watched, Corinne did a slow circle while taking in the sights through slightly widened eyes, her half glasses once again in their customary perch atop her nose. "I don't suppose Triple-A comes out this far into the middle of nowhere."

Laughing, I hefted tire and jack, manhandling them around to the correct side of the car. "I've got it covered."

She leveled me a look of pure speculation. "Yes, I believe you do." She continued to watch as I loosened the lugs holding the wheel on slightly before readying the jack. "Another of Ice's lessons learned?"

"Exactly. My father thought I'd have a husband to do these things for me, so he never bothered to teach them to me. When Ice found out...well, let's just say she made sure that I'd never be at the mercy of some friendly trucker with a tire iron and less than charitable thoughts."

"Smart woman, that Ice."

"You know it."

As I crouched down to set the jack beneath the car, I heard the door open and looked up just in time to see Rio emerge from the sedan, the makeshift bandages still pressed against her injuries. Her eyes flashing something other than pain, she took what appeared to be a menacing step toward me, either to pummel me senseless in payment for what I'd had the audacity to say to her, or to take the job of changing the tire into her own hands.

What little remained of my good humor snapped and I found myself slowly rising to my feet, lug wrench in hand. "If I need your help, Rio, I'll ask for it. So just...go bleed somewhere else, will you? You're blocking my light."

To my utter surprise, the standoff was over almost before it began. Lowering her eyes for a split second, Rio took several steps backward until she was even with the car's hood. When she finally raised her head back up, I saw something—perhaps the tiniest shard of respect—glimmering there. While we weren't suddenly best buddies by any means, I had the definite feeling that the playing field had been leveled, if only just a little.

The look of amused pride Corinne gave me caused a flush to heat my face and I crouched back down to hide it, fiddling with the jack and lug wrench I still had in my hand, and cursing her under my breath.

A short time later, it was done. After putting the tools and remains of the shredded tire back into the trunk and packing our belongings in there as well, I strolled around to the front of the car, taking a close look at the bumper, which was sitting snuggly against the bolder which stopped us.

Aside from a tiny scratch in the dusty chrome, the bumper was none the worse for the wearing. The same could not be said, however, for the boulder, which was sporting a very large fissure at the point of impact.

"They sure don't make 'em like this anymore," I said, shaking my head in amazement.

"That's a fact," Corinne agreed from beside me.

After a moment, I turned to find Rio looking silently at us both. Taking a chance, I stepped over to her, stopping just outside her comfort zone. "I...um...Would you mind if I took a turn behind the wheel for awhile? Give your cuts some more time to stop bleeding?"

Her eyes narrowed, then, just as quickly, relaxed as she nodded, somewhat reluctantly, I thought. Still, a nod was a nod, and I practically jumped at the chance, quickly opening the driver's side door and sliding into the seat. Because Rio was twice my size, my feet didn't come anywhere near to the pedals on the floor. Reaching down, I pulled a hidden lever and eased the heavy bench seat forward to accommodate my smaller frame.

Hands on the wheel and feet easily reaching the gas and brake pedals, I grinned with pleasure, no longer feeling like a small child behind the wheel of Daddy's sedan. "All aboard! Next stop...um...where *is* our next stop, anyway?"

"Tucson," Corinne answered as she slid into the back seat, groaning with relief. "Angel, my varicose veins thank you for the extra leg room back here. My bunions sing your praises as well."

"As long as they don't ask me to kiss them."

"You should be so lucky."

The passenger side door opened then, and Rio made as if to sit beside me. Halfway down, however, she got well and truly stuck, obviously not expecting that I would have pulled the seat so far up in the interim.

As her fanny hovered a good five inches above the seat, unable to move up or down, I tasted the blood that came from literally biting back my hysterical laughter. Looking at Corinne through the rearview mirror was quite possibly the worst thing I could have done. The speculative, totally evil look on her face almost sent me into convulsions.

When her fingers moved in a deliberate, exaggerated pinching motion, I lost all control, doubling over the steering wheel and choking on my laughter so hard I thought my lungs were going to fly clear out of my chest and land on the dashboard like a pair of glistening, overstressed balloons.

With a titanic grunt and a mighty heave, Rio freed herself from the car, then spun around quickly to glare at us both; her blood-caked face, blackening eyes, and massively swollen nose only serving to make her look more menacing.

"Asthma!" I wheezed, fanning my heated and tear-streaked face as I tried desperately to gain some control over my hysteria.

"Horrible case," Corinne deadpanned from her seat behind me. "We're just hoping the desert air does the poor dear some good."

Falling into the role I'd begun, I gave Rio my best impersonation of a woman trying desperately to breathe.

It was a pretty damn good impersonation, if I do say so myself. Especially given the fact that at that particular moment in time, I *was* a woman trying desperately to breathe.

"Perhaps it would be best, Rio, if you consented to share the back seat with me. Let the diminutive one sit all crouched up in front while you and I recline in luxury back here."

Had I the breath for it, I would have shot Corinne a look hot enough to curl her hair. Since breathing was still a priority, however, I settled for a nice mental fantasy of tying her down and beating her senseless with her own teakettle.

Diminutive indeed.

I didn't even bother to turn my head when an imperious finger tapped me on the shoulder.

"Drive on, Jeeves. Tucson awaits."

Adding a fireplace poker to my little fantasy, I grinned as I started up the car and pulled back onto the highway.

"Stop here," came the imperious command from the backseat as I tried to navigate the spaghetti-snarl of intersecting freeways that marked the entrance to Tucson.

"Where here? Do you have a particular exit in mind, Corinne, or will the overpass do? I'm sure the trucks behind us would be more than happy to turn this car into an accordion, if that's the look you're after." I'll freely admit to sounding a bit snappish, but I believe you would have too, had you spent the past five hours in vehicular hell, listening to two overgrown children sniping back and forth behind you. I spared a brief moment to wonder if it was some sort of cosmic payback for my own childhood spent doing much the same thing during long road trips with my parents.

"Keep driving," came the expected countermand from Rio, whose voice sounded like it was coming from the bottom of a very deep, very full well.

"Get off at the next exit, Angel. I refuse to be bled upon any more by this overgrown, pig-headed, sorry excuse for an adult."

"Keep driving. I'm fine."

Gritting my teeth against the overwhelming urge to just pull over and boot both of them out onto the middle of the crowded highway, I instead arrowed the car to the next exit and followed the long, curving ramp until it led me out onto a wide, nearly deserted street. Pulling off to the side of the road, I turned the engine off, left the keys in the ignition, opened the door, and stepped out onto the pavement, intending to put as much distance between myself and the "battling Bickersons" as possible before my head exploded.

It didn't matter that I seemed to be walking into some modern-dress version of an Old West ghost town, where bars and chains adorned the dusty, empty windows and doors. It didn't matter that most of the signs were in Spanish and therefore incomprehensible to me. It didn't even matter that I could literally feel the unseen eyes assessing me and making my flesh go tight against my bones.

All that mattered was the blessed silence which surrounded me, all the more dear for bringing with it warm sunshine and fresh air. Closing my eyes and tilting my face up to the sun, I let its warm rays bathe the tension from my body.

"Angel?" came a voice from behind me. "What are you doing out there?"

When I didn't answer, the car door opened and I heard the sound of sensible shoes hitting the pavement. A moment later, Corinne was by my side. "Angel? Are you alright?"

"As soon as this headache goes away, I'll be just peachy."

"How...? Oh, because of the discussion?"

I turned to look at her. "That wasn't a discussion, Corinne. I know discussions. I've had discussions. That wasn't one of them. It was a war. Between two grown adults. In a car. For five hours."

"I get the point."

"Good. Because I don't think I could summon up the energy to explain it again." I rubbed at my temples, trying to force the headache back down.

It wasn't working.

"She's bleeding pretty badly, Angel."

"Yes, Corinne, I'm aware of that. I'm *very* aware of that. The problem is, however, that the both of you seem to be much more interested in arguing about it than actually *doing* something about it. So, just go back in the car and beat each other senseless over it. I'll be back later to take whomever's left to the hospital, alright?"

"Angel...."

"No, Corinne." I sighed, forcefully cooling down my temper. "Look. I know Rio's bleeding badly, and I'd love to be able to do something about it. I really would. But, as you can see, I'm in a town I've never been in before and whose signs I can't even read. So I hope you'll excuse me if I'm not quite at my best in this situation."

"You're right. And I do apologize for my part in all this, if it helps any. Rio is as pig-headed as they come, but she comes by her hatred of hospitals honestly. Her mother was murdered in one."

"What happened?" I asked, eyes wide.

"Her mother was an ER nurse at the time. A man came in demanding drugs and shot her for the narcotic key in her hand. Rio hasn't gone near a hospital since."

"God...that's horrible!"

"Yes, it is."

Turning my head for a moment, I chanced to see a squat, low-slung and windowless building which looked more like a bomb-shelter than a business establishment. Attached to the roof was a huge billboard, pockmarked by bullet holes and weathered almost to splinters courtesy of the constantly beating sun, which simply read: *La Clinica.*

"Will that do? As a compromise, I mean?"

As Corinne followed my pointing finger, a smile broke out over her face. "It will do nicely, I think. And if not, I believe I have the fireplace poker stashed in the trunk somewhere."

"You'll have to wait in line behind me," I said, grinning. "I think there's a tire iron back there with her name on it."

Laughing, she slapped me gently on the shoulder, then made her way back to the car. I stayed where I was, enjoying the last bit of quiet and sunshine for as long as I possibly could.

The resolution was surprisingly anti-climactic.

After a brief, nearly silent conversation, Rio exited the car and brushed by me on her way to the clinic, still holding a crimson handkerchief against her bleeding nose. After a brief, sharp knock, the clinic door opened and the building seemed to swallow her whole, as if she never was, and never would be again.

Her smirk truly insufferable, Corinne waggled her fingers at me as she passed by, leaving me to play the caboose on this dysfunctional little train upon which I found myself. Shaking my head and biting back a smile, lest it somehow be misinterpreted as admiration (which it was, but she didn't need to know that), I followed her into the clinic.

While austere in the extreme from the outside, when viewed from the interior, the clinic was a marvel of modern design. Shining and spotless, it was filled to the rafters with enough medical equipment to ensure quick and accurate treatment for any who came through its doors seeking aid.

I stepped inside just in time to see Rio's broad form being ushered through a set of interior doors by a pair of orderlies clad in blue scrubs. The receptionist smiled as I entered, gesturing with a wave of her hand toward the bank of immaculate, if not very comfortable, chairs lined up in rows along two of the walls. Corinne was already seated and flipping idly through one of the many magazines sitting on several tables near the center of the room.

"Do we need to fill out some forms or something?" I asked, sitting down next to her. Except for us, the waiting area was empty of human habitation.

"I'm sure we'll find out soon enough," Corinne replied, turning another page with a wetted finger and examining intently the ad displayed there. "Advertising's become quite the fictional enterprise of late. To look at this ad, simply drinking the beverage in question seems to promise that not only will one feel truly refreshed, but that a makeover, tummy tuck, and breast enhancement comes free as part of the package. Almost makes me want to try a sip. My body could use a bit of a tune-up."

I laughed gently, appreciating her attempt to get my mind off my current surroundings. I hated hospitals, clinics, medical offices of all kinds. Having a lover unfortunately prone to spontaneous bullet holes made my hatred an honest one, I believe.

"Here," Corinne snapped, slipping a slightly tattered magazine in my hands. "Read this and stop fidgeting. You're making me seasick."

"You know I can't read Spanish, Corinne," I replied, leafing through the magazine.

"Then learn. I've no doubt that Rio's treatment will take quite awhile and there's really very little else to do."

"Yes, mother," I sighed, slumping back into my chair and flipping through the magazine's glossy pages trying to make sense of what I was seeing and failing miserably.

At least my headache was gone.

Several hours and a whole rack of magazines later, a heavily drugged Rio was wheeled out into the waiting room looking like the last survivor of a really intense Mardi Gras. Her face was a scattered sunburst of colors, which complimented the metallic splint that tented itself over her newly set nose.

A dapper young man wearing a long white labcoat over his scrubs, his name embroidered in red thread over the breast, gave us both a pleasant smile as he stopped and locked the wheelchair a couple feet away from us. "Are you here for Rio?"

"Yes," I answered. "Is she gonna be alright?"

"Well, she'll have a pretty big headache after the happy pills wear off, but yeah, she should be fine in a week or two. Speaking of which...." His smile became even more broad as he slipped a prescription into my hand. "More happy pills. She can have one every four hours or so, but they'll make her very sleepy, so make sure she isn't driving or doing anything else that requires concentration."

Corinne took the slip of paper from my hand and slid it into her purse as I looked from Rio to the doctor. "Is there anything special we should do for her?"

"Well, her nose is splinted and packed pretty tight, so make sure she doesn't have any trouble breathing, especially when she's asleep. She's probably swallowed a good deal of blood as well, so try and keep her head tilted to the side in case any of it decides to come back up the hard way."

I nodded my understanding of his instructions. "Anything else?"

"Other than keeping a close eye on her, not really. Like I said, it won't be too long before she's back to her old self again." Catching my grimace, he grinned. "Afraid I'd say that, weren't you?"

"Well...."

Laughing, he clapped me briefly on my shoulder and then stepped back. "Good luck."

"We'll need it." Reaching out, I grasped his proffered hand in gratitude. "Thanks."

"*De nada.* Carlos will escort Rio to your car."

"It's the beige sedan parked across the street," Corrine remarked, handing the buff orderly the keys.

Taking them, he smiled and nodded, then wheeled Rio out of the clinic.

As the doctor walked back through the doors and into the treatment rooms beyond, I accompanied Corinne up to the receptionist's desk. "The damages?" she asked, taking out her wallet.

"None, *senora.* This is a free clinic set up for those who can't afford to pay for medical services."

"We *can* afford to pay," Corrine replied, undeterred. "A nice round figure, if you please."

"But...."

Ignoring the woman, she pulled out ten crisp one-hundred-dollar bills, laid them out one by one atop the cluttered desk, and smirked as the receptionist's dark, almond eyes grew quite wide. "Round enough?"

"But...."

"Round enough," Corinne answered for her, obviously not

taking "but" for an answer. "Thank you for your most gracious hospitality." And with that, she closed her purse, turned on her heel, and left the clinic without so much as a glance behind, leaving me to helplessly shrug at the round-eyed receptionist who stared in disbelief at the small mountain of money lying in front of her.

After a long moment, she looked up at me. I grinned. "It's just her way."

"*Dios mio.*"

I chuckled. "You might be tempted to think so." A thought popped into my head. "Can I ask you a favor?"

"Anything, *senora*! Anything!"

"I...just need some directions. See, Rio's our guide here. I've never been this far south before. Is there a place nearby where we could stop over for the night? It's probably best if we continue our journey when she's awake enough to help."

"Oh, *si. Si.* I know of a nice little place not too far from here, *senora*. Just outside of town and easy to get to. Let me write the directions down for you."

A short time later, armed with wonderfully explicit directions, I made my way through the crawling after-work traffic toward the place where we would stay the night.

"Nice place," I remarked as Corinne and I navigated a very drunken and half asleep Rio into the large room and onto one of the king-sized beds.

As soon as she hit the mattress, Rio turned onto her side and began to snore, long and loud, through her widely opened mouth.

"I still say we should have gotten two rooms," Corinne remarked, making as if to put her hands over her ears. "Elderly librarians with short tempers aren't known to be at their best without the requisite eight hours of sleep per night."

"Angels aren't either," I replied, wincing as a particularly loud snore nearly broke the windows.

"We could always smother her with a pillow," Corinne observed.

"I didn't think suffocation was your style."

"For this, I'm willing to change my M.O."

"Perhaps. But where would we hide the body?"

She laughed. "You have a point. I'd say we could just

leave her outside, but someone would likely just toss her back in again."

Chuckling, I walked through the large suite and pulled back the heavy curtains protecting the interior from the harsh desert sun. A sun which was just beginning to set behind the low mesa to the west of the hotel. A need gripped me and I turned to my friend. "Can you watch her for a few minutes?"

"Of course. Running out on me already, are you?"

"No. I just...." I could feel myself blushing. "I'd like to see the sun set."

Her eyes held nothing but honest love and deep compassion. "I understand, Angel. Take your time. Just realize that in payment, I'll expect you to clean up whatever mess she might make in the night."

I grinned. "Deal."

"Then be off with you, before I decide to make you share her bed as well."

And so I did.

Though the mesa wasn't very tall, the trail was steep enough, and my legs burned pleasantly as I made it to the top. I faced away from the city, and the view of the desert from the summit was breathtaking; nothing but open land as far as the eye could see, free from any form of human habitation.

The view of the sky as the sun set was even more spectacular. Deep, blood red swirled and mixed with royal purple to form a gorgeous vista I couldn't quite keep my eyes away from. It was better by far than any sunset I'd ever seen.

After making sure that the boulder at my feet wasn't sheltering a snake or other venomous creature, I slowly sat down on it, watching as the sun made its triumphal march behind the mountains still further to the west.

"You'd like it here, Ice," I whispered to my absent partner. "So wild and free. No walls. No bars. Nothing but...peace. And beauty." A sudden chill came over me, at odds with the still-gentle warmth of the evening, and I wrapped my arms around my body. "I miss you, you know. So much. I keep telling myself that it's for the best, and we'll see each other soon. My brain listens, but my heart...well, it's got a mind of its own, you know?"

I felt the warm trickle of tears on my cheeks as the sky became a beautiful prism for my teary eyes alone. "I think I'd give anything just to feel your arms around me." I laughed a little. "I know that can't happen right now, but you can't blame a girl for wishing, huh?"

Wiping my eyes, I stood as the sun made its final descent behind the mountain. "I'll be patient, my love. Just...don't wait too long, ok?"

And as the sun finally set, casting the world below in shadow, a warm desert breeze enveloped me like a hug from my absent lover, chasing the chill away and leaving me with a profound sense of stillness and peace.

I could feel a smile form even as the tears dried gently on my cheeks.

"I love you, Ice. Hurry home."

The next morning, Rio was back to her old self. She awoke snarling, refused any of the pain medication we'd picked up from a pharmacy on our way to the hotel, pulled the packing and splint from her nose, and barked out orders at us, a right proper Drill Instructor to a squad of completely inept recruits.

Though her surly mood should have bothered me, it didn't. That gift of peace I'd received the night before proved itself tenacious, and I hugged it to me as one would a blanket on a cold winter's night, refusing to allow her poor temper and bad manners to take it from me.

Besides, within five hours—hopefully much less—our journey would come to an end, and God willing, I'd never have to put up with her again in such close and inescapable quarters.

Corinne wasn't nearly so gracious, but a look from me held her tongue.

We were quickly on the road, with Rio once again in her accustomed space behind the wheel. The miles fairly flew by as within me a keen sense of anticipation grew from a small seedling to full, blooming life.

We headed south, and south again, taking progressively smaller and smaller roads, passing nothing but desert vegetation and the very occasional car coming north. Just when I felt sure that the Mexican border was to be our destination, we took a turn to the west on a very narrow road that the desert did its level best to reclaim, washing it over with sand which heralded the road's infrequent usage. We drove west for several miles, threading our way through the foothills of several small mesas that stood like sawed-off chess pieces on the world's largest board.

Another slow, meandering curve brought us out into open land again, and I saw something I never expected in a desert.

Trees.

Row upon row of perfectly manicured trees. Trees whose abundant greenery stood in stark contrast to the sun-washed brown of the surrounding desert. Trees whose sweet scent came to me through the car's open windows and brought with it the images of....

"Oranges? Are those orange trees?"

"None other," Corinne replied, taking a healthy breath herself and grinning.

"I didn't know you could grow oranges in Arizona!"

"Ahh, Angel. I daresay you haven't truly lived until you've tasted an Arizona orange. Sweet. Succulent. Simply bursting with juices. Rather like...."

"Don't say it, Corinne. Just...don't say it. Please."

"Spoil sport."

Choosing to ignore her teasing, I instead took in another deep breath, noticing that the scent of orange blossoms became heavier—cloying almost—the closer we came to the grove. It reminded me of the truth in the maxim: "Too much of a good thing isn't always a good thing" and I put a hand up to my nose to stifle a threatened sneeze.

A wide path cut through the grove at a right angle, and when we came out on the other side, desert reigned supreme once again. Off to my right, I saw the low, barbed wire fence of a corral, and beyond that, dust being kicked up as a herd of horses came our way, led by a beautiful stallion—or what I took to be a stallion, my knowledge of horses minimal at best—with a coat the color of freshly spilled blood and a mane and tail black as printer's ink.

He reared up high, displaying powerful, slashing hooves and shining, sweat drenched muscles, and I found myself falling in love with him at first glance. The entire herd raced us toward the breast of a small hillock and then stopped as their enclosure ended. We, of course, continued on, down into a valley that signaled the end of our journey.

A huge house sprung up from the desert floor as if birthed

from the very sand upon which it rested. It was bone white adobe with a red Spanish-tiled roof and heavily tinted hexagonal windows. Though only a single story, it was very long and sported three front doors, each framed by a long, fluid arch.

Other, smaller houses formed a rough square behind the main house, with the stables off to the right and, beyond that, what looked to be a row of greenhouses, which would require further exploration in the very near future.

As we pulled onto the long, circular driveway, I began to notice groups of people walking calmly, or purposefully, around the grounds. Though of all shapes, sizes, and ethnic origins, these people all had one thing very evidently in common.

"Where are the men?"

A sharp bark of laughter was heard from the peanut gallery, who currently took up residence in the driver's seat.

"This is a women's ranch, Angel," Corinne explained, shooting a glare toward the back of Rio's head. "Men aren't welcome."

Instead of saying anything aloud and giving Rio further ammunition to use against me in this personal war of hers, I settled for a simple nod, watching the women as they went about their day.

"My, my, my," came Corinne's soft, awed voice to my left. "And me without my camera."

Curious, I gazed at the view from her window. And what a view it was.

A large, in-ground pool shimmered clear blue in the brilliant sunlight. In and around the pool lay almost a dozen courageous (it was warm outside, but not *that* warm) souls all dressed in the exact same costume.

Their birthday suits.

If my eyes weren't so firmly attached to the back of my skull, they might surely have popped out of my head at the vision.

"Remind me to give the good Mr. Cavallo a nice big kiss when Ice finally drags him back this way, Angel. I think I may have found heaven."

I'll admit it was heavenly for me as well, at first. While looking at the women, I pictured Ice's long, naked body cutting through the sparkling water with the ease of a born athlete.

I pictured her climbing the ladder with sinuous grace, water rolling off her in sparkling sheets.

I pictured the smile that would cross her face as she saw me standing by the edge of the pool, waiting.

I pictured three dozen other naked women clustering around the bronze-limbed goddess who was my lover, blocking her from my view and touching her in all the places currently denied to me.

I blinked.

Then coughed.

Amazing how one woman's heaven could so easily become another's private hell.

As the car completed its entrance onto the ranch, the pool-side view was mercifully cut off from my line of vision and I let out a deep breath of relief with the loss of it. After pulling to a complete stop, Rio turned off the engine and was out of the car so fast, I wondered briefly if she'd been sitting on a hornet's nest, or something equally unpleasant.

Probably just the company she was forced to keep, I told myself with a mental shrug. I could hardly fault her for it, after all, since I was feeling the same way myself.

I got out of the car just in time to see her all but swallowed up by a group of cooing women. Watching her back straighten and her shoulders broaden under all the compassionate attention she was receiving, I—quite uncharitably—wondered what tale of her injuries she was conjuring to earn such fawning responses.

Enough, Angel. Bitterness isn't one of your more charming assets, so just stick it back in the festering pit it came from and leave it there, alright?

My jaw set with newfound resolution, I reached behind the front seat and popped the trunk, then went around to the back to retrieve my luggage, setting each piece carefully down on the immaculate driveway, then doing the same for Corinne's bags.

Having lost what passed for our hostess, I was at a loss for what to do next.

"Think it'd be considered impolite if we just burst right in and announced ourselves?" I asked Corinne as I continued to stare after Rio and her admirers.

"I don't think that will be necessary, Angel."

I looked up just in time to see a woman come out from the house. She was dressed in faded jeans, a white shirt and dark leather vest, her face shaded by the wide brim of a white Stetson perched comfortably over her long, dark hair.

Squinting into the bright sunlight, I put a hand above my

eyes, trying to see her more clearly and place the feeling of familiarity that washed over me as she walked toward the two of us.

"Welcome to *Akalan*, Angel."

It was the voice that did it. Even more than the respectful touch to the brim of the hat, or the smile which made the woman's features suddenly recognizable.

"Montana?" I asked, so far beyond stunned that I couldn't even see it from where I was standing. "Is that really you?"

"In the flesh," she said, grinning. "It's good to see you again. You've changed since I saw you last."

Feeling tears well up in my eyes, I reached out and embraced her tightly, pleased when she didn't stiffen or pull away. In my joy, I'd forgotten about her natural reserve, so much like my lover's that it almost hurt to hug her.

"God, it's good to see you," I said, finally pulling away and wiping my eyes with the heel of my hand. "Why are you here?"

At her laughter, I blushed, realizing a bit belatedly exactly how my question sounded.

"I mean...I thought you were in Montana?"

"I was, until three weeks ago," she replied, sharing a warm embrace with Corinne.

"What happened three weeks ago?"

"I received a call from a lawyer who expounded on the joys of wintering in the warmth and sunshine of Arizona."

"Donita?"

"None other. And, since the alternative was another winter spent up to my neck in snow, I allowed myself to see the wisdom of her words, and here I am."

"You came here for me, didn't you," I said, as another piece of the puzzle fell neatly into place.

"I won't deny that was a factor in my decision."

"But your home...."

Smiling, she held up a hand. "*Akalan* is as much my home as the ranch in Montana, Angel. Or even the one in the hills of western Pennsylvania. Where I am at any given point in time doesn't much matter. What I can do and who I can help, however, does."

"But...."

Her smile broadened. "Look around you, Angel. What do you see?"

Following her gentle request, I looked around, then back to

her, eyebrows raised, not sure exactly where she was leading.

"No answer? I'll tell you what I see, then." I watched, fascinated, as her dark eyes scanned the grounds, missing nothing. "Where some might look and see only empty, arid desert and, yes, beautiful women...."

"Beautiful *naked* women," Corinne corrected from beside me.

"Point taken," Montana replied, smirking slightly. "I see hope, Angel. Simple as that."

"Hope for what?" I asked, honestly curious. While I liked and very much respected Montana, I knew her far less than the other Amazons who had befriended me. Part of the reason, of course, was that she was released so soon into my own sentence. And the rest, as I believe I've already mentioned, was due to her own reserved, quiet nature.

"Hope for the future. Hope for the community. Hope for safety, security, friendship." Her broad shoulders lifted in a shrug. "Hope as individual as the woman who wields it." When her gaze returned to me, it was soft with compassion and caring, yet bright with the passion of her convictions. "Above all else, Angel, this ranch is a place where hope is born and nurtured. Women come here from all walks of life. Many are bruised and battered, either emotionally or physically. Sometimes both. They aren't as much running to us as they are running away from the lives they've lived before. Communities like this offer a sense of safety, of protection, and belonging that can help to start healing in women with nowhere else to turn."

"It sounds wonderful," I said, completely taken with her vision.

"It can be. It can also be rough, dirty and thankless. But it's a job I wouldn't trade for any in the world."

"With these perks, I don't see why you ever would," Corinne remarked, frankly ogling a pair of scantily dressed women as they strolled past, arm in arm. They grinned back at her, waggling their fingers in invitation. "Oh yes, I'm going to love it here."

Montana laughed, something I'd never heard her do before, and I found myself charmed by the musical sweetness of it. "It's good to see you again, Corinne. You'll certainly liven this place up." Laying a hand on each of our shoulders, she gently guided us toward the house, our bags in hand. "Let's get you settled in and then we can talk more, alright?"

"You can talk," Corinne said. "I find myself in sudden and dire need of a refreshing swim."

"Or a cold shower, " I joked.

"Just you wait, you sorry excuse for an angel. One day, sooner than you might expect, you'll reach my age. And believe you me, I intend to be around long enough to see just what happens when you do."

Throwing back my head, I laughed, feeling better than I had in months. *Was this what you had in mind when you set this up, Ice?*

Then I laughed harder, though at myself.

Of course it was. Ice never did anything without a reason.

While I might have been safe in any one of several places, it was here where I could truly feel the beauty of hope once again.

Thank you, my love.

❖❖❖❖❖❖❖❖

In direct and no-doubt deliberate contrast to the sunny warmth of the outside world, the interior of the house was cool, quiet and dim, courtesy of the heavy blinds which hung over the tinted windows and seemed to possess the added benefit of muting sound as well as light.

The living room was huge and sunken, with heavily varnished bare wood floors and several large, comfortable-looking couches set up around a spectacular entertainment center, which would have looked comfortable even in a movie theater.

Behind the living room, bordered by an open rail, the kitchen stood. Its chrome appliances gleamed in the mellow, recessed lighting; appliances which looked large enough to hold and cook food enough to feed the hungry stomachs of an entire army and then some.

The dining room was to the left of the kitchen, dominated by a truly mammoth table with more than a dozen chairs drawn up tight against it, gently pressing against the shining, dark wood.

Long, dark hallways branched off to the left and right of the living room, and it was to the right that we were directed by Montana, following her into the cool dimness and passing by quite a number of closed doors on our way. My room was last on the left, Corinne's directly across from it on the right. The bathroom finished out the hall and had within it several stalls and at least two large showers that I could see, rather like a bathroom one would see in a college dormitory, I imagined.

While Corinne made a beeline for said bathroom, I entered the room that was to be mine for the duration of this newest adventure, taking in the neat, simple furnishings and pleasing earth tones with a satisfied eye. "This is wonderful, Montana. Thank you."

"My pleasure, Angel. I'm glad you like it." She watched quietly as I placed my luggage at the foot of the neatly made double bed. "I can leave you alone to unpack and get settled, or we can go back into the living room and talk a little more. It's your choice."

"The unpacking can wait," I announced, grinning. "My million and one questions can't."

She returned my smile. "Talk it is. C'mon. I'm sure Corinne will catch up to us when she's ready."

"If she doesn't make good on her threat to start an orgy at the pool," I replied, only half in jest. The look on Corinne's face as she took in the sights reminded me of nothing so much as a young child with his face pressed tight against a candy-store window.

"Without a doubt, Corinne is a treasure. She'll likely have more admirers than even she can handle by the end of the day."

"That'd be a first."

Laughing, she looped a casual arm around my own and guided me back down the long, cool hallway until it broadened out into the main living area of the house. "Make yourself comfortable on one of the couches. I'll get us something to drink."

Slipping into the cool comfort of one of the long couches, I leaned back against the soft fabric and closed my eyes, enjoying a brief moment of respite in an otherwise hectic day. When I opened them again, Montana was standing before me, hands wrapped around two tall glasses filled with liquid, lemons, and lots of ice.

She handed one of the drinks down to me, then joined me on the couch, taking a sip of her own beverage and looking inquiringly at me. "Lemon water," she explained. "It's the drink of choice down here. And pretty refreshing, as well."

As I took a tentative sip, I could feel my eyes widen in surprise. Montana wasn't kidding. "It's delicious!"

"Yup."

"Just lemons in water, huh? What'll they think of next?"

"Well, they've already thought of lemonade."

"True."

After a brief moment of silence, I looked over at her. "So, this ranch is a sort of shelter for battered women?"

"It serves that purpose on occasion, yes. But it serves several others as well."

"Such as?" I hoped I wasn't sounding too interrogatory with my questions. My curiosity has the oddest way of showing itself sometimes.

She didn't appear to be offended, though. "Some women use this ranch as a retreat; a temporary refuge, if you will, from the stresses of their everyday lives. For others, it's a permanent home; a separatist community where they can live their lives mostly free from the influence of males."

She smiled. "We're pretty self sufficient here, as you may have already guessed. The house is on Reservation land, deeded to us by the Yaqui. We grow our own produce and sell the surplus either to the Reservation or to the surrounding towns, which in turn gives us enough money to pay our utility bills, food, sundries, and the like. Every woman who comes here, no matter the reason, is expected to lend her aid to the community in the best way she can. In return, she receives free lodging and food, and, if needed, help with other expenses as they occur."

"Are children allowed?"

"No. If we hear of a woman in need who has children, we help her find assistance elsewhere. All the ranches are for adult women only."

I nodded, sipping my water and listening to the quiet hum of the air conditioner as it cycled on. "Are there any other Amazons here?" I asked softly, somehow loathe to disturb the tranquility of the silent house.

"Besides us, you mean?" she asked, grinning.

Looking down, I blushed a little. In all truth, I'd forgotten I was, in fact, an Amazon. It wasn't really something that came up in daily conversation outside of prison, and as that part of my life started to slip away into the past, some of my memories apparently had as well. "Yeah, besides us."

"Well...there's Rio, who you've already met...."

I turned to her, eyes wide. "Rio? Rio's an *Amazon*?"

"You say that like it's a bad thing."

"Oh! No! No, not at all. Really. I was just...surprised."

Her expression turned serious. "Is there a problem, Angel?"

"No problem. Really." I tried a broad smile on for size and then winced at how poorly it fit.

Montana's eyes narrowed. "Angel..."

"Really. It's just...a difference of opinion, that's all. Nothing to worry about."

"A difference of opinion about what." It wasn't a question, and I knew it.

I sighed, slumping into the seat. "I wish I knew."

"Did she say something? Do something?"

"Honestly, Montana, it's nothing to worry about. I'm sorry I said what I did. I'm sure Rio's an excellent Amazon. We just...we just didn't hit it off, I suppose. But that's alright. Not everyone has to like one another. I'm ok with that. Honestly." I held my free hand up to show my sincerity.

"I'll have a talk with her."

"No! Please! Please, don't do that. She didn't do anything wrong, and I'm sure everything will work itself out, eventually."

"Are you sure?"

"Positive."

After a long, assessing moment, she finally nodded, albeit reluctantly, I thought. "Alright. But if I see anything out of order, I *will* speak to her."

"Okay. Thank you."

As we lapsed into silence once again, I found myself looking around the house's interior, admiring the southwestern color scheme and the simple wall hangings that added color to the bone-white walls. "You must have to sell a lot of oranges to pay the mortgage on this place," I said in an attempt to steer the conversation into other, safer waters.

Her gentle laugh told me I'd succeeded. "I don't think the entire state of Arizona could produce *that* much citrus, Angel. No, this house was willed to me by the mother of a young woman I helped while in the Bog."

"Really?"

"Mm hm. The girl was very sweet, and kind. And quite beautiful as well." A melancholy smile spread itself over Montana's features. "She was such an innocent when she first arrived, like so many of them are."

"Like I was."

"Yes. You remind me of her, somewhat. She was arrested for possession. A short sentence, but as you know, in the Bog, even a month can seem like an eternity, especially if spent in the ill graces of some of the women there."

I nodded, not quite managing to suppress the shudder that came with my own memories of my first weeks in prison.

"When we finally managed to get in and pick up the pieces, I wasn't really sure how much was left. But she surprised me." Her smile was now proud. "She surprised all of us. The adversity made her stronger, and by the time she left us, it was as if a new woman had stepped out of the shell of the old."

"Where is she now?" I asked, sensing a sad ending, but needing to know.

"Dead. She returned here to be with her mother, and they were both killed in a car accident some years ago."

"I'm so sorry to hear that," I said, laying a hand atop hers.

"So was I." The sad smile returned.

"You loved her."

After a long moment, she nodded. "Yes I did. Very much."

"I'm sorry," I said again, at a loss. I wanted to hug her, but wasn't sure if she'd accept such a gesture from me. Instead, I settled for squeezing her hand harder, pleased when she looked at me, thanks in her eyes.

"I'm sorry for your loss as well, Angel," she said, finally. "I was quite pleased when I heard that you and Ice had made it into Canada. I had hoped that you had finally found your dreams."

It was my turn to smile sadly. "We did. For a while. Before Cavallo came in and started the whole avalanche." I sighed as the pain, a constant companion, settled itself on my shoulders once again, all the more heavy for the temporary respite. "I know it's been three months, but it still feels so unreal, you know? Like a dream, almost. Or a nightmare." I shook my head. "Most mornings, I still find myself waking up expecting to still be in the cabin, Ice sleeping next to me. And it's like I lose her all over again every time I *do* wake up. It makes me not want to go to sleep."

"I can understand that."

"Yeah. I guess you can." I absently wiped the tear rolling down my cheek.

"What happened to the woman who turned her in?"

"Ruby?" I laughed mirthlessly. "God, what a screw up. I find myself wanting to hate her. But I can't. No matter how much I try, I just can't. She acted out of love for me." I felt my fist curl and slam down on the forgiving cushion. "If I had only told her the truth in the beginning, none of this would ever have happened."

"You don't know that, Angel. For all you know, telling the truth would only have meant a sooner ending. Sometimes people see with their eyes and not with their hearts. Your friend might have meant well, but she didn't take the time to look beyond what she thought was the surface. You can't take all the blame for this upon yourself. It does no good."

"Maybe not," I replied, looking down at my lap.

"So what happened to her?"

"I'm not sure. I guess she's still in Canada. I doubt there'd be any reason for her to leave. Especially now." I closed my eyes against the memory of that horrible night, but it came anyway, mocking me with its stealth.

Corinne had gotten to me just as the last of the police cars pulled away into the night. I remembered screaming at the top of my lungs as she pulled me into a crushing embrace, holding me so tightly that I felt smothered against her body, unable to breathe.

I remembered trying desperately to pull free, but she held me with a strength I hadn't known she possessed, refusing to let me slip away. Knowing, I think, what I'd do if I did.

After a period of time—a moment, a day, a century—she loosened her hold, and I pulled away, as if scalded by her very presence. I turned, and she was there.

The one who betrayed me.

The one who tore my heart out and held it bleeding in her hands.

The one who drilled a great, gaping rent into my very soul.

And then I just...blacked out is the only way I can think to put it.

I didn't come back into myself until quite some time later.

Corinne was holding me once again. Of Ruby, there was no sign.

My right hand ached. When I looked at it, it was scraped, raw, bleeding, and swollen.

I knew I'd punched her. And part of me rejoiced.

Reading my mind as she always had, Corinne gently shook her head and then turned me to face the wall near the front windows. A wall which now bore a fist-sized hole in the plaster. A hole which was head-height on a person like Ruby. "You didn't hurt her, Angel. You wanted to, I know. But you didn't."

And that was all that was ever said on the subject.

And though I never saw Ruby again, to this day, my hand still aches when it rains, forever a reminder of the night I lost my soul and the woman, however unwittingly, who took it from me.

I wasn't sure how I wound up in Montana's strong arms, crying as if my very life depended upon this shedding of tears, but after a brief second of tense wonder, I simply surrendered to the inevitability of it and let the tears fall where they might.

Which, at the moment, happened to be all over Montana's neatly starched shirt.

She didn't seem to mind, however.

I hadn't spoken of the events of that night since that night. With Corinne and I, it was almost balletic, the way we would adroitly maneuver so as to avoid the issue. And who else, really, had there been to discuss it with? Donita likely already knew the whole story—albeit a vastly shortened version, considering her source was Ice. The only other person I'd spent recent time with was Rio, and quite frankly, I would have rather bitten through a high-tension wire than to cry on that particular shoulder.

Montana, however, was somehow safe. At least, I assumed as much, since my body was telling me something my mind didn't already know.

She reacted exactly right, simply holding me and stroking my hair until my cathartic release played itself out and left me empty, but in a good way. A way, I suppose, I had been unconsciously craving for the past three months.

Several moments passed before I finally pulled away and gave her a watery, half embarrassed smile as I wiped the remaining tears from my burning eyes. "I'm sorry for getting your shirt wet."

Her smile was kind. "Don't be. You've been needing to get that out for a long time, haven't you."

"Yeah. I suppose I have." I took in a deep, shuddering breath, then let it out, amazed with the lightness I felt deep inside, as if a festering wound had finally been lanced, the poison flowing out with my tears. "Thank you."

She shrugged. "That's what friends are for, right?"

I nodded. "Yeah. Thanks. Friend."

"You're welcome. Friend." Chuckling softly, she stretched. "Better now?"

"You don't know how much."

"Good. How about if I let you free to go exploring? Poke around a little, get a feel for the place. After all, it's gonna be your home for awhile."

I nodded again, smiling this time. "I'd like that."

"Alright then. Dinner's in about four hours or so. You'll hear the bell when it's ready." Getting up off the couch, she escorted me to one of the front doors and ushered me out. "Have fun."

"Thanks. I plan to."

The afternoon passed into evening rather quickly as I explored the grounds, poking my nose in anywhere and everywhere and generally making a nuisance out of myself.

As I'd known I would all along, my meanderings eventually led me to the stables and corral beyond. I spared several moments to watch a group of women industriously muck out the stalls, change out the food and water, and do whatever else needed doing to make the stables ready for the horses' return.

Then I moved on to the corral, climbing up the split rail fence to sit atop one of the posts and watch as a number of women put some of the horses through their paces. Of particular interest to me was a young, lithe, blonde woman who was racing her beautiful chestnut mare around three barrels set up in the central ring of the corral. Horse and rider moved in perfect symmetry, flowing like water around each barrel as women on the sidelines cheered and whooped. Another woman, broad and squat, pumped a triumphant fist in the air, a stopwatch clenched tightly between her palm and fingers.

Hats sailed into the air as the young woman slipped down from her horse, her boots kicking up clouds of dust as they reconnected with the desert floor. She was immediately engulfed by a crowd of cheering onlookers as her horse was gently led away by one of the stable-hands.

Several moments later, the crowd parted and the young woman walked out from the masses, dusting off her clothing and putting her hat back on her head, setting the brim with a casual hand. Walking in my direction, she stopped just shy of the fence and tilted her head up to look at me, smiling. "Hey, there," she said in a musical voice that was vaguely familiar to me, but one which I couldn't quite place.

"Hello. That was some riding you did there."

Her fair face colored a little as she shrugged and stuffed her hands into the pockets of her jeans. "It wasn't bad, I guess. I'll have to get a lot better, though, if I'm gonna have a chance in the Buckeye Rodeo."

"Well, you looked pretty damn good to me. I'm probably not the best authority on the subject, though."

She blushed again then laughed. "Maybe not on barrel racing, but you're pretty good at other things."

I could feel my eyes narrow. "Excuse me?"

"You don't remember me, do you?"

I winced. "No, I don't think so. I'm sorry."

"Don't be sorry. Please. I wouldn't expect you to remember me. I've changed a lot since you saw me last, even if it wasn't that long ago."

I peered down at her. "Alright. You've baited the hook and thrown in the line. Do you want me to just swim around a little before I go for it, or would you prefer it if I just grabbed on tight so you could reel me in?"

"Sorry." Her smile came again, bright and white. "My name's Ericka, and you saved my life, once."

"In the Bog?"

"Yup. Mouse and her buddies were set on having me for dessert, but you made sure they went home empty handed." She shook her head, her long blonde hair fanning out in amber waves behind her. "You were amazing. I'd never seen a woman fight like that before. It was...unbelievable."

It was my turn to blush and look down at my hands as the awe in her voice washed over me and brought with it, I'll readily confess, no small sense of pride. I remembered the incident vaguely, as I remembered most of those long ago fights in the Bog. There were so many that, after awhile, they all just tended to blend together into one long, nearly never-ending conflict.

My pride wasn't so much with my fighting abilities, such as they were—and are—but rather with the simple fact that I was given the opportunity to help in the first place. It felt good to know that I was a person others could look to for help, just as it felt good to remember that fact. Especially now, when all it seemed I could do was to seek out and rely upon the help of others.

"I didn't mean to embarrass you," she said softly, laying a gloved hand on my thigh in a gentle touch.

"You didn't. It's just...." I sighed. "That's not important now. I'm glad I could help."

"I'm glad you could, too. It was the closest I ever came, I think, to dying. Quickly, I mean. I'd been dying slowly for years."

"How do you mean?"

She shrugged again. "I was hooked on drugs for a long time. Cocaine, mostly. My arrest should have given me a wake-up call, but it didn't. Drugs were easier to get in the Bog than they were on the streets." Her laugh was mirthless. "Course, the price was higher. And when I finally decided to stop paying it, well...you walked in on the result. That's when I decided to quit. Cold turkey all the way. It was really hard, especially at first. But every time I was tempted to score some more coke, I remembered the look on your face when you walked into that room and started beating the crap out of those idiots. And I figured that if someone like you could care so much for someone like me, someone you didn't even know, then I figured maybe it was time that I started caring for myself, too."

"That's a wonderful story."

"Every word's the truth. You saved my life in more ways than one that day, Angel. And I told myself that if I ever got the opportunity to thank you, I would." She looked directly at me, the fire of sincerity burning in her bright hazel eyes. "Thank you. I mean that, from the bottom of my heart."

Jumping down off the fence-post, I pulled her into a tight hug and felt her return the embrace with strength and vigor. Pulling away, I smiled at her. "You're welcome, Ericka."

She blushed again. "Well, actually, they don't call me that anymore."

"No?"

"Nope. See, when I heard that you were an Amazon, I decided that I wanted to be one as well. Kinda schoolgirl crush-like of me, I know, but that's how I was back then. So I started working out to get back into shape again, and started hanging out with some of the other Amazons. And then, right after you were released, they made me an Amazon." She grinned, gesturing to herself. "I'll bet you can guess what they named me."

Taking a step back, I made a show of carefully examining her from tip to toe. "Cowgirl, right?"

"Got it in one."

"Figures. Amazons," I snorted, "not an original one in the bunch."

Her laugh and the dinner bell sounded at the same time, jolting me a little. She touched my shoulder in sympathy. "Did that to me the first couple of times, too." Then she looked down at herself, shaking her head. "Well, I'd better get cleaned up before Montana gives me fifty kinds of holy hell for tracking dirt through the house again. See you at dinner?"

"Sounds great!"

That night, sleep claimed me more easily than it had in a very long time. The evening had passed quickly and, for the most part, pleasantly as I spent the time exchanging spirited banter with Cowgirl, Montana, and Corinne and ignoring the other end of the table, where Rio held court, her fawning cronies slavish to her every word and action.

That I actually felt tired when it came time to turn in was a blessing in itself, and once the lights were turned off and a quiet goodnight was said to my absent lover, I turned to my side, closed my eyes, and remembered nothing until I woke up again.

Which, unfortunately, seemed to be smack-dab in the middle of the night, judging from the absolute lack of light from the direction of the window.

My heart rate was up, though not from fear. At least I didn't think so. A feeling more akin to anticipation washed through my body, standing the hairs up on my arms and behind my neck. I had the feeling of being watched, though I knew, beyond all shadow of a possible doubt, that I was most definitely alone.

Had it been a dream? Some nightmare which had evaporated back into the dark mist the second I opened my eyes?

No. Nightmares and I were old friends, especially of late. And this simply didn't feel like the aftereffects of one of their regular visits.

What then?

Cautiously, as soundlessly as I could, I turned from my side to my back...and almost jumped clean out of my skin when my cheek brushed against something soft, cool, and giving.

Scrabbling backward, I almost fell off the bed, my arm reaching somehow behind me to turn on the light. My free hand curled into a tight fist as I blinked against the bright light, breathing in quick pants through my nose as I waited for my eyes to adjust to the change.

"What the...?"

Lying on the pillow, completely devoid of thorns, lay one perfect, blood-red rose.

I stared at it dumbly for a long moment, my mind not comprehending what my eyes were seeing.

As if still asleep and dreaming, I watched as my hand slowly snaked out, fingers extended to their maximum length and gently brushing the stem before pulling away slightly, as if afraid they would be bitten. I looked on as they approached the rose again, this time taking it into a careful grip and pulling forward until the bloom was directly under my nose.

Inhaling deeply, I was unable to stop the smile which spread across my face.

"Ice," I sighed with pleasure as I took another deep breath, then gently brushed the incredibly soft petals against my cheek.

Then I stopped, abruptly, as I realized where I was and what I was doing.

My heart sped up again.

"Ice?"

Wide-eyed, I craned my neck until the vertebrae popped, scanning every inch of the room for my lover's dark presence.

My first waking impulse was confirmed, however.

I was completely alone.

Adrenaline shot me out of bed like a rocket, and my hand was twisting the doorknob open before my feet even realized they'd hit the floor. Yanking the door open wide, I stepped into the dim hallway, almost colliding with Corinne, who filled up part of said hallway, her head cocked at an odd angle, as if listening to something I couldn't hear.

The near collision brought Corinne's attention to me, and she took a long look at the rose that was still in my hand before dragging her eyes up to my own. "Secret admirer?" she asked, smirking.

"Where is she?"

"Your admirer? I may be good, Angel, but even I'm not *that* good. To ascertain where she might be, one would have to first know *who* she might be, yes?"

A harsh, barely restrained whisper from the living room cut off my retort and I pushed Corinne none-too-gently out of my way as I strode down the long hallway, preparing myself for the much-awaited sight of my lover.

What I received instead, however, was the vision of Montana and Rio at right angles to one another; the former standing calmly with a piece of white paper in one hand; the latter gesturing wildly, her face brick with barely controlled rage.

"Do it, Rio. Now. I won't ask you again," Montana said, her voice calm and uninflected.

"Fuck that, Montana. Everything was fine here before that blonde-headed bitch came down here."

"What's going on, Montana?" I said upon hearing my cue.

Rio whirled at the sound of my voice, her dark eyes absolutely blazing with anger. "You!"

Reaching out, Montana easily spun the much larger woman around to face her. "*Now*, Rio."

After a long moment, Rio's broad shoulders slumped in defeat. "Fine," she said, jerking away from Montana. Whirling again, she strode toward me, her fists clenched tightly at her side.

I braced myself for what was coming, both unwilling and unable to back down from her dangerous threat.

At the last second, she stepped left, jarring my shoulder with the side of her body. The rose in my hand flew loose from the impact, and, turning, I watched helplessly as she kicked it against the door, scattering the beautiful petals across the floor and crushing a few beneath her boot as she left the house, slamming the door behind her.

I turned slowly back. "Montana?"

"I'm sorry, Angel," she whispered.

"What's going on?"

Walking until she drew even with me, she handed me the sheet of paper she was holding.

It was a note. That much I could tell from my first quick scan. Unsigned, but that didn't matter, as I knew the bold handwriting as well as I knew the beat of my own heart.

If I were Cavallo, you'd all be dead.
Let me down like this again, and you'll wish I was.

"Ice wrote this," I said, stating the obvious.

"Yes. I found it stuck into my headboard with this." Holding her other hand out, she displayed a wicked-looking knife, its sharp edge glimmering malevolently in the dim lighting.

"Where is she?"

"Gone." She sighed. "Long gone."

"And you sent Rio to find her?"

"No. Rio's one of the best there is, but even *she* couldn't find Ice if she doesn't want to be found. Rio's in charge of security here. I sent her off to call for some reinforcements."

"But why? Why doesn't she want to be found? Why didn't she stay? I don't understand." I felt those damn tears wanting to fall again, but at that point, I think I was just too angry to give them the satisfaction of wetting my cheeks.

Montana sighed. "I don't understand either, Angel. The one thing I *do* understand is that she was testing us, testing our defenses. And we failed. Miserably."

"You can't blame yourself for this, Montana. It's Ice we're talking about, after all. I mean, she's...was...is...hell, I don't know anymore...an assassin. This kind of thing is what she used to get paid to do, remember?"

"Yes, Angel. I remember. But how can I be sure she was wrong? How can I be sure that even if we didn't stop her, we could stop Cavallo? Or, for that matter, any half-baked idiot or jealous boyfriend who came in here wanting to tear the place up?" She looked down at the knife in her hand, turning it over, and over again. "I used to think we were up to any threat. Now I know how foolish that idea was."

"Montana, you can't—"

"Yes, I can, Angel. I can and I will. The lives of every woman here, including you, are my responsibility." She looked at me once again, her jaw square and tight. "I failed this first test. Thank god we all lived through it. I'll be damned if I fail again. If you'll excuse me, I have some business to attend to."

Nodding to each of us in turn, she turned crisply and disappeared back down the opposite hall to what I assumed was her own room, leaving Corinne and myself to stare after her in shocked silence.

I spent most of the rest of the day shuttling wildly between anger and grief, hope and despair. Part of me was so angry at Ice that I wanted, given the impossible opportunity, to throttle her. Though I well understood her innate need to see to it that I was safe as it was possible for me to be, I didn't understand why that need had to come at the expense of my own innate need to see her, safe, whole, and, most importantly, free.

Much as it shames me to admit such a thing, part of me was glad Rio had bumped the rose from my hand and crushed it beneath the heel of her boot. The rest of me, however, spent long, painful moments on my knees, gathering up each and every petal I could find as some sort of tangible link to the woman who held my heart in her hands.

Since I knew that sleep wouldn't let me catch him quite so easily the second time around, I gave up even bothering to try, and instead showered and changed, then padded out to the kitchen, where work had already begun preparing meals for a new day as yet undawned.

Pitching in allowed the time to pass quickly and mindlessly, and before I knew it, I was up to my elbows in soapsuds, washing away the fruits of my morning labors.

The kitchen crew, at least for breakfast, was made up of an older, quieter group of women who seemed far more interested in getting the meal made and the dishes cleaned than expending energy on gossiping about who did what to whom, when, where, and how often.

That's not to say there wasn't talk, because there was, just not very much of it.

After the last dish was washed, dried, and put away, I escaped the suddenly too small confines of the house, and stepped out into the warm, bright desert day with a distinct feeling of relief. Taking in a deep, cleansing breath, I allowed my feet to take me where they would, not at all surprised to find myself once again perched atop a corral fence-post as the horses were released from their night-time abode.

The blood bay stallion, of course, led the way, and I felt a little smirk form, tipping my figurative hat to him for getting the plum job of being the only male around for miles. He snorted and bobbed his head at me, as if in agreement, before bounding away, most of the herd in tow.

I watched his antics with pleasure, enjoying the way the sunlight dappled his coat and brought the thick, corded muscles of his massive body into sharp relief. He reminded me, more than slightly, of the horse Ice had carved for me last Christmas—

almost a year ago, now.

God, has it really been a year? How could time have gotten away from me that quickly? How could...?

Any further thoughts along that maudlin line were halted as I felt a gentle nudge to my knee. Startled, I almost lost my balance, but maintained it by grabbing onto the nudger, which in this case happened to be the nose of a beautiful dappled gray pony, who indignantly snorted my fingers from her nostrils.

I couldn't help but laugh (almost losing my balance again, incidentally) as she appraised me with one huge, dark eye before lowering her head to nudge against my leg again, this time higher against my thigh, her nostrils snuffling as if in search of a treat.

"I'm sorry girl," I said with genuine regret. "I don't have anything for you."

A musical laugh sounded next to me, and I looked up to see Cowgirl astride a massive horse, the brim of her white Stetson tipped low to shade her face from the relentless sun. "Don't worry about Cleo, Angel. She thinks she's a puppy. C'mon, Cleo, give the woman some room. She's not your personal feed-bag."

"That's alright," I replied, giving the horse a scratch between the eyes. "I don't mind. She's kinda sweet."

"Oh, she's sweet alright. Keep paying attention to her like that and you'll find yourself with an eight foot shadow for the rest of your life."

"Don't mind the mean lady, Cleo," I stage whispered, continuing to scratch my newfound friend. "She's just jealous 'cause you only have eyes for me."

Cowgirl snorted as she led her horse around in a tight circle. "While I work on trying to get over my envy issues, would you like to take a ride with me? I need to fix some fence out on the back part of the corral and I'd enjoy the company."

I winced. "Well, as much as I love horses, I'm afraid I haven't ridden one since I was a kid."

"That's no problem. We'll just let you ride your new friend there. She's pretty forgiving."

I looked at Cleo, who tossed her head, then nudged me again.

"What the heck. Looks like I've been outvoted anyway."

Chapter
3

The sun was very close to setting as I walked my tired, sweaty, and saddle-sore body back toward the house. I was exhausted, beyond doubt, but pleasantly so. Cowgirl's gentle company managed to keep my mind away from sadder things, and her sweet voice belting out country song after country song kept me laughing and humming along, though I couldn't, as my father was wont to say, carry a tune in a bucket.

I stepped around Rio's car, which was once again parked in front of the house, and spared a quick wave to Corinne, who was lounging by the pool with a bevy of naked beauties attending her every whim. Grinning and shaking my head at her good fortune, I opened the door and stepped into the house, just in time to see an almost exact replay of the scene early that very morning, this time set in the living room.

Both turned to me as I entered, but any thoughts of simply reversing my steps and spending the night in the stables was erased as Montana beckoned me forward with a smile.

"I...um...didn't mean to interrupt. I'll just...be going to my room to wash up."

"No, that's alright, Angel. I'm actually glad you came back. I have some friends...."

Any further words were blocked out as I felt an unfamiliar, and somewhat gruff, hand clasp hard onto my left shoulder.

Already tired and wary from the resentful glare I was getting from Rio, my body reacted without thought, doing what it had been trained to do when it perceived a threat.

Reaching up, I grabbed the hand on my shoulder, twisting the wrist as I thrust my hip out to the left. With a smooth, controlled motion, as I'd been so carefully taught, I threw the body behind me over my hip, then straddled it, glaring down at the idiot who dared to grab me from behind like that.

A glare which quickly changed to a look of shocked disbelief as I recognized the woman I'd just thrown to the floor.

"Pony? Is that you?"

"Surprise?" she wheezed through the broad, proud grin threatening to split her face in half.

"*Pony*!" I yelled, grabbing her hand and hauling her back to her feet with adrenaline-fueled strength. "How did you...? Where did you...?" The rest of my babbling questions were lost as I pulled her tight against me in a hug.

Chuckling low in her throat, she returned the embrace before lifting me off of my feet and twirling me around before setting me back down again. "*Damn* it's good to see you again, Angel!" After giving each cheek a loud, smacking kiss, she pulled away to the length of her arms and boldly appraised me from head to toe, her eyes lingering longer in some places than others. "Lookin' good," she said, leering.

"You're not looking half bad yourself, Pony," I replied, laughing through my tears.

"I'll bet you say that to all the studs, Angel," came a very familiar, very loved, and very much missed voice behind me.

Stunned, I whirled, feeling my jaw unhinge as I did so. "Critter?"

"Hey there, stranger." Her smile as bright as the Arizona sunshine, she opened her arms and I ran willingly into them, feeling her hug engulf me like the warmest of blankets.

"I don't believe it," I blubbered. "I can't believe you're here. How...?"

"Thank Donita and a very shocked parole board," she said, her own eyes suspiciously bright. "They sprung Pony and I together. I think they're still trying to figure out why they did that."

"What about Sonny?"

Her smile faltered just a little. "We're hoping for a little better luck the next time around. She misses all of us, but she's doing ok." She smirked. "She found a new *looooove.*"

Laughing, I grabbed Pony's arm and pulled them both in for another tight hug, happy beyond belief that these two old, beloved, and cherished friends were with me once again, especially at a time when I needed them so very desperately.

After pulling away, I gave then each a long, assessing look. "Neither of you has changed a bit. Not a bit!"

"You sure as hell have!" Pony replied, poking at my belly and scowling. "Not that you weren't a knockout before, Angel, but you're positively *buff* now! What gives, woman? Ice put you on some steroids or something?"

I laughed. "No. Nothing like that. I came by these muscles honestly."

"Honestly? What'd ya do? Haul rocks around up there in bumfuck?"

"Pony!" Critter yelled, slapping Pony on the arm.

"Hey!" Pony yelped, rubbing her arm and scowling at Critter. "It's an honest question! When I first saved her ass, she was all skin and bones and baby fat. Now she's got more muscles than I do!"

Critter laughed. "God, Pony. You're so butch."

"You got a problem with that?" She turned back to me. "Spill it, Angel. What do I gotta do to get a body like that?"

"Well, for starters," I replied through the smirk that was forming, "you could build your own house."

"Bu...." Her eyes widened. "You *built* your own damn *house*?"

"Well, I didn't build it myself, no. But I helped. A lot." I winced over the memory of strained muscles and splinters and blisters and everything else that went along with building our cabin. That wince quickly turned to a grin, however, when I remembered the tender care Ice took with my injuries, and the many evenings spent face down and blissfully naked as my lover's hot hands expertly removed each and every bit of soreness from my abused muscles, replacing that soreness with languor, or passion, however she saw fit.

Looking up just in time to catch Critter's knowing smile, I felt a blush heat my face and quickly looked down again, trying to regain my composure.

Completely oblivious, Pony poked me again. "I can't believe you built your own damn house."

"Well, I did. I also chopped about a forest's worth of firewood, walked almost everywhere I needed to go, and swam two miles in the lake every morning and every evening in the summer."

Absolute silence reigned as Pony stared me with eyes the size of silver dollars. After a long moment, she covered her face and shook her head. "Never mind," she mumbled through her fingers. "Forget I asked. I'll just keep the body I got."

Grinning in absolute satisfaction, I turned to see Montana looking at us with an unreadable expression on her face. Of Rio, there was no sign at all. "Where's Rio?"

"She left."

"Left?" Pony asked. "Where the hell'd she go? We were supposed to go over the security measures, damnit!"

"Something's been eating at her all day," Critter supplied. "She's not like her usual self at all. Is there a problem?"

"It's been longer than all day," Montana replied, giving me a significant look.

That was something Pony *didn't* miss. She whirled back to me, dark eyes narrow and penetrating. "What's goin' on, Angel."

"Nothing, Pony. We just...we didn't hit it off real well, that's all."

"That's bullshit. You'd hit it off with the devil himself, Angel. What's *really* goin' on?"

I shrugged. "I don't know. There's obviously something about me that rubs her the wrong way. I don't know what it is, but I'm sure we can work it out eventually." I smiled. "Not everyone has to like me, you know."

"When I'm around, they do," Pony growled, fists clenched.

"Pony, calm down," Montana said. "It's gone beyond that now. You know how proud she is. When I had her bring you and Critter in, she got upset. She thinks I'm questioning her abilities."

"And she's blaming *Angel* for that? That's absolute bullshit! If she'd done her job right in the first place, she wouldn't have had to worry about it!"

"Pony—" This time, it was Critter's turn to try.

"Forget it, Critter. I don't know what damn bug flew up her ass, but I'm gonna pull it out for her. Through her throat."

"Pony, there's a lot going on."

"Fine. She can have a nice long time to think about it from the comfort of her own bed after I put her ass in traction."

As she turned to stomp away, I grabbed her arm, surprised at the ease with which I turned her back to me. "I appreciate this, Pony, but please, let me handle it myself, ok? When this whole thing cools down, I'll try and have a talk with her. You can even come along and hide in the shadows if you want. Just please...this is between Rio and I. Let's keep it there for now, alright?"

She scowled at me, obviously not ready to give up her anger, but finally nodded and gently pulled her arm away from my grasp. "Fine. But if you think I'm not gonna rag her ass over the security situation, you've got another thing coming. It's not just Cavallo we need to worry about, you know. There's a whole planet full of crazies who'd love to bomb this place off the fucking map. If she's not doin' her job right, then I'm gonna call her on it."

I returned the nod. "That's fine. I'm guessing that since you're down here, that's your job."

"Damn right it is."

Critter laughed, pushing Pony toward the door. "Go scare the venom out of a rattlesnake or something, Cujo, willya?"

"Fine," she grumped, then turned and left the house without another word.

Unable to stop myself, I just threw back my head and laughed, crossing my arms over my stomach. "God, I missed you guys!"

"We missed you too, Angel," Critter replied, slinging an arm over my shoulder and ruffling my hair. "We missed you, too."

"...and the next thing we knew, there she went, ass over elbows, right into the septic tank. The stink didn't come out for weeks! It followed her around like a cloud."

I collapsed against the pillows, weak with laughter, not even bothering to wipe away the tears of mirth that were coursing down my cheeks.

"Yup," Critter continued, her face the very essence of the word "smug." "Ol' Mousie was never the same after that. I told her she'd wind up smelling like shit one day. I was right, too. Literally."

Rolling over onto my stomach, I tried desperately to stretch out the cramps that were tearing at my abdominal muscles, already abused from a day of horse riding and hard physical labor. "Stop," I gasped. "Please. You're killing me over here."

"Sorry." She didn't sound very sorry at all.

But she did stop, which was a blessed relief. When my hysteria finally got itself back under control, I flipped on my back again and propped myself up on my elbows, fixing her with a pointed look. "You're bad."

"Sure am."

"Well," I said, sobering up a little, "much as I missed you guys, I don't miss waking up every morning wondering if someone like Mouse or Derby is waiting to rearrange my face for looking at her the wrong way." Shaking my head, I sighed. "I just wish I don't sometimes get that feeling when Rio's around."

"I wish you didn't either, Angel. I'm not sure what's going on with her. Rio's one of those really big people who scares the crap out of you to look at her, but she's really sweet underneath. At least, she used to be. God knows what's wrong with her now."

"So, you knew her before, then?"

"Yeah. In the Bog. She got there about a year after I did. She was huge even then, but those muscles were just for show. She couldn't fight worth a spit in the rain."

"Really?" I asked, finding that hard to believe.

"Yeah. Really. She might have been strong, but she was slow, and clumsy as all hell. The bullies held off at first, because of her size, but once they found out she couldn't fight, they were all over her like white on rice. It would have been pretty funny if it wasn't so damn sad to watch."

"What happened?"

"Ice happened. They were giving Rio all kinds of holy hell out by the weight area one day. A few of them were holding her down with the barbell she was lifting pushed against her chest. The rest were punching and kicking the crap out of her. The rest of us were kinda standing by because it seemed like she was big enough to take care of herself, but evidently Ice didn't think so, because she came out of the prison and before any of us could think to move, it was over." Her look of wonder was obvious as she thought about that incident. "Two of 'em wound up in the hospital. The rest...well...let's just say they weren't in any shape to bully a tadpole for a few months."

I snorted softly. "Why am I not surprised?"

Critter grinned. "I'd be surprised if you were." She shifted positions, coming to lie on her back next to me, our heads sharing the same pillow. "So anyway, Ice sorta took Rio under her wing and taught her how to fight. She took to it like a duck to water, and before we knew it, she was using those muscles for more than just impressing the ladies."

"Did she ever bully anybody once she could fight?"

"Rio? No. Not at all. Like I said, she's as sweet as they come. God, you should have seen the look on her face when Ice made her an Amazon. I thought she was gonna bust out crying in front of everyone."

I couldn't help but shake my head in amazed disbelief. The picture of Rio that Critter was painting was as different from my own version as night is to day. Suddenly, a thought popped into my head. "Critter, were Rio and Ice...?"

She looked at me for a long moment. "Are you asking me if they were lovers?"

I nodded.

Her brow furrowed, but after a moment, her expression cleared as understanding dawned. "You're afraid she's jealous, aren't you?"

"It would make sense, yes. An ex-lover having to play taxi-driver to the current lover, carting her to hell and back, then being told her skills aren't enough to protect her." I shrugged. "I'd probably be angry, too."

"Well, it would make sense, if that were the case. But, as far as I know, it's not. Rio worshipped the ground Ice walked on—hell, we all did—but they weren't an item. Friends, yes. Involved, no."

"Well, I guess that takes us back to square one again," I said, gently hitting the mattress with my hand.

Critter grasped my other hand, threading our fingers together. "Maybe she just has some personal stuff going on right now, Angel. Maybe all this just came at a bad time for her. Maybe after Pony settles things down here, that talk you were thinking about might not be such a bad idea."

"You're right. I just hope I can wait that long."

She laughed. "You've been with Ice for what...seven years now? If there's one thing you have in abundance, Angel, it's patience."

"A virtue that's being sorely tested right about now, let me assure you," I said, scowling.

Laughing again, she rolled over and kissed me soundly on the lips, then jumped up off the bed. "Lemme go see if Pony needs me for anything, then I think it's time to hit the bed. It's been a long day. Night, Angel."

"Night, Critter."

A jaunty wave, and she made for the door.

"Critter?"

"Yeah?"

"Thanks."

A half-cocky smile graced her lips as she sketched a half-bow in my direction. "Anytime, Angel. Anytime."

The next several days passed quickly and without incident as I gradually became accustomed to my new, if temporary, home. I spent most mornings in the kitchen with Corinne, helping to prepare breakfast for the thirty or so women who stayed at the ranch. It was the only real time we had to spend together, so I valued each morning for the chance it gave me to be with her, no matter how briefly.

Critter and Pony were busy as well, reinforcing ranch security with Rio. To her credit, Rio seemed nothing if not extremely dedicated to her job, throwing herself into it one thousand percent of the way and making sure that mistakes like that of a week ago would not be repeated on her watch.

I didn't have the heart to tell her that, where Ice was concerned, those mistakes would always be repeated. Not that it would have mattered, really. She would likely have smacked me senseless if I did.

She seemed a bit calmer with Pony around, though, so I had hope for an eventual reconciliation between us, given the opportunity.

I'd spend a good bit of the daylight hours at the corral, watching the horses, feeding and grooming any that needed it, and generally keeping myself busy and my mind off my absent lover, as best as I was able.

My best was frequently not good enough, and the ache in my chest only got stronger the more time passed without seeing her. I often found myself talking to her, much as one would a deceased loved one, sharing bits of my day with her, and telling her how much I missed her.

An evening ritual had also developed. I'd saddle up my newfound equine friend and set out for the westernmost part of the corral to watch the sun set over the distant mountains. The sight never failed to take my breath away, and it was the one time in the day when I felt closest to Ice.

I shed more than a few tears on those solitary treks, but always returned home feeling better for having gone.

One night, long after the sun had set, I escaped from the too-warm and too-noisy confines of the main house, taking in the cool quiet of the desert and feeling my body calm instantly as the peaceful night drew me in and made me welcome in its darkness.

I headed toward the stables, several carrots in hand, knowing that Cleo's placid, silent company was just what the doctor ordered for me.

As I entered the cool comfort of the stables, taking in the smell of hay and horses with almost absent pleasure, I heard an odd, rhythmic thumping noise that let me know that I wasn't the only two-footed animal in the place.

Still, the building was relatively well-lit and the horses seemed unconcerned, so I paid no significant mind to the noises and instead moved to answer the anxious greetings of Cleo, who could smell carrots, it was said, from a continent away. With a head cold. In a hurricane.

As she strained her neck near to breaking in order to quickly lip up the treats I had for her, I couldn't help but laugh at her antics and give her a fond and happy scratch between the eyes.

When she inhaled what was in my hand, she nudged my chest, snuffling for more. I laughed again, delighted, and as I pushed her insistent nose away, I heard the noises in the rear of the stable stop.

A moment later, a long, wide shadow fell over me.

I looked up to find Rio standing by the open doors, her black eyes glittering with anger, a large knife in her hand.

As I turned to face her, a smirk curled one corner of her upper lip. "Evening, blondie." She gave an exaggerated look around. "Where are your little protectors? Aren't you all joined at the hip or somethin'?"

Pulling away from Cleo, I squared myself to face her. "What do you want, Rio?" I could feel my body tense, but I fought it, trying to remain as calm as possible.

The knife flashed as she gestured with it. "Your head on a platter would do, for starters."

Though I kept my gaze pinned to her, in the periphery of my vision, I could see several implements that could be used as weapons should I need one in a pinch. That thought calmed me, relaxing my bunched muscles. "Well, you certainly brought the right tool for the job."

She looked down at the knife as if just realizing it was in her hand. After a second, she dropped it to the ground. "I don't think I'll be needing it on the likes of you."

I felt myself shrug. It was amazing how cool and centered I felt. Of course, hearing the low tones of my lover in my thoughts helped immeasurably as well. "Your decision, I guess." As she started to come forward, fists clenched, I held up a hand.

Stunned, she stopped in her tracks and stared at me.

"Before you start rearranging my limbs for me, I have a question."

She squinted at me. "Are you nuts?"

"Maybe. But I still have a question."

She scowled. "What?"

"Why?"

"Why *what*?"

"Why are you doing this? Why do you hate me so much? I've obviously done something to offend you. I figure if you're going to rip me to shreds, you could at least be nice enough to answer that."

She shook her head, not even considering the question. "You wouldn't understand."

Then she came at me, her arms open wide for a classic bull rush. It was a move I'd seen a hundred times before. I was, I'll admit, a little disappointed at her lack of originality.

I was working under no illusions, however. If she got close enough to get her arms around me, I'd be in for a world of hurt. Someone as big and as angry as Rio could easily kill me, even without meaning to do so. And even if she didn't, I was sure she'd have no qualms about beating me so badly that I'd wind up wishing I *was* dead.

Waiting until she was almost on me, I simply ducked beneath one of her outstretched arms, darting away and turning just in time to see her narrowly miss the stable wall.

"Try me, Rio," I said as she turned, her face twisted in a snarl of rage. "I might understand better than you think."

"Forget it, blondie." She rushed me again, this time in a more controlled maneuver, then swung one of her long arms out in a wicked cross that would have surely crushed my skull to bits if I hadn't ducked out of the way just in time.

Another punch came, and then another, but somehow I managed to evade them all.

She was strong, and quite obviously skilled, but no match for the woman I had made a habit of sparring with daily. Her swings seemed slow and almost clumsy in comparison to Ice's sinuous fluidity.

Still, I kept my eyes open and my hands poised, ready to try my best to deflect anything I wasn't quick enough to dodge.

Then a huge foot, topped by a tree-trunk sized leg, swung out to connect right at the nerve center of my right thigh. My leg gave out and I went down, quickly rolling away through the straw-strewn floor to evade a flurry of further kicks.

Just as I was about to trap myself in a corner, her foot slipped and she almost went down, her arms pinwheeling wildly for balance. Taking advantage of the opportunity presented, I stopped my roll and jumped back to my feet again, stiffened fingers working desperately to loosen the cramp she'd given me.

The knife glittered up at me through the straw on the floor, but after only a second of consideration, I looked away from that particular temptation. Never again would I go down that road.

Seeing my hesitation, she pounced, easing in and walloping me with a kick to the gut that, though partially blocked, sent me stumbling backwards for several feet while gasping for breath. I hit the wall then bounced off, managing to evade her wild left to my head as I did so.

When the right followed, as I knew it would, I threw my hands up, catching her at the elbow and using a little move Ice had taught me to spin her away from me and into the wall I had just moved away from.

She hit it with a force to rattle the timbers then turned, slightly dazed and badly out of breath.

"Talk to me, Rio," I said, circling away from her and back toward the shadowy part of the stables where there was much more room. "Tell me why you're doing this."

Gritting her teeth, she pushed away from the wall then kicked up the knife that lay at her feet. "Shut up and fight, bitch," she growled, stepping forward and slashing wildly at me.

I danced away. "I *am* fighting, Rio. I'm fighting to understand why you're doing this." I evaded another slash then ducked around the corner, using the maneuver to kick out at her as she came around to get me.

While my original goal, the knife in her hand, was missed, I did manage to get her a good one in the gut, which brought me precious seconds to regroup.

"Ice taught you to be an Amazon. Did she also teach you to come after unarmed women for no reason?"

"You don't know *anything* about what she taught me!"

"Oh, I think I do," I countered, circling. "Because she taught me the same things she taught you."

"You're not an Amazon! You'll *never* be an Amazon!"

"How can you say that? You don't even know me, Rio."

We continued to circle one another in and out of the shadows, the knife always between us, and my eyes never straying from it.

"Oh, I know all about you, bitch. I know that you're no Amazon. An Amazon doesn't suck the life out of people. An Amazon doesn't make people weak and soft."

"Who have I done this to, Rio?"

"Ice, goddamn it!" she screamed, her face red with rage. "Even you're not that stupid!"

"Maybe I am, because I still don't understand."

"It's all your fault, bitch. It's your fault Cavallo's still alive. It's your fault she got arrested. You made her weak. You made her soft." Each short sentence was punctuated with a thrust of her knife. "The Ice I know wouldn't play house with some blonde snatch and let the cops get the jump on her. The Ice I know would never have let Cavallo go after she had her gun to his head. The Ice I know...."

The click was loud in the echoing confines of the large stable. I froze in place as I saw the glittering silver of a gun materialize out of the shadows and press its malignant barrel against Rio's right temple. "Go ahead and finish what you were saying, Rio." The dark, velvet purr of my lover floated out of the shadows, causing every hair in my body to stand at stiff and almost painful attention as my muscles clenched and unclenched in pure animal reaction to her sudden presence. "The Ice you know...what?"

Rio was as stiff as I'd ever seen another human being. Her eyes were wide and rolling, and the dim lighting of the stables sparkled off the fat beads of sweat forming at her hairline and upper lip. Her mouth opened and closed, but only a strangled wheeze managed to escape. I could literally smell her abject terror, even over the heavy scent of hay and horses.

"Go ahead, Rio. Finish."

Another strangled wheeze was her answer.

A soft, mocking laugh filtered through. "What's the matter, Rio? Cat got your tongue? You seemed just fine a minute ago."

"I...."

"Ice," I said softly, taking a short step forward. Though it might have been insane, I found myself suddenly having a sort of strange sympathy for the woman who'd been trying to murder me just moments before. "Please...."

"Well, since you don't want to talk to me, Rio, maybe I'll talk to you instead, hmm?" The gun disappeared back into the shadows where my lover stood, and a black-gloved hand grabbed Rio's shirt and turned the terrified woman to face in Ice's direction. "Apparently you've forgotten a few things I've taught you, my friend."

"Ice...." I tried again.

"Rule number one. Never pick up a knife unless you plan on using it on someone." A booted foot slashed out of the darkness and the knife flew from Rio's hand, spinning over my head and landing in a hay bale several feet behind me.

"Rule number two. Never threaten an innocent woman."

Rio's breath exploded from her lungs in an agonized croak as she bent nearly double from the fist Ice drove into her belly.

She was quickly yanked back up once again, however.

"Rule number three." The soft, dark laugh sounded again. "Ah yes. I never mentioned rule number three to you before, did I? No matter. Now's as good a time to learn it as any, right?"

I could see her huge body spasm as she was shaken, hard.

"Rule number three. It's the simplest of them all, really. Touch Angel. You die. Got it?"

Rio was shaken again when she remained silent.

"I asked you a question, Rio. Answer me."

"Yes," she whispered. "I...understand."

"Good." There was a smile in Ice's voice, but I knew that it was a smile I would never wish to see. "Now, it seems we have a little problem, don't we? You broke Rule Number Three, and it's the most important one of all."

"Please...." Rio and I spoke at the same time, but Ice continued to ignore us both.

"It occurs to me that instead of threatening Angel, you should be on your knees thanking her, Rio. Because if it weren't for her 'softening' me, your brains would be splattered all over this stable. And I think we both know that, don't we?"

Another silence. Another vicious shake.

"Don't we?"

"Y...yes."

"Good. So. I'm gonna be nice just this once and let you use your 'get out of Hell free' card. Just make sure you never, *ever* even *think* of doing it again. Because I promise you this, Rio. You *will* die."

As if shot from the mouth of a large cannon, Rio literally flew the length of the stables, landing against the far wall and slumping bonelessly to the ground.

The stables went silent once again, and for a very long moment, I feared Ice had slipped away once again. Somehow, though, I could still feel her presence. That strange sensation I always felt when she was there persisted, giving me hope and the strength I needed to cross those last few feet and step into the shadows.

Before I could, though, she stepped out into the light, birthed from the darkness as if demon-spawned. Her pale eyes glittered coldly and a cloud of energy dark as the shadows from which she'd materialized wrapped itself tight around her like a shroud.

She was dressed completely in black, her hair pulled back into a tight braid that brought the beautiful, chiseled planes of her face into sharp relief.

"Ice?"

Almost as if pulled from the depths of a nightmare, her gaze sharpened and focused on me for the first time. And then, before my own eyes, it seemed to soften as she took me in. The tight, coiling energy surrounding her seemed somehow to dim, and the slightest of smiles graced her lips. "Hey," she said, her voice little more than a whisper.

Satan himself couldn't have stopped me from running into her welcoming arms.

Crushing our bodies together, I wrapped myself around her like a strange, four-limbed octopus, breathing in the scent of her and listening to the slow beating of her powerful heart beneath my ear. "Don't go," I whispered, knowing I was begging, but not caring. "Please stay."

Her long arms came around me, strengthening our bodies' embrace, and I could feel the gentle brush of her lips against my hair. Her ribs expanded as she took in a deep breath, then expelled it as a gentle sigh that ruffled through my hair, warming my scalp.

A moment later, I felt her muscles loosen as she gently separated our bodies along their lengths. Her chin lowered slightly as she looked down at me. "Please," I whispered again, laying my hand atop the one that cupped my cheek, "stay. At least for tonight."

The intensity of her gaze stripped bare my soul, leaving me a trembling supplicant to her dark majesty.

When those eyes zeroed in on my lips, I felt a flash-fire of arousal sweep through me with an almost painful intensity, calling up from deep within visions of dangerous, wild things which lashed out from their penumbral lairs to feast upon the blood of innocents.

A gloved hand moved to my chin and suddenly that dark, roiling energy was transferred to me through the searing touch of hot, wet, hungry lips moving against mine, consuming me to ashes where I stood.

"Stay here." Her voice was husky and raw and wanting as she pulled away from me, from us.

I couldn't have moved if I had wanted to. My feet had grown roots that fastened me to the dirt-packed floor. I watched, helplessly, my fingers brushing lips which felt nothing save the power of Ice's kiss, as she crossed from light to shadows and back to light again, walking with firm purpose toward the back of the stables.

Bending down, she pulled Rio easily up by the front of her shirt and then ducked close to whisper something in my erstwhile tormentor's ear. Though I couldn't hear what was being said, the look of dumb, pathetic gratitude in Rio's eyes as she nearly bowed deep in my lover's presence gave me all the information I needed to know about that particular conversation.

She was sent stumbling from the stables, an arm clutched hard against her belly. Ice turned, her eyes quickly scanning the building's interior. A brief smile crossed her face, and before I could think to move, a blanket-roll came sailing forth from the darkness, only missing my head because my hands happened to get in the way.

I looked down dumbly at it for a moment, and when I looked up again, Ice had disappeared.

The fear that she'd left broke my legs' paralysis, but before

I could take more than a few stumbling steps forward, she returned again, astride the blood bay stallion I'd spent so many hours admiring.

She rode him barebacked, her powerful legs gently resting against his muscled sides, her long fingers twined in his dusky black mane. He held her easily, not even twitching with the weight on his back, as if he had been born and bred for that very purpose.

His neck proudly arched, he looked down at me, and his dark eyes alight with some sort of half-amused knowledge. Or perhaps it was mischief. As I've said previously, my knowledge of horses is quite minimal.

He stepped strongly forward at Ice's gentle command, and the next thing I knew, a gloved hand had clasped me securely and I was lifted onto his back with an ease which never fails, to this very day, to both awe and thrill me.

"Hang on," came the low-voiced command as my hands were wrapped around Ice's lean waist, the bedroll crushed comfortably between us.

"Forever," I whispered, resting my cheek against her back as she urged the stallion onward and out of the stable.

The corral gate was open, and since I knew it hadn't been that way when I entered the stables, I surmised that it was one of the little tasks Ice had sent Rio on when she pushed her on her way. With a soft "Yah!", Ice sent us on our way, and my gentle hug became a hanging-on-for-dear-life white knuckled death-clutch as the earth flew quickly beneath the horse's galloping hooves.

"Oooo I'm gonna die, I'm gonna die, I'm gonna die. I don't wanna die. Ohhh nooo, I don't wanna die."

I could hear the chuckle rumble through her as she clasped my hands more tightly in her own and let the stallion have his head. Soft tendrils of hair blew loose from her braid and brushed against my nose and cheeks, reminding me of happier times and calming me right down to my soul.

Closing my eyes, I burrowed my face into her hair and allowed the scent of her to lead me onward into the unknown.

Some time later—frankly, I was too terrified to bother knowing exactly how much—the stallion's frantic gait changed to a steady rocking walk, and then to a gentle halt.

Before I knew it, I felt my arms unwrapped from around the waist of my anchor. Then strong hands lifted me and lowered me gently down to the ground once again. Prying my eyes open as I attempted to gather what remained of my wits, I looked around, taking in the beauty of the secluded spot Ice had chosen for us.

And secluded it most definitely was. A three hundred sixty degree panoramic view brought with it no signs of civilization whatsoever. We could have been on the moon for all the life I saw.

Sentient life, that is. Tall, soft grasses with feathery tops grew in abundance atop the broad, flat mesa upon which I found myself. Overhead, the sky was an immense, jeweled tapestry. Without lights to dim its splendor, nor buildings or tall trees to shrink its vastness, it seemed to fill up the entire world in a way I'd never seen before, making me feel very tiny and very insignificant in comparison.

A long, warm body wrapped itself around me from behind, halting my reflexive shiver unborn.

I was hugged briefly, then had the blanket roll taken gently from my hands. As I looked on in silence, Ice unbuckled the straps from the roll, then set the blankets out on the ground, going down to one knee to smooth them out and tack them down with a few judiciously applied rocks to the corners.

Then she looked up at me, the barest ghost of a smile caressing the corners of her lips, and held a hand out. Moonbathed, her face was a curious combination of gentle light and murky shadow, but her eyes, clear and bright, were the only home I ever needed.

I went to her, feeling strangely innocent; a bride on her wedding night accepting the gentle invitation of her betrothed.

A large, gloved hand clasped itself warmly around mine and a gentle kiss was placed atop my knuckles. Her smile broadened then as she looked up at me with that crooked grin that even now never fails to still my heart for the briefest of moments and always brings an instant answering smile to my own face.

"C'mere," she whispered, her voice barely heard over the gentle hiss of the wind against the tall grasses.

I lowered myself slowly to my knees, feeling the soft leather of her hand trail warmly up my arm and down my side to clasp securely at my waist, steadying me.

I looked up at her, my goddess of the night, as the moonlight anointed her from behind and created a brilliant, shimmering halo around her body. The expression of absolute adoration in her eyes as she looked down at me stole the breath from my lungs and the strength from my muscles.

The world around me ceased to exist. Time was only measured by the beating of my heart. "I love you," I said simply, in a tone I knew was very close to awe.

Truer words were never spoken; dearer words were never meant.

"I know," she returned in kind.

We came together as one being then, emerging from the darkness of our separate selves to meld once again in a language neither of us needed to speak. A language of love and building passion. A language of giving and taking and intimate knowledge. A language which eased hurts and filled to overflowing the empty spaces left behind.

Lips met lips in sensual urgency as hands fumbled at buttons and buckles. I almost screamed in relief as my shirt was torn open in a great rending of seams which echoed through the still desert night, borne up by the currents of the softly blowing wind.

Chill air was replaced by the inhuman heat of my lover's hands as she teased and taunted, running long, strong, and vastly knowing fingers over my breasts and circling my nipples with merciless abandon until I all but cried out my surrender.

A low chuckle filled the night air, and I was eased gently onto my back as her lips left my mouth and blazed a hot and needy trail down the length of my jaw before finally settling at the sensitized flesh of my neck. My hands fisted the coarse blankets beneath me as strong teeth made their presence felt and a darting tongue danced along my pulse point, causing stars the heavens had never seen to begin dancing behind my tightly clenched eyes.

"Dear god," I gasped, and writhed helplessly as her hands left my breasts and moved lower to remove the impediment of my jeans while her teeth and tongue continued to work their magic on my trembling flesh.

A moment of panic froze my movements as I felt her body leave mine, but when I opened my eyes, a hard, sharp wave of intense arousal swept through me, stronger by far than any tidal wave that had ever been birthed from the depths of a churning, frothy sea.

A silver-gilded goddess knelt above me, her nimble fingers removing the last of her clothing and allowing the moonlight to trail along her magnificent body in a lover's possessive touch.

I couldn't stop the moan which came forth from between dry lips as I watched her hands run freely down her breasts and belly, following the moonlight's anointed path and making me wish with all of my being to be given the power to shine down on her so intimately, if only for just a moment.

With a growl I didn't even know I had in me, I bolted upright and wrapped my hands around her waist, stealing her from the moon's embrace and bringing the wild, primal beauty of her into my arms, where it belonged.

I heard her quiet moan as I nipped and licked the satin skin of her muscled belly; felt her hands twine in my hair as my tongue found a home in the well of her navel; smiled against her skin as her hips thrust gently forward in unmistakable response to my attentions.

Unable to wait even the length of one more beat of my heart, I lowered my chin to trail ardent kisses down her lower belly, and to seek out the scent and taste of her, something so missed and so needed and so very much cherished that tears formed in the corners of my eyes for the sheer joy of finding it once again within my reach.

And then, finally, after so long waiting and wanting, the taste of her was finally on my tongue. I moaned in utter bliss, hearing the soft, answering moan from above as Ice's fingers tightened in my hair while her hips began a slow, gentle rocking which brought more of her into my mouth and filled me with indescribable, heart-clenching joy.

My hands wandered down from her waist, over her hips, and down to clench the tightly bunched muscles at the backs of her thighs. I could feel those muscles quiver beneath my palms as she tried to fight the combined hold that gravity and my mouth had over her.

Smiling slightly, I redoubled my efforts, pursing my lips and taking her deep within as my tongue danced against her, long and slow.

The trembling in her legs soon became violent tremors. Her hands clenched reflexively, the incredible strength of her pulling me tightly against her and driving my tongue deeper and then deeper still.

Until finally the edge was reached and, with a long, low moan, she released against my tongue in a great, shuddering wave that brought tears of happiness to eyes long used to sadder emotions.

Her legs gave out, finally, and I helped her down as best I could until she was sitting back on her heels and looking at me with an expression of half-dazed wonder, hands lying limply on her thighs.

A giddy sort of joy rose from my up from my belly and curved my lips in a wide grin. "Gotcha, didn't I," I said, mock-buffing my nails against my chest.

"That you did," she growled, her crooked smile broadening my own. "That you most certainly did."

I laughed, a gleeful chuckle. "I'll have to remember to write this down, then. It's not often that I...."

Any further words were swallowed as a six foot ball of naked, sexual heat seared my lips with her own and powered me once again onto my back. "Turnabout is always fair play, sweet Angel," a low voice rumbled into my ear. "And I intend to...play...a great deal."

I would have gulped, had I the saliva for it. Instead, I gasped, then moaned as a tongue traced a path around my ear, followed quickly by the gentle bite of teeth which suckled and worried at my lobe. Her hand wandered, once again teasing my breasts, finding each nipple with unerring intimacy until it was all I could do just to remember my own name for the fire she was fanning deep within. "Do you like this game, my Angel?"

"Yes, I...god!...there!...I...oh!...do. Very...oh yes, please...much...."

Her laughter rolled through me. "Good."

My body was the sun, burning hot and bright as her hands remapped its peaks and valleys, never stilling, never lingering too long before moving on in their quest.

Her body was the moon, bathing me in its magnificent radiance.

And when she finally entered me, thrusting with a strength and a tenderness which were hers and hers alone, I gave up a sobbing prayer of thanks to the heavens, which birthed us and brought her back to me, fully whole, fully strong, and fully alive.

My release came quickly beneath the tender mercies of her skilled and knowing touches. The second was building before the first even died out.

I needed more, needed the power of her love, and she gave it willingly, not stopping even after a second climax left me breathless and shaking.

I felt her strength against me as she moved to straddle one

of my thighs, her breath warm and moist on my sweat-drenched cheeks. "I love you, Angel," she whispered, as she began a gentle rocking against me, building a rhythm between our bodies. "So very, very much."

Turning my head, I captured her lips with mine, sinking my hands into the thickness of her hair as our love and passion built strongly once again. Our bodies, wet with sweat, slid against one another with a delicious friction. The coarse fabric of the blanket created a friction of its own as it slid against my back and hips in time to Ice's ever increasing thrusts.

Radiant energy passed from one to the other of us, binding us closer still, until finally our mouths separated when the need for air became too much. Her eyes glittered as she thrust herself against me, soft grunts speaking their own passionate language to the depths of my soul and beyond. Her fingers danced within me as she moved, inviting me to share this journey to the stars with her.

"Together?" I whispered, gasping deep as my muscles clenched and tightened, promising the release my very soul hungered for.

"Always," she answered, feeding me her own climax through the deep indigo of her eyes.

We stayed frozen for a long moment, two statues locked together by an unbreakable bond, until finally Ice's eyelids fluttered and closed and she slumped down full upon me, chest heaving as she regained her breath.

As I attempted to bring my own breathing back under control, I turned my head and nuzzled the sweet flesh at the juncture of her neck and shoulder. I smiled slightly as I felt a shudder run the length of her body, then kissed the spot in question, eliciting a smaller, but nonetheless easily felt, tremor.

Growling slightly, she pulled away and turned, using her arms to gather me close against her, breast to breast and belly to belly. "You alright?" A tender kiss was placed, like a benediction, on my forehead.

"I'm...wonderful." As if she couldn't tell it by the dopey, blissed-out grin I was sure was on my face.

"That you are," she said, chuckling.

"You're not so bad yourself, sweetheart," I replied in my most saucy tone, only wanting to hear that laugh tickle my ears again.

I was well rewarded as her low laughter filled the cool night air, warming my insides right down to my toes. Unfortunately, the same could not be said about my outsides. As the cool wind wafted across my sweat-soaked skin, I shivered from the chill.

"Cold?" She pulled me more tightly against her body, enveloping me in the heat of her.

"A little."

A long arm detached itself from my waist, and a bare second later, I was wrapped in one of the blankets, snug as a babe in her mother's warm arms.

"Better?"

"Mmm. Much."

"Good."

As I listened to the slowing beat of my lover's heart, my eyelids grew heavy as I found myself in a place filled with wondrous beauty and infinite peace, a place only found within the safety of Ice's embrace.

As I drifted in this place, my mind wandered from thought to thought until one stood out and caused me to stiffen. "Ice?"

"Mmm?" came the contented murmur of my lover's sleepy voice.

"As much as I can't believe I'm saying this, do you think maybe we'd better go back now? Before Montana calls in the National Guard, I mean?"

"All taken care of." I felt her stretch against me, then settle back, tangling our legs together and taking in a deep, contented sigh.

I pulled my head back slightly to look up into her eyes. "Rio?"

"Rio."

I nodded and then nestled into her warm body, smiling slightly as I felt her rest against my hair. "Thank you, by the way."

"For what?"

"Being my knight in...um...black cotton."

Snorting softly, she shook her head, her chin brushing gently along the top of my scalp.

"How long were you there?"

"Since before you came into the stables."

Shock ran through my body, and I pulled away again to look up at her. "Then why...?"

She shrugged. "You were handling it."

I could feel my jaw hang suspended, like that of a gaping

fish, as I continued to stare at her. Though a woman of relatively few words, sometimes those she chose to utter made me feel more than fifty feet tall.

Smirking slightly, she brought a hand up and gently closed my mouth. "Don't want a scorpion crawling in there."

If any threat in the world could have broken the spell I was under, it was that one. Had Ice not been holding me, I would have jumped clear up to the moon. Though I'd never seen one up close and personal, my hatred of scorpions was already legendary, if to no one other than myself.

And now, apparently, to Ice as well. "Don't worry. There aren't any around here."

I could feel my eyes narrow. "How do you know?"

"I just know," was the soft-voiced reply.

"Alright then. But if I get stung on the butt, you know who's going to be sucking the poison out."

"With pleasure." Her tone of voice caused me to think that perhaps finding such an insect was suddenly quite high on her list of priorities.

I grabbed her in a tight hold. "Don't even think about thinking about it."

An evil little smirk was her only answer.

Stealing a kiss from her lips, I laid my head back down against her shoulder, reveling in the smoothness of her skin against mine and the scent of our loving which surrounded us both. The brush of her fingers against my hair as she started a slow, gentle stroking caused yet another smile to break out across my face. I knew, without any sense of false modesty whatsoever, that I was the most loved and cherished person in all the world at that very moment in time.

A moment I hoped would last an entire forever's worth of forever.

After several long moments spent in silence, listening to the gentle hiss of the wind against the grass, my mind turned back to other things. Less pleasant things. Things that had no business being spoken of after what we just shared—and were continuing to share—but nevertheless just wouldn't go away.

Ice must have felt the change, because her hand stilled and she pulled away just far enough to look into my eyes. "What is it?"

I laughed to keep from crying, and she knew that too, because her eyes narrowed and her head tilted as her hand came up to cup my cheek.

"What Rio said back in the stables," I said through a tremor in my voice, "was it true? Did I make you soft? Weak?" I sighed heavily, lowering my head so as to avoid looking into her eyes. "So much of this is my fault."

The hand on my cheek lowered to grip my jaw, forcing my gaze back up. Though her touch remained gentle, her eyes were anything but, reminding me of nothing so much as the roiling black clouds that preceded a midsummer's furious storm. "Don't you...*ever*...say that...again."

"But—"

"*Never*. Do you hear me?" Her body, once sated and soft, was now hard and stiff with anger.

I felt her stiffen further, fury literally radiating from every pore, and as I felt her muscles begin to move in what I knew was a prelude to escape, I did the only thing my heart would allow. I threw myself on top of her and held on as tightly as I could. "I'm sorry," I said, half sobbing. "Please, don't leave. I'm sorry. Please."

After a long moment of intense inner struggle, she relaxed somewhat beneath me, though her eyes still blazed out their anger.

"I'm sorry. I should never have said something like that. I don't know why I did. Please...."

When several more moments passed in silence, I sighed and rolled away, berating myself internally for picking the exact wrong time to forget how to keep my damned mouth shut.

As if agreeing with me, the wind blew harder suddenly, and even though I was still half covered by the blanket, it was as if I was naked to the world without the living heat of my lover pressed so close against me. I fought against the forming shiver, but it came anyway, making me even more miserable than I already was.

Not more than a second later, I was once again enfolded in wonderful warmth as she eased up behind me, grasping me tight and pulling me close. "Never doubt my love for you, Angel." The low, serious timbre of her voice hummed through me, warming me even more. "Never doubt yourself. Never doubt the gifts you've given me."

Her arms tightened their hold around my body. "You haven't made me weaker, Angel. You've made me stronger. You've taught me how to feel again. And how to love again."

My scalp tingled from the kiss she pressed onto it. "You are a gift beyond price to me, Angel. And anyone who doesn't believe that, or can't accept it...can just go straight to Hell." I felt her chest and belly press against my back as she took in a deep breath of air, then let it out slowly. "And if need be, I'll put them there myself."

Tears trailed down my face. "You're...incredible."

"'You're not so bad yourself, sweetheart.'"

The mimicry was damn near perfect and my laughter flowed freely, easing the last of my soul's somber aches.

Turning easily within the nest of her arms, I pressed my lips to hers in a kiss of profound gratitude that quickly grew into something stronger and more passionate.

The sounds of laughter and tears were slowly replaced by the soft sounds of loving in the cool of a sweet desert night.

The house was tomb-silent as I stepped inside and closed the door gently behind me. Pushing up the sleeves of the too-large shirt Ice had given me to replace the one she'd ripped to shreds (and let me tell you, the added benefit of seeing Ice sitting astride that stallion in nothing but her jeans and a smile more than made up for the destruction of a one-time favorite shirt) I broke out of my bliss-induced haze just long enough to wonder at the silence and chance a look around.

Nearly a dozen women looked back at me from their places on the couches and chairs in the sunken living room. The expressions of awe on some of the faces caused me to whirl and look behind me, thinking that perhaps Ice had reconsidered and decided to spend the night after all.

But no, the door remained resolutely closed, and I remained alone and standing on something that was quickly coming to resemble a stage.

A piercing whistle shattered the unnatural stillness, and when I whirled back around, I saw Cowgirl coming to her feet, a knowing and incorrigible grin on her face. Throwing me a wink, she brought her hands together and started clapping.

Others stood, joining her, and soon the entire house was filled with wolf whistles, thunderous applause, and comments ribald enough to sear the skin from my face.

In a state of embarrassment more acute than any I've ever

known, I whirled around again, intending to charge right back outside to escape the spontaneous combustion that was threatening to consume me on the spot. Only to find the way blocked by a leering Pony and a grinning Critter who stared at me, arms crossed against their chests and feet spread wide against any possibility of an escape.

"Don't make me hurt you again, Pony," I half-growled as I slapped away the hand that was intending to turn me around to face the music, as it were.

"Ooo. More butch lessons from Ice, I see." Her leer grew more pronounced as she tried again. "Were they before or after she...?"

"Pony...," Critter warned, seeing the glint in my eye.

"C'mon, Critter! It ain't every day someone survives a knife fight with Rio and goes riding off into the desert to get banged by Ice, ya know. I'm just expressing my admiration here."

Critter barked out her laughter. "God, Pony, you are so damned crude."

"I call 'em like I see 'em, babe."

"Keep calling 'them' like that and you'll never see 'them' again," I warned through gritted teeth.

"Enough!"

Turning at the sudden silence in the room, I saw Montana and Corinne striding toward me, identical expressions of serious resolution on their faces. "Everyone to bed," Montana ordered, sweeping the group with her lancing gaze. "Now."

With some good-natured protesting, the group broke up and filtered through the house to return to their rooms and bed down for the night.

"Don't you have things you should be attending to?" Montana asked as she arrived at my side, pinning Pony to the door she was guarding with a very pointed look.

My friend paled slightly, then blushed, ducking her head very much like a chastised schoolgirl. If there was a pebble on the ground, I think she would have kicked it. "Yes."

"Then I suggest you attend to them."

Muttering something a touch too soft to be easily comprehended, she spun on her heel and took the ready escape I had been seeking just a moment before, closing the door swiftly behind her.

Corinne closed the distance between us, took my hand, and

gently ushered me through the house and into my own room, Montana trailing silently behind. Once the three of us were safely ensconced in my room, Corinne released my hand and smiled. "Are you alright?"

"I didn't think it was possible to die from embarrassment," I said, chuckling slightly. "Now I'm not so sure." I ran my hand through my still damp hair. "But yeah, I'm alright."

Reaching out, she gave me an "around the shoulders" type hug, something most unusual for her. When I looked up as she pulled away, her eyes twinkled and she fingered the fabric of the black top I wore.

I could feel my eyes widen when the realization sunk in. I couldn't help but grin. "Who knew there was such a pile of warm mush beneath that granite exterior?" I joked, enjoying the blush that briefly suffused her face.

Easily evading her kidding slap, I turned my head to see Montana studying me intently. I felt a blush of my own coming on, and thanked god that the shirt I was wearing, high necked as it was, covered what was no doubt a multitude of sins.

"Are you sure you're all right?" she asked.

"Pretty much, yes. Is there a reason you're asking?"

"Do you want to press charges?"

I could feel my head cock as I looked at her. "For being kidded? I don't think you can arrest someone for embarrassing you. Can you?"

"I was speaking about Rio," she replied with an air of exaggerated patience.

"Oh. Rio." I could feel the bridge of my nose crinkle with distaste. Still.... "Um...I don't think that'll be necessary. I think she's pretty much learned her lesson, don't you?"

"This isn't about learning lessons, Angel. She came after you with a knife. She could have killed you."

"She could have, yes. But she didn't."

"Again, you're missing the point."

Holding up a hand for quiet, I sank wearily down onto the bed. "No I'm not, Montana. I understand your point. And your concern. Believe me, I do. It's just that...." Steepling my fingers together, I sighed, then looked up at her. "I think people are entitled to second chances. She made a mistake, and I know it was a big one. But it was a mistake just the same. In the end, she realized her mistake and no harm was done."

Corinne snorted. "From what I was given to understand,

Angel, Rio didn't exactly 'realize' her mistake on her own. She had it beaten into her."

"She didn't...." I sighed again. "Ice was very angry."

"And she had every damn right to be," Corinne growled.

I looked up, surprised. Swearing was very unusual for her. As was growling.

"What? She's just lucky Ice stepped in. Were it me, I would have killed her. *Then* asked questions."

Smiling slightly, I reached up and took her hand in mine, giving it a fond squeeze. "So no, Montana. I don't want to press charges. I think that whatever crime she committed has been more than paid for already."

After staring hard at me for another long, tense, and silent moment, Montana finally nodded. "Fine. I'll have her pack her things and be out of here by sunrise." Then she turned to leave.

"No! Wait. Montana, that's not necessary, is it?"

She turned back to me, a strong sheen of regret easily evident in her eyes. "Rio has broken every oath she has sworn to uphold, Angel. She's turned the Amazon name into a mockery. That's not something I can just overlook, no matter how much I might wish to."

Corinne, beside me, looked thoughtful. "Perhaps if she was stripped of her membership, yet allowed to make restitution with the possibility of regaining her status within the group?"

Montana frowned slightly, but after a moment, her expression cleared. "You've given me something to think about, Corinne. I'll let everyone know of my decision in the morning." Looking at me, she smiled slightly. "I'm glad you weren't harmed, Angel. You're a very special person."

"Thanks," I replied, returning her smile. "You're pretty special, too."

As soon as the door closed quietly behind her, I let out the deep breath I'd been holding and fell back onto the bed, my feet still planted firmly on the floor, my arms flung wide. "God. What a mess."

"It could have been worse," Corinne observed, coming to sit down beside me and shoving one of my arms out of the way.

"True. I could be lying dead in a pile of horse manure right now."

Chuckling softly, she grabbed my hand and gave it a pat. Reaching out with her free hand, she again plucked at the long-sleeved black shirt I wore, rubbing the fabric between her fingers. "So...how was she?"

"Corinne!" My shock was, of course, feigned. This was Corinne, after all.

"Now whose mind is in the gutter, hmmm?" Her grin was merciless. "I simply wish to know how she's doing, Angel. Not what she's like in bed. I have a pretty good idea of that already."

Moaning, I covered my face with my hands, feeling the heat of embarrassment warm the skin of my palms. "Is tonight 'Kill the Blonde' night and someone forgot to mention it to me?" As plaintive wails went, it was a pretty good one, if I do say so myself.

She laughed then ruffled her fingers through my hair. "So?"

"She's...good. I think those months in jail affected her more than she's willing to let on—she's lost a bit of weight—but otherwise, she's doing all right."

"Now tell me something I *don't* know," she teased.

Pulling my hands away from my face, I sighed. So much for snuggling down under the covers and letting the memories of the wonderful night I had just spent with Ice lull me to sleep. Rolling over to my side, I tried a diversionary tactic. "We really didn't spend that much time talking, Corinne."

"Nice parry, Angel. And I just might be willing to buy that load of fertilizer you're trying to sell. If it was coming from anyone else. Now spill it."

"Can't it wait until tomorrow? Please? I'm exhausted." Maybe the old "end around" would work.

"I'll just bet you are, my dear." Nope. Didn't work.

"Fine," I said, rolling back onto my back. "What is it you want to know?"

"Everything you do, of course."

Chuckling, I shook my head, eyeing her. "Is that all?"

"Pretty much, yes."

And so I told her everything I knew, which wasn't, of course, very much at all. I explained to her how, by Ice's telling, Cavallo was a small cog in a very big wheel. The spokes of that wheel were made up of bribery, kickback schemes, money laundering, jury tampering and other like crimes all situated within the judicial arm of the state government, and, in some cases, the federal government as well. Not only was Cavallo himself participating in many, if not all, of the criminal activities taking place, he was also, it was believed, in possession of a very important list. A list that contained the names of many of his co-

conspirators, some of which he was also practicing his own extortion schemes on in return for his silence in those matters.

A very special, very secret probe, made up of members of both the state and federal governments, was very interested in what Cavallo knew. *Very* interested. And they figured that if they could just get a hold of him, they could make him crack.

"That doesn't sound very plausible. They already had their chance at him. He didn't crack."

"Oh, but he did, Corinne. Ice said he sang like a canary."

"Then why...?"

"He was under the influence of narcotics at the time. They'd just finished plucking eight bullets out of him, remember?"

"Ahh yes, now that you mention it."

"So, his statements were inadmissible as evidence, and by the time they got around to trying again, his lawyer had him trussed up and gagged and that was the end of that."

"Well, if they want him so badly, why don't they just get off of their fat posteriors and hunt him down themselves?"

"Believe me, Corinne, I asked that question a time or ten myself."

"And?"

I shrugged. "Ice guesses it's because they don't know who the good guys are anymore. That's not the reason they've given her, but it's the one she thinks is the truth."

"The F.B.I doesn't even trust its own staff?" Corinne's eyes were round with disbelief behind her glasses.

"Makes you think, doesn't it?"

She shook her head. "And they call *us* criminals."

I laughed softly, though in truth, the situation was as far from amusing as it was possible to get.

"So, they offer Ice a deal she can't refuse and set her up as a tasty little sacrificial lamb."

"That's about the gist of it, yeah."

"And if she should fail...."

A leaden ball settled itself into my stomach. Failing was definitely number one on my list of things not to even consider.

Corinne gazed at me with eyes filled with compassion. "Forget I said that."

Nodding, I gave her a grateful smile, shoving the notion to the deepest recesses of my mind, where it would linger and, I was sure, come out in nightmares, each worse than the last until a cold sweat would become my nightly companion.

Giving my hand a final squeeze, Corinne stood up and smiled down at me. "Thank you for indulging my rampant curiosity, Angel. I'll leave you to your dreams. May they be sweet ones."

"Thanks, Corinne. Yours too."

Her gentle smile became a leering grin. "Living in a house surrounded by a bevy of naked bathing beauties? How could they be anything but?"

As she gently closed the door on my laughter, I dragged myself up from the bed and walked to the window, pulling the heavy blinds aside just enough to look out into the dark desert night. "Thanks," I whispered before turning away slipping under the covers, allowing the scent of my lover still clinging to the shirt I wore to lull me into the place dreams were born.

And they were sweet.

The next several days passed quickly and, I'll be the first to admit, almost without notice, wrapped up as I was in a haze of sweet memories. After learning of Montana's decision to allow Rio to stay on, albeit without her membership in the Amazons, part of me wanted very much to finally clear the air with my one-time nemesis. Every time I thought to approach her, however, Pony or Critter would sweep down and give the poor woman yet another backbreaking chore to accomplish.

Still, on the few occasions our eyes chanced to meet, her expression was one of such supreme sorrow and regret that I felt my heart going out to her in a way it had never done for the people who had tormented me in the past. So I made myself a firm promise that we would get together and talk. Soon.

Early one afternoon, as I was making my way from the house to the stables, a bit of commotion stirred the women walking the grounds, and when I turned around to look, a dusty pickup was pulling the last several yards into the driveway.

As soon as it stopped, an attractive young woman—blonde, with a California tan and a beaming smile—hopped down from the cab. Seemingly from nowhere, Cowgirl blew by me and, with a loud whoop of joy, leapt into the woman's arms, pinning her against the truck and melding their lips together in a kiss that sent the already warm temperature up another ten degrees.

"Cheeto," came Montana's voice from behind my right shoulder.

Turning my head, I looked at her, a question in my eyes.

"Don't ask," she replied, smirking.

"Probably best that I don't," I agreed.

After a very long, heated moment, the strangely-named Amazon—at least I assumed she was an Amazon, though her parents could well have been flower children with a fondness for Frito-Lay products for all I knew—released Cowgirl, grinned broadly, and waved to the rest of us.

Then, walking over to the passenger's side of the truck, Cheeto opened the door and helped a young woman exit the cab, holding the woman's arm until her feet gingerly came into contact with the ground.

A gasp went through the small crowd of onlookers as the young woman looked up, tucking a length of light brown hair behind one ear and smiling shyly at the gathered women.

I heard my own gasp join the rest as I saw the tragically marred beauty of the woman before me. Dark eyes peered out through swollen, blackened flesh. Her cheeks were puffed out to what I believed to be at least twice their normal size, the left one sporting a knot the size of a cue ball. Ugly black bruising stained the skin of her jaws and neck, where it disappeared beneath the collar of her shirt.

"Bastard." The snarled epithet came from somewhere behind me, and I could feel the crowd's anger radiate through the yard.

The young woman dropped her gaze, her hand wandering, birdlike, to her throat. If it weren't for the horrific bruising which covered her face like some demon's patchwork quilt, I'm sure her blush would have been readily seen.

From beside me, a woman stepped forward, taking the stranger into a tender embrace. As if breaking a dam, others came forward, and still others, until the woman was surrounded by a circle of support.

"Her name is Nia," Montana explained, low voiced, as I looked on, my jaw hanging agape. "Unfortunately, she's an all too frequent visitor to *Akalan.*"

"Who did this to her?"

"Her husband."

"Oh no," I half-moaned, half-whispered as my mind was suddenly deluged with scenes I spent long years trying to forget.

Scenes of Peter standing over me, teeth clenched in an animal's snarl, eyes bulging, hands tightly fisted—waiting to lash out...waiting...waiting...waiting.

I closed my eyes against the strength of those images, then opened them quickly when the small group of women brushed by me, Nia safely ensconced between them.

"Are you alright, Angel?" Montana's voice was soft with concern.

I turned a weak smile toward her. "Yeah. Just dealing with some memories."

She nodded sagely, but remained quiet.

"You said she's been here before?"

"Many times, yes." Now her voice held a note of deep sadness.

"The same man...?"

"Yes."

"So why does...?" But I trailed off, the question unfinished. It was the same question I'd asked myself a million or more times in my own life, and one for which there was no ready answer. Did she feel trapped, as I had, with nowhere to turn? Did she feel somehow deserving of his fists, his fury? Did she believe his tearful recriminations, his promises to do better, his pleas for just one more chance to show his love?

I'd believed each and every one of those things in my own marriage. And though it shames me now to admit such things, back then, it seemed my only chance for survival. The woman I am now would never, I hope, accept the lies nor cower before the cruelties, but the woman I was then felt she had no choice in the matter.

Hindsight is, as is often said, viewed through perfect vision.

After a brief squeeze to my shoulder, Montana left me alone with my thoughts.

Nighttime came quickly and, as I was settling down for some well-earned rest, a soft knock came to my door. "C'mon in."

The door opened slowly, and Nia peeked in, freezing as soon as she saw me. "Oh. I'm sorry. You're getting ready to sleep. I'll just...."

"No, that's alright," I replied, hastening to sit up. "Please.

Come in."

"Are you sure?"

My heart breaking at her timidity, I gave her my brightest smile. "Sure I'm sure." Pulling my arm from beneath the blankets, I patted the bed. "Make yourself comfortable."

"I...um...just came to see if I could borrow some toothpaste. I...don't have any and I...kinda saw your light on under the door."

"Help yourself," I replied, gesturing to my toiletries laid out neatly on the dresser-top.

With the bearing of a beaten dog, she made her way over to the dresser, retrieved the requested item, and after looking at me for another long, assessing moment, finally sat down gingerly on the bed, as if expecting me to kick her off at any second

"I don't think we've been properly introduced. I'm Angel."

Keeping my smile as bright and friendly as possible, I slowly extended my hand, watching as wary eyes took the gesture in. After a moment, she wiped her own hand off on her pants and extended it to meet mine. I began to clasp it gently, then stopped, looking down.

Only by the grace of some beneficent god was I able to keep the gasp in my throat. Though a woman I knew to be younger than myself by at least two years, her hand had the look of a crippled octogenarian beset with a horrible case of arthritis.

I knew without asking, however, that no disease laid its touch on those once supple fingers. Rather, they were deliberately broken and then refused treatment, left to heal as best they could. The end result was a crooked tangle of swollen joints only vaguely resembling the hand it used to be.

Noticing my stare—how could she not?—Nia smiled hesitantly, and retrieved her hand. "I...got it stuck in a...."

"Don't," I whispered, on the verge of tears. "Please."

"Don't what?" she asked, her expression the very picture of innocence. An innocence I wasn't even close to buying.

"Don't lie. Not here. Not to me. Please."

"But, I'm...."

"Please."

I watched as her shoulders slumped and her head bowed. "Maybe I should just go."

"Is that what you want to do?"

She looked at me for a long, silent moment. "No. Not really."

I smiled again. "Then stay."

Her smile was tiny, but it reached the dark of her eyes. "Alright. Thank you."

We sat in silence for a moment as I cast about for a conversation opener. "So...have you settled in ok?"

The smile broadened. "Yeah. The Amazons are so nice. They always make me feel at home here." She looked down at the bedspread, tracing an abstract pattern on its surface. "And safe, too." Then she looked back up at me. "You're one, aren't you? I think I remember them talking about you the last time I was here."

"Good things, I hope."

"Oh yeah. Very good things."

I grinned. "Guilty as charged. So to speak."

Her hand went up to tuck a strand of hair behind her ear—a nervous gesture that I well recognized, having done the same thing a million or so times myself. "If you don't mind my asking, what did...?"

"I killed my husband."

Amazing how I could state that without any inflection in my voice whatsoever.

"You k.... For money?"

I caught myself laughing. "Not quite. We didn't have two nickels to rub together between us."

Her eyes were round within their swollen, black mask. "Then why?"

Could I speak of this thing aloud? Could I let it see the light of day in a way it never had before? Even with Ice, I had never spoken of it. It was something which was intuitively known, resting comfortably between us, yet not needing to be explored. A pink and purple elephant which grew smaller with each passing year.

In the end, however, I didn't seem to have much choice in the matter. It was almost as if fate had decreed that I save my story for someone who really needed to hear it. And it appeared that person was Nia.

"He was raping me at the time," I replied in a voice I scarcely credited as my own.

"But...that's impossible! You were married!"

Though a thousand sharp retorts entered into my mind, I found I couldn't utter even one. Not to a woman who had endured just as much as I had, and probably even more. "Rape is rape, Nia," I said, in the softest tone I could manage. "It really doesn't matter who's doing it at the time."

"But how...?"

I shrugged. "He wanted something I wouldn't give him. So he took it." My gaze turned inward, viewing a movie meant for my eyes only. My arms came up to cross my chest, my hands gripping my shoulders in a hug of solace against the memories. "I didn't mean to kill him. I just wanted him to stop. But...." Tears threatened, but I fought them back, heaving a great sigh and letting it go. "He just wouldn't listen."

"What happened?" Her voice was timid, unsure, delicate almost.

The movie continued to play, drawing me back to that night with vivid clarity. The sounds were there. The sights. The scents of alcohol and cigarettes. "I begged him...god...over and over...begged him to please stop...please stop hurting me. He wouldn't listen." I took in another deep breath, still fighting tears of anger and anguish, trapped in the past as surely as a rabbit in a snare. "A bat.... I kept a bat by the side of the bed. He worked nights, and I was...afraid. Afraid that someone would break in and...do exactly what he was doing to me. I didn't think. I couldn't.... I just reached out and grabbed it. And hit him. To make him stop, you know?" I felt my fists clench at the bed linen, wadding it up tight against palms wet with sweat. "And it worked. He stopped. He just...slumped down on top of me."

The tears fell, hot and scalding down my cheeks. I lifted a hand, brushing against them almost absently. "I remember not being able to breathe. So I just...pushed...him away from me. I remember him rolling off, like a rag-doll, almost. And I realized, when I looked down at him, that I'd done more than just hurt him."

I looked up at her, wishing with all my heart, mind, and soul that the eyes I was seeking out were a pale blue fire instead of the deep, somber brown I was actually seeing.

"I'd killed him."

"No," she whispered.

"Yes. He was my husband, and I killed him."

The look in her eyes changed then, and to my horror, I saw the tiniest spark of speculation brighten their somber depths.

"No," I said, reaching out and grasping her wrist firmly. "No. That's not even something to consider, Nia. Take it from me. It was the worst mistake I've ever made in my life."

The speculative gleam remained, though she tried her hardest to eclipse it with a look of practiced innocence. "There isn't anything to consider. Richard loves me. He'd never do something like that to me."

I met her stare, suddenly feeling old beyond my years. My hand floated up to her cheek, pausing when she flinched away. "Love doesn't hurt, Nia. Not like that."

It was as if my words had drawn a veil across her eyes. She stiffened, then pulled away from me, as if I had somehow become suddenly dangerous, a thing to be feared.

And perhaps, in a very important way, I had.

"I think I'll...go back to my room now. It's been a long day and I'm really tired. Thanks for letting me borrow this," she said, standing and waving the toothpaste tube. "I'll get it back to you in the morning."

Like a seasoned general who knows that losing a battle just might mean winning the war, I backed down and gave her a smile and a nod. "You're welcome. Thanks for coming by to talk. It's good to meet you."

Her smile became a bit shyer, a bit more genuine. "It's good to meet you, too. Goodnight."

"Night."

Though the house was still and quiet, I spent the night wrapped up in a misery of memories, wishing for nothing so much as a pair of strong, loving arms to hold me close and chase away the demons of the darkness.

The days marched on in their interminable fashion; tin soldiers with no watch-spring to wind them down. Where I thought our night-time conversation would make Nia wary of my company, she seemed, instead, to seek me out, albeit tentatively, much like a child who wants desperately to jump from the high dive, yet can only manage a walk to the very edge before turning and scampering away in fright.

We talked of many things. Her childhood, which was very much like my own, yet very much different as well. Her marriage and life with Richard, the man she called her husband when words like "jailer" and "keeper" would have been much more appropriate. To my mind, anyway. Her hopes and dreams, which seemed to all revolve around this man in one way or another.

In many ways, being with Nia saddened me. It was so hard seeing someone in such a high state of denial, especially when I had been in much the same state earlier in my life. In other ways, though, it showed me just how far I'd come from the woman I used to be all those years ago.

My chores at the ranch kept me busy, and almost before I realized it, another Thanksgiving was nigh. Living on Native American land with a group of women of many different nationalities changed the "flavor" of the holiday, to be sure, but because each and every one of us had something to be thankful for, the festivities went full steam ahead.

I woke up that morning feeling rather out of sorts. I wasn't exactly sure why until an offhand mention by Corinne brought home the differences between this Thanksgiving and the last, the first one I had prepared with my own hands, in my own home, my lover by my side instead of just in my memories.

Corinne, Critter, and Pony tried their best to keep my mind and hands busy, and for a time, I'll admit that I was able to lose myself in the pleasant tasks that went with a feast's preparation.

But after the meal was cooked and laid out on the table, after everyone had gathered and thanks were given, I'm afraid that the feast I had spent all day preparing suddenly lost its appeal, especially where my stomach was concerned.

After pushing the food around on my place while trying to give the impression that I actually consumed some of it, I threw my napkin down on the still-full place and made as if to rise from the table, well before even the quickest of eaters had thought to go back for seconds.

A gentle touch to my shoulder made me turn, and when I looked up, it was Montana's face I saw. "If you're through, do you have a minute?" she asked quietly.

I nodded quickly, fully expecting to be the first tapped for clean-up duty. I didn't mind, really, since it was another task that would hopefully keep my mind carefully numb. Holidays without the ones you love most deeply can be the most depressing of days. At least they are for me.

I know that sounds incredibly selfish and more than just a bit petty, and in many ways, it probably is. Looking back over that time through the wonderful gift of hindsight we're all blessed with, I had so many things to be thankful for. I was free. I was warm, dry, and well-fed. I was surrounded by people who loved me and cherished me for who I was. I was safe from harm and free from danger.

Why, then, did I feel so incredibly alone?

Rising to my feet, I followed close behind Montana. Instead of leading me into the kitchen, however, she instead ushered me down one of the darkened halls and into a room I hadn't yet seen. Soft lighting glowed from a small lamp on an equally small table set next to a deep-set window, heavily shuttered against the blinding sun. The walls were a soft white, the carpet a peaceful pale blue. Bookshelves lined three of the four walls, and several comfortable looking chairs sat to either side of the table.

I loved it on sight.

Walking over to the table, she picked up the handset of a cordless phone, returned, and handed it to me, smiling slightly.

Taking the phone, I stared at her. "What do you want me to do with this?"

Her smile broadened, becoming a grin. "Normally, you put it up to your head and talk into it."

"Fun-ny." Even so, I decided to do as she suggested and put the phone to my ear. "Hello?"

"Hey."

My hand went numb and I felt all the blood rush from my face, leaving me slightly dizzy. "Ice? Is that really you?" Tears clouded my vision, but I didn't care. I barely noticed as Montana quietly left the study, closing the door softly behind her.

"Happy Thanksgiving, my Angel."

"Oh god, it *is* you. Hi, sweetheart. How *are* you?"

"Doin' alright. How 'bout you?"

"I'm...." My throat closed for a moment. "I'm crying right now, but otherwise I'm ok."

"Don't cry, Angel." The note in her voice only served to cause more tears to fall.

"No, they're happy tears. I've just missed you. So much."

"I miss you too, sweet Angel."

The sound of breaking glass came over the line, then, followed by loud, masculine laughter and the slightly discordant strains of music. "Where are you?"

"Mexican cantina," came the succinct answer. "The Yellow Dog, if the missing letters are any indication."

"Charming," I replied, grinning like a madwoman behind my tears.

"Definitely high society."

More breaking glass, more riotous laughter.

"How are...things?" I asked finally, feeling like some absurd extra in a James Bond movie.

"Slow. Cavallo's on the run. One of my 'helpers' tipped off the wrong man." The disgust was plain in her voice.

"Where are your 'helpers' now?"

There was a moment of silence, and I pictured her craning her neck to see through the crowd. "About one tequila away from passing out. Again."

"And they're supposed to be *helping* you?"

Her snort sounded softly over the phone line. "Guarding me, actually."

"That's even worse!"

"Not really. It's better for me when they're out of my hair."

I sighed. "I suppose that's true."

A silence settled between us then, though it was a comfortable one. That might seem silly, being quiet over the telephone, but since it was, at that point, my only connection to her, I took it willingly.

"Ice?" I asked when the sounds of laughter came through the line once again.

"Mm?"

"If those guys are as bad as you say they are...."

"Worse."

I chuckled. "Ok, worse. But...couldn't you just...you know...give them the slip? Come back over the border? We don't have to go to Canada. I mean, the desert here is huge. No one would ever find us. And...I really like it here. We could...."

"I can't do that, Angel," her soft voice broke in.

"But why?" God, did I really sound as petulant as I thought I sounded?

"You know why."

"No I don't, Ice. I don't know why. You've got a chance to be free of all this. Why can't you just walk away? It would be so easy."

"For how long?"

That question stopped me dead in my tracks. "What?"

"For how long, Angel? How long do we run? How long do we hide? How long do we look over our shoulders until some other well-meaning neighbor does something without thinking? Until Cavallo finds our trail again and tries to finish what he started?" Her sigh was heavy and filled with emotion. "I won't put you through that anymore, Angel. I won't put *us* through that. Not anymore."

"But...."

"No, Angel. Whatever happens, it ends here."

A shiver ran down my spine at the chord of utter resolution in her tone. Running my free hand over a bare arm, I wasn't surprised to feel the gooseflesh pebbling my skin.

"No more running, Angel." Her voice was hoarse, raspy. "No more."

By some sort of weird telephonic osmosis, the immense weight of that promise came to rest on my soul. It took up the burden gratefully while the rest of me seemed at a loss. "You shouldn't have to go through this alone, Ice," I whispered faintly, knowing she would hear me. "Not while I'm sitting safe up here. It's not fair. Not by a long shot."

"I'm never alone, Angel. You live in my heart. Don't you know that by now?"

Have you ever had one of those moments when you were so filled with absolute, spellbinding joy that your entire body just goes numb from the sheer enormity of it?

I was having one of those moments. I stared at the phone dumbly, as if it had just sprouted wings and was threatening to fly off.

When a loud burst of static shot through the line, I almost dropped it, and by the time I managed to collect my scattered wits and put the receiver back up to my ear, I heard a woman's voice speaking in very rapid Spanish.

Then the line went dead.

"Ice?"

Nothing, of course.

"Ice? Are you there?"

When the fact that that particular corpse had no hope of being revived filtered through my still-benumbed brain, I slowly replaced the phone back on its cradle, brushing my fingers against the warm plastic just briefly before letting go entirely.

I felt the very tips of my fingers then trail lightly against my lips, as if to seal in a phantom kiss. Her last words to me rolled through my mind over and over, unceasing and powerful as waves crashing against a distant shore.

"Wow," I whispered the four walls surrounding me, my voice as awed as a child's on Christmas morning.

Chapter 4

Some time later, I found myself out past the well-lit courtyard, drawing the darkness around me like a well-loved coat. The moon hung pregnant and low. *Low enough to touch,* I thought as I tried to do just that, my hand obscuring its deep-pitted face for a moment. The night wind was cool upon my skin. I felt alive, awake, aware, much like the desert around me.

A slight scuffle behind me heralded the presence of a nighttime visitor. *Took 'em long enough.* I chuckled inwardly, waiting with the patience of Job for my watcher to reveal herself as I continued to stare at the moon.

"Um...hello?"

Smiling slightly, I turned to watch Nia step diffidently to my side, her own smile shy and slightly off-center.

"Hi, Nia. What brings you out here so late at night?"

"They...um...wondered if you were ok. But no one wanted to go and find out for themselves." She shrugged. "I said I'd do it. So, here I am."

"That's very sweet of you, Nia. But I'm all right. Really." Looking back up into the sky, I breathed deep of the fresh, cool air. "Just enjoying the peace and quiet."

She laughed softly. "Yeah, it's pretty much of a zoo in there. Everybody's fighting over who has to do the dishes and what to watch on TV."

"Why doesn't that surprise me?"

She laughed again, a free and unfettered sound that clashed with the healing bruises on her face. After a moment, her expression became more serious. "Did you...talk to Ice?"

I looked back at her with some surprise. In the several conversations we'd had, Ice's name was never mentioned.

"That's what they were guessing back at the house." Her tone became slightly defensive, as if she'd taken my surprise for anger.

"It's ok," I hastened to assure her. "I just wasn't aware you knew who Ice was."

"Are you kidding? Everybody knows who Ice is!"

I couldn't help but laugh at her enthusiasm. "Oh they do, do they?"

"Sure. I mean, you can't hang around the Amazons for ten minutes without hearing about her. It's like she's some kind of god or something."

"She's not a god, Nia. She's a woman. An extraordinary woman, perhaps, but a woman just the same."

"That's not what they say."

Smiling, I put a hand on her arm, pleased when she didn't flinch away. "Take it from me."

After a moment, she nodded then craned her neck to look up at the sky. Letting my hand drop away from her wrist, I joined her in her study and a somewhat content silence fell between us.

"Are you scared?"

Her question was so softly uttered that at first I thought it was only the wind. But when I turned my head, I saw her looking directly at me, her dark eyes questioning.

"Of what?"

Dropping her eyes from mine, she studied the dirt beneath her feet. "I...um...heard what she did to Rio in the stables the other day."

I blinked as my mind scrambled for a foothold in the conversation I seemed to be having.

"They say she almost killed her," she continued, still staring at the ground.

"They say that, huh?"

She nodded. "Yeah."

"Rio wasn't in any danger of dying." I knew that as well as I knew my own name. "Ice was very angry."

She looked up, not quite meeting my eyes. "Because Rio

was threatening you, right?"

"Yes. That's right."

"The Amazons say she's a very violent woman sometimes."

"Rio?"

"No. Ice."

"She can be." Again, I spoke honestly, feeling no need to sugarcoat a fundamental truth.

This time, she met my gaze dead on. "And that doesn't scare you?"

A simple question, yes. But the answer was anything *but* simple. But if that night on the dock, seemingly so long ago, had taught me anything, it was that my perceived fear *of* Ice was really a fear *for* Ice. "Not in the way you're thinking, no," I answered finally, knowing she wouldn't be pleased with the answer, but having none other to give.

The look she gave me in return was one of patent disbelief and I'll admit that I felt my jaw stiffen at the seeing of it. "Those stories you told me about your husband. Isn't being with someone like Ice sort of like jumping from the frying pan into the fire?"

"Nothing could be further from the truth, Nia. Ice would rip out her own heart before she'd raise so much as a finger against me."

"But how can you say that? How do you know?"

When my voice came, it was my heart that spoke the words. "Because she loves me."

And that was the most fundamental truth of all.

After a very long moment, she finally looked away. Her body seemed smaller somehow, as if my words had deflated something she held very tightly within her. "Oh."

Sensing her need to be alone to ponder what I'd just told her, I laid a gentle hand on her shoulder, and when she looked up, gave her the slightest of smiles. "I'm going to go back inside. Will you be okay out here?"

Returning my smile, she nodded. "Yeah. I'll be along in a little bit."

"Alright then. Happy Thanksgiving, Nia."

Her smile broadened. "You too, Angel. And...thanks. For giving me something to think about."

"Anytime."

As I walked back into the house and prepared myself for bed, another Thanksgiving day passed into the mists of time, with an ending much sweeter than its beginning.

And for that, I was truly thankful.

It seemed that my head had hardly warmed the pillow when I found myself awake again. Craning my neck, I caught the none-too-faint noises of a door closing and feet quickly marching down the hall, sounds which had woken me from my sleep.

Slipping out of bed and tugging my T-shirt down to cover everything that needed covering, I quickly padded across the room and opened my door just in time to see Pony blow, like a hurricane, into the room next to mine. *Nia's room,* my mind helpfully supplied as I crossed glances with Critter, who was following close behind, a no nonsense expression setting her face in somber lines.

Shouting, followed by a high, breathless scream vaporized the last of the sleep clinging to my system and, startled, I ran from my room into Nia's. Pony was standing above the bed, her face brick with rage. In one tightly clenched fist lay the sheet that had once covered Nia's body. The other hung loose by her side, though her muscles bulged beneath the tight shirt she wore, telling their own story about the state of her anger.

Nia was curled in a fetal ball on the bed, her hands wrapped tight around her head. She was moaning loudly in what I took to be sheer terror.

"Back off!" I yelled to Pony, pushing past Critter and slipping into bed beside Nia. I tried to gather her up into my arms, but at the first touch of my hand, she screamed again and jerked away, rolling over to the very edge of the bed and staring at us all with wide, blank eyes.

"What the *hell* is going on here?" I demanded, more than a little angry myself.

"Tell her, Nia!" Pony shouted. "Tell her what you did!"

Nia's only answer was a moan.

"Go on! Tell her!" The veins in her neck stood out in stark relief against the flushed rose of her skin. "Tell her, damnit!"

"Pony, stop! Please! You're scaring her to death!"

"She deserves it! She deserves more than that! She...*goddamnit*!" Throwing the twisted sheet down onto the bed, she turned and stalked over to the window, whipping the heavy blinds aside and peering out into the coming dawn.

I turned my head from that scene to bestow a totally bewildered look on Critter, the only one among us who seemed to have retained at least some semblance of sanity.

"She called Richard to come and get her. Even worse, she gave him directions to the ranch."

"What?" In utter disbelief, I turned to Nia, who was once again huddled in a tight ball, apparently well past the point of responding to anything. I turned back to Critter. "How do you know?"

"Another Amazon, Tweaker, was with Cheeto in Las Vegas when they picked up Nia. Tweaker stayed behind to make sure Richard didn't follow them back to the ranch. Last night, she overheard him talking to a group of his buddies, saying that his wife had called him and he was going back down to, as he put it, 'break the bitch out.'" She ran one hand through her hair, sighing deeply. "That was about four hours ago. Tweaker's tracking them as we speak."

"How many?"

"Six. In three cars."

"Shit."

She sighed again. "Yeah."

Pony turned slowly from the window, letting the blinds drop back into place. "That bitch has put every single woman on this ranch in danger." She laughed mirthlessly. "It's not like any of us was surprised when she called that overgrown shitbag. She's done it more times than I can count." Her fists clenched again. "But this...this...." Her jaw clamped down so tightly, I thought her teeth would shatter. "*Motherfucker*!" She turned back to the window again.

Resisting the urge to get up and try to offer comfort to Pony—a useless gesture in any event—I settled for relaxing slightly and looking up at Critter. "What now?"

It was Pony who answered, however, still staring out the window. "We're gonna make sure that fucker forgets this place even exists." When she turned to face us, all traces of anger were gone. In its place stood calm resolution. "Critter, wake up Cheeto and have her help get all the women from the cottages in here. Once everyone's inside, lock the doors and don't let anybody leave. Not for any reason. Got it?"

Critter nodded.

"I'll wake Montana and gather the rest of the Amazons. We'll stop that bastard in his tracks. Understood?"

"Understood."

"Alright then. Let's get to it."

"What about me?" I asked, slightly miffed at being left out of the plans.

"You stay with her. Make sure she doesn't do anything stupid." The sneer on her face was quite pronounced.

Feeling myself stiffen, I came to my feet before I quite realized I was even standing. "Pony? Could I speak to you for a moment? Outside?"

Open-mouthed, she looked at me as if I'd grown another head.

"Now."

After a long, silent battle of wills, Pony backed down slightly, nodded brusquely, and stalked out of the room. I glanced at Critter. "Will you stay with her for a minute? I don't think it's a good idea to leave her alone right now."

"No problem," she said, favoring me with a slight smile that had more than a touch of awe mixed in.

When I walked out into the hallway, it was to find it lined with women, each with a shocked expression on her face. I looked at Corinne, who was standing closest.

"I'll help with Nia," she whispered, and I gave her a grateful nod. If anyone had any hope of comforting Nia, it was Corinne. She just has a way of reaching out to the unreachable. It's a gift, and one I'd gladly pay good money to have.

Ignoring the rest of the women, I followed Pony down the hallway, through the living room and out into the cool dawn. When she stopped, I stopped, staying several feet behind her and staring at a back she had turned to me. "Pony," I said softly.

Her fists clenched and the broad, thick muscles in her back bulged under her shirt, but she didn't turn around.

"Pony, please."

When she finally turned, her expression was a curious mixture of anger, respect, and a curious sadness. "Little Angel's all grown up, huh?" she said, a bittersweet smile on her lips.

"Pony...it's not like that...."

"Isn't it?"

"No. It isn't."

"Then maybe you could explain it to me, Angel. Because the last time I checked, I was responsible for security here. Which means that in a situation like this, *everybody* listens to me. Even Montana. Or are you above that now?"

"I'm not above anything. You know that."

"All I know is what I saw, Angel. And what I heard."

I laughed a little. "Funny. I was going to say the same thing."

Dark, narrowed eyes stared back at me. "What do you mean?"

"Pony, do you realize how much you terrified Nia back there?"

"So? You heard what she did!"

"Yes, I did. But do you also realize that what you did to her, how you yelled at her, was probably almost exactly like something her husband would do? I know it's exactly what Peter used to do to me."

Her lips parted slightly as her eyes widened. Obviously, it was something she hadn't considered.

"Look. I know you were angry. You have every right to be. What she did was foolish and thoughtless. But it's also in the past. What we have to do now is to work on some way of rectifying her mistake."

"That's what I'm tryin' to do, Angel! Or do you think I'm just givin' orders cause I feel like it?"

"I realize that, Pony. But...." How to put this tactfully.

"But what?"

So much for tact. I sighed heavily. "Listen. Keeping Nia locked up here isn't any better than the relationship you just got her out of. I know you don't like it. I don't like it either. It's dangerous. But the fact of the matter is that Nia *did* call her husband. And she needs to be given the choice to see him or not. If you take that choice away from her, can you really say that that's any better than what he would do to her?"

"Sure I can," she replied, sneering. "I'm doing it because I want to protect her, and everyone else."

"And I'm sure that sometime in his life, her husband thought the same thing. Either way, it's wrong. Nia is an adult. She needs to be treated like one."

"Then she damn well needs to start acting like one!"

I took a step closer. "That's not for you or me to decide, Pony. You need to let her make this choice. It's the right thing to do, and I think you know that."

I could see the knowledge come to her face. I could also see, by the set of her jaw and the tenseness of her body, how hard she was still trying to fight it. "I don't have time to be anybody's babysitter," she said finally, grudgingly.

I couldn't help smiling. "You won't have to. I'll do it."

"Oh no. No. No. No. No. No. Forget it, Angel. Not a chance in hell."

"Pony...."

"Forget it, I said! No way, Angel. I do that, and I might as well let that bastard husband of hers put a gun up to my head and pull the trigger. At least then I'll only die once. You get hurt out there, and Ice will cut me up into little bitty pieces, then kill me, then resurrect me, then kill me all over again. Nope. Not happening. Sorry."

"Pony, listen to me."

"Nope. Sorry."

I looked at her, struck with the almost unbearable urge to laugh. I could almost picture her on some playground somewhere sticking her fingers in her ears and shouting, "I'm not listening! I can't hear you! LaLaLaLa!"

I guessed my struggle against laughter must have shown up on my face, because she halted her rant in midstream, planted her fists on her hips, and stared at me. "What's so damn funny?"

I wiped the smirk off my face, feeling oddly chastised, like a child with her grasping appendage caught in a baked goods container. "Nothing."

"Yeah. Right."

Clearing my throat, I struggled to get the conversation back on course. "At least hear me out, Pony."

"Can you handle a gun?"

"No."

"Then forget it. Period. End of story."

As she turned to leave, I reached out, grabbed her arm, and turned her back to face me. She looked at me, down at her arm, and then back up at me. "You know, I'm really getting tired of you doing that to me."

I dropped my hand to my side. "At least hear me out," I repeated. "Please."

Crossing her arms over her chest, she leveled her best glare at me. "Fine. Start talking."

"Nia trusts me. And I think, in some way, she respects me as well. We share the same history. If I take her out there, maybe she'll be able to see exactly the kind of person her husband is. And maybe she'll stop going back to him."

To her credit, she was really listening to what I had to say.

"That's a hell of a lot of maybes for you to risk your life like that, Angel."

"You're risking your life too, aren't you?"

"Yeah. But I'll have a gun in my hands."

"And I'll have twenty women with guns all around me. I think that evens the odds a little." I reached out again, and this time, she accepted my touch. "I wouldn't suggest this if I didn't believe it would work, Pony. All I'm asking is for you to have a little faith in me and believe it, too."

"And if I don't?"

"Then I'll do as you ask and stay inside. No questions asked."

As she looked at me, I could almost see the gears turning inside her head. After a moment, the faintest of grins curved her lips. "You know the name of a good shrink?"

"What?" I asked, blinking at the non sequitur.

"I think I need to have my head examined."

When the meaning of her words caught up to me, I laughed out loud, crushed her to me in a grateful embrace, and kissed her soundly on the lips. "Thank you, Pony! You won't regret this!"

Laughing again, I pulled away, turned, and ran for the house.

When I found she wasn't behind me, I turned again, to find her just where I'd left her, mouth agape, her eyes glassy. "Pony?"

"Bu... Wa... He..." For a brief moment, I saw only the whites of her eyes, and I thought sure she was about to faint. Then she blinked, shook herself, and looked around to see if anyone had caught her brief lapse into insanity.

Unable to help myself, I laughed again, then completed my trek to the house, grinning like a madwoman.

Stepping inside Nia's room, I wasn't surprised to see her safely ensconced within Corinne's all-encompassing embrace. The dampness of Corinne's nightgown attested to the many tears shed by the younger woman, and when I softly closed the door behind me, she gifted me with a tremulous smile, her head tight against Corinne's generous chest.

"How are you feeling?" I asked as I came to sit beside them both, laying a hand on Corinne's warm arm in thanks.

"A little better now, thanks," she said very softly, her eyes not quite meeting mine. Straightening a little, and wiping her eyes with the back of her hand, she pulled away from Corinne's hold, still not meeting my eyes. "Listen, I'm sorry about all this. I know you must think I'm some kind of nut for calling Richard."

"I'm not here to judge you, Nia. None of us are. I think I can understand a little bit why you called him. I might have done the same thing, once. That's not the problem here."

As I fell silent, she finally met my eyes, her own round and dark and full of tears.

Though part of me felt for her, I had to harden my heart just a little. "The problem, Nia, is that your mistake in giving your husband directions to the ranch could put some innocent women in danger. Do you understand that? And why it's so?"

"But Richard wouldn't...."

"Stop it, Nia," Corinne interjected, reaching out and tipping the young woman's chin up, forcing those round eyes to meet hers. "Right now. If you wish to continue to lie to yourself, feel free. But don't force the burden of those untruths on others who don't deserve it."

"I don't know what you're talking about," Nia mumbled, but I could see that she did, in fact, know. Guilt was written in bold strokes across her face and her eyes wandered downward, despite Corinne's firm grip on her chin.

Knowing that continuing further down this path would only lead to Nia withdrawing into herself once again, I decided to try a different direction. Summoning up my friendliest smile, I turned it toward her and held out my hand. "C'mon. Let's get dressed."

Her eyes narrowed, suspicion seen easily within their clear depths. "Why?"

I affected an offhand shrug. "Well, since your husband and his friends are coming down to pick you up, don't you think it might be better to meet them in something a little more...substantial...than your nightgown?"

That "Angel just sprouted another head" look came back again, directed at me through two sets of eyes this time. I seemed to be getting that look a lot lately. I shrugged again, inwardly. *Whatever works.*

"You mean you're just gonna let him waltz right in here and take me?" Nia asked finally.

"Isn't that what you want?" When I wanted to, I could look very innocent indeed. In the periphery of my vision, I saw Corinne quickly hide a smirk behind her free hand. Ok, maybe not to people who knew me really well. "I mean, you *did* call him to come get you, right?"

"Yeah," she replied, though her voice didn't sound quite so sure as before.

"Let's get a move on, then."

But Nia didn't move. Not an inch.

"Well?"

"Maybe I changed my mind?"

Corinne snorted. "It's a little too late for that, my dear."

"Corinne...."

"No, Angel. I'm right. It's about time we stopped coddling this woman. She's made her bed. The best thing for all concerned is to let her lie in it. We've all had to do it a time or two. Perhaps it's best to allow her her turn."

Nia straightened. "But maybe I made a mistake! You said you could forgive a mistake!" She was talking to us both, and we both knew it.

It was Corinne who answered. "Forgiveness is one thing, Nia. Forcing others to live with the consequences of that mistake is another matter entirely."

Nia's eyes brimmed with tears again, and I watched, not without some sadness, as they spilled past the barrier of her lids and trickled down her bruise-shadowed cheeks. "So what do I do?"

I sighed then held out my hand again. "Do you trust me, Nia?"

After a very long moment, she nodded, sniffling. "Yes."

"Then come on and let's get dressed."

"But...."

"Please."

Her gaze was timid as she looked from me, to Corinne, and back. "Ok," she whispered, her expression much like that of a condemned prisoner taking her final walk. She took my hand and I helped her to stand, then gave her a gentle push in the direction of her closet. Giving her an encouraging smile, I then turned and made for my own room to change into something more suitable for the occasion.

Since I didn't have any suits of armor or bulletproof vests handy, I settled for a pair of jeans and a T-shirt. Ok. One of

Ice's T-shirts. I suppose you could say that I'd suddenly developed a taste for larger clothing. Go figure.

When I looked up after brushing out my hair, I saw Corinne standing behind me, her face expressionless. "What?" I asked, turning and laying the brush down on the dresser.

"Please tell me you're not going out there, Angel."

"I'm sorry, Corinne. I can't tell you that."

As I moved to walk past her and out into the hallway, she laid a hand on my arm, stopping my forward progress. "Don't do this, Angel. The others are more than capable of handling that piece of excrement without your involvement. Don't put yourself in danger when there's no need."

Turning toward her, I gently removed the hand from my arm and stood with it clasped in my own. "I need to do this, Corinne. Nia trusts me, and maybe, just maybe, I can get her to see her husband through the eyes of reality instead of that little fantasy she insists on putting before the world. She's made her mistakes, and she's paying for them, but I think she deserves this shot." I looked down at our joined hands. "I wasn't able to prevent things from going too far with Peter. Maybe my being there with her will keep her from making the same mistake I did." I looked up at her. "I need to do this. I don't need your blessing. But I do need your love."

As I watched, her face softened, her smile beautiful and tender. "You always have that, Angel." She squeezed my hand, then let go, giving me a gentle shove out into the hallway. "You'd best get going before I change my mind and do something that will doubtless land me in the ICU, courtesy of Ice's fist."

I laughed, pressing a quick kiss against her cheek. "Never happen, my friend."

Her return smile was wicked. "Never say never, Angel."

"I'll keep that in mind," was my retort as I stepped fully into the hallway and went to collect Nia, who was coming out of her own room at the same time. She looked more than a little green around the gills, but when our eyes met, I could see her swallow convulsively, then straighten her neck and tilt her chin slightly in a rather impressive display of confidence.

Smiling, I gently touched her arm. "Let's take care of business."

As we walked down the hall, we passed a large group of women filtering into the house, some with mild looks of alarm on their faces, others just looking for the first available place to lay their heads, it still being rather early in the morning.

I caught Critter's eye, and she gave me a brief smile and a short nod before turning away to deal with her charges. Cheeto entered the house as Nia and I left it, ushering still more half-asleep women into the house. She gave us both a small, polite nod before brushing by to continue her duties.

The sky was a stunning blood red as the sun shone its crescent over the tops of the far-off mountain ranges. Looking at it, I wondered if the color was an omen, then shivered internally at my own ghoulish thoughts.

The air was cool and crisp, a slight breeze ruffling my hair and leaving goose bumps in its wake as it brushed gently against my skin.

The courtyard was a bustle of activity, with women moving to and fro, their faces set with serious purpose. Taking Nia's hand in mine, I moved out beyond the crowd and headed toward the stables, where I could see Pony and the others assembling.

It was a mixed group of women gathering there—both Amazons and several permanent residents of the ranch, each of whom looked supremely confident and capable, even in the face of what was sure to be a dangerous situation. They formed a single-file line facing Pony, who was kneeling on the ground in front of a long box from which she removed weapons, handing one to each woman in turn as they approached.

I could feel Nia stiffen beside me, her hand becoming warm and clammy as it rested in mine. I turned my head to see her staring at each weapon as it emerged from the box, her eyes wide and frightened. Smiling slightly, I tightened the grip of our hands and started forward again, determined to drag her behind me if I needed to. Thankfully, after a minor stumble, she quickly began walking under her own power.

Just as we were about to reach the group, the corral gate opened and Cowgirl rode out atop her spirited horse. Seeing us, she grinned, tipped her hat, twirled her rifle once in an impressive maneuver, and gently urged her horse into a trot in the direction of the orchard, giving us all a cheery wave as she passed.

A moment later, Montana emerged from the corral, seated astride a truly magnificent dappled gray mare that sported a snow-white mane and tail. Twitching her lips in a semblance of a smile, she touched the brim of her hat in a very Cooper-esque fashion, settled her rifle comfortably against her thighs, and, with a quiet "hut", sent her own mount after Cowgirl's.

We started forward again and, hearing our approaching footsteps, Pony gave us both a wave and a jaunty grin before standing up and brushing the desert sand from her knees. "Great day for a bloodbath," she joked with a gallows humor I well remembered, if couldn't quite appreciate, given the circumstances. "We're just about ready."

Soft footsteps from the interior of the stables heralded Rio's approach, and when she stepped from the shadows into the newly risen sun with a gun in her hands large enough to bring down an entire herd of stampeding elephants, I'll admit my heart considered fainting dead away and taking the rest of my body with it.

She stared at me for a long moment, her dark eyes wary and watchful, before apparently realizing why my face was as white as the sun-bleached steer's head that hung above the stable doors. Blushing sheepishly, she lowered the barrel of her shotgun until it faced the desert floor and held up her free hand, palm out, facing me.

It was then that my lungs remembered what their true purpose was and I took in a grateful breath, happy when that simple action dissipated the dizziness I was beginning to feel.

"Sorry," she mouthed, before turning her attention to Pony and dragging the now-empty wooden box back into the stable.

"Are you ok?" Nia asked.

"Um...yeah. I just...you know...saw...something."

She giggled a little, which relaxed us both. When Rio stepped out again into the sunlight, her gun was pointed carefully at the ground. Our glances crossed briefly, and then she turned, taking her place at Pony's left shoulder as the women moved out of the courtyard and onto the path that would lead them to the orchard.

I turned to Nia. "You ready?"

Looking up at me, her expression was, by turns, doomed and hopeful. "You don't suppose I could just...go back to my room and pretend this day never happened, do you?"

"Well, you could do that, yes."

For a brief second, her eyes lit up brighter than a joyful child's on his birthday. Then she sighed. "But if I keep hiding from my mistakes, nothing's ever going to get better for me, is it?"

"Nobody knows what direction someone's life will take," I

said with as much compassion as I could. "Not even their own. But this seems like a good place to start, yes."

She looked as if she were biting into a lemon. "Somehow, I knew you'd say that."

"Ms. Predictability," I said through my grin, "that's me."

The shade beneath the orange trees was cool, dim, and fragrant. I tried my best to blend in with the thick foliage around me, but I knew that unless these trees were suffering from a spectacular case of fungal rot, my blue jeans and black T-shirt could never be mistaken for part of the scenery. Nia, who was standing by my side as if glued there, was much better dressed for the occasion, sporting brown slacks and a green top. She was so frightened, however, that I didn't have the heart to tell her that standing next to me was like keeping company with a neon billboard. Or a bull's-eye.

Squinting against the dappled sunlight that occasionally filtered through the grove, I tried to spot the other women who were ensconced, as I was, within the thick fall of heavy foliage, but it was like looking for a needle in a haystack. Except for Pony, who was standing behind the tree in front of me, and Rio, who was standing across the small road that led through the trees, it was as if the rest of the women had never been there at all.

Standing plastered against me, I felt Nia shift and then shift again.

"What's wrong?" I whispered.

"I gotta pee," she replied in a five-year-old's voice as she continued to squirm against the pressure in her bladder.

The only thing that kept me from exploding with laughter was the vivid memory of my own similar situation while waiting to cross into Canada two years before. Some of my mirth must have shown on my face, however, because she scowled at me.

"It's not funny."

"No, I know it's not," I hastened to reassure her, "but you're kinda gonna have to hold it for a little...."

My helpful advice was interrupted by a horse's quiet nicker. Pony turned to me, her face set. "They're coming."

Nodding, I looked back at Nia. Her face was chalky white, her expression slightly ill. "I...um...don't think 'holding it' is gonna be a problem anymore."

Resisting the urge to step delicately away from her, I settled instead for a sympathetic smile. "Well, that's one less thing to worry about, right?"

The sounds of trucks barreling down the unpaved road made whatever she might have said into a very moot point. Feeling her stiffen beside me, I knew without even the slightest hint of a doubt that she was readying herself to bolt. Much as I wanted to restrain her, I knew I couldn't. Not and remain true to my own ideals, not to mention the spirit and intent of Montana's ranch.

To my immense surprise, though, instead of fleeing, she simply looked at me. "Please," she whispered. "Don't.... Don't make me do this. Please...."

"You don't have to do anything you don't want to, Nia," I replied, gently as I could while sparing a glance over my shoulder to track the progress of the oncoming trucks that I could barely see past the line of trees blocking my vision.

"I can't...I'm so...so scared." Her hands knotted in the fabric of her shirt, twisting so hard the fabric came very close to tearing. "He.... He...."

Ignoring the action at my back, I turned my attention fully on Nia, sensing an epiphany in the making.

Her eyes were wide and dark and full of tears as she stared at me, past me, staring at something my own eyes couldn't see. "He hurts me," she whispered, as if saying it louder would seal her fate.

Blindly grabbing the front of my shirt, she buried her flushed face into my chest. I cradled her to me, knowing exactly what she was going through and crying a little for us both.

Her moans turned to muffled sobs and I comforted her as best I could, all the while tracking the action behind me by sound alone. When the trucks skid to a stop and a door opened, I turned, taking Nia with me, and shuffled forward slightly to a break in the heavy leaves blocking my vision.

It's amazing how such monsters wear the mask of the ordinary so easily. And that's just what he was.

Ordinary.

Ordinary face, ordinary body, ordinary clothes. A man you'd pass on the street without looking twice. Without wondering if perhaps he beat the holy hell out of his wife for the unpardonable sin of breathing too loudly.

I strained my ears to hear his voice and was not surprised to hear that it, too, was ordinary.

"Get those horses outta the way, bitch. You're blockin' the road."

"You're trespassing on private property," Montana coolly responded.

"I don't see any signs," he scoffed, spitting off to the side.

"There aren't any," Montana agreed.

"Then who says it's private property?"

"I do."

"And who are you? The fucking Queen of Sheba?"

"I might be."

"Just let me pass, dyke, before I run you and your fucking horses over."

"I suggest you do as I say and go back the way you came."

Crossing his arms over his chest, he squinted at her. "Or what?"

I heard the shot before I saw Montana's gun move, and watched as Richard danced away from the puff of desert dust blew up from where his foot had been a split-second before. When he looked up at her, his mouth was a perfect "O" of shock, and for a brief instant, he had the look of a schoolboy just caught with his father's *Penthouse*.

"Go home, Richard," Montana said, her voice full and deep and unbending.

"Not without my wife," he snarled, finally gathering his wits about him. "You fucking kidnapped her and I'm not leaving till I get what I came for."

"She wasn't kidnapped, Richard. You know that as well as I do."

His face flushed red. "Bullshit. You bunch of man-hating dykes kidnapped her like you always do, twisting her mind against me, filling her head with all kinds of shit until she finally gets wise and comes back to me. Now give me what I came for or I'll burn this place down and all you fucking dyke bitches with it."

"I can't give you what you don't own. Go home."

"The fuck I will." Spitting once again, he turned and gestured to his buddies, who were staring at him through the dusty windows of their trucks. "Let's just go the fuck around. We'll be in and out before they know what hit 'em."

This is it.

Straightening, I pulled away from Nia's death-grip on me

and instead took her hand. "C'mon."

"What? Where?"

"We're going to stop this. Now. Before anyone gets hurt."

Her eyes were wide as saucers as she stared up at me. "We who?"

"Just c'mon," I replied, turning and half-pulling her along behind me.

"Where the hell are you going?" Pony hissed, reaching out to grab me as I strode by.

Ignoring her, I kept on walking, determined to halt this fiasco in its tracks. As if sensing my mood, both horses tossed their heads a little and backed away, leaving me a clear path ahead. I stepped forward, taking Nia along for the ride, until the sun shone warm upon my face. Then I stopped and watched as Richard's body froze, half in and half out of his truck.

After staring at us for a long moment, a cruel grin twisted his lips and he slowly pulled out of the car, straightening and crossing his arms over his chest. "About damn time. I knew you dykes didn't have the balls to pull this off. Come on, woman. Get your ass in the car now."

It nearly broke my heart to see Nia cringe before this maggot in the guise of a man. Her pulse was fast and thready beneath the touch of my fingers and her body trembled in fright.

Richard's cocky sneer turned quickly into a scowl. "You mind what I say, Nia. Get in the car. Now."

"Maybe she's afraid you'll beat the crap out of her again," Cowgirl observed from atop her horse.

"Shut your trap, bitch, before I shut it for you!"

"I'd like to see you try it," Cowgirl replied, smirking.

Obviously shaking off the temptation, he looked back at his wife. "Don't make me come after you, Nia. Your ass is already in enough hot water as it is, making me come all the way down here. Don't make it worse on yourself." His voice was almost soft, his words almost kind, but the false compassion didn't even come close to reaching his eyes.

Taking in a deep breath, Nia straightened somewhat and pulled away from me. I nearly panicked, until I heard a word sounding suspiciously like "no" come from her mouth.

Apparently, Richard heard the same thing, because both his arms and his jaw dropped as his eyes widened. "What?"

"I said no, Richard. I'm sorry you came all this way for nothing, but I've changed my mind."

Disbelieving, I turned and watch as her lips moved. Yes, she was the one saying the words, in a voice that sounded very much like hers, but with something—fortitude, perhaps? desperation? doom?—delivered a subtle change to the tone of her voice; a subtle, but undeniable force to the words she was giving voice to.

Across the clearing, Richard made as if to clean out his ears. His neck stuck out—rather like a turkey's I thought—as he tried again to stare her down. "I better not have heard what I think I just heard, bitch."

"I'm not coming back to you, Richard. Not now. Not ever. I'm...really sorry I called you, but...just go now. Please? It's over."

His face went white, then quickly flushed to a deep red before settling, finally, for a truly impressive purple shade. "It's over when I say it's over, you fucking cunt!"

Fists clenched in fury, he closed the gap between us in long strides, coming so close so quickly that I didn't even have time to get scared. Instead, I found myself watching as he shot out an arm as if to grab Nia by the throat and choke the life out of her.

In a completely reflexive motion, my own arm darted out and stopped his fist dead in its tracks. As if in slow motion, his head turned in my direction, his expression one of patent disbelief that someone—a woman no less—could actually be doing this to him.

My muscles strained against his rage-fueled strength, but the knowledge of what he'd do if I let go made my task, if not easy, at least bearable.

"You better let go of my hand, bitch, before I rip your fucking head off."

Before I could answer, steely fingers bit into my shoulder and I was wrenched away from the scene and into Pony's somewhat prepared arms.

"You like beating on women, big man?" Rio's voice roared out. "Why don't you pick on someone who can fight back, huh?"

Struggling out of Pony's tight grip, I looked over to see Nia being hugged tight by another Amazon whose name I didn't know. Quickly, I turned back to the scene unfolding before me.

"Come on, ya cheap little prick," Rio taunted. "Hit me. I dare ya."

Obviously stunned at the sudden change in game plan, Richard's only answer was to blink stupidly at her.

"Coward," she spat. "What's a matter, little man? Your balls crawled up inside your asshole, did they?" She said this last as a loud aside, deliberately turning her head toward the rest of us and living him an opening big enough to drive a tractor-trailer through.

I almost shouted a warning as he gathered himself and launched at her, but she turned in more than enough time, stopping his advance with a hook to the face that flattened his nose and sent him stumbling backwards several steps, blood spewing from between the fingers now covering his broken face.

That action, apparently, got his friends' attentions, because the clearing was then filled with the sounds of truck doors opening as six men stepped out into the light of the day, their expressions murderous.

That sound, however, was quickly overtaken by the music of a dozen Amazons exploding from the trees, their rifles cocked, ready, and aimed at the idiots who thought to help their unfortunate "friend."

"Show's over, boys," Montana drawled. "Get back in your trucks before the coyotes eat what's left of you after we're through with target practice."

If the situation hadn't been so serious, I would have laughed as the men slipped meekly back into their trucks almost as a single unit, all the testosterone suddenly gone from their puffed up little bodies.

"Well, well, well," Rio remarked conversationally as the last of the men was safely tucked away inside his truck, "looks like your buddies have about as much guts as you do, wife beater. Maybe next time, you'll pick your friends a little better, huh?" Her laugh was loud in the otherwise silent clearing. "C'mon, prick. Lay one on me like you do your wife. Or ain't ya got the sack for it anymore?"

I watched as her muscles rippled like mercury beneath the heavy denim of her work shirt as her body prepared itself to react in whatever way she demanded. Unlike the last time I'd seen her fight, Ice's teachings were plain to see in the loose, limber set of her body and the alert cock of her head. "Whatcha waiting for, big man? An engraved invitation? You like hitting women, right? Well, I'm a woman. So hit me!"

With a roar of rage, he came at her, fists swinging furiously. They grappled for a few moments before Richard got in a lucky shot to Rio's head. His smirk was short-lived, however, as a thunderous right to the gut blasted the air from his lungs and doubled him over, the remains of his breakfast littering the ground between his feet.

"Had enough yet, pussy?" Rio taunted. "Or would ya like to go another round?"

After several long moments, he finally straightened, blood still pouring from his nose like water from a spigot. "Last chance, Nia!" he shouted, to the disbelief of us all. "Get in the damn car, woman!"

No one was more surprised than I was when Nia actually pulled away from her rescuer's embrace and slowly walked toward her ailing husband. She stopped less than two feet away, and reached out an arm as if to touch him. At the last minute, she lowered it and looked at him instead. "I'm sorry, Richard. I really am."

"Not half as sorry as you're gonna be, I can tell you that. Now get your ass in the car. Move!"

She slowly shook her head. "No. Never again. You're not gonna hurt me ever again."

His smile was evil and dark. "That's what you think."

Whatever he might have thought to do next was interrupted abruptly as a knee came up between his legs and robbed all the fight from his body. Gibbering high in his throat, his hands cupped his injured groin as his legs gave out and dumped him onto the hard desert ground.

"That was for calling me a bitch, you bastard."

Her knee came up again, this time landing against the side of his face and landing him on his back. "And that was for every time you made fun of me and yelled at me and made me feel worthless."

The leg lashed out, again, and again, and again, raining blows against his unprotected body as she screamed out every sin he'd committed against her person.

I felt myself move, but Rio beat me to the punch, and in two quick strides, managed to wrap the enraged woman tight against her massive body, pulling her quickly away from the writhing body of her husband as Nia continued to scream her hatred out into the desert.

Two other Amazons came forward and half-dragged, half-carried Richard over to the lead truck, opening the passenger door and shoving his mostly unconscious body inside.

Not more than a split-second passed before the trucks

started up and pulled away in a shower of dust and sand.

A huge cheer went up through the clearing, the women shaking their rifles and shouting their triumph for a job well done.

"It's not over yet, you know," Pony said from her place next to me. "He'll be back. Not tomorrow, maybe, but soon. We might have won this battle, but the war isn't even close to being over."

"I know," I agreed. "But at least Nia knows what it's like to stand up for herself. That's a pretty important battle to win."

Grinning, she clapped me on the shoulder. "That it is, my friend. That it is."

Were I a novelist, I would entitle this chapter "The Blooming of Nia." Since I'm not, however, I'll settle for saying that after her confrontation with her husband, a new Nia stood upon the ashes of the old, rather like a phoenix rising up from the flames.

Of course, not all the changes were good ones, but that was to be expected, I suppose. Having married quite young, Nia had lost the best of her teenage years as she suffered beneath the oppressive and dangerous weight that was her husband.

And when that weight was finally lifted, that's exactly what she became.

A teenager.

The woman who would meekly carry out any task asked of her had suddenly developed an unbendable will, especially when it came to being asked to do things she didn't particularly care for. And that was a very long list, indeed.

Her favorite expression was fast becoming "you don't own me, so stop telling me what to do."

Which was, in a way, understandable, given all she'd been through in her young life. It didn't make putting up with her sudden attitude any easier though, except, perhaps, for Montana, who treated Nia the same way she treated everyone else: with patient compassion and total honesty.

Nia also developed somewhat of a crush on Rio, much to Rio's acute embarrassment (though truth to tell, the rest of us were quite amused). She followed her around like an overgrown puppy, asking—and at times begging—Rio to teach her how to fight, offering to do chores she otherwise would avoid like the plague, and generally ensuring that Rio walked around looking like she'd just suffered a severe sunburn to the face.

"Please tell me I wasn't ever like that," I observed one morning as Rio tried unsuccessfully to shoo her unneeded helper away for the third time in as many minutes.

"Never," Critter said from her place next to me on the couch.

"Thank god," Pony chimed in. "I don't think we ever would have survived it."

"Well, they do make a cute couple," Corinne added, her smirk quite pronounced.

Hearing the remark, Rio turned to us with an expression that was half murderous intent, half heartfelt plea.

Taking pity on this mercurial, moody, and sometimes violent woman who I was, nonetheless, coming to see as a friend, I levered myself up from my space on the couch and walked over to Nia, touching her arm briefly. "C'mon. Remember I promised to help teach you how to ride today?"

She turned to look at me as if realizing for the first time that I was even in the room. "Oh. Yeah," was her less than enthusiastic reply. "Can we do that another time? Rio's gonna...."

"The only thing Rio's gonna be doing is helping me with the security schedules," Pony interjected, coming to stand beside me. When Nia's face lit up at the prospect, Pony scowled. "Boring stuff. Really...really um...."

"Boring," Critter finished, nodding. "A yawn a minute. Puts me right out every time."

"I don't know about that," came a sweet voice from the couch. "I always found them to be particularly...."

Four identical glares convinced Corinne to temporarily shelve that line of thought, and with a slightly wicked grin, she absented herself from the rest of the conversation altogether, to our great relief.

"So, what do you say, Nia? It's a beautiful day outside. How about if we go on a nice trail ride, and by the time you get back, Rio should be finished with her job."

She looked over at Rio, who nodded vigorously.

"Alright. I guess that's ok, then."

Grinning in triumph, I looped my arm inside Nia's and drew her away from her newest obsession, leaving three profoundly relieved Amazons behind.

The next several days passed in like fashion, with Rio becoming very proficient at the game of hide and seek. If her body hadn't been so large, I would have half-expected to see her stuffed into one of the cabinets under the sink in the bathroom, that being the only place she could have even a modicum of privacy. At least until Nia thought of asking to attend to her there as well.

Christmas was fast approaching, and the prospect of spending it without Ice by my side turned a fairly stable mood into a downright depressed and surly one. Rather than biting the hands that fed and sheltered me, I decided that solitude was the best course of action, at least until I could come up with something better to assuage my depression.

Cleo and I became fast friends. I rode her daily, sometimes from dawn till dusk, taking in all of the treasures that the Arizona desert had to offer. Being out there in the wild without another human being around for miles gave me a strange, but welcomed sense of peace. It was there that I felt free to drop my mask of geniality and scream and rant and rave at the injustices that kept me apart from the other half of my soul.

Oh, I yelled at Ice as well, damning her for that selfless nobility which called her to put my life and my happiness before her own and wound up causing both of us to suffer for it. Even jail seemed a better place than where I found myself, and after three years of freedom, I actually began to look at my time in the Bog with a sense of happiness rather than the dread I was used to feeling.

That scared me, I'll be the first to admit, but I was truly at a loss as to what to do about it. Speaking to my friends, even to Corinne, about it was out of the question. They each had burdens of their own, and I wasn't about to add to them by forcing them to accompany me on this journey of self-pity I found myself on.

One day, as I was walking back from the stables after an early morning ride, I chanced to see Nia slipping into one of the community cars parked in front of the main house. She must have seen me through the rearview mirror, because as I passed, she reached out the open window and snagged the sleeve of my shirt, turning me to face her. "Hey, Angel! I'm blowin' this one donkey town for a little while. You wanna come with me?"

"Where?" I asked as I disengaged myself from her rather manic clasp.

Her grin lit up her whole face. "Mexico. I'm in the mood to party!"

I looked at her. "Mexico? As in...."

"You know," she replied, rolling her eyes, "that place south of the border where everyone speaks Spanish and they serve a mean tequila? Whadda ya say, huh? I was gonna go alone, but you look like you could use a little good cheer yourself."

"I...ah...don't think getting drunk is a really good idea for me right now."

After looking at me for a moment longer, she shrugged and started the engine. "Suit yourself. I'm outta here."

"No! Wait!" I knew I couldn't just let her go. Not into a land of strangers whose language she didn't even speak. At least I assumed she didn't speak it. Not that it mattered, really. Newly borne independence was one thing. Foolhardiness was another thing entirely.

Her eyes narrowed. "What now."

"Why Mexico? Isn't there someplace around here that...."

"Are you kidding? Look around, Angel. This place is dead. There's nothing around here for miles. I'm bored and I want some action. So, if you'll excuse me, I'm outta here."

"Wait! Please! I...um...." I scratched the back of my neck, trying to think quickly. "Why not? Sounds like fun. It might do me some good to get out of here for a while. You know, see new sights, stuff like that. Just wait here till I...get my wallet."

Her suspicion was evident as she stared at me for a long beat before finally blinking and nodding, not without some reluctance, I thought. "Alright. Just hurry up. You're not back in five minutes and I'm leaving without you."

"Great! Thanks!" Grinning, I jumped away from the car and took off for the house at a dead run. "Be right back!"

Running full speed into the house, I managed a full-bore collision with Rio, who was getting ready to come outside. Normally, running into Rio would have been akin to running into a brick wall, but with momentum behind me, I managed to accidentally tackle her, sending us both back into the sunken living room where we flipped over the back of the couch and landed, in a tangled heap, on the floor.

"My, my, my," came a dry as dust voice above us. "You really must tell me your secret, Rio. Flash a little brawn and you have women literally falling into your arms."

The woman beneath me flushed a brilliant crimson before scrabbling away from me as if I were the fire and she'd just gotten burned. She jumped to her feet, her eyes darting around the room. "I'm sorry. I...uh...I..."

Laughing a little at her expression, I hauled myself up with a little help from Corinne. "It's alright, Rio. I'm sorry I smashed into you like that."

"Where's the fire?" Pony demanded, rushing into the living room with Critter close at her heels. Sliding to a stop, she put her hands on her hips and stared balefully at us, obviously trying to piece together what had happened to leave the three of us looking so...rumpled.

"No fire," I hastened to respond. "Just a little accident. I...um...lost my footing."

My glare cut off Corinne's snicker before it even left her lips.

A horn blaring ended our impasse and reminded me why I blew into the house like a fanged, flying mammal out of the kingdom of Hades in the first place. "Pony, I'm glad you're here. I need your help."

"What's up?"

I signed. "It's Nia. She's bound and determined to go down to Mexico and she's not taking no for an answer."

"Mexico? Why?"

"She's bored. She wants to 'party.'" My fingers formed sarcastic quotes around that word.

"Damn. She won't last two seconds down there."

"I know. That's why I said I'd join her and came in here to find you."

"Shit," Pony replied. "Alright, Rio, you go out there and stall her. Tell her you'll go with her. Just don't let her leave till I get there."

"No way! You're nuts, Pony! I'm tryin' to get *away* from her, remember?"

"Rio...just do it, ok?"

"God damn it," she muttered. "You owe me big time, woman."

"Yeah, yeah. Put it on my tab. Just go stall her, alright?"

With a melodramatic sigh, Rio turned away, grumbling phrases perhaps best left to the imagination.

After the door slammed, Pony turned to look at Critter, who

shrugged. "Well, we were planning on going down there anyway to pick up medications."

At my questioning look, Critter—bless her heart—stepped in to explain. "In Mexico, you don't need a prescription to get prescription drugs. You can just go down to the local drug store and pick up what you need."

"And they don't stop you at the border?" I asked, amazed.

Critter grinned. "Nope. They tell you you can't bring back more than a month's supply, but those guys don't know what a month's supply is, so it's not that difficult."

"Interesting."

"Yup. So, I figure since we were planning on going down there anyway, we might as well kill two birds with one stone, so to speak."

"Great! Just let me get my wallet and I'll meet you at the car."

"Hold up there, Angel," Pony stated as I turned away. "You don't need to come down with us. We'll keep an eye on Nia while you stay up here."

I turned back slowly. "Are you saying I can't go?"

She sighed. "Look, Angel, I don't want to fight with you about it. But face facts here. With your coloring, you just scream 'American tourist'. They'd be after you like flies on horseshit."

"Wonderful image, Pony," Critter said, disgusted. "Thanks."

"Hey! I'm serious here! It's the truth and you know it."

"What about her?" I asked, cocking my thumb at Critter.

Pony scowled. "That's different."

"Yeah? How? Because her hair's blonde and curly and mine's blonde and straight?"

She sighed again. "Critter, you tell her."

"I would, if I knew what the answer was."

"Fat lot of good you are," Pony muttered.

"I try." Critter's smile was sweet as sunshine.

After a moment, Pony threw up her hands in defeat. "Blondes," was all she said. Funny how she could make a color sound so much like a curse.

To her, though, it probably was.

Since my only knowledge of Mexico came from honeymoon pictures and episodes of "The Love Boat," I was expecting a country rife with pristine beaches and crystal blue Caribbean waters. In fact, on the way down, I cursed myself roundly for having neglected to bring along a bathing suit.

As is true with life, however, what I was expecting and what I received were two different things entirely.

My first surprise of the day came about when we walked across the border. Where I had expected a few somber looking guards with weapons and a snarling dog or two, I got instead a...turnstile. Unmanned. Apparently, in this part of Mexico at least, they didn't care what you brought in with you; they only cared about what you brought out.

The second surprise came shortly thereafter, and almost made me turn and run back for the border.

Instead of white sand beaches and beautiful, tanned, and oiled bodies, I saw something that could only be Timothy Leary's version of a carnival midway. A riot of color and a cacophony of sound, streets too narrow for cars to pass through were lined on both sides with booths and hucksters as far as the eye could see in any direction.

Dark men in worn clothing beckoned from the front of each booth, using heavily accented and broken English to lure unsuspecting American consumers to part with their money on a wide variety of less than tasteful merchandise.

Pony was, of course, right, damn the woman. With my blonde hair and fair skin, I seemed to be a magnet for male attention no matter where or how quickly I walked. I was pinched, pulled, patted, and prodded as I attempted to pass by inconspicuously.

I might as well have been naked and wearing a neon sign with the word "sucker" plastered across my chest. Things came to a head when two vendors, ostensibly selling woven horse blankets most likely made in Taiwan, each grabbed one of my arms and turned me into a rope in the game of tug-of-war they were holding at my expense.

Rio put an end to it all in her own special fashion, intimidating the hell out of both men (not to mention every single vendor on either side of the street we were on) by yelling something in rapid Spanish, relieving me of my human tethers, and cracking their heads together before dumping them, stunned, into the noisome street.

Then she used her bulk as a human battering ram and got us through the market maze with no further trouble at all.

It was almost as if we'd jumped from the frying pan into the fire, though, when we finally made our way safely out of the incredibly loud and confusing maze of stalls and into the more wide open areas of the town. I'm afraid I then became the epitome of every relatively well-to-do American tourist as I stared around me, slack jawed with shock.

Squalor and absolute, unmitigated poverty was all around me as I stared at the crumbling buildings, which made up this small town. People shuffled to and fro, many with the kind of blank stares that only come from hunger and total despair. Many were half-clothed, and most were barefoot.

I suddenly felt very much ashamed of myself, spending long days in self pity while the people around me could only wish to have a life as good as the one I've led, rough spots and all. Tears sprang unbidden to my eyes, and I lowered my head so as to keep from drawing even more attention to myself with my unwanted emotional display.

"C'mon," Pony said from beside me, quickly grabbing my arm and hurrying me down a narrow, pitted side street. "There's a pharmacy right around the corner. We'll stop there."

Beggars filled the streets, many of them missing limbs, and others with a multitude of open sores running down arms and legs and faces. Several congregated outside the very pharmacy we were headed toward, just feet away from medication that could help them, yet without a penny to their name with which to purchase it.

The bitter irony of the situation caused even more tears to fall until I found myself blinded by them and stumbled along only by the grace of Pony's firm support.

Turning my head slightly, I could just see Nia through the haze of my tears. She looked both frightened and repulsed by the scene surrounding her, and as I watched, she grabbed onto Rio in a white-knuckled grip that the larger woman didn't even bother trying to draw away from.

"We need to help them," I whispered to Critter, who came along beside me and wrapped a compassionate arm around my waist. "We can't just leave them like this. Someone needs to do something."

"We would if we could, Angel. But there isn't enough money in the world to help these people, I'm afraid. We do what we can, but it's never enough."

"God," I replied, shuddering.

The pharmacy itself was cool, bright, and surprisingly modern. The woman behind the counter smiled pleasantly as we entered, and greeted Rio with enthusiasm, obviously remembering her from a previous trip. With her clean, pressed clothing and carefully applied make-up, she stood as out of place among the town's other denizens as a clock would if placed high in the crotch of a tree.

Part of me wanted to rant at the woman for having the audacity to be so well dressed and so well fed while right outside her door, people were suffering and dying in the most horrid of ways. But a bigger part of me kept silent and I damned myself, feeling more ashamed than at any other time in my life.

The transaction was quickly completed, and before I knew it, a box full of medical supplies was pressed into my hands. Pony, Critter and Rio each held their own boxes. Rio led the way out of the store then did something I will never forget even if I live to be one hundred and ten.

She stopped.

Gently placing her box on the ground, she called to the people huddled in shop doorways. They flocked to her, faces wreathed in joyful smiles, seeming truly human to me for the first time since I'd set foot in the town.

They came to her as if to a Savior, reaching out with grimy, trembling hands to touch some part of her, be it skin or cloth or hair, tears brimming in their dark, shining eyes.

She greeted each by name and touched them back, enfolding some in delicate hugs, pressing kisses to weathered cheeks, and shaking hands with others.

Though I didn't understand a word of what was being said, I knew in my heart I was witnessing a true miracle.

When she had greeted every last person, she knelt down and opened her box, then began distributing the medical supplies she'd just purchased to the people gathered around us. She seemed to know exactly who needed what and handed each item over with a kind word and a bright smile. There was no jostling, no fighting as each person waited patiently to receive Rio's offering.

When one box was emptied, she beckoned, and another was placed on the ground until all the boxes, save one, were unloaded, the contents given to the people who needed them the most.

The rest of us helped pass out the supplies as Rio directed us, and were treated to our own smiles and softly spoken words of gratitude. I felt completely unworthy of such thanks, having played no part in this wonder happening around me, but I accepted the gratitude nonetheless, though on Rio's behalf, rather than my own.

When we were almost finished, I felt a slight tug on my jeans, and when I looked down, a young girl was smiling up at me. Squatting down to her level, I tried my best to ask what it was she needed. Stick-thin arms flung themselves around my neck and a small body nestled into my own as a gentle kiss brushed the skin of my cheek. "Thank you," she whispered in heavily accented English before shyly pulling away and running off to stand behind her mother.

I almost lost it then, and probably would have if Rio hadn't chosen that moment to stand and dust off her hands.

The small crowd cheered, and amidst many shouts of "*muchas gracias*!" they dispersed back into the crumbling bowels of the town to leave us standing alone on the street.

I looked over at Rio, a new-found respect shining in my eyes. She blushed a deep red and gave me the smallest of grins before hefting the lone remaining box and beckoning us to follow her yet again.

This time, I went willingly, a much humbled and wiser woman for the incredible gift I'd been given.

After leading us on a seemingly aimless trek through narrow, twisting streets, Rio brought us to an older, and paradoxically better kept, section of the town. The streets, while old, were for the most part clean and in good repair. The businesses lining those streets were brightly lit and pleasant to look at, with wonderful smells emanating from within some of them.

It was to one such building that Rio led us, and I grinned as I stepped beneath the brightly colored awning, its stiff cloth flapping in the mild, fragrant breeze. The entrance revealed a bar that was cool, dim, inviting, and crowded, mostly with men who's attentions were drawn to a soccer game currently being broadcast on several televisions dotting the bar's interior. Many of them turned to look at us as we entered and more than a few of the gazes lingered before Rio's fierce scowl convinced them soccer was a much more important thing to watch than women.

For the first time in their lives, no doubt.

The bartender, a short, rather rotund man with a thick shock of black hair and a bristling moustache which hid half his genial face, came quickly from behind the bar and led us all over to a large, empty table, while speaking all the while to Rio in rapid-fire Spanish.

After we were all seated, he returned with several menus, then with two bottles of Tequila, six shot glasses, salt, and a bowl of limes, which he set down on the table in front of us.

"Alright! This is more like it!" Nia crowed as she reached for one of the bottles, scowling as Rio intercepted it and deftly removed the top. Going around the table, she filled each glass almost to the brim before going back to her chair and resuming her seat.

After watching the others prepare the salt and limes, and copying their actions, I was ready as Rio lifted her glass in a toast. "Here's to swimmin' with bowlegged women."

Laughing, we touched glasses and, as they say, knocked the shots back after taking a healthy lick of salt. Breathing fire, my eyes watering, I slammed the glass down. Then I picked up the lime, shoved it into my mouth, and bit down, thanking god when the sourness of it cut through the taste of rocket fuel that managed to make its way up to my sinuses.

Bad as my reaction was, however, it didn't come close to matching Nia's. The young woman was receiving a thorough back-pounding by Rio as she lay half slumped over the table, choking and sputtering as the others looked on, laughing.

As soon as her breath returned to her, however, she reached out and swiped the bottle, pouring herself a healthy shot and downing it before anyone could think to stop her. Managing to keep her reaction to the shot somewhat under control this time, she sank back into the chair and smirked at the rest of us while wiping her mouth with the back of her hand. "Niiiiiice."

While Critter and Pony simply shook their heads and reached for the bottle, Rio looked as if she desperately wanted to throttle someone—preferably the someone sitting to her immediate left. Thankfully for Nia, however, she chose to drink instead.

Never one to feel comfortable in a crowd of men, especially boisterous men, I was surprised to find myself gradually relaxing as late afternoon turned into early evening. Whether it was from the effects of the wonderful dinner we'd been served or the additional two shots of Tequila I'd managed to down, I wasn't sure, but never being one to look a gift equine in the cuspids, I simply went with the feeling and didn't ponder it over much.

My five companions were certainly feeling no pain, particularly Nia, who now viewed her little corner of the world through reddened, half-lidded eyes while a goofy, drunken grin seemed to have taken up permanent residence on her face.

Increasingly outlandish tales were being traded back and forth across the table, but rather than participate, I was quite content to sit back and relax, determined to enjoy my brief respite of good cheer while it lasted.

Which, as is almost always the case with me of late, didn't last nearly long enough.

Seven men, the largest larger even than Rio, entered into the bar, their expressions belligerent. I found myself stiffening in my seat and was pleased to see my companions do the same, except for Nia, who was too far gone to be able to resemble anything other than a limp rag doll at that stage.

"Trouble," Critter muttered to my left, stating the obvious.

"Maybe now'd be a good time to leave," I replied, sotto voce.

"You got that right." Turning, she tapped a bleary Pony on the shoulder and then jerked her head toward the door.

Pony nodded and reached out to shake Nia's arm. "Wake up, little Miss Sunshine. It's time to head back home."

Lifting her head slowly off the table, Nia peered owlishly at all of us. "Wha—?"

"We're leaving."

That woke her up fully. "What? No way! The party's just getting started!" As if to prove her point, she grabbed the second (or was it third?) bottle of Tequila, brought it to her lips, and upended it, guzzling down a quarter of the contents in a single gulp. "C'mon ya bunch of old ladies! Drink up! What are you waitin' for? Christmas?"

Laughing uproariously at her feeble joke, she slammed the bottle back on the table, which, unfortunately, attracted the attentions of the goon squad steamrolling their way toward the bar.

"This doesn't look like it's gonna be fun," Critter whispered to me as they made an abrupt detour toward our table.

"Anyone ever tell you you have an innate gift for understatement?"

Her grin flashed. "A time or three."

"Good. Wouldn't have wanted to be the first."

A second later, a hand the size of which would have put a Daisy Canned Ham to shame reached for Nia's bottle and snatched it up, returning it a brief instant later, totally empty. A loud belch blasted over our heads and I swore I saw several carefully tended plants wither and die away under the assault.

"Hey!" Nia shouted as the bottle collided with the table. "Get your own bottle, you...." Turning, she craned her neck back as her chin lifted high, then higher. "Wow. Look guys! A walking mountain of shit!"

Her drunken giggles were cut off when the man reached down and grabbed her by the back of her shirt. Hauling her up out of her chair, he belched once again, in her face this time, before tossing her to his buddies who stood behind him. Then he turned his attention to the rest of us.

A leer barely had its chance to curve his lips before Rio flattened them for him with a sweet right cross to the jaw. His stumble backward into the bodies of his cronies allowed Nia to slip nimbly away. When she was in range, Rio grabbed her roughly by the shirt and shoved her behind her large body. The rest of us closed ranks in a tight formation around her.

Wiping the trickle of blood from the corner of his mouth with the back of his hand, the walking mountain smiled at us; a smile very much like something I'd seen Ice use on occasion, white and dangerous, like the smile of a shark as it spots a floundering seal. Or, in our case, a group of seals.

"Ohhh shit," Critter breathed.

The group came at us en masse, each more than double our size (except, of course, for Rio, who towered over everyone save the largest of the group). As was usual in these types of fights, the littlest one came for me. While that fact should, perhaps, have threatened my ego slightly, I found myself once again thanking God for small favors (pun intended) and chopping the cocky little banty rooster down a peg or two as he tried to grab for parts of my anatomy which were reserved for someone a lot taller, a lot stronger, and a hell of a lot meaner than he could ever hope to be.

The look on his face as he toppled over from a foot to his chest should have pleased me less than it did, but I went with it, happy to be feeling anything positive at all at that point.

A chair flew past my head, and when I looked up, I saw that the entire bar had erupted into a massive brawl complete with flying bodies and flying furniture.

As my friends seemed to be holding their own quite well, I concentrated on keeping Nia in my sights and defending us both against the onslaught of testosterone-fueled flesh which came after us, fists clenched and teeth gritted. It was easier that I'd had a right to hope, and I felt my muscles respond eagerly to their call to action, slipping into time honored rhythms of advance, block, and retreat as if I'd been born to do that very thing.

The fight hadn't been going on very long when a young man blew in from the outside and shouted loudly into the din. The only words I heard were "prisa," "amigos," and "policía!" And those words I understood only too well. The brawl stopped almost immediately as the men broke away from each other and dove for the windows and doors of the bar, leaving only a few of us still standing.

Unfortunately, one of the ones still standing chose to take advantage of the brief lapse of concentration the announcement had brought and landed a solid uppercut to Rio's chin. I looked up in time to see the whites of her eyes flash before she tumbled bonelessly to the ground in an unconscious heap.

Time seemed to slow down then. As I jumped to cover Rio's helpless body with my own, from the corner of my eye, I saw Nia pick up a miraculously unbroken bottle from our table and grasp it by the neck.

"You son of a bitch!" she shouted, rushing past me before I could stop her and smashing the bottle against the man's head.

Everything went dark for me then, as my body hit Rio's, and his body fell on top of mine, making me the unfortunate meat in a rather unappetizing sandwich and chasing the breath from my lungs in an undignified whoosh.

It might have been a second, it might have been a century, but when the man's body was finally rolled off of mine, I thought I would weep for the simple joy of being able to breathe freely once again. I was hauled up to my feet by the scruff of my neck and stood watching as Pony's wild, frightened eyes bore down into mine. "Are you alright, Angel?" Her voice sounded like it was coming from the end of a very long tunnel, but as oxygen began to clear the cobwebs from my brain, I nodded.

"Are you sure? How many fingers am I holding up?"

"Um...seven?"

My feeble joke only caused her eyes to widen further and, taking pity on my distraught friend, I laid a hand on her arm and gave it a brief squeeze. "I'm alright. Really. Just a little winded."

Just then, the bartender, who'd spent the duration of the brawl tucked safely behind his bar, rushed up to us, jabbering so quickly, my head started to spin again. "What's he saying?"

"There's a back door that leads to an alley. He's begging us to leave now before the police come," Critter replied, holding on to a struggling Nia. "Goddamn it, Nia, stop struggling."

"Let me go then!" Nia hissed, redoubling her efforts to break free.

"Not a chance. We're getting out of here."

"Not without Rio!"

"She's coming with us," Pony stated, looking back at me. "Can you help me with her? She's too heavy for me to carry by myself."

"Just tell me what to do."

"Grab her feet. I'll grab her arms. We'll drag her until we get outside. Then we'll figure out something else."

"Too late," I heard Critter shout a split second before the doors blew open and what seemed to be an entire army of Mexican police entered, their guns drawn and pointing in our direction.

"Motherfucker," Pony grunted, dropping Rio's hands and raising her own.

In a word, that pretty much summed it up.

"I don't feel so good."

"There's the toilet. Go puke in it."

"I don't know why you've got such a pissy attitude. If it wasn't for me, tall, dark, and gruesome would have finished your ass for sure!"

"If it wasn't for you, we wouldn't be in this fucking mess in the first place."

"Says who?"

"Says me."

"Yeah, well who died and made you God, huh?"

Closing my eyes, I rested my head back against the crumbling cement wall that made up my new, and hopefully temporary, home—a prison cell. Rio and Nia had been at it since Rio'd regained consciousness in the back of what passed for a police van in these parts and I was trying my level best to get their voices out of my head before I really did something to earn my stay here.

As if reading my mind, Critter leaned over to whisper in my ear. "Wonder how long a term murder gets around here?"

"I heard that," Rio growled at Critter and received an abbreviated peace sign for her troubles. Her scowl deepened.

I felt something tickle my hand, and opened my eyes just in time to see a cockroach the size of a sparrow skitter across it in search of more hospitable surroundings. "I hate bugs," I said through gritted teeth.

"Welcome to Chez Roach Motel. Ya check in, but ya don't check out."

"That's not even close to being funny, Nia," Critter remarked.

"Sor-ry!"

I looked over at Critter. "You know the saying 'be careful what you wish for'?"

"Yeah."

"Remind me to have it tattooed across my forehead when we get out of here, ok?"

"Easy for you to say," Pony interjected from her place by the cell's barred door. "You're not on parole. If we don't find a way of getting out of here before something worse happens, me and Critter will wind up back in the Bog faster than shit through a goose."

"We'll get out of here," I replied with a confidence I didn't really feel.

She spun around to look at me. "Yeah? How? Gonna get Scotty to beam us out or something?"

"Pony, calm down, please," Critter said. "It's not Angel's fault we're here."

Pony sagged against the bars, sighing. "I know. It's just...damn. I just got outta prison. I really don't want to be back in here so damn soon." Straightening, she returned to wearing a hole in the ground with her incessant pacing.

As a brief silence descended, I looked around the room once again. Three walls of crumbling cement stared blindly back at me, painted in a color that might once have been just about anything, but which time and harsh conditions had reduced to that dirty beige no-color which characterized many a prison cell and cheap motel. Bars made up the fourth wall and brought with them memories that I was trying desperately to fight against receiving.

A splintered wooden bench ran the length of the back wall, and in the far corner, a hole in the ground that doubled as a toilet rounded out the décor. The wet, cement floor was a moving tide of roaches, beetles, and insects I didn't even want to try and identify, even to take my mind off of less pleasant thoughts.

Like what was going to happen to us. Like how we were going to get out of here. Like if I was going to ever see Ice again.

The sound of Nia losing the contents of her stomach brought the distraction I needed.

"Montana knows where we are, right?" I asked Critter, who was staring at Nia with an expression of deep distaste.

"Wha—? Oh. Yeah. Pony told her we'd be picking up some meds down here and we'd be back by midnight at the latest." Sighing, she looked at her watch. "Which is an hour from now."

"So, once she realizes we're overdue, she'll put together a search, right?"

"We'd just damn well better be way the fuck gone from here by then," Pony replied, still looking out into the dim, empty hallway.

"Why's that?"

She turned to face us, her expression serious as a heart attack. "There are plenty of places to bury the bodies on that ranch of hers, Angel."

I gave a nervous sort of laugh. "C'mon, Pony. She's not that bad."

"No," she agreed, nodding. "She's worse."

"Worse than spending the rest of our lives in this hell hole?"

Her expression never changed as she turned back around to stare into the hallway once again.

Chapter 5

I must have fallen asleep shortly after Pony's pronouncement of doom, because when I next opened my eyes, it was to find myself crushed between the wall and Critter, who was snoring lightly and drooling on my shirt.

Yawning—and cursing myself for the indrawn breath given the stench sharing the cell with us—I gently removed Critter's lolling head from my shoulder and eased my tired and stiff body off the bench.

Pony was still awake and still pressed, face first, against the bars, her head turned to face down the long hallway.

"Morning," I whispered, padding over to her and laying a gentle hand on her tense back.

Turning, she favored me with a slight smile before looking back down the hallway again. "Mornin'. Sleep well?"

"Not...exactly. What time is it, anyway?"

"A little after four," she replied, not even bothering to check her watch.

I sighed. "Means Montana's on the hunt by now."

"That's what I'm worried about."

Yawning again, I rubbed her back and tried to see past the bars. Only a dim, blank nothingness greeted me. "I wonder what time this place gets cracking in the mornings?"

As if in response to my query, a bank of bright lights

snapped on, temporarily blinding my dilated pupils with their brilliance. As I rubbed my smarting eyes, I heard the sound of keys rattling, followed by a barred door opening and several sets of booted feet beginning their trek down the tiled corridor.

As the steps came closer, Pony's already tense back stiffened even more and I heard her gasp slightly for air.

"What is it?" I asked, feeling a tendril of fear curl into my belly.

She turned her head to face me, her eyes huge, her face as white as a freshly laundered sheet. "You know when we were talking about Montana versus spending the rest of our lives in here?"

"Yes...."

"Those...," her throat bobbed as she took a hard swallow "...were the good choices."

"What's going on?" I demanded, pushing myself against the bars and craning my neck to look as far as I could down the now brightly lit hall. All I could see were shadows moving steadily closer.

"Never mind that now. Help me get everyone up and ready to move."

"But—" Whatever I might have said was cut off abruptly as Pony grabbed my arm and yanked me away from the bars. Bowing to the inevitable, I set to waking up Critter and Nia while Pony worked on Rio.

Critter was easy. One shake, and she was wide-awake and ready for action. Nia, however, was a different story altogether. Trying to wake her up was like trying to rouse a corpse. Not effective in the slightest, in other words.

Fully awake, Rio took matters into her own hands by simply hauling Nia up off the bench and plopping her, so to speak, on her own two feet, then bracing the younger woman until she could more or less stand on her own.

For awhile there, it was a toss up as to who was the more green: Pony, who looked like she'd spent the night with her head in a bottle, or Nia, who actually had.

With my back to the bars, I listened as the bootsteps came closer and closer until they stopped just outside. A jangle of keys, and then I heard the cell door being opened, its rusting hinges squealing loudly in protest.

Pivoting on my heel, I turned in time to see several large guards file through, handcuffs and belly-chains in their hands.

As they entered the cell, they fanned out, surrounding the five of us, their faces expressionless.

"Je*sus*."

The epithet whispered by Critter took my attention from one of the guards, a brutally ugly man with a thick, red, and twisted scar running from temple to jaw, and I followed her line of sight back to the cell's entrance.

If looking caused Lot's wife to be turned to salt, it caused me to be turned into rock. Everything in me froze—my heart, my lungs, my muscles, the blood in my veins. An atom bomb could have exploded from an inch away and I would never have known it.

My life stood before me, a vision in monochrome.

From the low, slanted visor of her stiff peaked cap to the tips of her highly polished boots, to the wide gun belt which coiled around her lean hips like Eden's tempting snake, to the deep, burnished tan of her skin, she looked like every bad girl's fantasy come to life, drawn by an incredibly talented hand all in shades of charcoal brown.

Though I couldn't see her eyes, I knew they were flashing as silver as the mirrored sunglasses which covered them.

The set of her jaw and the tense, coiled power of her body fairly radiated her emotions to those with eyes to see beyond simple (if indeed anything about her could be considered as mundane as "simple") outward appearances.

Anger. And something else. Something more.

Fear.

No, not for herself. Never for herself.

When one considers themselves as living on borrowed time, things like pain and death and captivity hold very little sway over them.

Fear for those they hold dear, however, is a major force that steers the course of their lives.

This maxim holds doubly true for the woman who shares my soul. I see it in her eyes every morning when she thinks me asleep and so lowers her guard for those few precious moments. I see it each and every time we make love and her arms come up to enfold me, holding me close as if I were the most cherished object on earth. I see it, too, each night when we slide between the cool, fragrant sheets of our bed and she tenderly kisses me, then spoons against my body to keep me safe from the demons of the night.

I knew that same look was in her eyes then, hidden behind the blank lenses of the glasses she was wearing. Knew it as well as I knew my own name and the sound of my own heart as it beat in my ears. Where others looked and saw rage, I looked and saw fear and so, though perhaps I should have been, I wasn't afraid.

"*Formación y asimiento fuera de sus muñecas. No intente cualquier cosa estúpida o usted morirá.*"

I marveled at the way the foreign words rolled from her lips like warm honey. Though I didn't understand a word of what she said, I was enraptured. Not so intent as I at the sound of her voice, but rather the words she was speaking and the meaning behind them, the others hastened to form a line and yanked me into the middle of it. My wrists were thrust upwards, and then cuffed, pretty as you please.

As we stood like soldiers at attention before the Queen, the prison guards wrapped the chains around our bellies and shackled our bound wrists to them. Then we were chained together, and almost before I knew what was happening, we were wordlessly paraded, single file, out of our cell and down the long, featureless hallway.

In short order, we were led through the building and out into early morning darkness. Though the air outside was quite chilly, the fear-induced body heat of my companions fore and aft kept me quite toasty. It wouldn't have mattered if my skin froze up and shattered, though. What power did the elements have when the woman who held my heart stood scant feet away?

A dusty, beaten van bearing the logo of some Mexican government agency stood idling in the cool morning air. Two of the guards opened the rear doors, and with a quick jerk of her chin, Ice started us moving forward again. I stumbled a bit going in, but her strong hand on my back eased my steps, and I wore the touch of her like a brand upon my skin.

When we were finally all in and settled on the narrow bench that ran along the van's interior, the doors were slammed and locked, throwing us into total blackness.

Five sets of held breaths were simultaneously expelled.

"We're dead," Pony grumbled morosely to my left.

"Dead as dog shit," Rio agreed to my right.

"Wonderful image, Rio. Thanks," Critter chimed in.

"Can I throw up now?" was Nia's contribution.

"***No***!" came the reply. In stereo.

As for me, well, let's just say I was trying hard to smother my grin, as well as the fire my lover's simple, innocent touch had managed to spark in me.

And as the truck slipped into gear and pulled away with the feeling somewhat akin to being in a coffee can being shot into outer space, I slumped back against the interior wall and just enjoyed the ride.

An hour or so later (at least, that's what my kidneys and the fillings in my teeth were telling me), the van pulled to a merciful stop...somewhere. We could have driven to Timbuktu or Outer Mongolia for all I knew, trapped as I was in the back of a windowless van with four women who were trying desperately not to throw up, either from fear or from an overabundance of alcohol. Or both. The stench of it was almost overwhelming, and I found myself wishing for nothing so much as a simple breath of fresh air.

A short wait, and then the doors were flung unceremoniously open, temporarily blinding me with the brightness of the sun as it shone in on the black interior. I tried to cover my eyes, but with my hands bound to my waist, the task was a fruitless one indeed, so I settled instead for squinting.

Ice's long form cast an ominous shadow over us, backlit as it was from the brilliant sun shining over her left shoulder. I rose with the rest, relieved to finally be standing once again, and more or less followed them—not having much choice in the matter at any rate—into the outside world once again.

Stepping outside, I chanced a look around, taking in only empty desert as far as my eyes could see. Bringing my attention back to the situation at hand, I saw Ice standing in front of Rio with an expression any sane person would characterize as murderous.

For her part, Rio was standing so stiff and so straight it was as if someone had poured molten lava down her spinal canal and allowed it to harden into cement. Her normally bronzed face was ashen with fear and I found my heart, yet again, going out to her.

After a long, lingering look, Ice next moved to Pony, who looked like fainting was a distinct possibility in her very near future. Pony had known Ice longer than the rest of us, and had always held an extremely deep and abiding respect for the woman who was my lover. To disappoint Ice was a fate far worse than death could ever be for her.

Ice knew that and if only to spare her feelings, stepped past after giving her a brief, but significant, look. Nia came next, and though she was trying hard not to show it, I could feel her fear in the trembling of her body.

And then, it was my turn.

Though hidden behind the mirrored lenses of her sunglasses, I could feel her eyes rake over me. My skin tingled, feeling exposed and totally vulnerable to her gaze. Her serious expression didn't change one iota, and I felt a curious combination of fear and longing flutter through me on butterflies' delicate wings.

After a long, tense moment, her expression softened just slightly as her hand came up to brush gentle fingers against my cheek.

I felt weak with relief, my legs nearly buckling beneath me. My head tilted upward as hers lowered and our lips brushed together in a kiss of tender welcome.

Thoroughly overwhelmed, it took me a moment to realize that the sounds I thought to be bells were actually chains rattling as Nia struggled to step between us.

"You son of a bitch! What do you think you're doing? Leave her alone, damnit!"

Three woman around me gasped as Nia managed to land a glancing blow to Ice's turned back, and Pony and Rio moved as far away from the young woman as the meager length of their chains would allow, as if she were a plague-bearer and marked for certain death.

Casually reaching behind her, Ice grabbed a handful of Nia's shirt and easily held her off without breaking the sensual tangle of our lips.

Only when she was good and ready did she pull away from me and turn to deal with the struggling Nia, peering at her over the tops of glasses, which she'd lowered slightly. "Did anyone ever tell you that it's rude to interrupt?" she asked mildly.

Nia's mouth opened, then closed, then opened again.

"Something you want to say to me?"

"Your eyes...."

A finely arched eyebrow disappeared into Ice's hairline. "Yes?"

"They're so...so...um...blue!"

Ice just looked at her.

"And you're...I mean...um...your voice...it sounds...um...."

Unable to help myself, I burst out in laughter, thoroughly enjoying the young troublemaker's first taste of the indomitable Morgan Steele. The others looked at me as if I'd grown a third head, which, of course, only made me laugh harder.

After a moment, I decided to relieve Nia of her misery. "Nia, I'd like to introduce you to Ice."

She turned wide eyes to me. "Ice? Ice as in your.... *That* Ice?"

Grinning, I nodded. "That Ice, yes. Ice, this is Nia, a...friend of ours."

"So I've heard," Ice replied, smirking slightly.

In response, Nia flushed a brilliant scarlet and looked as if she wished a giant sinkhole would conveniently appear just beneath her feet and swallow her whole.

Turning her attention back to me, Ice produced a key from her gun belt and unlocked my shackles. Then she pulled me into a tight embrace, her muscles trembling faintly. The rapid beat of her heart against my ear told me all I needed to know about her emotional state at that moment.

I knew the one thing we both needed at the moment was a bit of privacy, so when she pulled away and placed an arm around my waist, I went with her willingly, and with a lightness in my step which hadn't been there for months.

Before we reached the vehicle's long shadow, Ice tossed the key carelessly over her shoulder. "We have some unfinished business," she said, not bothering to look behind her. "Don't even think of running."

I couldn't help but grin slightly as I imagined the expressions on the faces of the women behind me.

I had thought, perhaps, that we would step inside the van, but Ice instead turned me so that my back rested comfortably against one of the side panels. Reaching down, she clasped my waist and smiled slightly. "Hey," she whispered.

I tried for casual, at first. "Hey, yourself." Grinning a little, I bumped her knee with mine. "Come here often?"

Gifting me with a dazzling grin, she just shook her head, snorting softly through her nose as she removed her sunglasses and tucked them neatly into her right breast pocket.

Unable to help myself, I threw my body against hers, melding myself to her as I felt those strong arms wrap themselves around me, enfolding me in a living cage filled with warmth, tenderness, and love. It was a place I never wanted to leave, so I wrapped my own arms around her lean muscled frame and held on for dear life. Tears came, and I let them fall, heedless of anything save for the beat of her heart in my ear, the feel of her body against my own, and the cherished scent of her skin.

"Shhhh," she whispered, pressing a kiss to my hair. "Don't cry, Angel."

"But I missed you." It was all I could get out before my sobs made words impossible to form.

"I know, sweetheart. I missed you, too. So much."

"Please don't send me away," I whispered in desperation against her chest. "I couldn't bear it if you did. Being without you is killing me inside."

Looking back on these words as I write them, I suppose I should feel the flush of embarrassment heating my face. I'll be the first to admit that I sounded like a small, lost child rather than the strong adult I thought myself to be at the time.

I should, perhaps. But I don't. All I can feel, clear and sharp as if it were happening now, is and was the anguish lancing through me at the thought of spending even one more moment away from her.

She didn't answer me, which was fine, because I wasn't expecting one.

After a long, quiet moment, we pulled away at the same time. Reaching out, she tenderly wiped the tears from my cheeks, the look of adoration in her eyes making me feel as tall as a Titan.

"I'm sorry," I murmured. "I shouldn't be putting any more pressure on you."

She favored me with that wonderful half-smile of hers, that crooked grin that I see every time I close my eyes. "'s ok."

"No it isn't. But I'm too happy to argue about it now." I felt my nose crinkle as I grinned right back at her, so happy and so much in love that I thought I would burst with the intensity of feeling running through me. I fingered the sharp crease of her uniform shirt. "Do I want to know?"

Her grin broadened. "Let's just say that Officer Martinez is probably waking up from a nice, long nap right about now."

"Naked."

"Hey! I left his underwear on."

I laughed. "Well, that's something, I suppose."

She shrugged. "Better than busting you out with my gun. I don't think they would have taken too kindly to that."

"Probably not." I looked up at her again after a short pause. "Montana?"

"Through Donita. Who's rather pissed that you're out of the country, by the way."

Suddenly embarrassed, I looked down at my dusty boots. "I know. It was stupid. But I had to do something. The waiting and wondering was...well, it was...hard." I could feel tears threatening again, but held them back through sheer force of will. I looked back up at her. "Don't blame the others, Ice. Pony and Critter both tried to talk me out of coming with them. I just wouldn't listen."

Shaking her head slowly, she put her glasses back on, denying me the intimacy of her eyes. "I don't blame them for that, Angel. You made your own decision and I know you'll deal with the consequences, whatever they might be."

I found myself nodding, though inside I felt a faint tendril of nervousness seep its way into my belly at the sudden, almost ominous turn of the conversation.

"What I can't forgive, nor will I forget, is the idiocy of going out to get drunk down here. Medical supplies, I can understand. They're needed. But unless someone has a damn good reason for walking in to that bar...."

Her voice trailed off, but I didn't need to be some sort of psychic Boy Scout to follow the trail her thoughts laid out. I felt my heart pick up its pace as I watched her stare out somewhere over my left shoulder, her fists slowly clenching and unclenching in time to the muscles in her jaw.

"We didn't think," I finally mumbled, acutely embarrassed.

She peered at me over the rims of her glasses, her eyes flashing silver. "That's right."

Without another word being said, she stepped past me and back into the sun as she rounded the van.

Like a scolded puppy, I tagged at her heels and stopped behind her as she halted in front of the rest of our friends. To a woman, their faces were pale as cream, even in the light of the blinding desert sun. Ice's body was tense and I prepared myself for the explosion I knew would follow.

One we all deserved, myself no less than the rest.

We all were left wanting, however, when she abruptly jerked open the van's doors and gestured with a sharp tilt of her chin.

"Inside. Now."

If those women had been a team competing in the twenty-foot dash, they would have won hands down.

"Not you," she said, grasping me by the arm as I attempted to follow my colleagues. "You ride up front with me. The rest of you keep your mouths shut and your ears open. Be ready to put those chains back on if we get stopped for any reason. Got me?"

She slammed the doors closed on their group nod.

Still grasping my arm, though gently, she led me around to the van's passenger side, opened the door, and helped me in. After I was securely in the rather threadbare seat, she closed the door and walked around to her side, then hopped in behind the wheel.

Still silent, she started the engine, put the truck in gear, and pulled away in a great fan of desert grit.

As we drove down the rutted, half-paved roads, I kept my silence, but couldn't help stealing glances at her chiseled profile, watching the interplay of muscles as her jaw clenched tight, and at her hands, whose knuckles stood white against the burnished tan of her skin as she gripped the wheel with frightful intensity.

My lips ached to form words that my mouth refused to utter. Words of apology and recrimination. Promises to do better next time. Pleas not to be sent back.

My mind knew, however, what my heart wouldn't admit. That Ice wasn't ready to hear my words. That beneath her anger lay a vast wellspring of fear for my well-being and, even, the well-being of the others with us. That anything I might say now would only run up against the stone wall of her anger and fear, and fall shattered to the ground, ignored.

So instead I settled myself more comfortably into the seat and stared out at the blank scenery coming toward me through the windows, trying hard not to cry.

She must have sensed that, though, because after a moment, one hand came off the wheel, reached out, and clasped mine in a tender tangle of fingers. "I love you, Angel," she said, her voice raspy. "Never forget that. No matter what."

"I won't," I whispered, tearing up.

"Good." Withdrawing her hand from mine, she placed it back on the wheel as silence descended once again, more comfortable because of her gift of love.

We drove on for quite awhile in that silence, with nothing but the silent desert for company. I felt myself getting sleepy, but fought hard against it, wanting to savor every second with Ice by my side. With the thought that perhaps some music would keep me awake, I looked toward the dash, only to see an empty hole where the radio should have been. *So much for that....*

Swallowing hard, I then cleared my throat. "Where...are we going?"

She spared me a brief glance before returning her attention to the road. "The legal crossing's too dangerous. There's an out-of-the-way place I know that should be safe for you to cross back over. We're almost there." Her voice was quiet, but determined. Whatever emotions she was feeling were carefully concealed beneath the stone exterior she was displaying.

My jaw opened to say something, but another glance from my lover closed it with a clack of teeth on teeth. I sighed, then slumped in my seat, my mind, like a spider, already beginning to spin out this plan or that, all with the express purpose of making myself invaluable to her here. I just had to find the right one.

"Shit."

Though the word was softly uttered, it was more than enough to pull me from my thoughts and plans. "What? What is it?"

"Roadblock."

Leaning forward in my seat, I strained my eyes, but the best I could come up with was a wink of sunlight on metal. I looked over at Ice, then back at the road. "How do you know?" I asked finally.

"I can see it. Straight ahead. About five miles. Maybe less."

Since staring out into the sun was only giving me a headache, I gave up on it rather quickly and simply took Ice at her word—an effortless task, to be sure.

"Is it for us?"

"I can't be sure. But I doubt it. I left the guard pretty far from civilization. More likely, they're set up to catch people trying to cross over illegally."

"How do we handle it?"

Her hand came off the steering wheel and to the gun at her hip. Her fingers gently eased the strap away from the holster.

"If I tell you, be ready to run."

Her softly spoken words caused a burst of adrenaline to rush through my body, quickening my heart rate and breathing, suffusing my muscles with life-giving energy. I sat up straighter in the seat, only now able to catch the beginnings of what looked to be a good sized line of cars snaking out from a central point on the road in front of us. Off to one side, a patrol car sat, it's lights flashing and illuminating the desert in a red wash of color.

Something occurred to me, and I looked over at my lover. "Ice?"

"Mmm?"

"If these guys really *are* just looking for illegals, what are they gonna think of an Anglo like myself sitting in the front of a police van? Unbound?"

"You've got a point," she replied, gradually slowing the van until it came to a stop behind the last car. Turning to me, her right hand lashed out in a move too quick to follow, and before I knew it, my shirt was ripped nearly in half, though by some miracle, my breasts were still covered.

Mostly.

"Happy to see me?" Though the situation was dire, I just couldn't help myself. That little evil spot inside me chose the most perverse situations in which to come out to play.

She gave me a little smirk before returning her gaze to the line of cars in front of her, doubtless trying to figure out the puzzle of the roadblock and leaving me to figure out the puzzle of my suddenly torn top on my own.

Light soon dawned. "Ohhh! You're gonna play at being the person Nia thought you were, aren't you? A disgusting pig with a taste for blondes?"

The next glance she shot me was over the rim of her glasses. "Actually, I kept you from being beaten to a bloody pulp by the animals in the back of the van, but if you want to go the sexual prey route, be my guest." Her smile was a predator's grin, flashing white and full of teeth.

The contradictory sensations that surged through my body amazed even me. I didn't have time to dwell on them though, as the van started to inch forward, bringing us closer to our unwanted destination.

"Which way do you think I should play it?" Though that might have sounded flirty, I was, in point of fact, utterly serious.

"You'll figure it out when the time comes," she replied offhandedly.

I stared back at her, a little stunned. “I don’t even understand the language, Ice. You have that much faith in me?”

The look I received swallowed me whole.

"Always."

Into each person’s life, I believe, come moments that you wish time would freeze long enough for you to savor them in all their perfection.

This was one of those moments for me.

After an interminable wait which saw me nearly pulling my hair out in frustration and nerves, it was finally our turn. A tall, broad man who strained the seams of his uniform walked up to the driver’s side and lowered his head, peering in. His eyes were covered by mirrored sunglasses and his mouth was mostly hidden by a huge, bristly moustache that was just showing the first flecks of gray. All of this made him very hard to read, which was, I suspect, his intention.

All of which made it difficult, of course, to choose a course of action. I finally decided on a combination of defiance and innocence. Not a likely pairing, I know, but one that I’d used to great success all my years in the Bog. My situation being what it was, it wasn’t very hard to slip back into that role, and the ease with which I adopted it again would have no doubt frightened me, had I the time or the wherewithal to ponder it closely.

In any event, whatever he saw in me must have appeased him, because after sparing me the briefest of glances, he muttered something to Ice, and she produced a sheaf of papers she’d stowed next to her seat. Our transfer papers, I guessed.

He leafed through them, grunting, and then made some hand gesture which caused Ice to open the door and step out. After the door was closed, he stuck his head back in and barked something at me that I hadn’t a prayer of understanding.

Which, I suppose, was just as well since I probably wouldn’t have liked it anyway.

I almost fell out of the van in a most undignified manner when, scarce moments later, the door I was leaning against opened without warning and I was lowered gently from my seat out onto the ground. The hands which steadied me were familiar, and so I relaxed as I was led around the van to the rear, where the others were standing, apparently waiting for something. Or someone.

How they'd managed to cuff themselves back together in so short a time, I'll never know, but I was grateful for the foresight. I hoped Ice was grateful for it, too. I imagine she was, though, being Ice, she's never said a thing about it one way or another.

To me, at least.

Pony and the rest—even Nia, to my immense surprise—stared back at me with hard, flat eyes, seeming every inch the hardened criminals they had once been. The smirk Rio tossed at me could only have been taught by my lover.

The officer shouted something to Pony, who in turn, looked at me. "He wants you to point out the person who did that to you."

All right, Angel. Showtime. Don't screw this up or we're all in a whole heap of trouble.

"Tell him that it happened during the fight at the bar."

Pony translated, and the officer looked over at me, eyes narrow with suspicion. I gave him my best "innocent" expression and prayed that it would be enough.

Apparently, it wasn't good enough.

"He wants to know why you'd lie to protect animals like us."

"I have no reason to lie to you, sir."

Hearing the translation, he scowled, crossed in front of the group, and reached out to grab me. And was promptly stopped by Ice, who smoothly intercepted him while nudging me partially behind her broad back. Whatever she said to him made his scowl deepen, but it halted his grab for me, and for that, I was grateful.

He spit out his comments in a scathing tone, and the smirk on Ice's face when she turned to translate was quite pronounced. "He wants to know how someone who would stand up to a bunch of men in a bar could suddenly become too frightened to fend off a group of women."

Laughing a bit inside, I allowed my own smirk to form. "Tell him that you weren't protecting *me* from *them*. You were protecting *them* from *me*."

One corner of his moustache twitching as he heard the translation, the officer did a slow head turn until the other women in our group were in his sights.

They all nodded, quickly, Pony even taking the further step

of wincing and rubbing her belly where, I gathered, I'd managed to land a good one during my "fight" in the van.

He looked over at me, and I glared back at him, my fists clenched. Then he looked over at Ice, who nodded. His moustache bristled again, and this time, his smile was plain as the flashing of his teeth in the sun. A laugh sounding almost like a rifle shot erupted from his belly, followed by another, and then another, until he was laughing uproariously and wiping tears of mirth from streaming eyes.

After several long moments, he finally regained control and clapped me on the shoulder, saying something to Ice. Then, transfer papers in hand, he walked back to his patrol car and slipped inside, no doubt to confirm our story with the powers that be.

"What did he say to you?" I murmured out of the side of my mouth, while at the same time keeping a close eye on one of the other officers, who leered at me while holding his high-powered rifle casually in one hand.

"Told me to watch out for myself, that I had a wildcat on my hands," she replied in like fashion, her glare wiping the leer from the young man's face in record time as he found something else more interesting—not to mention much safer—to occupy his attentions.

I could feel the grin pull at my lips as my back unconsciously straightened. "Hm. Wildcat, huh? Not too shabby for spur of the moment."

"Watch it, or I'll have you declawed."

I gave her a soft hiss and then settled myself down to wait. It was the most dangerous part of this whole charade, and I knew it. If the guard Ice had "persuaded" to give up his truck somehow woke up and found his way to civilization more quickly than she thought he would, we were going to find ourselves in a whole mess of trouble, and that right quick.

Ice's body next to my own, however, was completely relaxed, so, as always, I took my cue from her and tried my best not to betray my nervousness and, in so doing, shoot our plan in the foot, as it were.

Still, I could feel my heart speed up in my chest when the officer finally exited his patrol car and walked back toward us, papers in hand and face unreadable.

After several excruciatingly long moments, during which I saw my life flash before my eyes, each time with an ending more gruesome than the last, he finally handed the papers back to Ice and waved us through the roadblock. Before he left, he looked down at me one more time and chuckled, shaking his head.

I tried not to let my sigh of relief show as he walked away and Ice opened up the back of the van, gesturing the others inside. Nia was grinning like a madwoman at the thought that we'd pulled it off.

The others just looked plain sick.

"So, where are we headed now?" I asked with feigned casualness as my kidneys did their level best to make an abrupt exit through my ears. My breasts were complaining loudly as well, since the only protection they'd heretofore had, that being my top, was no longer very much help at all.

To call what we were driving on a "road" would do a great disservice to roads everywhere. And if the van we were riding in ever had any shocks, they had run screaming quite some time ago. Like when Roosevelt was President.

Teddy Roosevelt.

She glanced at me briefly before returning her attention to the rutted road-wannabe. "The mountains. The boarder's too dangerous to be crossed safely now. I'll keep you all with me until I can think up something better to do."

Though I wanted to shout for joy, I knew such an outburst wouldn't be appreciated by her in the least. So I settled for a smile, well knowing she could see it, even if it looked like she was staring straight ahead. "I can't say that I'm disappointed to hear that," I said softly, needing her to hear the truth, though I'm sure she knew it already.

"I can," she replied, just as softly.

Though I knew they were coming, I didn't anticipate the sting those quietly uttered words would bring with them.

"Ice...."

Her name slipped from my lips quite without my permission, but once it was said, I didn't regret it.

"No, Angel." She held up a hand, requesting silence, before returning it to the wheel. She sighed, her shoulders slumping a little before straightening proudly. "This mission I'm on...it's more dangerous than anything I've ever done before. Not just to me, but to all of us. I work alone. I always have. Even now.

Especially now."

"But those police officers...?"

She laughed; a mirthless sound if ever there was one. "Dead."

I gasped in horror. "Both of them?"

"Both."

"How?"

Her jaw tensed in anger, muscles pulsing just beneath the skin. "They listened to someone I warned them against. They left without me knowing, and by the time I got there...." She sighed again. "There wasn't anything I could do."

"But they were police officers!"

She turned her face toward mine. "Police officers die just as easily as the rest of us, Angel."

"I know that. What I mean is...the government will have to do something now, won't they?"

That mirthless, terrible laugh sounded again. "Not hardly. They were as expendable as I am. Little tin soldiers in their war against Organized Crime and government corruption. A dime a dozen."

I didn't begrudge her her bitterness. How could I? Every word she spoke was the truth.

Still....

"You're not expendable, Ice."

She snorted. "Me? Sure I am."

I felt my own jaw tense as my hands curled into fists tight enough to send my short nails scraping against the flesh of my palms. "Not to me you aren't."

As she opened her mouth to speak, I cut her off at the pass. "And not to those women in the back of this van. We may not be as important in the general scheme of things as the government, but damnit, we should count for something."

Her expression didn't change, but I fancied I saw her throat move as she swallowed.

"Angel," she said finally, her voice suspiciously hoarse, "you count for everything."

If I'd thought to add strength to my argument, her words disarmed me just as easily as if I'd been up against her with a gun in my hand.

The words dried to dust in my throat; dust that the salt of my tears helped wash away.

The van finally pulled to a shuddering stop in front of what appeared to be a small, cinderblock house. Flat-topped and with narrow loopholes for windows, it looked more bomb shelter than palace, but since panhandlers can't be discriminators, I simply called it "home" and left it at that.

With a feeling of profound relief, I opened the door and slid to the ground, squatting to loosen the cramps in my stiffened muscles. Twin pistol shots signaled my knees' gratitude for the maneuver. I regained my feet as the other women walked past looking hot, sweaty, and generally miserable. Attaching myself to the end of the line, I waited patiently with the others as Ice produced the keys to the little house and opened the door.

We filed in like obedient schoolchildren trying to stay on the good side of a headmaster who *had* no good side.

The interior was cool, dim, spare, and stamped with Ice's particular brand of almost regimental neatness.

"Sit."

Four bodies broke all land speed records and packed in like overripe sardines on the single couch in the small living room. Only Ice and I were left standing in this game of "musical chairs," sans music, of course.

Pony opened her mouth to speak, but closed it quickly when Ice held up a hand.

"Quiet."

Walking over to the small table beside the couch (and causing a bit of a group flinch as she did so), Ice picked up the cellular phone resting there, opened it up, and punched a single key. Bringing the phone up to her ear, she closed her eyes and listened for a long moment.

"They're safe.... Yeah.... Alright."

She snapped the phone shut, replaced it on the table, and walked across to the other side of the room, eyes still closed. Her anger burned in the tightness of her jaw and the set of her shoulders, but I could see the invisible struggle going on. The struggle not to lash out, not to do something she'd later regret, no matter how much her body was begging her to do just that.

When she finally opened her eyes, they were glowing with a preternatural calm that was at distinct odds with the messages her body was sending. And which only served to make the rest of us that much more nervous, myself included.

"You'll be staying with me until I can find a safe way to get you all back across the border. I'll leave Montana to deal with you then. Until that time," and here she smiled; one of those grins that makes your guts tie themselves into a tiny little ball and your blood freeze in your veins, "you belong to me. That means that you do what I tell you, when I tell you, and how I tell you to do it. Am I making myself clear?"

Everyone, save Nia, nodded.

Ice's eyes narrowed. "Is there a problem?"

"Yeah," Nia shot right back. I didn't know whether to applaud her bravery, or mourn her foolhardiness. "Why are you acting like some kind of psycho drill instructor anyway? I mean, yeah, we made a mistake. So what? It's not like you haven't made any yourself."

That smile flashed again, dark and dangerous. "Yeah. I make plenty of 'em."

"Like rescuing shit-for-brains there from the big house," Pony muttered half under her breath. She received an elbow in the ribs for her effort and set to scowling at Critter.

"So what's the big deal, then?"

Picturing my lover exploding into a million pieces with the effort of containing her anger, I took a chance, and stepped in. "The big deal, Nia, is that this 'mistake' could have cost us all our lives, or at the very least, our freedom. Ice risked a great deal to get us out of there. Even more than you know. And now, because we couldn't make it safely back over the border, we've managed to throw a very large monkey wrench into some very important things she has to do, putting us all into even more danger. Is that a big enough deal for you?"

Sitting back, she crossed her arms over her chest. "I was just asking."

I sighed. "I know, Nia. And I'm sorry for yelling like that. It's just...you need to understand that this isn't a game we're playing here. The person Ice needs to deal with is very, *very* dangerous. He's killed a lot of people, and he's almost killed her. Twice."

Nia's eyes widened as she lost her sullen expression, and I could tell I was getting through to her. Biting my lip, I decided to take one more chance, something that would either convince her totally or land me into even more hot water than I was already treading in. Or both.

Turning, I walked back to my lover and smiled slightly at

her, begging her with my eyes to trust me just this once. When her body relaxed some of its coiled tension, I reached out and gently untucked the uniform shirt from her pants, baring her abdomen and the scars that had taken up permanent residence there.

"This isn't a game, Nia. This is real. As real as it gets."

Nia's face went white with shock as she stared unblinking at the tapestry of wounds stitched over taut skin and muscle. A tapestry which told its own tale of the woman who bore it.

"Do you understand now?"

She nodded swiftly. "Yes."

"And will you do as Ice asks, without any questions or attitude?"

She nodded again.

"Good."

Smiling at my lover, I gently tucked her shirt back in, taking care to straighten the seams exactly as they had been before I'd disturbed them. "Thanks," I mouthed, catching a glint of amused pride in her eyes before turning back to the group, all of whom were staring back at me, open-mouthed.

They were looking at me as if I'd totally lost my mind; as if I'd baited a caged bear with a stick and had gotten away with it.

Perhaps, in a way, I had.

After a long moment of silence, it was Critter who finally broke the ice—no pun intended—by clearing her throat. "So...what now?"

A quiet jingle sounded as Ice tossed Critter the keys. "My car's out back. You and Rio go into town for some provisions: clothes, food and the like. Rio knows the way. Get in, get what you need, and get back here. Don't stop for anything else, understand?"

"Gotcha." Standing, she collected Rio with a nod, and together they left the house.

Ice turned her gaze to Pony. "I want you to go out there and strip that van into something unrecognizable. There are tools in the shed out back. Take Nia with you. It's about time she learned to run something other than her mouth."

"Will do."

Nia, for her part, evidently learned her lesson and simply followed wordlessly behind Pony.

"Should...I go with them?"

"No. You're staying with me. I've got something I've gotta

do. C'mon."

I followed her into a room that could only be her bedroom and grinned when she began to unbutton her shirt. "Alright! This kind of job I could really get into!"

A second later, I found myself with a face full of shirt.

"Later, wildcat. We've got some business to take care of first."

"Business before pleasure, huh?" I mock-sighed, pulling the shirt off of my head, but taking the opportunity presented to pull in a deep breath of her scent which clung to the fabric. "Alright. I suppose I'll have to deal with that. As long as it's worth it later."

I hardly had time to blink before I was wrapped up in six feet worth of half-naked woman. My lips were captured in a kiss that sent my senses, and my thoughts, reeling out of control like some monstrous roller coaster whose breaks had been stripped away.

Pulling away finally, she looked at me, a smug twinkle in her eyes.

"What's my name again?" I asked, only half in jest.

Chuckling softly, she released me and turned away to finish undressing as I watched her with a pleasure I can't fully articulate.

Oh yeah. It'd be worth it.

I shifted in my seat, then shifted again, all the while trying to keep my feet away from the empty Styrofoam cup which rolled back and forth along the floorboards in time with the car's bumpy movements. There were teeth marks in the Styrofoam, teeth marks made by a man who was now dead.

It was an eerie feeling, staring at something as innocuous as a simple cup with its residue of coffee indelibly marked on the outside where some of it had spilled over.

He was alive when he drank that.

My thoughts were crazy from lack of sleep and too much building tension.

But he's not alive anymore.

My overworked, overtired mind pictured in vivid clarity the man sitting in this very car and draining the last dregs of his coffee before tossing the cup mindlessly onto the floor, never dreaming that it would be the last cup he would ever drink.

I shivered all over, my flesh going tight against the bone. *How morbid.*

"Are you alright?"

A hand on my thigh almost caused me to jump out of said flesh, and I spared a few seconds swallowing my heart back down into my chest. "Oh! I'm sorry. You startled me."

"I can see that. What's wrong? That cup down there tryin' to bite you or something?"

I tried to laugh, but it didn't come out sounding much like one. Truth be told, I felt a bit foolish and savagely crushed the cup under my foot, banishing with it the strange thoughts I'd been having. "I'm just a little overtired, I think. Didn't get much sleep last night."

"Understandable," she replied, taking her eyes off the road just long enough to glance at the crushed cup, then at me, before returning to the view from the windshield. "I'll be as quick as I can, then we'll go back to the house and you can relax, alright?"

I found myself grinning. "Relaxing wasn't quite what I had in mind, unless that's what they're calling it these days. I'm so out of touch, being an ex-con and all."

"Oh yeah, you're a regular Lizzie Borden, alright."

"Hey!"

Laughing softly, she squeezed my leg and continued driving as a comfortable silence fell between us. I placed my hand over hers as it lay comfortably on my thigh and concentrated on the smooth heat of her flesh in mine and not on the fact that we were driving in a dead man's car with a dead man's things littering the interior.

Ice hadn't told me very much about the "business" she had to take care of, just that she was going to meet with someone who had some information for her. The reasons didn't really matter to me at that point. I was just too happy to be sitting next to her to worry about anything else.

The town, when we finally arrived, looked pretty much like any small city I'd encountered in my travels, save for the fact that all the signs were, of course, in Spanish. When we entered, Ice dropped any pretense of ease, straightening almost imperceptibly in her seat, muscles tense, nerve endings on high alert. Her nostrils flared, reminding me of a wolf scenting danger—or prey—on the wind.

She made a circuitous sweep of the area, driving around a

several block area, her narrowed eyes missing nothing. On our second loop, my eyes caught a glimpse of an unmistakable curly blonde head exiting one of the small shops lining the street. "Hey! Isn't that—?"

"Yeah. Hang on." An abrupt U-turn in the middle of the near-empty street bought us up behind the car where Critter was storing her newly gotten gain. "Stay here. I'll be right back."

I watched through interested eyes as Ice approached Critter and spoke intently to her. Critter nodded a few times, then, with a jaunty wave to me, disappeared back inside the shop. Ice returned to the car and slid inside, then silently pulled away from the curb, her expression set and determined. It was a side of her I hadn't seen in quite awhile. The weight of the world was once again heavy on her shoulders, but as always, she seemed to flourish under the burden. There wcs a peculiar glint in her eye, the kind I'd seen often in the Bog when she was getting ready to knock one inmate or other down a few pegs.

I won't say that that glint didn't concern me, because that would be a lie. But I will say that over the years, I've become much more comfortable with it.

A final sweep around the block, and we parked against the curb directly across the street from a rather ostentatious looking establishment which had, of all things, a green awning of the type you see outside trendy restaurants, and intricate scrollwork etched over the door. Only the heavy bars across the windows and door dimmed the ambience of the place.

Stepping out of the car as soon as the motor was off, I crossed around the car and joined Ice as she started across the street, heading straight for the shop I'd been admiring.

When we entered, my first thoughts were that we were in an incredibly eclectic jewelry store. But when I saw handguns, transistor radios, and a plethora of other goods of better and lesser quality, I realized quickly that we were in quite a different type of store altogether.

A short, rather handsome man, nattily dressed, beamed when he saw us enter and came out from behind the counter, his hand already extended. "Morgan! So good to see you again." Though of obvious Mexican descent, his English was unaccented and spoke of an American education.

"Pedro," Ice replied, squeezing his hand briefly, then releasing it and turning to me. "Angel, this is Pedro Nunez, loan shark...."

"Ah—I prefer 'lending counselor,' actually."

"...and Pawn Shop owner."

"Purveyor of slightly used fine goods and sundries, if you don't mind."

"Whatever. Pedro, this is my partner, Angel."

"A perfect name for such an angelic vision of beauty indeed," he replied, taking my hand and bringing it up to his lips.

I wanted to laugh at his overdone theatrics, but not wanting to alienate him, I settled for as demure a smile as I could manage, though I drew the line at a feminine titter. "It's...very nice to meet you, Mr. Nunez," I replied as soon as I regained possession of my hand.

"Oh, please, dear lady. Call me Pedro. I insist on it."

"Alright," I replied, nodding. "Pedro it is."

"Good! Excellent." He rubbed his hands together. "May I get you anything? Tea perhaps? Wine? I have an excellent—"

"Information," Ice replied in her usual let's-just-stop-stomping-around-shrubbery-and-get-to-the-point manner.

His smile faltered a little, then returned, bright as day. "Ah yes, of course. If you'll both follow me into my office...?"

As he put his hand on my lower back to escort me to his office, the door opened. A young couple, freshly engaged I guessed, based on that "new glow" of love coloring both of their faces, stepped in and headed for the jewelry display.

"Ah—customers. If you'll excuse me for just a moment, I must attend to them. Please, make yourselves at home and feel free to look around. A special discount for you, my friends." And with a final, glib smile, he left.

"Interesting," was the only word I could come up with.

"That's one way of putting it," Ice replied, smirking.

"Old...friend?"

Her smirk became a snort. "Hardly. We've spoken a few times, on the recommendation of a friend of mine. Seems most of Pedro's debt collectors have gotten better offers to be on Cavallo's goon squad. He's a bit pissed."

"Ahh. So now they're breaking kneecaps for the competition, huh?"

"From what I've heard, yes. Got a few tips that he's starting to become the laughing stock of the loan sharking business."

"So...he feeds you information in the hopes that you'll take care of his little problem for him."

"Somethin' like that, yeah." She didn't sound entirely convinced, however.

"Something wrong?"

"I don't know yet. Just keep alert."

"Will do."

Several moments later, he returned to us, all slick smiles and oozing charm. "I apologize for the interruption, but, as they say, business is business, and I *am* a businessman. Shall we?"

We started for the back again, when Ice froze.

I stopped as well. "What is it?"

"Get down."

Her words were aided by a firm push to my shoulder, and I dropped to my belly immediately.

The rear door blew open and two men stepped through, already firing their automatic weapons into the shop. It was obvious that Ice had already removed her own gun (which I hadn't known she was even carrying until that very second), because she returned fire immediately, hitting one of the men in the chest and blowing him back out the door.

The sounds of gunfire and shattered glass filled the air, and I covered my head with my arms in blind reflex.

There were several more rapid bursts of gunfire and breaking glass, before all went mercifully silent save for the ringing in my ears. I vaulted to my feet immediately, almost bumping into my, thankfully, very much alive partner, who steadied me with her free hand.

"Ice, thank god you're alright. Are you...you're bleeding!"

She spared her shoulder a cursory glance. "I'm alright. Just got hit by some flying glass." She returned her gaze to the second gunman, who was sprawled on the floor, a massive quantity of blood splattered across his belly. Stepping over, she shoved him with her foot. His body lolled like a rag doll's. He appeared quite dead.

Swallowing back the bile in my throat, I turned away just in time to see Pedro rise to his feet, swaying slightly as he brushed glass from his hair. It was obvious he'd gotten his bell rung, but he didn't appear to be hurt too badly otherwise.

"Get in the back room now, before any reinforcements come."

"But Ice, I—"

"I said *now*!"

Without waiting to hear my response, she launched herself

at Pedro, pinning him against the wall, one hand around his throat and the other holding her gun that was pressed up against his temple. "You set me up, you bastard!"

"I...please...." His voice came out in a pathetic wheeze, and after arguing with myself for all of a second, I walked over to them, intent on getting Ice to back down enough to let the man breathe.

"You lost any right to beg when you double-crossed me, pig. It's time to say goodbye."

"My family!" was all he was able to get out before Ice's hand squeezed his throat closed and slammed him back against the wall hard enough to cause already fractured glass in one of the cases to shatter and fall to the ground in a rain of trumpery diamonds.

"Ice, please!" I yelled, my voice almost lost to the sound of glass shattering.

"I told you to get *back*!" Ice returned, her face set in a snarl of rage.

"I won't stand here and let you kill a man in cold blood, Ice."

"Oh, no, my blood isn't cold, Angel. Not at all. In fact, it's red *hot*." Though she was speaking directly to me, her eyes were flame, and far, far away.

"Ice, please...." Pedro's face was the color of brick, his lips, a deep plum. His eyes were bulging from their sockets and sweat formed in fat beads along his hairline. "Please...don't do this," I whispered. "He might be beyond begging, but I'm not. Please...don't kill him."

As I watched, her fingers tightened infinitesimally around his neck, her knuckles white, the tendons in her wrist standing out in bas-relief against the bronze tan of her skin. Then slowly, like a fan winding down after it has been turned off, her grip began to ease until she'd released him entirely and he fell to the floor, breath coming in great, whooping gasps.

"Thank God," I whispered, closing my eyes as relief swept through me in a great tide of emotion.

After a moment, she holstered her gun and, reaching down, pulled Pedro back up to his feet using the lapels of his suit jacket instead of his neck. "Tell me what I wanna know, Pedro," she snarled, her face an inch from his.

"M...My family! He was going to kill my family!"

"I don't give a *shit* about your family, you bastard! Tell me where Cavallo is!"

"I...I don't...."

"*Tell me*!" The shake she gave him probably scrambled what was left of his brains and I was about to step in once again.

"The...he's in the desert! They call it *Scorpion's Nest*! That's all I know! I swear!"

"Thank you." Releasing him, she pulled out her gun again, causing both of us to gasp. Reaching into his suit pocket, she removed his handkerchief and proceeded to wipe her prints off the gun. Then, grabbing his hand, she pressed the gun into it, closing his fingers around the grip and looking him straight in the eye. "Now, when the police come, those bastards over there broke in and tried to rob you. You killed them in self-defense. Got it?"

"Yes! Yes, I got it! Anything!"

Her grin was menacing. "Good. Because if I hear that you told any other story, to *anyone*," she placed his finger on the trigger, with hers over top, and forced the gun upward until the nose was touching the skin beneath his chin, "I'll kill ya."

"I won't. I swear!" He was a talking statue at that point, his eyes spinning crazily in his head as the rest of his body was stiff as marble.

With her free hand, she patted his cheek. "Good boy."

Releasing her grip on both the gun and his suit, she stepped back, and, after a tottering second, the whites of his eyes showed and he slid down the wall to the floor in a dead faint.

"C'mon," she said, turning for the door and grabbing my wrist just as the first sounds of sirens became audible in the shop. "Let's go."

She led me over to the first body before releasing my hand. "Go on ahead, and don't step in the blood. We don't want to leave tracks behind."

Oh, like that was going to be a problem.

Or maybe it would be, since in order to avoid the generous pools of blood, I had to keep my eyes open as I stepped over the man's corpse.

The back door opened into a narrow, trash-strewn alley. The second gunman, equally dead, lay sprawled across the noisome pavement, his head resting against the brick wall of the next shop down.

The putrid stench of rotting garbage filled the air, and I resisted the urge to vomit right then and there. Instead, I looked down to the left, to where our car was parked.

It looked as if a bomb had fallen on top of it. The tires were shredded, the body full of bullet holes, and the windows shattered. "Ice?"

She spared the car a quick glance. "Yeah, I know. C'mon, this way. Hurry."

The sirens were getting steadily louder as I followed her down the alley, my feet slipping in who knows what as I tried to keep up with her long-limbed strides.

As the narrow alley gave way to a wider street, I hear the unmistakable squeal of tires. I was just about to turn and run when Ice grabbed me, lifted me bodily off the ground, and practically threw me into a car that suddenly appeared out of nowhere, the back door levering open as it came even with us. Landing squarely atop Critter, I scrambled to make room for Ice, who dove headlong in behind me.

Grabbing the door and slamming it shut, she shouted "Move!" to Rio, who promptly accelerated, throwing us all back hard against the seat as she took off down the thankfully empty back street.

"Take a roundabout route," Ice ordered. "Make sure we're not followed."

"Right," Rio replied, driving expertly through the twisting maze of city streets with one eye always on the rearview mirrors.

I turned to Critter. "How did you...?"

She grinned at me and then shifted her gaze, significantly, to Ice.

I looked over at my lover. "You *knew*?"

"Let's just say I believe in covering my bases." Her expression became serious and I knew there was something lurking behind the silvered blue of her eyes, something she wouldn't, or couldn't, say. Not here. Not now.

I gave her a slight smile and nodded, letting her know I saw her thoughts and letting her know further that I would be willing to wait for her to express them, if that time should ever come.

Sighing, I slumped back in the seat, my body tired and achy and plummeting quickly down from its adrenaline-induced rush. My eyes were gritty and they longed to close, but every time I allowed myself that luxury, the images of the men Ice had killed would come floating out of the darkness to superimpose themselves over the image of Ice slowly strangling Pedro.

Needless to say, it wasn't a very pleasant ride home.

"Why don't you sit here and take off your shirt," I said, leading my lover into the bathroom and closing the door behind us, "and I'll see what I can do about cleaning out that cut of yours."

Without a word, she sat on the closed lid of the toilet as asked, sure fingers making short work of the buttons on her shirt and easing it off of her broad, bronzed shoulders. She hadn't spoken a word since ordering Rio to take the long route home, an order Rio followed to the letter, turning a twenty-minute jaunt into a two-hour trek.

She seemed deep in thought, buried beneath the weight of whatever emotions were going on behind the razor-sharp glare of her eyes.

I stole glances at her as I cleansed the dried blood from the long, narrow slice in her upper arm. She appeared absorbed in her hands, staring at them intently, turning them over, and back, and over again as I worked.

When I was finished, I replaced the supplies and moved to the front of her, squatting down between her spread thighs. "Hey," I said softly, looking up into her closed face. "You ok?"

The barest ghost of a smile graced her lips as her eyes cleared and focused on mine. "Yeah. I'm alright."

Things fell silent once again as I searched my mind for an opening gambit. "They say I'm a good listener."

Her smile became a tad more pronounced after a moment. "They do, huh?"

"Yep. Best listener in three countries."

She laughed softly, then dropped her gaze and looked back down at her hands, rubbing them together. After a moment, she spoke, so softly that I had to strain to hear her, even though we were inches apart.

"I used to think that if I tried hard enough, I could get it off."

"What?" I asked, in the same quiet tone.

"Blood. On my hands. So much blood," she whispered, clenching her hands into tight fists. "No matter how much I try, though, it's always there. Always." She met my eyes then, her own glittering with such agony that my heart wrenched powerfully and tears sprang unbidden to my eyes. "Sometimes in the night, I ache to touch you, to hold you. But how can I taint you with all this blood?"

Taking her hands, I gentled them open, stroking each palm, each finger, before lifting them and placing them on my face, cupping them to my cheeks and nuzzling each in turn. "You don't taint me, Ice. You complete me. In ways I never dreamed possible."

Her eyes darkened and she attempted to pull her hands back. I held fast, pitting my own strength and my own will against hers. An uneven match, yes, by far, but one I was determined to win.

"No," she said.

"Yes, Ice. Yes. You always tell me who I am to you. I think it's time I tell you who you are to me." I locked gazes with her, not allowing her to look away or to shrink back inside her self imposed prison of guilt. "You are my hope. My strength. The joy in my life. You're my teacher. My guide. And my light."

She shook her head slowly, trying to negate my statement.

"Yes, you are. No matter how much you want to believe it's not so, it is. Whenever I find myself in a very dark place, all I have to do is look at you, or think of you, and it's like seeing the sun after a month of rain. Because you're inside me, so very deep, that I can never be alone, even if we're miles apart." I smiled up at her, the joy of that truth shining from my face. "Don't you see, Ice? You don't taint me. You never could. And you know why?"

Lifting her right hand from my face, I placed a kiss in the palm, then placed it over my heart. "Because you're here. In my heart. And with every beat, more of you comes in, until I'm totally full with the joy of loving you. *All* of you, Ice. The part that's happy, and the part that's angry. The part that loves, and the part that hates. The part that forgives, and the part that seeks vengeance."

Releasing her hand, I placed my own on her face, tenderly holding it in my palms. "All of you."

There was a look of wonder on her face, but it was the wonder of a man alone in the desert who views an oasis from afar and yet is, perhaps, afraid to walk to it, afraid to reach out to find only an illusion where the promise of life once stood shining bright with hope.

Knowing further words would never convince her, I let my heart speak instead. Rising from my crouch between her legs, I moved our faces together and covered her lips with my own in a kiss as full of tender promise as I could possibly make it.

After what seemed a small eternity, she responded, moaning softly as the hand, which had been cupping my cheek, threaded its way through my hair, melding us more closely together and deepening the kiss we shared. Deepening, too, the bond between us.

An eternal bond.

After a long moment, she pulled away and looked down at me, her face still filled with wonder. But this time, the wonder was of a man who has found out that the oasis is, indeed, real after all. "I...think I needed that," she commented softly, her voice husky.

"Dear god, so did I," I responded with the fervor of one newly converted.

"Would you...could I hold you? For just a little while?"

Her simple request filled me with a joy I couldn't even begin to describe, and I know my face showed it in the beaming smile I could feel growing there. "You don't know how much I'd love that."

Her answering smile was almost shy as she reached out to take my hand.

The bedroom was cool and dim, and carried a slight hint of my lover's scent on the still air. I breathed of it deeply, then followed as Ice sat down on the narrow bed, then stretched out on her back, her feet hanging slightly over the edge, even with her head resting cocked against the wall.

"Like being back in the Bog, huh?" I joked, grabbing one foot playfully.

"It's not so bad," she responded softly, crossing her ankles and resting her clasped hands on the flat plane of her belly.

Taking her word for it, I crossed to the side of the bed and, at the last second, stripped off my shirt, needing more than anything to feel her skin, soft and smooth, against my own. Her eyes glittered as she watched me, and her arms opened wide and welcoming as I lowered myself onto the narrow bed. I melded myself to her side, throwing a leg over her thighs and wrapping an arm around her belly as I laid my head once again on her chest.

It was a sense of homecoming as brilliant and as perfect as sunlight upon new-fallen snow and I felt tears sting at my eyes from the sheer beauty filling my soul to overflowing.

Her hand came up to stroke my hair, her touch warm and tender and loving. My body flowed through with warmth and as sweet an ache as I can ever remember having. I willed my tears not to fall, well knowing that she'd stop the minute she felt their heat on her skin.

"I love you, Angel," she whispered.

It was the last thing I remembered as the day finally called in its marker and I fell asleep to the music of her heart beating in my ear.

I love you too, Ice. More than you'll ever know.

A knock to the door roused me from my unintended slumber, and when I opened my eyes, I saw the door crack open and a shaft of light lance its way into the pitch-dark bedroom. Pony's head materialized almost out of nowhere, a small grin gracing her lips. "Dinner's almost ready, if you're hungry."

"We'll be out in a bit," Ice replied, stretching her long body slightly and settling herself back on the bed.

Nodding, Pony closed the door, casting the room back into darkness once again.

"Hey, sleepyhead. Get a good rest?" Her voice burred out of the darkness above me and sent a warm, welcoming tingle down the length of my body.

I was glad the darkness hid my blush. "Sorry. I didn't mean...."

"Don't be sorry, Angel. You needed the rest."

"But...."

"Shhh. It wasn't any hardship to hold you as you slept. Believe me."

Bowing to her superior logic, I laid my head back down on her chest, breathing in the scent of her with undeniable pleasure. Not surprisingly, my hand had crept upward as I slept and now lay covering one of her breasts. I trailed my fingers lightly over the warm, soft flesh, smiling as I felt her unmistakable response.

Since she didn't seem inclined to halt the proceedings, I felt myself growing bolder, and repeated my actions as I lowered my head just slightly to lay a line of gentle kisses down her exposed chest.

She tasted of salt and sunlight and mysteries to be explored. I felt my hunger growing, but it wasn't for food. Her fingers tightening in my hair, she guided me gently, and when I closed my lips around her, suckling, the soft sigh of pleasure she allowed was a homecoming all its own.

I would have continued growing still bolder in my attentions had my stomach not chosen that very moment to announce its own demands; demands having very little to do with the hunger that was consuming the rest of my body.

Releasing her fingers from my hair, Ice gentled herself out from under me.

"Hey! I was enjoying that!"

"I think your belly would enjoy something a little more nutritious first."

"Then my belly can just walk itself out to the kitchen, 'cause the rest of me's staying right here." I reached for her again, only to be halted by tender hands.

"Food first. Fun later."

"Awww...!"

She chuckled softly. "I'm not going anywhere, Angel. We have all night."

As my eyes adjusted to the darkness, I could see the faint shadow of her face above me. "Promise?"

Her smile was full of love. "Promise."

"Alright then. What are we waiting for?" I asked, as I scrambled off the bed and grabbed my shirt while tossing Ice's at her.

Catching her shirt, she exited the bed much more gracefully than I. Yanking the garment over her head, and smoothing it on, she paused to run her fingers through her hair, settling it back into order. An action which caused my hormones to dash off a rather pointed note to my stomach for spoiling their fun.

My stomach growled in response to the missive, which sent the hormones back into hiding, cowards that they were.

"Ready?"

"Oh, yeah."

We both knew I was talking about far more than food.

Dinner, as it turned out, was fantastic. Rio proved herself an excellent chef, and all but ruined me for any other Mexican food anywhere. The brief respite we'd had seemed to have relaxed Ice, which, in turn, allowed the others to relax as well.

The conversation was pleasant, if forgettable, and even Pony lightened up enough to crack a joke here and there. All were invariably horrid, but at least it was better than sitting there looking as if her best friend had died and she was next on the list.

After the meal was consumed and the dishes were washed and put away, though the night was still quite young, everyone claimed exhaustion and were ready for sleep. There was a second bedroom in the house, with two single beds, where the policemen guarding Ice had slept. To Rio's immense relief, Ice doled out sleeping assignments, which had Critter and Nia sharing the bedroom and Rio and Pony sleeping in the living room.

As Ice went off to make some phone calls, Pony and Rio took a last walk around the outside of the house, checking for any signs of trouble. I chatted with Critter for a bit while Nia washed up, and once the bathroom was free, I decided to treat myself to a long, hot shower to wash the last of the day's pressures away.

Not that anything as simple as a shower could wash away the images of blood and death the day had wrought, but perhaps a physical cleansing could affect a spiritual one as well.

At least, that was my hope.

Stepping into the shower, I closed the curtain behind me and grabbed the soap as the hot, steaming water cascaded down over me. Hot water, a luxury I would never again take for granted, no matter how long I lived.

As I drew the sweet-smelling soap over my body, the images of the day began to be replaced by other, more personal visions. Scenes of bodies wrapped tight in loving, of sweating skin gliding effortlessly together, of lush moisture and quiet moans.

So wrapped up was I in this waking dream that I didn't, at first, notice that fantasy had become reality as if my thoughts had willed it so. I stiffened at first, at the belated awareness of a body pressed close behind me, but the feel of that body and the tender strength in the hands which captured the soap from my own turned my muscles from cement into jelly within a beat of my heart.

Strong, tanned hands worked the bar into a full, foaming lather and then replaced it on the ledge. Those same hands then traced a silken path over my body, teasing my breasts in maddening circles until I thought I would go insane with need.

Unable to take the sensual teasing any longer, I grasped her hands and drew them up my body until they cupped my breasts. Long fingers glided effortlessly over my nipples, lightly pinching, lightly pulling. My breathing kept time with soft sighs and whispered moans.

Soft lips and sharp teeth nipped at the skin of my neck and shoulder, her tongue darting and teasing and tasting as I squirmed beneath her hands.

Then she turned me to face her. Cupping my face in her large, gentle hands, she lowered her head and melded our mouths together as the water cascaded down over both of us. I tasted the sharp tang of minerals and the sweet hunger of her lips as she opened them and drew in my tongue for a tender duel.

Her breasts, full and firm, brushed against my sensitized skin, sending prickles of sensation through my body and pooling the moisture building between my legs. Her hands left my face and trailed over my spine, reaching lower to curve over my hips and pull our bodies tight together along their lengths. Soap and water provided a delightful slickness, and we slid together as if dancing to a sound only our hearts could hear.

God, I ached for her. An ache as strong and as needing as anything I'd ever felt before. It consumed me. It robbed my breath from me. It made my heart thunder in my chest, my body throbbing with every forceful contraction.

Our mouths still entangled in a passionate kiss, she lifted me slightly off my feet, and as my legs spread of their own accord, she placed her long, strong thigh between them, and rested me back down on top of it. I groaned in pleasure as she steadied me and then moved against me, my back pressed flat against the warm, slick tiles of the stall.

Sure, tender hands glided me along the length of her thigh and I gasped at the sensations that raced through my body, turning it to a searing flame, which knew no bounds. Slowly at first, then gaining delightful speed, she pressed into me, her warm, supple flesh and iron hard muscles relentless in pursuit of my pleasure, and hers as well.

Moaning softly, she broke the lock of our lips and rested her forehead against the tile next to mine, turning her head and tracing her tongue along the shell of my ear. "Come for me, sweet Angel," she growled low in my ear, searing my nerve endings as she suckled on my lobe. "Let me feel you."

Gasping for badly needed breath, I tipped my head back, well past any semblance of rational thought, baring my neck to the assault of her lips and tongue and teeth, my hips gliding in a timeless, primal rhythm of hunger and aching desire.

Her tongue lapped at the hollow of my throat, and then at the pulse point bounding strongly, rapidly in my neck. And when her teeth gently bit down on the flesh she'd so lovingly captured, it was the trigger that released me as the darkness behind my eyelids burst into a brilliant pattern of light and shadow.

My soul was free, floating on a sea of bliss and sensation. Ice was my anchor, her warm hands and softly murmured words of love keeping me tethered to the real world as my spirit soared to the heavens and beyond.

Slowly, so slowly, I came back to earth to find myself tight in Ice's fiercely tender embrace. The water had since turned cold and the icy spray sent uncontrollable shivers through me. A quick hand cut off the water, and before I knew what was happening, I was borne up in strong arms and carried out of the stall.

I was placed gently on the floor and steadied as she reached for a large, fluffy towel. She dried me carefully, tenderly, making me feel like the most cherished person on earth, then wrapped me in the towel and lifted me into her arms again, the look of absolute adoration on her face almost painful in its intensity.

We walked down the short, dark hallway, Ice uncaring in her nakedness. She shut the bedroom door behind us with her foot, and placed me gently on the bed, her expression sweet and loving. "How ya doing?" she asked, brushing the bangs from my eyes.

"Oh, I'm...I'm...wonderful."

Her smile was slow and sweet. "I'm glad."

"So am I," I replied with fervor.

Tousling my hair, she straightened and stepped away slightly, stretching her shoulders back and rolling her neck to loosen the bunched muscles there. I looked on silently, drawn, as always, by the sheer magnificence of her naked body. The cold water and her undeniable arousal had done wonderful things to it, as I'm sure you can imagine, and as I watched, spellbound, a single bead of water, fat with moisture, rolled slowly between her breasts, down the muscled ridges of her abdomen, and nestled in the well of her navel.

I watched that journey through blazing eyes, licking lips suddenly desperate for moisture. Catching me in my fantasies, a secret smile spread over her face, and she crossed to the night-stand. My eyes were glued to her; glued to every sensual shift of muscle over silken skin, glued to the light sway of her hips and to the inky trail of wet hair as it spilled down her tapered back. My hands closed in fists, fighting desperately against the need to just reach out and pull her to me and ravish her senseless.

Opening a small drawer set in the nightstand, she reached in and pulled out an object that made my whole body implode with renewed, raging desire. Holding it in the dim light of the small bedside lamp, she shook the straps free, then looked at me, eye-brow raised and a tiny smile playing over her lips.

"Yes," I gulped, suddenly wondering where all the air had gone in the room, "please."

I spared a brief second to wonder just how she'd come by such a prize, but that thought was quickly lost in the blaze of her eyes as she closed the drawer and crossed back over to my side of the bed. She handed the phallus to me, and I took it with faintly trembling hands. It was of medium size, medium length, and double-ended, with the slightly shorter end to be inserted into the wearer.

I ran my fingers lightly over the warm, pliant skin, then looked up at her, smiling with anticipation. Eyes dark and glittering, nostrils flaring just slightly, she slowly lifted one long leg and planted her foot on the bed, opening herself to me.

She was glistening with moisture, so open and ready for my touch. I spread her fully to my heated gaze, drawing a finger through the lush wetness and watching as a shudder ran through her body. Unable to help myself, I leaned forward and drank deeply of her, moaning with the taste of her readiness on my lips and tongue. Strong fingers threaded themselves through my hair, holding me to her as her hips rocked against my feasting mouth.

I couldn't get enough of her, this woman who was hot, and wet, and oh so very sweet. The more she offered, the more I took, like a greedy beggar at the feast of a king.

And as I felt her reach that place of no return, I reached up and eased the phallus into her, filling her full as I tasted the musky beginnings of her climax on my tongue. Her body shuddered, her inner walls clenching down hard on the toy in my hand and her hips thrusting uncontrollably against me. Her growl of release was sweet music to my ears.

When her shudders slowed, then halted completely, I pulled away after pressing a tender kiss into her flesh. Then I looked up at her, grinning cheekily. She stared down at me, her gaze half-lidded and searing as her fingers worked the harness over her hips and buckled it into place.

I found myself on my back, not quite sure how I'd gotten there, with Ice looming over me on all fours, like some great hungry predator with prey in her grasp. Her lips covered mine in a kiss of boundless passion as her fingers worked to unwrap me from my towel.

That task finally completed to her satisfaction, she lowered herself, lapping up each and every bead of moisture that had escaped the towel's absorption, attending to her duties with great relish. Her tongue and lips seemed to be everywhere at once, and I shivered, my body taut and aching with desire. She blazed a heated trail down my body, pausing at each breast to suckle and nip, before moving lower, ever lower. When her tongue delved, thrusting, into the recess of my navel, I thought I would release then and there from the sheer erotic power of it.

Lower she moved, her tongue grazing the insides of my thighs, over my knees and calves and down to my toes. As she took the first one into the heat of her mouth, the release denied before came blazing full force and I cried out, as the contractions flared through me like a windswept fire on a grassy plain.

She was relentless, though, this woman who was my lover, moving back up my body with the same slow, sure deliberation, until she reached the place where I was all fire and pulsing need. She took me into her mouth, growling as she tasted me, her tongue darting and teasing and stroking and dancing, pushing me higher than I'd ever thought I'd go, and then, still higher, responding to my cries with deep moans of her own.

My body finally reached its straining limit and stiffened forcefully as another climax seared its way through me on tendrils of hungry fire. She held me tenderly in her mouth as my climax ended, then moved back up my body quickly, nestling against me and looking down into my eyes, her own ablaze with love. My spent muscles trembling, I relaxed beneath the secure, warm weight of her body, my eyes closing as I felt her tenderly stroke my hair and face, gentling me and bringing me back home.

"God, I love you."

I don't know if those whispered words were meant to reach my ears or not, but reach them they did and caused a smile to break over my face. I opened my eyes to see hers, brilliant with unshed tears. Reaching up, I cupped her face and ran a tender thumb across her cheek, catching a single tear as it escaped beyond her lashes. "And I love you. More than the air I breathe."

Smiling through her tears, she lowered her head and kissed me. It was a kiss of promise and of unbounded love, delivered from her heart to mine in the sweetest of ways.

Though there was nothing passionate in this sharing of breath, incredibly, my body began to respond again just from her nearness and warmth. "Please," I whispered with the last of my breath. "I need to feel you inside me." It was a need that had become all-encompassing, a last act of completion to put my heart and soul fully at rest.

Still kissing me tenderly, almost reverently, she shifted most of her weight off of me and ran her hands slowly down my body, the tips of her fingers caressing peaks and valleys and everywhere in between with a grace that was, to me, beauty incarnate.

Her hand finally nestled between my legs, preparing me for her entrance into me. I was well past ready, and she smiled when she felt the evidence presented her. Gentle hands spread my legs as she continued to press kisses deep into my mouth, our tongues dancing a slow, sensual ballet.

Then she was covering me with her body once more, resting her weight on her arms as she looked down at me, an unasked question clear in the smoky depths of her eyes.

"Yes," I whispered, wanting nothing more than what she so silently, so lovingly offered. "Please, yes."

One hand disappeared from my sight, and I soon felt the smooth, rounded tip of the phallus being drawn through my heated wetness. A brief moment later, it was poised at the entrance to my body. Leaning down, her hair forming a curtain around our faces, she kissed me deeply and slid smoothly within, filling me more completely, more wonderfully, than I'd ever before felt.

Fully sheathed, she hovered there, waiting for my body to adjust, her deep and passionate kisses taking my mind from muscles strained to their limit and onto something infinitely more pleasurable.

She fit into me perfectly, like a puzzle piece, and my body adjusted quickly to this new sensation, quickly demanding more. I trailed my fingers down her muscled back until I had her hips in my hands. Grasping those hips, I pulled her to me. "Now," I growled into her ear.

Groaning, she did as I asked, pulling smoothly out before thrusting in once again. The pleasure was indescribable, and I nearly cried with the joy of feeling it.

Together, we set up a perfect rhythm. We kissed passionately until neither of us had the breath for it and were forced to pull away. Ice's head rested next to mine as she thrust into my willing body, her sweat-soaked hair gliding wetly over my cheeks and lips, its fragrance as intoxicating as the scent of our loving which hovered in the air surrounding us.

I pulled her to me, quick and forcefully, needing everything she could give to me, and more besides. She responded as if born to do this very thing, surging into me with unbridled desire, unleashing the darkness and lightness inside of her, the passion and the tenderness, the power and the strength. All of this she delivered to me as her soft grunts and low moans filled my hearing like a symphony.

She crested first, her back arching, her neck thrown back to expose her throat to me, her hips thrusting blindly, forcefully, without thought or intent. Sweat poured down from her and dripped onto me, a baptism of fire and passion.

A bare second later, I too was drawn into the whirling vortex where life as I'd come to know it ceased to exist, and only pleasure resided.

I think I must have passed out for a moment, because when I came back into my body again, it was to find her full weight atop me, her chest heaving in time to her exhausted gasps for air. When she felt me move, she attempted to roll from me, but I was having none of it and wrapped my arms around her, my body still throbbing around the phallus as it rested, still, deep within me.

"No. Stay. Please," I gasped, badly out of breath myself. "Need this. Need you."

She settled back over me, a living blanket of love, warmth, and safety, and from that moment on, I knew no more until the sun rose once again.

Chapter 6

The next morning, I woke up to something unexpected and very, very much welcomed. As my fuzzy thoughts came to sharper awareness, I realized that the gentle thumping beneath my ear was the sound of Ice's heart beating. The tickle on my back was the feel of her hand as she gently rubbed aimless circles across my flesh. Though we'd been together for nearly eight years by that time, I could count on one hand the number of times I'd woken up in her arms, and probably still have a finger or two left over.

Her fingers hesitated briefly as she became aware of my awakened state, then resumed their gentle caress of my skin. "Morning, sweet Angel." The deep tenor of her voice rumbled up from her chest, filling me with a most comfortable warmth.

"Mmm. Morning yourself, my love."

"Sleep well?"

"Like a baby. You?"

"Very well, thanks."

Her touch tickled slightly, and I shivered, then stretched, wincing slightly at the twinge of soreness I felt.

She stiffened beneath me, as always, zoning in on my emotions with uncanny accuracy. "Are you alright?"

Cocking my head, I smiled up at her reassuringly. "I'm great. Just a little sore."

Her face immediately froze as her eyes darted away from mine. "I'm...."

"Don't," I warned, laying two fingers across her full lips. "Don't say it. Don't even think it." Shifting a bit so I could see her more easily, I slid my fingers beneath her chin to direct her gaze back to me. "Ice, last night was one of the most wonderful in my life. Please don't say you're sorry for making it that way."

She finally met my gaze, but the look of shadowed guilt still haunted the pristine blue depths of her eyes.

Smiling, I gently squeezed her jaw between my fingers. "C'mon, Ice. Wasn't it you who said that there are two kinds of sore? The good kind and the bad kind?"

The guilt in her eyes faded a little. I stretched again, my grin broadening at the telltale signs of a body well loved. "This is most definitely," I added, yawning, "the good kind."

That got the smile I was looking for, and I reached up to capture it with my lips, savoring the warm contact for a long, wonderful moment, before pulling away and resting my head on her chest once again. "So," I began, trying hard to sound nonchalant, "what are our plans for today?"

She laughed softly. "Your plans, Angel, are to get some more sleep. We've got a long drive ahead of us."

I lifted my head to stare at her, sure that my fear could be easily read, and not caring. "Not back to the border...."

Her eyes were gentle, her hand tender as it stroked my hair. "No. Not back to the border."

"Thank God," I replied on a sigh of relief as I rested my head back down on her warm skin.

I held up a hand. "And before you say anything, I know that it's dangerous. And I know I'd probably be safer with Montana on the other side of the border. But that doesn't matter. None of it matters. Not as long as I don't become a distraction or a danger to you by remaining here." I looked up at her again, meeting her eyes dead on. "Will I?"

She returned my look measure for measure, her eyes showing no deceit or guile. "I'll always worry, Angel. As I have from the first day you set foot outside of the Bog and decided to make your life with me. I'll always bear the guilt of having you live through the mistakes of my past."

"You never forced me into this, Ice," I replied with some heat. "It was my own decision from the word 'go.'"

"I know." Her words were barely above a whisper. "And

part of me will always damn myself for not taking that decision out of your hands when I could have. But now...." Her hand lifted, then dropped back to rest on my shoulder. "...now...I wouldn't trade one second with you, in danger or out, for anything in the world."

I knew I was beaming, but I couldn't stop myself. For a woman of so few words, she had the ability to make my heart overflow with love and joy with the simplest of phrases. "So, we're in this together, then?"

After a moment, she nodded. "Together."

Lifting my head, I sealed the vow with a kiss, which led quickly into another kiss, and then another, and still another, until my twinges of soreness were replaced with twinges of a far more pleasurable kind. We made long, slow love by the increasing light of the rising sun, and afterwards, Ice's plans for me were realized.

I slept.

"I'll get you, my pretty! And your little dog, too!! Ahahahahaha!"

I shot a scathing look to my left and then glanced back into the mirror held before me, realizing that Critter was correct in her assessment. In fact, it wouldn't be an exaggeration to say that the Wicked Witch of the West was the goddess Aphrodite compared to how I looked with that particular wig on my head.

"At least I don't look like a family of rats set up condos in my hair," I replied, just to lob my own truth back at her.

She didn't even try to volley, knowing I was right. Instead, she grinned sheepishly, and shrugged. "They looked better on the mannequins we stole them from."

I turned to her, eyes wide. "You *stole* these?" I wasn't sure which shocked me more. *That* she stole, or *what* she stole.

"Well...not in the traditional sense, no."

"I think you're gonna have to explain that one to me."

Before she could answer, the door to the bathroom burst open and Pony strode in. "What the hell are you two...oh Jesus, give me that!" Snatching the wig from Critter's head with one hand, she grabbed a brush with the other and began combing out the tangled mess that might once have borne a faint resemblance to actual hair.

In mere moments, she transformed it from rat's nest to work of art.

Critter and I stared on, dumbfounded.

"You're scaring me, Pon," Critter said, looking very scared indeed. As if her lover had vanished into thin air and a rather butch Martha Stewart had appeared in her place.

She shot us a look that was the epitome of the word "withering," and put some final touches on her masterpiece. "My father was a barber and my mother owned a beauty shop. I can't help it if some of the shit they tried to teach me actually sunk in."

Finishing her masterful transformation of the first wig, she held out her hand for the second. "Gimme."

"With pleasure," I replied, pulling the wig off of my head and handing it to her, watching as she applied her talents to that one as well.

The wigs were Ice's idea. And it was a good one, to be sure.

From what I was told, the area called the *Scorpion's Nest* was a rather large, and mostly empty, part of the desert, dotted here and there with tiny towns. Trying to find one man in such a place was akin, I was told, to searching for a crystal of sugar on a white sand beach.

To find him, we'd need the help of the townspeople. We'd also need to remain as anonymous as possible so as not to arouse undue suspicion. Suspicion which could get back to Cavallo and cause him to either go deeper to ground, or come out, full force, against us.

Suspicion which would be raised if a couple of blonde-haired, light-eyed women just suddenly showed up in the middle of nowhere and started asking questions.

Of course, the wigs wouldn't cure all of the difficulties inherent in such a task. Such as the fact that neither Critter nor I could speak more than a couple words of Spanish.

Still, Rio, Pony, and Nia were all brunettes, like Ice, though unlike my lover, their eyes were brown or a dark hazel. All of them also spoke fluent Spanish. Since Critter and I would be with them like bees on honey, it was my hope that we'd go unnoticed in that particular crowd. Unless, of course, we came off looking like a couple of cast extras in a grade B horror flick.

Beckoning me to her, Pony replaced the wig on my head just as the door opened and Nia stepped through, her arms full of clothing. "Cool!" she remarked, grinning at me. "Cher-ette on an acid trip!"

Pony and I scowled at her, which, of course, did absolutely no good whatsoever. In fact, the twin scowls only caused her to launch into a particularly horrid rendition of "Gypsies, Tramps and Thieves" that nearly cracked the mirror in my hands.

All of my life, I was sure that there was no one more tone deaf than my own dearly departed father. Pretty crappy time to find out just exactly how wrong I was on that particular subject.

Mournful pleas for silence only spurred her on until finally Pony had had enough and shoved her bodily out of the bathroom, slamming the door behind her and locking it tight against further intrusion. Nia's laughter echoed in the hallway, but that soon faded away, leaving only blessed silence in its wake.

"That woman is in serious need of a shrink," Pony groused as she turned Critter away from her and replaced her wig over her lover's blonde hair. After fussing with it, she stepped back and appraised her lover, a wide grin curving her lips. "The gypsy fortune-teller look. I like. I *like*!"

"Down, Fido," she joked, turning to me. "Well? What do you think?"

I grinned as she faced me. In actuality, Pony wasn't all that far off in her assessment. "Would you read my palm, Madame Fifi?"

Slapping my hand away, she grabbed for my mirror instead. "Hopeless, the lot of you. Just hopeless." Looking in the mirror, she scowled as she straightened her bangs. "I look like an idiot."

"No, that would be me," I assured her, remembering my own image in the mirror.

"You don't look like an idiot, Angel. You look...um...."

"Freakish? Demented? Insane?"

"Groovy!" she shouted, grinning. "Nia was right, now that I think about it."

My hands went to my hips. "Sing one word of one Cher song and I'll tie your lips in a knot."

Pony snickered, which earned her a growl from Critter. No fool, Pony, she shut up mid-smirk. Clearing her throat, she offered up the pile of clothes Nia had left behind after her unceremonious eviction. "Try these on and come outside after you're done," she stated, obviously trying to regain some sort of control over the situation. "We'll be leaving as soon as Ice and Rio get back."

"Where'd they go, anyway?" Critter asked as she picked out

a garish purple wannabe silk top and held it up against her chest, eyeing me with eyebrows raised.

I shook my head in a very definite and vigorous negative. Sighing, she threw the shirt back into the pile, and rooted for another one.

"To pick up another car, since the other one got trashed to shit yesterday."

Shaking her head in mock disgust, Critter grabbed another shirt, this one a teal number that was slightly better than the purple one. Slightly. As in the width of a hair. "Sometimes, Pon, I wish I was your mother. I'd have you over my knee for that mouth of yours."

"You can have me over your knee any time you like, babe," Pony replied, waggling her eyebrows and leering. "You bring the paddle, I'll bring the edible soap."

Snorting, I turned and rooted through the pile of clothes for something to wear while Critter pushed her leering lover out of the cramped bathroom, closing and locking the door behind her and ignoring the indignant pounding that issued forth soon thereafter.

"Why I put up with that woman, I'll never know."

"Cause you love her."

She grinned. "Yeah. I do."

"I've been through the desert on a horse with no name. It felt good to get out of the rain. In the desert...."

"Nia...."

"...you can remember your name, cause...."

"Nia!"

"...la la la la la la la, la la la, la, la..."

"Nia!"

The discordant voice trailed off and I was shot a sullen look through the rearview mirror. Under other circumstances, being the cause of a friend's upset would have concerned me.

These weren't those circumstances.

Four hours into our trip through a featureless, monotonous desert, and the little men with jackhammers were just about to break out of my skull through my temples.

It wasn't so much the absolute and utter boredom of the trip thus far. It wasn't the "hair-trigger" shock absorbers that did everything *but* absorb the shock of the rutted and broken road. It wasn't even the blinding sun which insisted on glaring at me through the window, forcing me to squint so hard that my cheek and eye muscles threatened to freeze that way permanently.

No, it was something worse than all of those things put together.

It was the grating sound of Nia's voice as she ran through her rather extensive mental and vocal catalogue of what she called "traveling songs." I rather thought that "songs to commit suicide by" was a more apt title, since that is certainly what I was contemplating doing after the third encore of "Send in the Clowns" assaulted my eardrums.

When that was swiftly followed up by "Don't Cry Out Loud," thoughts of merciful suicide gave way to thoughts of vengeful homicide, complete with vivid (and curiously satisfying) mental pictures.

Ice seemed totally unaffected, but I really expected nothing less. Her focus on the task at hand was the stuff of which legends are made, and this task was no different than the rest.

As blessed silence descended, I leaned my throbbing head back against the cracked vinyl of the bench seat and closed my eyes against the harsh desert sun, willing my headache away.

With only the sounds of the humming motor for company, I felt myself begin to drift into a light sleep, the pain behind my eyes dimming as my breathing evened out.

Just before sleep could fully claim me, however, I felt a not so gentle prod to my kidney area. Thinking that Nia was just shifting her legs, I ignored it.

Until the prod came again, and then again, becoming less gentle with each repetition. Then the humming started, softly at first, though discordant and grating in my ears. As my eyes opened, I could feel my fists curl tightly of their own volition to match the clenching of my jaw. Anger welled within me, deep and strong, banishing the last of my sleepiness with its searing heat.

I could tell my eyes were flashing, even without benefit of a mirror, and I could feel my body, stiff from so many hours in the car, start to turn toward the back, where the source of my frustrations sat, in her own little world.

Whatever I might have done (and truthfully, I don't think it would have been all that much) was stopped almost unborn by a firm, warm hand on my thigh. My anger drained away like water through a sieve as I gazed into liquid crystal eyes peering into my own over the rims of mirrored sunglasses.

The look in those eyes convinced me to think up a different plan. So I did. Quickly.

"Nia?" I said, calm as I could.

"What?"

"I was thinking." Oh boy, was I.

"About what?"

Was it possible for her to sound more petulant?

"Well...since we're in Mexico and I need to fit in here...."

A derisive snort.

"Yeah, right."

It was possible alright.

Calm, Angel. Be calm. Think happy thoughts. Happy. Happy. Happy.

"Do you think you can teach me some Spanish? You know, just enough to get by?"

Mercifully, the kicking stopped, followed shortly thereafter by the humming.

"Really?"

"Yes, really. I know hello, goodbye, thank you, a few swear words, and I can count to ten...I think. None of which is going to get me very far."

She laughed softly.

"So...could you help me? Please?"

"Sure! That would be cool!"

Thank you, God.

"Hey! There's this great song my Spanish teacher in Elementary School taught us. Let me see if I can remember how it starts."

I sagged back against the seat, defeated.

In a deliberate ploy for sympathy, I rolled my head in Ice's direction, just in time to see her turn attention back to the road, the corner of her mouth lifting just slightly.

I scowled at her, knowing she could feel it.

Just you wait, love of my life. You'll pay for that smirk. Later.

Two hours and one crash course in "Spanish for the tone-deaf" later, my grateful eyes spied a town coming up quickly on the left. If two houses sandwiching an ancient gas station could be considered a town, that is.

"Ice, do you think we could...?"

She had already started to pull into the gas station before I could even finish my question, a small smile playing over her lips.

"If I didn't know you any better, I'd think you were enjoying this," I muttered out of the corner of my mouth.

Silence was my only reply.

Sighing, I turned my head and peered back out the window, only to have almost half my face taken off by Nia's swiftly thrust hand pointing forward.

"Where are they going?"

Blinking and shielding my eyes from the glare of the merciless sun, I could see Rio's car shoot past in a long cloud of desert dust.

"Yeah. Where *are* they going?"

"There's another town about fifty miles down the road. They'll scout it out and we'll all meet up beyond that and compare notes."

"So I guess this isn't just your average 'potty break and stretch your legs' type stop, is it?"

She laughed softly, turning to face me as she pulled the car smoothly in front of some antique gas pumps. "It's that, too."

I returned her chuckle with one of my own. "Good, because my kidneys were getting ready to file a grievance with their union, and I don't think either one of us would like it if they went on strike."

As soon as the car stopped, I eased myself out, groaning in combined pain and relief, my over-stressed tendons singing out their anger like a guitar string turned one notch too tight. Stretching toward the sky, I chanced to look around and saw the opportunity to put my newfound (not to mention hard-won) bilingualism to its first test.

"Hmm. Let's see. Pedro's Gas and Market. Hot Food. Cold Drinks. P...." I blinked, rubbed my eyes, and looked again, trying to convince myself that what I thought I was seeing was not, in fact, what I *was* seeing.

The words refused to change, though.

I turned, looking for Nia, only to see her disappear quickly into the market, searching, no doubt, for a bathroom. Ice was busy inserting the gasoline nozzle into the tank.

I turned back to the sign. "Hot Food. Cold Drinks. Petting...Zoo." My eyes roved lower. "Rattlesnakes. Tarantulas. Scorpions."

A shudder of revulsion skittered down my spine on spider's legs. I turned quickly away from the sign, only to come nose to chest with my lover, who embraced me quickly to keep me from bowling us both over. "Where's the fire?"

"Oh! Sorry," I mumbled into her shirt, hiding my blush from her keen eyes. "It's...um...nothing."

"Mm. Hm." Gently grasping my arms, she stepped back apace. "Thought you were gonna go...." She cocked her head in the direction of the restrooms.

"I...um...changed my mind."

Her eyebrow hiked itself up over the rim of her glasses. As I watched, she turned her head just slightly, and I knew she was reading the same sign I'd just turned away from. I blushed again at my own foolishness.

After a second, she looked back at me. "I don't think they'll have them crawling around on the floor, Angel."

"Maybe not," I replied, my voice full of doubt, "but I'm not real sure if I want to frequent the establishment of someone who thinks that petting scorpions is a money-making venture."

Her laugh was low, and gentle, and soothing. "I don't think you have anything to worry about." She looped an arm casually over my shoulders, holding me close to her side. "Besides, I haven't heard Nia scream."

"She died silently," I replied darkly. "They're probably burying her in the back right now."

She laughed again, more loudly this time, and bumped me with her hip. "C'mon, Angel-mine. I've got some gas to pay for, and you've got some kidneys to relieve."

"Sure, fine," I grumbled. "Just remember I don't want an open casket at the funeral."

Goodbye, cruel world.

It was coming down evening as I spread my blanket atop a long, flat rock that sat on a small hill overlooking the Mexican desert. The rest of the afternoon had been relatively uneventful.

After Ice had finished her business with the gas station owner, she'd driven us back out into the desert to meet up with

Rio and company, who'd parked by the side of the road five miles past the town they'd stopped in, ostensibly to fix a flat tire.

From there, we'd continued on for another few hours until we pulled off the road and found ourselves in a small, secluded valley surrounded by small hillocks on every side. It soon became obvious we were going to camp out for the night. Nia surprised me. Rather uncharitably, I'd figured her for a city girl, objecting to any hint of living rough.

Such wasn't the case. She took to the idea much like a fish takes to water, and pitched in quickly, helping us unload the gear and set up camp, as if she'd been doing it her whole life.

The ground was cleared in short order, the tents—three in all—were quickly pitched, and a fire was started, surrounded by a ring of desert stones. Pony and Nia set to cooking up something for dinner as Ice, Critter and Rio stood off to one side, deep in conversation.

With no more chores to keep me occupied, I decided to take a blanket to the top of the westernmost hill and watch the sun set. It had become a habit since my introduction to the desert, and one that I was loathe to break.

So I sat on my rock, which was still warm from the strong sun of the day, and watched the sky turn a myriad of colors as the sun moved inexorably closer to the horizon. Closing my eyes, I tilted my head back and felt the last heat of the sun stroke my face as the cooling desert wind gently ruffled the hair (I'd removed the god awful wig the moment we made camp with a sense of blessed relief) back from my brow.

Suddenly, I felt a warm, soft sweatshirt drape itself around my shoulders, bringing with it the scent of the woman I loved. I opened my eyes slowly, a smile curving my lips unbidden as I saw Ice standing above and behind me, her eyes brilliant with the last of the sun's dying rays reflecting in them.

"Hey," I said, surprising myself with the huskiness of my voice.

"Hey yourself," she replied, smiling in that cockeyed way I so adored. "Mind some company?"

"Not at all."

Lowering herself behind me, I watched as her long legs appeared to either side of my own, and sighed blissfully as her arms wrapped themselves around my waist and pulled me slightly back until I was resting against her chest, wrapped in the warm nest of her arms, legs, and body.

"Mmmm, I like this."

"Ya do, huh?" Her head lowered until her chin was resting on my shoulder. Her hair tickled against my cheeks, and the warmth of her body sent tingling heat through my own.

"Yup. A warm rock, a sunset, and you. There are worse things a body could wish for."

"Mm. Guess so." She squeezed me once, and then we both fell silent as the sun shone its last and sunk beyond the rim of the world for another day.

We celebrated the event with a kiss. More kisses followed, until they merged into one, single, passionate melding of lips and quickening breath.

Who knows how far we might have gone if a shout of "dinner's ready!" hadn't come from the valley floor below us?

"It's a conspiracy," I muttered darkly, rearranging my T-shirt and buttoning my jeans as I made a concentrated effort to dampen down the fire raging though me.

Laughing softly in response, Ice rose gracefully to her feet and then pulled me up with deceptive ease. Pressing one more gentle kiss to lips still flushed with passion, she slipped an arm around my waist, and together we made our way down the hill to where our friends waited.

"Oh...dear...*God!*" I managed to gasp out as the last of the tremors washed though my body, leaving me weak and breathless and not quite all there.

The tremors—more like the spastic twitches of someone touching an electrified fence than anything else—started anew as Ice made her way up my sweat-slicked body, pausing here and there to kiss and nip several of the more sensitive spots as she did so.

Her dark head popped out from beneath the sleeping bag, her eyes twinkling and still dark from the love we'd made. Stretching out full length next to me, she tenderly stroked my stomach and breasts, getting me used to my own skin again as she gentled me and brought me back home.

The expression on her face was love mixed with just a tinge of smugness.

Not that I blamed her in the slightest. With an alchemist's

precision and consummate skill, she'd managed, in just a few short moments, to turn me from a human being into a boneless octopus.

"You alright?" she asked after a moment, the husky timbre of her voice and the warm glow of her eyes filling me with a different sort of heat, no less welcomed than the fire we'd just shared.

"Mmm. Perfect, as always," I managed to mumble, my lips and tongue only grudgingly giving up their afterglow lassitude. "This camping out stuff has some merit to it, lemme clue ya."

Her subtle smirk became a full-out grin as she reached up and gently ruffled my hair.

"We'll have to do it more often then."

Returning her grin, I rolled to my side and buried my face in the warm valley of her breasts. "I like that idea."

The flannel material of the sleeping bag tickled my face as Ice pulled it up to cover my rapidly cooling body. Her arm then wrapped around my waist, strong fingers stroking random, nonsense patterns against the damp skin of my back.

I had almost fallen asleep to the music of her heart when a thought intruded my fog-drenched thoughts and I stirred, untucking my head and looking up at my lover, who was staring ahead, seemingly lost in thought. "Ice?"

She blinked, coming back into herself and looking down at me, her gaze sharp and attentive. "Yes?"

"What's the plan? For tomorrow, I mean. Did Rio get any good information?"

"Actually, she did." Pulling back slightly, she stretched, arching her back. I winced at the sound of several vertebrae slipping back into place. "Seems that our friend Cavallo has been hiring some local thugs as henchmen. Looks like some of his own men weren't too keen on spending god knows how long stuck in the middle of nowhere without any place to spend their ill-gotten gain."

"Is that good for us?"

She shrugged. "Depends. They'll be harder to spot, but I'll take them over a trained professional any day. They're generally easier to outsmart." The gleam in her eyes told me everything I needed to know about how much she was going to enjoy testing them.

"So...what happens now?"

"There's an open air market that opens every Saturday.

Rio's contact says it's a pretty big deal, especially since it's close to Christmas. People from the surrounding towns and farms come to sell their produce and other wares. Rumor has it that Cavallo will send some of his men down to pick up some supplies that he can't get from the smaller markets where he's hiding."

"Where *is* he hiding?"

Her eyes went far away again. "I don't know. Yet. But if those idiots do manage to make an appearance, I'll track him down to his lair." A cold smile curved her lips, chilling me to the bone.

Unable to stop myself, I reached up and stroked her face with the tips of my fingers, trying to bring her back from whatever darkness she'd gone into.

After a long moment, she was back and looking down at me with a bit of chagrin in her eyes. "Sorry."

"No need," I replied, smiling and keeping my hand cupped to her cheek. I felt my smile turn into a cheeky grin. "So, what will the rest of us mere mortals be doing while you're making the world safe for humanity yet again?"

She laughed softly, reaching up to squeeze my hand and then bringing it to her lips to lay a kiss to my palm. "Helping me."

My jaw dropped. "Excuse me? Would you mind repeating that?"

She laughed again. "You heard me."

"Well, yeah, I *heard* you, but...."

Her face turned serious. "Angel, it's one thing to go into a guarded compound with the express purpose of assassinating someone. It's a different thing entirely to go into that same compound and try to bring that person out alive. I'm gonna need help, and I trust you guys to provide that for me."

"You know we will, Ice. No matter what."

She smiled. "I know."

The vow was sealed with a kiss.

I awoke the next morning to the sight of the morning sun filtering its way through the nylon fabric of the tent. I could tell straightaway that the air was brisk and cool, but I was warm, tucked in a soft nest of sleeping bags and blankets. I was alone, of course, but that realization didn't really bother me, as I knew without doubt that Ice was somewhere very close. The thought of her and the love we had shared well into the night brought a smile to my lips as I stretched and yawned. The scent of bacon cooking over a Mexican wood fire assailed my senses and caused my mouth immediately to water.

Yup, this camping stuff is pretty much alright in my book.

Just as I was considering rolling over and catching a few more winks, the tent flap eased open and Ice ducked in, her hands occupied with carrying a plate of food and a tin mug of what smelled like coffee. Straightening almost to her full height (it was a pretty tall tent), she looked down at me, a smile gracing her lips.

She looked magnificent in her soft, warn jeans, ribbed black T, and roomy flannel worn open over her rangy, muscled frame. Her black hair was loose and flowing over her broad shoulders, and her face sported a sun-kissed glow, giving her the appearance of rugged immortality that I just couldn't seem to tear my eyes away from.

Not that I wanted to, of course.

Her beauty always took my breath away, and I would gladly live with that particular affliction for the rest of my days and beyond.

Quirking an eyebrow at my blatant appraisal, she lowered herself gracefully down to the floor of the tent to sit cross-legged next to me, balancing plate and cup on her knees.

"Sorry," I managed to finally get out, blushing under the weight of her return, if patient, stare. "Um...is that for me?"

"Sure is," she replied, nodding. "If you're hungry."

"I could eat," I allowed, untangling myself from my comfy nest and sitting up. The cool air from the outside hit my naked body with a slap, causing an all-over shiver. "Brr."

Putting the plate and cup on the ground, she pulled her shirt from her body and drew it over mine, helping my arms through the sleeves and deftly buttoning it over my chest and belly. I couldn't help but laugh as I held out my arms, a full four inches of spare fabric dangling uselessly over the tips of my fingers.

Rolling her eyes and shaking her head, she helped me roll the cuffs up so that my hands were finally exposed, then handed me the breakfast she'd brought with her.

"Oh, this is *good*," I managed, around mouthfuls of eggs and bacon washed down by strong, bracing coffee. "Remind me to thank the cook."

"If you don't kill her first," she replied, eyes twinkling mischief.

"Nia made this?" I asked, disbelieving. In all the time I'd known her, I'd never seen her anywhere near a kitchen, let alone actually in one.

"Yup. She's pretty handy with a cook fire."

"Wow," was all I could think to say in return.

Ice left after I was finished, taking my dirty dishes with her to clean. Left to my own devices, I got up and dressed quickly, more due to the cold rather than any particular hurry. After pulling on the damnable wig over my hair and straightening it to the best of my ability, I opened the tent flap and walked out into the morning air, squinting at the bright sunlight shining down on the campsite.

My friends were working like a group of industrious bees clearing out a hive. As I walked over to where Ice was stowing some gear in the trunk, I couldn't help but notice Pony and Critter dismantling one of the tents, grinning and giggling like a couple of schoolgirls. Their faces and eyes had a glow about them. Almost as if....

"Did they share a tent last night?" I asked my partner, handing her our sleeping bags and blankets.

Looking back over her shoulder, Ice smirked. "And a good deal more than that, if this morning's any indication."

"But...how?"

Ice shrugged. "Rio got tired of Pony's whining, so she switched."

"But what about Nia?" Looking back at the campsite, I saw Rio and Nia working together to scatter the ashes of the cook fire, chatting amiably.

"Rio said that Nia was a perfect gentle...person."

"Amazing." Reaching up, I scratched the back of my neck. "Guess the crush is gone then." Just to be sure, I looked over my shoulder once again, only to see something I didn't expect.

Nia was staring past me and to my right, the expression on her face giving a whole new meaning to the word "dreamy." When our eyes met, she looked quickly away, guilt stamped clear on her youthful features. "Uh oh."

"What?" Ice asked, turning around, then looking back at me, her eyebrows drawing twin question marks across her forehead.

"Another one's fallen for you," I replied in my best "long suffering" tone.

She snorted. Rolling her eyes, she turned back to her work. "You're dreaming, Angel."

"Oh, I don't think so, my beautiful love. I'm wide awake, thank you very much."

"You're seeing things, then."

"I have perfect vision, as you well know."

She looked over at Nia, then back at me.

"You'll see," I warned, adding a smirk that told her more than any words could say.

"Wow! This place reminds me of the flea markets my mother used to drag me to when I was a kid!"

I found myself agreeing with Nia's assessment as Ice circled around the perimeter of the market and headed for the area designated for parking.

Multi-hued banners flapped cheerily in the brisk November wind, providing an almost musical counterpoint to the sounds of booths being set up, children's laughter, and the frenzied barking of the dogs who ran pell-mell around the grounds chasing whatever caught their fancy.

The tantalizing scents of grilling meat and vegetables immediately brought to mind the days of my less than wanton youth, when Sundays (after church, of course) were reserved for the almost holy rite of flea market and garage sale hopping. One of the all-time great bargain hunters, my grandmother. She never met a hand-lettered sign nailed to a telephone pole that she didn't like, much to my chagrin. Weekly trips to the plethora of open-air flea markets, which dotted the flat Indiana landscape like boils, were treated with much the same reverence the Crusaders must have felt when they quested after the Holy Grail. And many's the day I would spend trying on someone else's cast off dresses—always three sizes too big so I could grow into them—and wishing, with a sense of desperation common to children and trapped animals, that I was *anywhere* else. Like a dentist's office getting all of my teeth drilled without benefit of Novocaine, for example.

Ice startled me out of my musings when she touched my leg briefly before opening her door and slipping silently out of the car. Reaching for the door handle, I joined my partner, shivering slightly in the surprisingly chilled air and pulling my corduroy overshirt tighter across my body, thankful for its warmth.

Ice looked down at me, her eyes once again hidden behind mirrored sunglasses. "Ready?"

"As soon as you tell me what it is I'm supposed to be ready for, then yeah," I replied, grinning.

Smirking at me, she pulled out a large wad of Mexican currency and handed it over to me. "Don't spend it all in one place."

I looked down at the cash in my hand, then up at my lover. "Say again?"

"Shop," she replied, folding my fingers over the money before it had a chance to scatter over the marketplace. "You know...look at things, haggle, spend money."

"And this is helping you...how, again?"

She smiled. "Angel, I trust your instincts. You might not know this place or these people, but you *do* know when something doesn't feel right to you. And for this thing to have at least a minute chance of working, I need to be able to rely on those instincts to help me out. So..." her grin broadened, "...have fun. Go shopping. Have some lunch. Just keep your eyes and ears open, and if you spot anything even the least bit 'off' to you, lemme know. And take Nia with you, if you would. She can help translate anything you might have a hard time understanding, and you're the only one I trust to make sure she stays out of trouble."

Though my intent expression didn't change, the smile inside me grew. Her words of trust weren't often voiced, but when they were, I felt like a kid on Christmas morning, filled with joy and happiness at the receiving of them.

"I think I can do that," I replied, casually as I could.

She gave my shoulder a squeeze. "Good. Let's go then."

Stealing a quick kiss from her cheek for luck, I grabbed Nia's hand and walked into the fray.

The scents, sights, and sounds of the open-air market drew me in like a moth to the flame. Everywhere my gaze landed, there was something else to snare my attention. I could tell right away that rather than the flea markets of my long ago youth—*Venus Old Lady Traps*, my father used to call them in one of his rare moments of good humor—this market seemed to run along the lines of craft fairs my mother was sometimes known to drive miles out of her way to attend.

Woodcrafters and painters vied for space with rug weavers and furniture makers. Booths with every inch of available space crowded with fresh produce were book-ended by leatherworkers and garment weavers displaying their wares on tables and crates.

As several hours had passed since I had eaten breakfast, my nose, as it often did, took charge of the situation. It led me to a booth, behind which stood a man who made Methuselah look like a toddler fresh out of diapers. His smile was wide and bereft of teeth, but his dark eyes sparkled with intelligence and kindliness. In each hand, he held a thin wooden skewer pushed through thick chunks of sizzling pork, hot peppers, onions, and cherry tomatoes. The food looked wonderful and smelled even better. With a grin and a flourish, he presented us each with a skewer.

"Gracias," I replied in my rudimentary Spanish as I took hold of the treat, my mouth watering.

His grin broadened as he waved his hands at us in the universal sign to sample his wares.

Switching the skewer to my other hand, I fumbled for the pocket where I'd stored the money Ice had given me while at the same time wracking my brain for the phrase "how much?" in Spanish.

Seeing the money appear in my hand, the man put his hand up and shook his head in the negative, saying something too rapidly for me to understand and frowning slightly. I looked to Nia for help.

Walking over to me, she brought her lips close to my ear. "You'll offend him if you give him money. He gave us this food as a gift."

"Are you sure?" I whispered back.

"Positive."

After a moment, I nodded reluctantly, and Nia stepped away, thanking the man for both of us. His sunny grin returned and he waved at us before two more customers drew his attention away.

Stuffing the money back in my pocket, I savored my prize and bit into the succulent meat, feeling my eyes rolling back in my head as I did so. The combination of flavors was heaven to my tongue and I groaned in delight. "God, this is wonderful!"

"Yeah, it is pretty good, isn't it?" Nia replied, taking her own healthy bite. "Maybe I'll ask if he'll share his recipe later."

"Great idea!"

Turning, we both strolled down the wide path between booths, adroitly sidestepping various passersby as we walked along, filling our bellies. I kept my eyes and ears open, as Ice had taught me to do, hoping that if there *was* any trouble, I would find it before it found me.

And find it I did, not more than fifteen minutes later, as Nia stopped to examine an incredibly beautiful woven rug. Looking around, I spied three very large men heading in my direction, though two aisles to the left of where I was currently standing. The expressions on the men's faces left no doubt that Christmas cheer had passed them by. In fact, it had probably run off screaming into the night once it had set proverbial eyes on them.

I watched through narrowed eyes as they pushed a succession of people out of their way, including a young boy who fell and hit his head hard on one of the tables. His mother quickly scooped him up and darted into the dubious safety of the crowd, the tears streaming down her face matching her son's.

Laughing cruelly, the trio continued on its way, wreaking havoc on the stalls and patrons they passed, grabbing up merchandise and either tucking it away or smashing it beyond repair on the rocky ground beneath their boots.

Taking my eyes off them for a moment, confident that I could pick up their trail by following the evidence of their destruction alone, I grabbed Nia's arm and spun her around to face me. "Get Ice."

"What?" she asked, trying ineffectually to pluck my hand from her arm. "Why?"

"I don't have time to explain. Just do it. Please."

"But...."

"Please."

She looked at me doubtfully for a long moment, but something in my eyes must have convinced her, because she then relaxed. "Ok. I'll find her." She hesitated, smirking. "I assume you're talking about tall, dark, and gorgeous, and not the cold stuff that comes in cubes, right?"

I tightened my grip. "Nia...."

"Alright! Alright! I will! Just leggo my arm, will ya?"

Releasing her, I gave her a gentle shove back the way we'd come before turning away.

The thugs' trail was, as I'd predicted, rather easy to find and follow again. Like a modern day Sherlock Holmes, I followed the simple clues of the men's passing and caught up to them at a booth that seemed to specialize in produce and dried meats, fish, and the like.

Ducking quickly across the way so as not to be caught looking, I found myself amidst a large display of wind chimes of every size, shape, and description. The very air of my passing set them to jingling, but the men I'd followed didn't spare a glance my way, for which I was thankful.

As I pretended to carefully examine the merchandise before me, I watched as the biggest of the men grabbed the poor merchant by the front of his shirt, shaking him much as a dog would a dirty sock, while his cohorts grabbed wooden packing crates and began stuffing them with all the food they could get their meaty hands on.

A very large part of me wanted to rush out from my hiding place and put a stop to the blatant theft. Deep down inside, though, I knew that if I did that, and these were the men we were looking for, my chivalry—for wont of a better term—would only cause more problems than it was likely to solve and we'd likely lose the only shot we had of tracking Cavallo to his hideout.

So I stayed where I was, albeit with some reluctance, and watched with gritted teeth and fisted hands as the thugs cleared the poor man out of nearly everything he had.

Throwing the merchant back into his now denuded stall, the trio laughed and picked up their crates, shouting insults easily understood in any language in which they were uttered.

Damnit, Nia. Where the hell are you?

The men were quickly gone from my sight, though the sounds of their malicious laughter were easily heard over the subdued noise of the crowd.

After a final look around convinced me the cavalry wasn't coming over the hill anytime soon, I took in a deep breath and ducked out from my cover, intent on following those men to the highway, if necessary. I caught up to them quickly, though staying a good distance back. Not that it mattered. They weren't looking anywhere but straight ahead anyway, their mission, apparently, accomplished.

I followed them until they got to the gate, then paused a moment, considering. In the end, though, there really wasn't any other choice in the matter. Though I didn't have keys to the car and couldn't very well follow the men to wherever it was they were going next, I could at least get a description of the car they were driving and give Ice the general direction in which they were headed.

Nodding once at my decision, I stepped past the last row of booths, only to have my wrist grasped firmly by a warm hand, stopping me dead in my tracks. Whirling, I saw Ice, a smile in her eyes, if not on her lips. She pulled me close, then turned and gave a short nod. Rio and Nia appeared out of the shadows of the booth behind us, and set off at a determined pace after the men I'd been following.

"Good job," Ice said softly when they'd cleared the gate and were gone from my view.

"Thanks," I replied, smiling at her praise and leaning into her strong, muscled body for just a moment. "So...are we going after them?"

"Nope."

Pulling away, I looked up at her. "No?"

"Rio and Nia will handle it."

"But.... I don't understand. Aren't they the right guys?"

"Most likely."

"Then why aren't we going after them?"

Sometimes Ice's peculiar brand of circular logic made my head spin.

Now was definitely one of those times.

"Well?"

"They're bait."

"Excuse me?"

She looked down at me, a subtle smile playing over her lips. "Bait. Cavallo might have an ego larger than this entire country, but he's not entirely stupid. He knows he's being followed. He just doesn't know by whom."

A light dawned somewhere within the recesses of my whirling brain. "I get it. He thinks he's being followed, so he sends out a couple of overbearing goons who make a deliberate racket to snare in anyone who might be interested in his whereabouts. The trackers follow the bait, and he sends the real guys in later, when the coast is clear."

Her smile bloomed fully, reaching the pale glitter of her eyes. "Exactly right."

I could feel my brow furrow. "But that means that Rio and Nia could be heading into a trap. Why did you let them go after those guys?"

"Just in case Cavallo *has* gotten stupid in his old age."

"And if he hasn't?"

She gave my hand a squeeze before releasing it. "Rio knows this desert better than any of us. If they're leading her into a trap, she'll know."

"I hope you're right." Though Rio and I weren't the best of friends by any yardstick one wished to use, I'd come to respect the large, quiet woman a great deal. I didn't want to see her hurt. Nia either, despite my oft-voiced thoughts to the contrary.

"I am."

And because it was Ice saying these things, I gave up my reservations and simply believed.

"So...I guess it's back to more shopping, huh?" I tried out my best nonchalant voice, but I'm afraid my grin gave me away.

Rolling her eyes, my lover quirked a grin right back at me. "Guess so."

I affected a sigh. "Well, alright. It'll be a hardship, but I'll manage to muddle through. Somehow."

Smirking, she gave me a gentle shove back in the direction I'd come. "Stay around this general area. If you see anything that doesn't sit right with you, come find me. I won't be too far away."

"Will do."

As I walked away, something bright and shiny caught the periphery of my vision. Like some sort of overgrown crow drawn to a bit of aluminum foil with which to feather its nest, I headed unerringly in the direction that had caught my interest.

The booth was small and set a bit back from the rest. As I moved closer, it became quickly obvious that a master silversmith had chosen this place to display his exquisite handiwork. I looked around in utter awe as I came to a stop in front of the long display table. Most of the pieces were jewelry of some kind; bracelets, pendants, arm cuffs, and rings being the most predominant. They were similar, though much better in quality, to pieces I'd seen in some of the more expensive jewelry stores at one time or another in my life, especially in the southwest. The price tags for such works of art started in the mid-hundreds and only went up from there. I hesitated to see how much these were going for.

Rather than look for price tags, I decided to examine the artist himself, who was sitting on what looked to be a wooden beer keg while working on his latest creation. He was young, that much I could tell at first glance. With a trimmed shock of thick black hair that shone blue in the intense light of the sun, he was short of stature but wiry and well-muscled in his tight white t-shirt, faded jeans, and dusty boots.

As if sensing my gaze, he looked up and favored me with a boyish grin that touched the inky black depths of his deep-set eyes. Charmed, I couldn't help but smile back, noticing as I did the strong resemblance he bore to Rio. It was obvious that they shared the same ancestry, though I doubted they were in any way related.

Saying nothing, he looked back down and began his sculpting work anew, apparently content with my intrusion. I watched his hands as he worked, his fingers thick and square and blunt. Sure, strong, and swift, yet so unlike Ice's long fingers that moved with almost liquid grace while undertaking much the same task, though her medium of choice was wood and not silver.

As I watched, I made sure that I was also aware of my surroundings at all times. My eyes were in constant motion, scanning the market and the people therein, looking for something, anything, which would set my internal "danger" meter off.

So far, everything seemed quiet.

The market seemed to have recovered quickly from the upset the thugs had caused, as public gatherings sometimes will once the shouting is all over and there's nothing more to see.

By the time I looked back at the object of my attention, he had finished the piece he was working on and was rubbing it briskly with a buffing cloth. Silver peeked from behind the soft cloth, winking cheerily in the sun. I could tell it was a bracelet by the vague outline that shone through as he worked. More like a wrist cuff, actually, almost two inches wide with a carved design along the face.

Giving me a boyish, almost shy, grin, he held out the object for my inspection, a quick motion of his head inviting me to take it into my own hands for a closer examination. Smiling back, I reached out and then stopped, my fingers scant inches from their goal. I could feel my jaw hang open as my gaze zeroed in on the design on the bracelet.

The rim of the rising sun was carved in bas-relief along the face. And below that, an intricately carved and absolutely beautiful tree, spreading its limbs to the sun.

A bonsai tree.

Close enough to the one Ice had carved on our headboard to have been its twin.

I looked up from the bracelet to the artist who created it. His black eyes, just seconds before youthful and innocent, seemed almost ancient in their wisdom. It wasn't as if he was looking at me. It was as if he was looking *through* me, beyond the flesh and blood and bone and into that space where my soul resided.

I felt a prickle of fear skitter up my spine.

"How did...?" I trailed off, realizing in my shock that I was speaking English.

He smiled, pressing the bracelet into my hands and backing a half step away, diluting somewhat the tension between us. "Sometimes, things just are," he said, likewise in English, his voice soft and warm. "It belongs to you, now."

"Oh no," I demurred, holding the bracelet out to him. "I couldn't possibly...."

He held his hands up, refusing to take it back. "I saw this vision in my mind, and when you came, I knew it was meant for you to have." He cocked his head slightly. "There is someone close to you for whom that design has deep meaning, yes?"

Stunned, I could only nod.

"Good. Then I have chosen wisely. Please. Accept my gift to you both. It is a tradition of my people."

"But...I...."

"I give this to you, knowing it will be cherished. What more can I ask?"

I laughed a little, as much to break the tension as anything else. "Well, money's nice, too...."

He laughed then, looking much more like the young man he was—to my great relief—than the wizened ancient he'd appeared just seconds before. "Yes, money has its uses. And rest assured that the compensation I receive from well-to-do jewelers to the north guarantees that I'm rarely without it. But, if art is not sometimes done for art's sake, it quickly loses much of its meaning." He grinned. "To me, at least. So take this, with my good wishes, and enjoy it. Or throw it away. It's yours."

I knew the look in his eyes very well indeed. It was the same expression Ice used when a subject was closed beyond all possibility of ever being reopened again. In this century or any other, for that matter. It was an expression to which there was, really, only one answer.

Graceful concession.

"Thank you."

Another charming, boyish smile, and then he dismissed me, though not unkindly, by returning his full attention to his work.

At somewhat of a loss, I looked back down at the bracelet in my hand, viewing it from every possible angle under the brilliant light of the midday sun. I imagined, as I did so, how it would look on Ice's wrist, the silver gleaming brightly against the deep, burnished tan of her skin.

Ice didn't wear jewelry as a rule. In fact, in all the time I'd known her, I'd never seen her so much as eye a piece, much less don one.

Still, I had a feeling that this particular object just might change all that.

And if it didn't, it wasn't as if I'd lost any money in the deal.

"And speaking of money," I muttered to myself after giving my benefactor one last look. "I think I know someone who'll appreciate some right about now."

After a quick glance around and noting that the coast was still clear, I set off in the direction of the booth the thugs had torn apart earlier. The proprietor was still there, sitting on an overturned crate, his shoulders slumped in disconsolation. Several people were gathered around him, speaking in low and sympathetic tones. My heart went out to him, this poor man who had likely lost enough potential income to keep his family through the winter.

Stepping through the small crowd, I pulled all the money Ice had given me out of my pocket and thrust it into his trembling hands. "For you," I said in my faltering, grade school Spanish. "Merry Christmas."

He looked up at me with moist eyes the size and shape of saucers. His mouth hung open in a perfect oval as he stared.

Blushing to beat the band, tuba section and all, I bowed my head a little, smiled, and quickly turned on my heel before I started blubbering like some sort of idiot under the influence of a little too much Christmas cheer.

Half running down the wide, dirt-packed aisle, I looked quickly around me, then stopped dead in my tracks as I spied two figures entering through the main gate. Tall men, both, with regimental haircuts, broad shoulders, and clothes which, though they tried their best to look casual, were obviously quite expensive.

Thinking quickly, I ducked into a corner booth, breathing fast and trying desperately to fight against the memories their presence brought with them. Images of staring down the barrel of a gun as I tried to protect Corinne with my own body. Images of my unconscious lover being dragged away as I begged and pleaded with them to please leave her alone.

"Alright, Angel," I whispered, the sound of my own voice calming me somewhat. "Now's not the time to be having flashbacks, here. Those are the guys we've been waiting for. You know it. So let's just get on the ball and find Ice, alright?"

Thus fortified, I was about to turn when a warm pair of hands descended on my shoulders and almost sent the life screaming right out of me. "Good eyes," came a husky voice in my ear, as fragrant hair brushed softly against my cheek.

"Jesus, Ice," I breathed, relaxing back against her. "You almost gave me a heart attack."

With a gentle squeeze, Ice stepped back away from me and Critter and Pony gathered 'round. "That them?" Critter asked, looking somewhere beyond my field of vision.

"Yup," Ice replied softly.

"So, what do we do now?" Pony chimed in.

"I'll show you," she replied, reaching down to clasp my hand in hers, then starting out with that long-limbed, take-no-prisoners stride of hers, which left me half running every other step just to stay on my feet.

Before I knew it, we were out the gate and heading rapidly toward our car, parked toward the back.

"Um, Ice?" I queried when I was able to get my wind back.

"Mm?" she replied, unlocking the doors and opening them quickly.

"Aren't...aren't the guys we're after that-away?"

"Yes." She drew the word out.

"Then...why are we going in the opposite direction? Aren't we supposed to be keeping tabs on them?"

"That's exactly what we're doing."

I looked over my shoulder at Critter, who grinned and shrugged helplessly before ducking her head and getting into the back seat. Pony just smirked.

I looked back at my lover. "Wouldn't it be better to keep tabs on them where we could actually see them?"

Her smile put the Mona Lisa's to shame. "We will. Eventually."

Grumbling, I slipped into the car and slammed the door shut. Ice smirked when she slid inside and, when she lowered her glasses, her eyes were twinkling mischievously. I stuck my tongue out at her, and she chuckled, laying a warm hand on my thigh. "We'll wait here until they come out. That way, they won't see anyone following them out of the market. Then, when they pull out, we'll follow them at a safe distance."

"That makes sense," I allowed, not totally willing to let her off the hook just yet.

She, of course, wasn't buying my act. "Of course it does," she replied, giving me her own version of a cheeky grin before sliding her glasses back to their customary position and turning forward once again.

Still, her warm hand lay comfortable on my thigh, and when I reached down and covered it with my own (as if I could help myself) she squeezed our fingers gently together, and all was pretty much all right with my world.

We didn't have all that long to wait before the two men cleared the gate and started heading for their car, followed by several merchants each toting boxes full of goods. The car in question was a long sedan, which was likely black, but currently sported a reddish-yellow covering of desert dust. Parked among a bevy of bastardized trucks and cars whose showroom dates were no later than the nineteen seventies, it stuck out like a hammer-smashed grasping appendage.

Within minutes, the merchants had finished placing their boxes in the back seat and trunk of the car and were summarily waved off by the two men without so much as a "by your leave," as far as I could tell.

The men got into their car and were off in a spray of gravel and dust.

A moment later, Ice started up the car and pulled in behind several other shoppers who were heading toward home after a long day of bargaining. She'd taken the radios from both of the police cruisers before they shuffled off to auto heaven, and had reinstalled them in the two cars we now used. Unhooking the mike, she depressed the button as we drove at medium speed down a straight-as-an-arrow two-lane highway, following a short convoy of cars and light trucks. "You there?"

"Yeah," came Rio's voice over the radio.

"How'd it go?"

"They were the bait, alright. Led us on a good chase, but I backed off before it became too obvious. Heading back to you now."

"We're on our way out now, headed west toward the mountains. We're about two miles out."

"I'll continue on and swing in behind you, then."

"Alright. We're following a black sedan, two men inside."

"Will do. Out."

Racking the mike, Ice put both her hands on the wheel and raced the winter sun as it began its slow, meandering trek westward toward the mountain ranges in the near distance.

Conversation, what there was of it, was sparse, and I spent some time silently thanking Ice for sending Nia with Rio. Forty-five minutes into the trip, I saw Rio's beaten beige sedan pass us in the opposite direction, then U-turn across the highway and slide in behind the line of cars heading to the west.

We continued on for maybe another half-hour when Ice's radio crackled with an incoming call. Rio's urgent voice came over the speaker. "Shit. I know where he's going. Follow me."

As Ice slowed down, Rio crossed on a dotted yellow and slipped in front of our car. Up ahead and to the left, there was a turnoff, and when Rio signaled, Ice followed behind a line of two or three other cars and turned as well, leaving the rest of the unintentional caravan to continue on, still led by Cavallo's men.

We were in the foothills, and as the cars in front of Rio's continued forward, Rio herself pulled off, her front bumper almost touching the rocky hill which sprung up in front of us like a shark fin in an otherwise calm, if rather dirty, ocean.

The car hadn't even stopped rolling before she jumped out and sprinted up the rocky side of the hill (more like a small mountain, really) at a speed far quicker that one would think a body that large could possibly go.

Nia exited more slowly, simply staring up the mountain and the quickly retreating form of Rio with open-mouthed shock.

After pulling up along side the parked car, Ice exited at a more leisurely pace, but once she was free and clear, she went up after Rio, catching up to her rather quickly despite the other woman's rather large lead.

"Up?" Pony asked me, eyebrows raised.

"Up," I replied, already taking off.

"Figures," she muttered, climbing next to me with Critter and Nia joining in the chase.

The route to the top was steep, the footing very unsteady, and by the time I made it up, I was breathing heavily and bathed in a fine layer of sweat. I was inwardly pleased, however, to note that both Pony and Critter were both more winded than I, while Nia was still struggling to the top, her face florid and wet with sweat.

Covering the last few feet, I went to stand next to Ice, who was standing in a small stand of tough, gnarled pinion pines, and breathing as if she'd just taken a leisurely stroll down the lane. Where I might once have felt envy over her supreme display of physical fitness, I instead just grinned and shook my head.

"What?" she asked, eyebrow raised.

"Nothing," I replied, nudging her a little. "What's going on?"

Following my lover's pointing finger, I noticed a rather large dwelling surrounded on all sides by a high stone wall. The house itself looked to be made of pink adobe with a blue Spanish-tiled roof. It looked slightly run down, as if it hadn't been properly cared for in quite some time. Some of the roof tiles were missing, the yard was an overgrown proliferation of cacti, olive trees, and pinion pines, and the large in-ground pool was thick and green with algae and god knows what else.

As I watched, the black sedan pulled into the compound and stopped in the circular driveway near the front entrance to the house. Several men emerged from the home, all armed, to help remove the boxes the men had brought back with them.

Try as I might, I couldn't see Cavallo himself anywhere which, as I'm sure you might guess, didn't cause me much of a problem at all.

"How did you know?" I whispered to Rio, who stood to the other side of Ice.

When she looked back at me, her expression was one of self-loathing. "I didn't. But I should have." Her large hands were clenched into tight fists, which she beat uselessly against her tree-trunk thighs. "Buncha compounds like this all around here. Drug lords and dictators on the lam hide out here. Been doin' it for over fifty years or more. Didn't realize this was where he was holed up until we got close, though. Damnit."

"Rio, enough." Ice's voice was soft, but the note of command it held was undeniable and unalterable.

Rio's shoulders sagged.

"Do you know anything about this particular compound?" my lover asked, raking her eyes over the land in question.

The other woman's expression brightened slightly as she shoulders squared. "Matter of fact, I do. A friend of mine was caretaker here for about ten years before the drug lord who lived there went back home. As far as I know, it's been empty for two years, maybe three."

"Is your friend still around?"

"Yeah. Twenty miles or so back the way we came."

"Alright then. Let's head over there. I want an idea of what's inside before I make my move."

Knowing a conversation ender when I heard one, I spun away from the mountaintop view of the compound and then stilled my motion as I tried to mentally adjust to the picture my eyes were presenting me.

What I thought I was seeing was a large fogbank moving in from the east. If fog was yellow, that is. Which it isn't. Like fog, though, it had a mysterious quality to it and might have even been beautiful, in its own fashion, if not for the ugly yellow color.

Entranced and a little spooked, to be honest, I looked up. And saw something that, if possible, was even more strange.

It was as if someone had taken a ruler and drawn a perfectly straight line across the sky. To the west of the line, the sky was a clear, vibrant winter blue. To the east, a deep, black void. Black as night, but without any moon or stars to show the way.

It was something I'd never in my life seen before, and it was more than a little frightening.

As if to frighten me further, a freshening breeze blew up, and that breeze was cold. Icy cold.

I shivered inside the flannel Ice had given me and pulled it tighter against my sweat-drenched skin.

Pony was the next to turn, and like me, she froze when presented with the view. "Dust storm," she muttered disgustedly. "Shit."

"More than that," came Rio's voice from behind. "Monsoon. Bad one, by the looks of the sky."

"A monsoon?" Pony countered. "In December?"

"Mother Nature doesn't always read the White Man's calendar," Rio replied.

"She should damn well start, then."

Sensing that a storm of a different type was brewing, I stepped forward, drawing Rio's attention away from Pony. "So, what do we do?"

"We head east, like we were planning."

"Into the storm?" I asked, doubt coloring my voice.

Her dark, somber eyes met mine. "The only way through these mountains is to take that highway, which leads down into a deep valley and crosses a major river. It's fifty miles or more before the valley floor raises up. It's a flood plain. We'll never outrun the storm." She pointed ahead. "There's higher ground back to the east. It's a lot safer, even if it means going into the mouth of the storm."

I looked over at Ice, who nodded her acceptance of Rio's succinct assessment.

"Out of the frying pan and into the fire, huh?"

My lover smiled slightly before stepping up and laying a feather light touch to my back. "Let's go."

Driving through the dust storm was interesting, to say the least. It was like being in a fog bank and a snowstorm all rolled into one. One choking breath of that swirling dust, however, convinced me that Ice meant what she said when she ordered all windows and vents closed tightly.

Nia rode with us this time, though thankfully she was too busy gawking at this interesting weather phenomenon to break out into song. If I could be grateful to a storm for one thing, it would be that.

The dust soon thinned and then disappeared altogether. My sense of relief lasted, however, for all of about two seconds before the deluge hit.

No simple winter rainstorm, this. Nor even remotely like anything I'd ever been through before in my almost thirty years of living on this planet of ours.

About the only thing I can think to liken it to is going through one of those drive-thru car washes without using your windshield wipers. The rain came harder than it had any right to, completely swamping the car and making it utterly impossible to see anything but the rippling pool of water battering the windshield.

Lightening flashed in rapid-fire bursts, like the finale of a fireworks display in fuzzy monochrome. Thunder boomed and cracked so loudly that I clapped my hands over my ears and feared for the strength of the glass in the windows.

"Ice?" I asked, my voice high and wavering. Though loathe to disturb my partner's intense concentration, I was, quite frankly, scared to death. "Do you think we should maybe pull over until this lets up some?"

"Can't," came her succinct reply as she willed her keen eyes to see beyond the curtain of water the storm laid over the windshield.

"There's...um...c-canals on both sides." Nia's voice floated up from the back seat, even more breathy and timorous than my own.

I could have slapped myself for forgetting that. Long, narrow canals took the place of the shoulders on both sides of the highway, bringing rain and reservoir water into the outlying regions. So, pulling over was most definitely not an option.

Rigid with fear, I tugged on my seatbelt, making sure the connection was secure. I was absolutely sure that, with each passing second—time measured by the rapid, if useless swish-thump of the wipers, beating in perfect synchrony with my panicked heart—we would either plow into Rio's car, or someone else would hit us from behind.

We were flying blind, and we all knew it.

The radio crackled and Pony's voice filtered into the car. "We're out."

Quickly, I retrieved the mike. "What do you mean? Out of the storm?" Hope flared, high and bright, in my heart.

"We're stopped. A tree's down, blocking the highway."

"How do you know?"

"We just hit it."

"Jesus. Are you alright?"

Static crackled as a bolt of lightening landed frightfully close. I almost screamed as the thunder nearly shattered my eardrums with its frightful intensity.

"Yeah. No damage. We were going too slow. You'd better stop, Ice. You'll hit us."

Ice had already started slowing down, from the first moment Pony contacted us, and came to a gradual, safe stop in the middle of the highway.

"We're stopped." The relief coursing through me made me feel limp and drained.

"Good. Anyone behind you?"

"Like I can *see* anything?"

"Alright, alright, Angel. Take it easy."

My attention was quickly diverted as I watched Ice's hand go to the door lever and proceed to open it. "Ice, wait! You can't...."

My words were bitten off, literally, as my teeth came together sharply, pinning my tongue between them. The hot, metallic taste of blood flooded my mouth, then was quickly forgotten as my entire body was jerked forward, my head on a direct collision course with the dashboard as we were hit, hard, from behind.

The impact never happened, though, because we were hit again, this time from the side. Unrestrained, Ice's body flew across the interior and landed in my lap, pinning me against the door. Stars sparked in my vision as the back of my head collided with the window, but somehow my lover managed to prevent me from sustaining more damage by wrapping her long arms around me and tucking me against her snugly.

My indrawn breath of pain and relief was cut off midway as we were struck again, this time with twice as much force as the previous two collisions combined. The squealing groan of metal rending mixed in frightful cacophony with the splinter of fractured glass and Nia's high-pitched, terror-filled scream.

We were hit again, and then again as the storm set off a destructive chain reaction with us as the focus-point. I clutched at Ice the way a drowning man clutches his rescuer, knowing my fingernails were scourging her skin, but terrified beyond caring at that moment.

The final crash came and I felt the world around me tumble as the car began to raise up off its wheels. The next thing I knew, we were floating free.

After that, I knew nothing at all.

Something soft and fragrant tickled against my nose and then tickled again as my eyelashes fluttered against opening. When the nuisance wouldn't go away, I finally opened my eyes and scowled at the feathery stalk of grass that waved at me, courtesy of a warm, summer breeze.

My scowl quickly turned to a grin, though, and I rolled over on my back to look up at a pristine blue sky and a slight scattering of tiny clouds, which trailed lazily across a friendly summer sun.

I felt...perfect, I realized as the sounds of the breeze traveling through grass and leaves played a lazy, peaceful harmony. The long nap I'd apparently taken had left me feeling uncommonly refreshed. The minor aches and pains, which collected as I got older, seemed to have vanished, as if they never were.

I was clear-headed and light-hearted and filled with an absolute, incredible joy.

Rolling up to a sitting position, I gazed across the flat expanse of a pristine lake with waters so calm and so blue that the sight brought tears of happiness to my eyes. The lake was surrounded on all sides by a forest of stately, deep emerald evergreens whose laden boughs swayed and danced in the ever-present and deliciously scented breeze, which blew warm and gentle upon my skin.

Paradise.

Coming to my feet, I turned in a slow circle, the smile on my face growing so broad that I was sure it would freeze there. Not that I would have minded, of course.

Giggling like a schoolgirl, I watched the whimsical path of a beautiful butterfly as it flitted over a meadow filled with a million flowers in every color of the rainbow.

I was grasped with a sudden need to be in that meadow, to run through it and feel the soft, pollen-dusted petals as they brushed against my bare legs, and to smell the sweet fragrances of the flowers as I passed each one by.

With a joyous shout, I flung my arms wide and took off through the field, laughing until tears ran from my eyes, blurring the scene before me as if I were looking through a prism filled with a magical radiance. Temporarily blinded, I stumbled and fell, but the ground was like a soft, warm blanket, cradling me and cushioning me as I rolled, still laughing and covered with pollen, through the field.

Springing back to my feet, I continued my sprint, filled with an energy I'd never before felt. It was...amazing was the only word I could think to use. I could have been running for hours, or even days, but it was like the energy within me kept growing and growing until my body fairly buzzed with it.

The meadow's end lay only a short distance away, bordered by more of those tall, fragrant evergreens. As the warmth of the sun and the exercise had conspired to lay a faint sheen of sweat on my body, the promised coolness of the shaded emerald forest was perfection itself.

With a last, grateful look at the flowering field, I stepped into the cool, fragrant shadows of the giant trees. Soft fronds brushed my arms like welcoming friends. It was cool, quiet, and dim, yet tranquil and comforting the way a warm summer's night is comforting.

Up ahead, a short distance away, a faint rose glow came through the trees, drawing my attention and my footsteps in that direction.

The glow, which became subtly brighter as I made my zig-zag way toward its unknown source, gilded the trees at the edge of the small wood a dusky bronze, which was quite beautiful in its own way. I felt in some way drawn to it by an almost magnetic attraction, and before I knew it, my meandering pace had quickened to a ground-eating trot.

The trees fell away suddenly, giving way to a huge clearing.

And in the center of that clearing, glowing rose and gold and bronze, was the largest tree I'd ever seen in my life. Not so much tall, no, but broad and strong, as if sprung up from the very bedrock of the earth itself. Its thick, sturdy limbs grew out from the trunk in wild proliferation.

It seemed wild, and untamed, and, to my awestruck eyes, so very, very beautiful.

I felt a tug from somewhere deep down within me, and I took up my trot once again, feeling the radiant glow gently, tenderly caress my face and form as I moved ever closer.

Drawn on by a need and a longing beyond my understanding, I increased my speed, hands outstretched to their fullest limit and aching for something I couldn't name. A final step and I was there, my outstretched fingers brushing against the warm, smooth, living bark with a sense of profound relief.

Laying my palms flat against the trunk, I felt an intense surge of energy flow through me, bringing with it a sense of rightness, of completeness that, until now, I hadn't been aware I was lacking.

Startled, though unafraid, I took a brief step back, losing contact with the tree as I did so.

The immediate sense of loss was almost overwhelming, and

tears sprung quick to my eyes, blurring my vision once again.

"What's happening to me?" I whispered, overcome with a grief whose source was unknown.

Angel....

My head jerked up, and I took another step back, looking around me. "Who...who said that?"

Angel....

The voice seemed to come from everywhere and nowhere. I did a slow circle, eyes darting around the clearing, but as far as I could tell, I was completely alone.

"Please. Who's there? I won't harm you. Just please...."

Angel....

Drawing a bead on the origin of the voice, I turned quickly back to the tree.

Only, it wasn't a tree anymore.

In its place stood a woman of breathtaking beauty. She was tall, broad of shoulder and lean of hip. Her hair was black as night and flew freely from her brow in luxuriant waves. Her face was that of an artist's model, and her eyes...her eyes were the pale, intense blue of the hottest part of a flame.

"I know you," I breathed with surety, though the full knowledge of the woman before me danced tauntingly out of reach, like a word stuck on the tip of your tongue and refusing to come forth.

Angel....

The corner of her mouth turned up in a crooked smile, and she reached out one long arm, elegant fingers slightly curled, beckoning.

Without conscious thought, I felt my own arm raise in response as my feet moved me steps closer to the breathtaking woman in front of me.

Our fingers brushed together and memories of a forgotten lifetime crashed over me, literally bringing me, gasping, to my knees.

Angel....

The voice came again, only this time, I knew who it was that was calling to me.

"Ice?"

A radiant smile broke over her face like the beauty of the rising sun. She reached out again, beckoning.

Grinning like a fool, I jumped back to my feet, ignored her outstretched hand, and leapt into her arms, only to find myself tumbling into blackness once again.

I came to with a gasp that sent pain wracking through to the deepest levels of my body. My lungs were on fire, and I began choking and gagging so hard that I felt as if my lungs and guts were about to make an unseemly exit through my nose and mouth.

The only thing to come up, thankfully, was brackish water, and that in great amounts.

"Oh god," I gasped as my body convulsed again, trying desperately to expel everything I'd evidently ingested. "Help me."

In answer to my prayer, I was enfolded in a tender embrace by arms I knew and cherished. I felt a kiss being pressed into the crown of my head as those arms gathered me close against a muscled body, which was shaking as badly as I was.

"It's alright," came the whispered words. "You're gonna be alright."

Forcing my stinging eyes open, I tilted my head back and looked up into the cherished face of my lover. "Ice?"

She barked a half laugh, half sob which brought more tears from already swollen eyes. "Yeah, it's me."

"What happened?"

The lines of her face tensed in unimaginable pain. Her eyes closed and she gathered me still closer with an almost desperate strength. Laying her cheek atop my head, she rocked my pain-wracked body as I listened to the panicked beat of her valiant heart.

It all rushed back to me then. The monsoon. The accident. The feeling of flying, of falling, and ultimately, the total darkness that spiraled around me until it finally caught up and captured me in its inevitable grasp.

Something horrible had happened. To me. That much I knew.

I just needed to figure out what it was.

"Ice?"

Sensing no answer from that quarter, I opened my eyes again and gazed outward, past the comforting circle of my lover's arms and body.

I latched on to the first face I saw. "Critter?"

Like Ice, her eyes were red and swollen from crying. Giving me a watery smile, she moved closer, settled on her haunches, and grasped my hand, her thumb trailing tenderly over my knuckles. "Welcome back, Angel."

I could feel my brow creasing, though the action sent a fresh wave of pain through my skull. "What happened?"

She took in a deep breath and then let it out, hesitating. "What...what's the last thing you remember?" she asked at last.

"I remember the car flipping over. That's it, I think."

"It...um...flipped into the canal," she commented softly, sniffing back fresh tears.

"On it's fucking roof," came the voice of Pony as she moved in to kneel beside Critter. Her face was white with shock, and there was a suspicious wetness around her eyes. "Damnedest fucking thing I ever saw," she continued, shaking her head as she dragged a slightly trembling hand through soaked hair.

"What was?"

The two women exchanged glances. Critter nodded slightly, and Pony sighed.

"You guys were trapped. There wasn't enough room to get to the doors on either side," Pony explained. "Rio jumped in to see if she could get underneath, but the water was so damn fast she nearly got swept away."

"Rio? Is she...?" Though I looked around, I couldn't see the woman in question anywhere.

"Yeah," Critter interjected, squeezing my hand. "She's fine. Pony and I were able to drag her out before she got too far away."

"Where is she?"

"With Nia," Pony answered.

"Is Nia...?"

"She's fine, too. Banged up pretty good, but not too bad, considering."

"Considering what?"

They exchanged glances again, and Pony, once again, took up the gauntlet.

"We were going all kinds of crazy, trying to figure out how to get you all out of there. Rio kept wanting to jump back in and me and Critter kept holding her back." Her fists clenched. "We needed help, but none of the other assholes who caused this whole fucking mess wanted to help out. They were too damn busy pissing and moaning about their pitiful pieces of shit cars to pay any attention to us." Her face screwed up into an expression of bitter disgust.

Critter wrapped her free arm around Pony's waist and squeezed. She picked up the tale. "Rio found some rope in one of the other cars. We figured we'd try and tie it around one of the axles and maybe pull, somehow try to move the car and get you guys out."

"We were getting ready to do just that, too," Pony said, "when the damnedest thing happened." She shook her head, disbelief plain on her features.

"What?" I'm afraid I sounded a bit annoyed at that point, but my head was pounding, my lungs were still on fire with every breath I took, my body felt as if Ice had used it in place of her heavy-bag, and I felt as if I was going to throw up sometime in the very near future.

Pony, however, seemed oblivious. Her eyes were dark and far away. "We heard this loud *crack*, and the next thing we knew, Nia was flying through the air, pretty as you please. Rio caught her just before she would have hit the ground. She was soaked, and bleeding some, but she was alive." My friend's voice trailed off as she shook her head in patent disbelief.

"Then Ice came out through the back window she'd somehow kicked open," Critter said, softly. "You were in her arms. The water kept trying to sweep her away. I don't know how she managed, but somehow she did." She, too, shook her head. "Pony, Rio and I went down to take you from her, but she wouldn't give you up. She was in shock, I think." She took a deep breath and then let it out slowly. "We finally managed to get hold of you and bring you up here. You were...."

"Dead," Pony supplied, flatly, wiping at her eyes with savage hands.

"Wha-at?" My entire body went numb at her pronouncement. Ice's arms tightened convulsively around me, cutting off my breathing for a long, aching second before they finally loosened, though only infinitesimally, for which I was grateful.

"You weren't breathing," Critter supplied gently. "You guys were completely under water for a long time, and you were unconscious. You hit your head a good one on something."

That explained the unmerciful throbbing, which threatened to explode my skull into tiny little fragments.

"I tried...to get a pulse...and I couldn't find one," Critter continued, tears streaming liberally down her cheeks and dripping onto the still-wet pavement. "I...we...didn't know what to do. I mean...we all knew CPR, but...I'm afraid we panicked." Her face flushed a deep shade of red and self-disgust was very prominent in every tense line of her face and body.

"Critter..." I whispered.

Scrubbing her eyes, she shook her head, refusing my attempt at comfort.

Her face similarly flushed, Pony embraced the weeping Critter, and looked at me over the top of her lover's bowed head. "All the sudden, we heard this...this...roar. Like some kinda wild animal or something. Scared the shit outta me. Next thing I know, I'm flying backwards. Almost fell into the damn canal."

"What happened?" Those words seemed the extent of my vocabulary of late.

"Ice did," Pony replied. "Everything that we couldn't do, she did." Her voice was soft, reverent almost. "Somehow, she got some of the water outta you, then she started doing CPR, pounding on your chest and breathing into your mouth. She was like a demon, almost. Totally possessed."

Critter pulled slightly away from Pony and turned her face toward mine, her eyes bright with awe. "We...we tried to help, but she wouldn't let any of us near you. Just kept doing CPR and screaming at you not to leave her. It seemed like it went on like that for...god!...hours. She just kept screaming. Kept telling you you couldn't leave her. That it wasn't your time to go. That you were strong. That you could fight it." At that, she broke down into sobs that matched my own. "She begged you not to go."

Pony wrapped Critter in an embrace again, unmindful of her own tears. "It was taking too long," she whispered. "Too long. I...tried to pull her away. It seemed fruitless...too late. But she wouldn't listen. She wouldn't...." Her hand went up, unconsciously, to brush against a swollen, bruising area just below her right eye.

"Did she...?"

Pony hung her head. "I deserved it."

"Pony!"

Her chin raised and she met my eyes again, her own burning with a strange intensity. "I deserved it, Angel. I gave up. *She* never did."

"She believed in you," Critter added, her body still wracked with sobs. "Even when the rest of us had given up, she still believed."

Closing my eyes for a very long moment, I gingerly moved

my head, ignoring its outraged screaming, and wormed an arm free of my lover's desperate grip. Reaching up, I trailed my fingers across her icy cheek until I could cup her chin and turn her head toward my own. "Ice," I whispered, willing her eyes to open.

Her face was a tragedy's mask, set in harsh lines of grief. Her eyes and jaw were tightly clenched. Her nostrils flared as her breath came in quick pants.

"Ice," I whispered again, stroking her jaw. "Look at me. Please."

I continued my gentle stroking, loving her as best I could and willing her to feel that through the bond we shared. "Please, sweetheart. Please open your eyes."

Whether it was the tone of my voice or the realization that I was never going to give up until she did as I asked, her lashes finally fluttered open to reveal the deep, stormy blue of her eyes.

There was such a tumultuous wash of emotion in those beautiful eyes, but I could read each one as if it stood out as a beacon for my gaze alone.

Grief.

Pain.

Anguish.

Anger.

Self-loathing.

Fear.

And, swirling through all the negative, dark emotions, trapped like a ship battered by a winter storm, was the one thing that I needed to see, more than anything else in this world.

Love.

"Thank you," I said, meaning it from the bottom of my soul and beyond. Though it hurt to smile, I did, so filled with love was I for this woman who'd given everything to save my life, and never gave up.

Ever.

With a mystic's sight, I could see how trapped she felt; torn between holding me tightly and pulling away, thinking herself undeserving of my gratitude and love.

With a strength I didn't know I possessed, I drew my fingers along the base of her skull and pulled her head down even as I raised my own, trying not to wince as fresh pain flared through my head with the motion.

Our lips tangled, and at first, hers were as cold and unyielding as a marble statue. But, just as she never gave up on me, I wasn't about to let her hide away in whatever dark hell she'd built for herself.

As I'm sure you've noticed by now, I'm nothing if not persistent. I kept to my task with a single-minded devotion until finally, after eons had truly passed, I felt her begin to respond. Slowly, tentatively at first, to be sure, but within moments, it was as if I'd released a lion from its cage, all ferocious passion and primal need.

She built an inferno effortlessly within me as my body surged to renewed life with a passion and an intensity that matched her own, need for need, want for want.

There was nothing gentle about this fierce reclaiming of our souls. Nothing tender. Nothing soft or soothing. It was as if we both knew, by some strange metaphysical, karmic fusion, that neither of us could handle that right now.

No, the kiss we shared mingled our anger and our fear, our pain and our loss, our anguish and our love, all melded into a ball of white-hot intensity which flared far brighter and far hotter than any sun in any galaxy you'd care to name.

And when it was over, we were both left bruised and panting, hearts pounding and heads spinning, and locked together more tightly than ever before.

We were home.

The sounds of sirens, still far off but getting closer, served to break the spell. Pony's apologetic face slipped into my field of vision. "We...um...should start thinking about getting outta here."

It was an amazing thing, I mused, being held in Ice's arms as she methodically erected her defensive walls one by one. It was almost like watching a rose bloom, but in reverse, the petals closing in protectively to shield the soft heart inside. As I watched, her eyes turned from the stormy, turbulent blue of grief to a flat, steel gray of resolve, a color that perfectly matched the sky above.

As she prepared herself to stand, with me still firmly gathered in her arms, I noticed for the first time the cuts and scratches scattered liberally over the naked areas of her skin, including the deep one right at her hairline which was dripping a slow, thick trail of blood down the side of her face.

I was about to say something, but the look in her eyes warned against it, so instead I concentrated on losing my invalid status. "I...can stand." *I think.*

The briefest twitch of a raven brow, and then I felt her grip around me loosen as she gently placed me back on my feet.

My knees, traitors that they are, promptly buckled under my weight. The asphalt and I would have once again become rather intimate acquaintances had not Ice's preternatural strength come to my rescue. Gathering me in her arms once again, she shot me a look that was all business and brooked no arguments on any subject I might care to bring up.

Realizing that there were far worse places in the world to be than in the sure grip of my lover's arms, I wisely decided against tempting Fate, and simply gave in to the inevitable, leaning my head against her chest in complete surrender.

The barest trace of a smirk ghosted across her face at my antics and we turned toward our sole remaining car with all due haste.

Rio finished tossing her bolt cutters and the registration tag from the demolished car into the trunk and then moved to open each door in turn as we approached. Critter helped settle Ice and myself in the back seat and then joined us as Pony, Nia, and Rio took up the bench seat in the front.

The sirens drew still nearer as Rio started the engine and managed to maneuver the large sedan around the tall tree that blocked all but the very edge of the oncoming lane of the highway. For a long, terrifying moment, I was sure we were going to take another trip into the canal, but Rio handled the car with the ease of a professional, and before I knew it, we were on our way back to Ice's safe-house.

"Angel, lie still! I need to get these wet clothes off of you!"

"I can't," I replied peevishly, scowling up at Critter as she tried to wrestle me to the mattress. "My chest hurts and it's hard to breathe if I lay down flat."

Sighing, Critter dragged a hand through her soaking golden hair. Then she grabbed the waistband of my jeans and tugged. "At least lift up so I can get these pants off of you, okay? Ice will kill me if she comes back and you're still dressed."

"Oh all right," I grumped, slapping her hands away and unbuttoning the jeans myself. As I struggled to pull the wet, clingy fabric off of legs which felt like lead, the effort suddenly became too much and I slumped back against the beat, exhausted beyond reckoning.

To her credit, and though I more than deserved it, she didn't smirk at me. Instead, her eyes were kind and compassionate as she removed the sodden clothing from my shivering body. As the last piece came free, Ice entered the room, arms laden with towels and a thick comforter, which she laid down on the bed. Her face was expressionless as she nodded to Critter, thanking her silently for helping me undress.

Nodding, Critter pointed to the large gash in Ice's hairline which bleeding sluggishly. "You need to get that looked at."

"Later," my lover replied. Picking up two of the towels, she approached my side of the bed and began drying me off, her touch clinical, yet gentle. Her piercing gaze examined every inch of my body, with the exception of my eyes, which were continually avoided, no matter how much I tried to catch her own.

Soon, I was perfectly dry and well on my way to being warm as well, as Ice carefully tucked me beneath the covers of our bed and covered me with the extra quilt she'd liberated from somewhere. While the silence between us during these mundane tasks should have been comforting, it was anything but. I itched to draw her out, but my tired mind came up blank.

"You...should get out of those wet clothes," I finally managed, my voice soft and hoarse.

With a brief incline of her head, indicating she'd at least heard me, she gathered the wet towels and turned away, her every movement under tight control as she left the room.

Sighing, I slumped back onto the three pillows Ice had placed behind my head and shoulders to prevent me from lying flat. Fighting against giving in to the overwhelming exhaustion, I tried to keep my eyes open. The stuccoed ceiling above stared down at me complacently, giving me no answers.

Sighing again, I rolled to my side, facing the door and coughing a little as my lungs evidently protested the change in position. Settling down some, I stared into the darkened hallway and willed the woman I loved to appear.

Please, Ice. Don't shut me out.

As if my thoughts had willed it so, Ice reentered the room, one towel wrapped about her lean hips while the other pushed through the inky mass of her thick hair, drying it. I found myself gasping in horror at the patchwork of deep black bruises that covered her chest and belly to disappear beneath the towel wrapped around her lower body.

Hearing my gasp, my lover froze and followed my gaze, looking down at her own body for a long moment before catching my eyes once again. "They'll heal," she said softly, resuming her hair-drying task with casual indifference.

The silence hung heavy and thick between us, a white elephant we both pretended not to notice.

Tossing the damp towel down on the bed, she crossed the room in easy strides and crouched over the neatly stacked pile of clothing, rummaging for something clean to wear.

Getting dressed was not something I wanted to have happen. Naked, her body easily telling the tale of the tragedy we'd both survived made her vulnerable in a way that I needed at that moment. To allow her to cover those marks would be tantamount to accepting that this would always lie between us, undiscussed and unfinished. Given the chance, I feared, it would grow and fester if left alone, and that wasn't something I was about to have happen. Not now. Not ever.

"Ice," I said, in the strongest voice I could manage.

Her broad back stiffened for a moment, reading my plea for exactly what it was.

For a long moment, her next action was a tossup. Would she give in and bare her soul as easily as her body? Or would she ignore me and gird both against revealing the pain in her heart.

I held my breath against the second possibility until spots swum before my eyes.

Relief washed through me in an almost painful wave as her hands finally came away from the pile and she came to her feet with an animal grace, which never failed to thrill me. She turned, eyes as shuttered and as guarded as I'd ever seen them.

Smiling wanly, I held out a hand to her, willing her with my heart alone to step forward and take it.

And, after a second which spanned eternity, she did, clasping her warm, strong fingers around my smaller ones in a tender embrace.

Quickly, I made room for her on my side of the bed and tugged her hand gently, my smile grown broader as she gave in and sat next to me on the bed. I looked up into that breathtakingly beautiful face, memorizing each and every feature for the millionth time since I'd first set eyes upon her, and holding that image closer to my heart than even the blood that ran through it.

"Thank you," I said finally, though my voice was strained

and cracked through with emotion. Tears welled up in my eyes and spilled unhindered down my cheeks.

Two simple words, yet they encompassed so much meaning.

Thank you for not running away.

Thank you for saving my life.

Thank you for not giving up on me.

Thank you for loving me.

My lover's eyes were shiny with their own tears as she looked down at me. Her hand reached out to cup my cheek, one strong thumb wiping away the wetness on my face. "I'm so sorry," she whispered.

Looking into those shattered blue eyes was like taking a knife to the heart.

"No," I whispered, watching as those brilliant eyes slid closed, liberating one solitary tear to roll down her cheek. "Don't say that, Ice. Don't ever say that. You fought for me. You brought me back. Don't *ever* be sorry for that! You *saved* me!"

Jaw tightening, her proud head bowed, every line in her body negating my words.

Struggling to a sitting position, I took Ice's hand from my cheek and clasped it between both of my own, holding it to my chest so she could feel the strong and steady beat of my heart. "Now you listen to me, Ice. What happened today was an accident. Nothing more, nothing less. It wasn't your fault, it wasn't my fault, it wasn't Rio's fault, it wasn't *anyone's* fault. Blaming yourself for it won't change that fact, and I think you know that."

"If I had sent you back over the border when I got you out of that jail, none of this would ever have happened," Ice replied after a long moment, her voice a low, determined growl.

"Maybe that's true, Ice," I replied. "But none of this would have happened either if I hadn't come over the border in the first place. Or if Rio hadn't taken us to that bar. Or if Nia hadn't started that fight. Or if she hadn't had the idea to come down here in the first place. Or any of a million other things that all conspired to put all of us at that place at that time." I clasped her hand tighter, not willing to let go. "Don't you see? Responsibility for our actions lies with all of us, Ice. You can't take that on your shoulders, as much as you sometimes seem to want to. You have to let us shoulder some of it, too. That's what being in a partnership is all about, and I don't know about you, but I kinda like to think we *are* partners. In every sense of the word."

I could tell she was listening. I could sense it in the minute lessening of the tight coil of her body. I could hear it in the ease of her breathing. I could feel it in the slowing of the rapid pulse beneath my thumb.

Bringing our joined hands up to my lips, I touched a tender kiss to her fingers. "What you did today, Ice, was nothing short of miraculous. The only person who doesn't see that, or won't accept it, is you."

Her head raised slowly as her eyes opened, pinning me with glittering silver. "I'm no hero, Angel."

I smiled. "You don't know how wrong you are, Ice. You're a hero to all those women out there. You're a hero to Pop and to Corinne, and to so many others. You're a hero to that little boy whose life you saved out on that frozen pond. And, most of all, you're my hero. You're the white knight who came riding over the hill when I most needed her. The person who taught me how to stand up for myself and how to fight to be all I can be. The person who believes in my dreams and encourages me to follow them. The person who loves me and allows me to love her in return. The person who would give her last breath to protect me, and who would give up her own life to save mine."

My smile broadened. "That, my love, is a hero. And that's what you are. To me, and to a whole bunch of people out there. I believe it. They believe it. All you need to do is believe it as well."

Her dark head shook slowly in negation. "I...don't think I can."

"Sure you can," I replied, grinning and nudging her gently. "That's why you have me around, remember? To point these things out to you."

That got the smile I was looking for, even if it was just a ghost of the one I really wanted to see. Reaching out, I wrapped my arms around her shoulders, ever mindful of the horrid bruising on her breasts and belly. Not caring in the least, she pulled me to her and buried her face in my hair. "I love you, Angel," she whispered. Her lips brushed against my ear, causing a shiver to run down my spine and back up again.

"I love you too, Ice. More and more each day."

Leaning back, I managed to lay both of us down on the bed with my lover's head pillowed against my breast. It was a wonderful feeling, getting to hold her like that, and I fell asleep with a smile on my face.

Chapter 7

Pneumonia came calling, as I knew it would, setting up residence in my chest, throat, and head. I don't remember much about those long days and longer nights, especially since I spent most of them viewing the world through a haze of fevered delirium. What I do remember is that every time I opened my eyes, Ice was there to cool my fever, ease my aches, calm my cough, and love me through it all.

I also remember my fever breaking fully for the final time, leaving me incredibly clear-headed and incredibly exhausted. I remember turning my head on a sweat-soaked pillow, and looking down to see one of Ice's hands clasped so tightly in my own that I'd wondered if I'd cut off her fingers' circulation with my obvious death-clutch. She'd been sitting in a chair pulled up to the bed, and her head was resting on the mattress next to my hip. Her deep, even breathing proclaimed her fast asleep.

Smiling slightly, and a little teary-eyed, I reached with my free hand and laid the most tender of touches to her dark, bowed head, relishing the feel of her thick, silky hair beneath my fingers. "I love you," I whispered on the smallest of breaths, pleased I could do so without coughing.

Her head snapped up quickly, her eyes fully awake and fully aware as they came to rest on my face. After a moment, those magnificent eyes warmed and softened, and my entire world became the look in them.

If the essence of love could be distilled into just one thing, it would be the color of her eyes when she looks at me that way.

"Hey," she said softly, her voice rough from sleep.

"Hey yourself," I replied, grinning as if my face would break. Reaching up, I tangled a lock of her hair around my finger.

"How do you feel?"

"I feel...good."

And it was true. Every word.

How could I have felt any differently, wrapped up as I was in her love for me?

"*You* don't look so good, though," I said, gently tugging the lock of hair I held.

A ghost of her cocky grin came over a too-pale face. "I'm fine."

"Nothing a year's worth of sleep wouldn't cure, huh?" I teased.

"Nah," she replied, gently grasping the hand that held her hair and kissing my fingers before pulling away and standing. "Let me go get some dry sheets so you're not laying in a pool."

I nodded, accepting her need for some distance. An exhausted Ice was a brittle Ice, and I knew I'd probably gone one step too far in teasing her about her own state of health. Still, I had the feeling that once I was in a dry bed, I could convince her to lay down with me and rest. Especially if I told her it would help me rest better.

Which was, of course, only the absolute truth of the matter.

Scarcely a minute after Ice left, Critter entered, carrying a mug in her hands. When she saw me awake, she grinned and crossed the room quickly. "Welcome back, Angel! How do you feel?"

"Not bad," I allowed. "What day is it?"

"Saturday. You've been sick for a week."

I slumped back against the pillows, stunned. "A *week*?"

"Yup. You had us all pretty scared there for a while. Ice wanted to get you to a hospital back across the border, but you kept begging her not to." Putting the mug down on the bedside table, she sat next to me on the bed and rubbed my arm. "I think it took everything in her not to just pack up and leave here, but you can be pretty persuasive when you want to be."

"Was I really that bad?" I asked, cringing inwardly.

She tilted her head to the side, pondering. "Well...you made some very good points, Angel. If Ice gave up on her deal with the Feds, the two of you would never have any peace."

I felt my eyes widen as I stared at her. "I said that?"

"Yup."

"Ice told me that. Not so long ago. When *I* was the one arguing that we should just leave."

She smiled. "Guess you listened, huh?"

"Guess so." I peeked up at her through my lashes. "Was she angry with me?"

Critter snorted. "Are you nuts? God, Angel, she was so worked up with worry over you, it was all any of us could to do just get her to drink something. Forget about eating or sleeping."

My chagrin must have shown clearly on my face, because she reached out and cupped my cheek. "It's her way, Angel. You know that. You're the most important thing in her life, and she wouldn't have it any other way."

I nodded, accepting the truth in her words. The only thing, which made it better, was that Ice meant as much to me and she knew it.

"Besides, you're better now, so things should get back to normal around here." She paused. "Or...as normal as things ever are with you guys."

Laughing, I poked her in the thigh for her impertinence. Then I sobered, as a new thought occurred to me. "If it's been a week, what happened with Cavallo? We were so close...."

"Relax," Critter soothed. "We still are. Rio and Pony have been keeping an eye on him. He's not going anywhere anytime soon." She shifted a little on the bed, crossing her legs. "A few days ago, Rio took Nia over to that friend of hers who used to work at the house Cavallo's saying in. Now we've got the whole layout, inside and out. So when it comes time to do the deed," she grinned, "we're ready."

Ice returned then, her arms filled with fresh linens.

"Let me help," Critter said, jumping up from her perch next to me and grabbing the bottom sheet from the stack. "No, you just stay there," she said as I struggled to get up. "We're pros at this by now. We'll be done in a jiffy."

Giving in to the inevitable, I laid my tired body back down and accepted my passive role in the whole thing. In short order, they were done and I was left feeling much better for their efforts. The tea Critter had brought for Ice was by that time cold, and after she'd gone off to get a refill, I looked over at my lover, on her feet through sheer, brute strength of will. I flipped back the sheets and patted the bed. "It's been a week since I've remembered feeling you close to me. I sure could use some of that now."

I knew by the look in her eyes that she knew I had ulterior motives, but I think she also knew my words for truth. I simply needed to feel her against me, like I needed air in my lungs and blood in my veins.

And, smiling at me slightly, she acquiesced and I found myself wrapped up in the only world in which I wanted to live.

Forever.

The next several days were devoted to recovering my lost strength, and trying to get Ice to keep still long enough to do something about the deep, dark circles that had taken up semi-permanent residence beneath her eyes.

The second task consumed a great deal more energy than the first, but was, for me, much more rewarding. I was actually quite proud of myself for accomplishing the gargantuan job of getting her to relax in bed with me for seven hours straight two nights in a row. Of course, the hours before and after the "relaxation" period were anything *but* relaxing, but heck, making love for hours on end does help get a body back into shape, right?

One day, while Ice was off with Rio scouting out Cavallo's place, I made myself a little nook in what passed for a front yard of the hovel we were living in and sat outside, letting the gentle breeze and warming sun do its magic on my body. Coming outside with a small sack in her hand and a smile on her face, Critter plopped down beside me on my blanket. "How ya feelin'?"

"Almost back to my old self, I think."

"Good to hear. You had us worried there for awhile."

"So you've said. I think I'm over the worst of it, though. It doesn't hurt anymore when I breathe, and hey! I even managed a run in the desert with Ice! Well, not really a run. More like a slow, groaning jog, but it's progress, right?"

Critter grinned. "Yup." She tossed the small, cloth sack into my lap. "I don't know if you've forgotten about this, but you gave it to me the other day. I found it when I was washing some clothes."

Curiously, I lifted the package, noting its weight was heavy for its size, and opened it. Reaching inside, my fingers brushed against something cool and solid, and when I pulled the object out, I saw it was the bracelet I'd been given the day of the accident. I looked upon it with awe. If anything, it was even more beautiful than it was the first time I'd seen it.

"Thank you, Critter," I breathed. "I thought it was lost forever. I forgot I gave it to you. I was gonna give it to Ice for...shit!"

"Shit?" Critter asked, laughing. "Doesn't sound like a very fair trade, if you ask me. Even for Ice's."

I spared her a mock glare. "I mean I was going to give it to her for Christmas. But if I've been sick for a week, Christmas is already over, isn't it?"

"'Fraid so," my friend replied, sobering. "It was last Wednesday."

"Damn." I could feel my shoulders slump under the weight of the unhappy news. Christmas at the Moore household was pretty much a grab bag from year to year. I had vowed while still a child that when I grew up, every single Christmas would be as special as it was possible for me to make it. And though I knew enough not to blame myself for being out of commission this particular Christmas, there was still a sadness there because a day I held so dear in my heard passed by without my knowledge.

Critter laid a warm hand on my shoulder. "It's alright, Angel. None of us was really in the mood to celebrate anyway. And we pretty much figured that Ice's heroics during that accident and your heroics in battling death and coming back to us pretty much beat any store-bought gift all to hell anyway." Leaning over, she gathered me into a soft embrace. "We love you, Angel, and we know you love us. Isn't that pretty much what Christmas is all about?"

After a long moment, I nodded against her chest, acknowledging the truth in her words to me.

Pulling back slightly, she grinned. "There ya go, then. So...are ya gonna give it to her?"

"Yeah, I think so. Maybe when she gets back."

"Which would be right about now. I think that's their car trailing all that dust down there." Grinning and clapping me on the back, she stood up. "I'll leave you two lovebirds alone.

Don't do anything I wouldn't."

"As soon as you let me know what that might be," I replied with a cheeky smile, "I'll be sure and not do it."

A lurid wink later, I was on my own once again.

Replacing the bracelet back in its little cloth bag, I laid it to the side and stretched my legs out, enjoying the pull of muscle in my thighs and calves and the warmth of sunlight on my skin.

She wasn't noisy. She never is. But I knew the second she came close. Call it a third eye, or some sixth sense. Call it crazy, or karma, or pheromones, if you want.

I'll just call it love and leave it at that.

Though my eyes were closed to the brilliance of the sun, I still followed her movements easily, my mind playing a pleasing mental picture of a long, rangy body as it dropped to the ground beside me with incommunicable fluid grace. I pictured her eyes, darkened with concern, and the little furrow between her brows and the tense set of her mouth that spoke of the same.

Opening my eyes to that exact picture, I found myself smiling with the joy of knowing her so well. "Hey there."

"Hey yourself," she returned, her eyes intent. "You alright?"

Leaning over, I stole a kiss from the softest lips in the world and then sat back, a smug grin on my face. "Just perfect, thanks."

Her eyes brightened as a smile tugged at one corner of her mouth. "Glad to hear it."

"Me too." I shifted a little so that I was facing her. "So, is Cavallo still behaving himself?"

"Seems to be. I want to get this wrapped up soon, though. He's gotten too lucky too often. It's about time he paid the piper." That shark-like grin flickered briefly across her face before disappearing once again into whatever darkness housed it.

Nodding, I picked up the sack from beside my leg and fumbled with it a bit. "I'm...um...sorry I missed Christmas."

"You didn't miss it. You just don't remember it."

I nudged her. "Same difference, smart aleck."

"Not to me, it isn't."

My eyes widened as I realized what she meant. "Oh. I'm...."

One long finger covered my lips. "Don't. Don't be sorry. No one takes any blame, remember?"

As much as I hated getting shot in the foot with my own

words, I couldn't help but admit she was right. If I forbid her to feel guilt, I couldn't either. Fair was, after all, fair. Even if I didn't like it.

"Ok, ok. I'm not sorry for not remembering Christmas. But I am sorry for not being able to give you this." I held the bag out to her. "I'd gotten it on the day of the accident. Critter kept it for me. I'd like you to have it."

She took the bag from me and opened the ties. Reaching in, she pulled out the bracelet and held it so that the sun played across the shining silver. I watched her throat move as she swallowed. "It's beautiful," she whispered, tracing the intricate engraving with the very tip of her index finger.

"A Native American silversmith made it. He said he saw the scene in a vision and knew I was the one to give the piece to. I don't know how much I believe in his mysticism, but I do know that it has 'you' written all over it. I know you're not much for wearing jewelry, and you don't have to wear this either, if you don't want to, but...oh!"

My ramblings were cut short in the sweetest of ways as my lover's lips covered my own in a tender, yet fiery, kiss of thanks.

After she pulled away, I watched through blurred eyes as she slipped the bracelet onto her wrist, adjusting it so that the cuff fit perfectly, the silver a breathtaking contrast to the bronze of her skin. "Thank you," she said simply, and her expression let me know just how deeply that expression went into her heart.

Suddenly shy with the intensity of her emotions, I felt myself color, and I smiled back, a little. "You're welcome."

"I have something for you, too," she said finally, reaching into the pack she wore at her waist. "I made it quite some time ago, but never got the chance to give it to you. It's something I thought of after I'd been shot this last time."

Pulling out a flannel-wrapped bundle, she handed it to me, her own eyes just a little shy, as they often were when giving me a gift. Especially one she had made with her own hands. Which were, of course, the best gifts I've ever received.

I opened the wrapping, then froze, tears immediately sparking my eyes as I looked down at the gift she'd so expertly made for me.

It was a wooden figurine, a little smaller than the palm of my hand, but heavy, and carved with exquisite attention to detail.

It was a carving of the two of us, together.

I was the figure behind, on my knees, angel's wings arched forward in an all-encompassing embrace of Ice, who was half-laying in my lap, her head back against my breast, her eyes closed, and the most beautiful expression of peace I'd ever seen on her face.

"You're my Angel," she whispered, raising a hand and tenderly drying the tears from my cheeks. "You always say that I'm the strong one, but this is what I see when I close my eyes at night. I love you, my Angel. And I always will. Merry Christmas."

Holding the precious figure against my heart, I once again closed the space between us and kissed her with all the love in my soul.

If I live to be a million, I'll never understand the magic she uses to make the impossible happen. To make me fall even more in love with her than I was the second before.

And I hope I never do.

Desert nights can be blacker than any other. Or so I've found during my relatively short time on this earth of ours. Even with a billion stars sparkling coldly overhead and a huge half-moon hanging low.

They can be quieter, too. Quiet enough so that the blood rushing through your ears with every beat of your heart is the only sound you hear. Except, perhaps, for your breathing coming harsh and fast and tasting almost electric as it rushes in and out of your mouth and nose.

And if you're scared, so scared that every second is a toss-up between vomiting and fainting, well, then the nights are blacker and quieter than ever.

And I was scared.

So scared that I felt a weird sense of detachment. The kind you feel when fever is sitting hot and heavy in your brain.

And yet at the same time, I felt totally grounded. My eyes, wide and dry and aching, darted everywhere at once, taking everything in, over and over, as if they'd never get the chance to prove their worth again. My body was wound tight, muscles trembling with the unconscious effort to keep still and silent. My heart thundered painfully in my ears, and the scent of my panic curled up around me, hot and sour like three-day-old summer sweat.

When a hand brushed against my back, I nearly jumped out of my skin. Only that same hand firmly gripping my upper arm kept me from making a mad, screaming dash back down the steep hill to the safety of the cars that waited below.

"It's only me," Critter's voice whispered mere inches from my ear. "How are you doing?"

Frozen shut, my jaw refused my summons to move. I couldn't even turn my head to look at her. All I could do was stare ahead into the blackness.

The pressure of her hand changed from a stern grip to a warm clasp. "It's alright. I'm scared, too."

Somehow, the tone of her voice gave my body the permission it needed to shake off—at least temporarily—the icy grip terror had over me. I was able to turn my head, and I could tell, just by looking, that she was speaking the truth. Her eyes were as wide as mine, and the area just above her upper lip shimmered with sweat, even though the night was anything but warm. She smiled at me a little. That sickly kind of smile a seasick pleasure cruiser gets just before he goes to the railing to evacuate his dinner into the ocean.

"I'm glad to know I'm not the only one," I finally managed to whisper.

"Not by a long shot. And I've *done* this kind of thing before."

I looked at her.

She blushed. "Well, not *exactly* this kind of thing, but I did break into a lot of places where I wasn't welcome back when I was younger."

"Oh. Yeah." Though it might sound strange, I'd managed to forget that most of my friends had criminal pasts. "How did you deal with the fear?"

"Alcohol," she replied with brutal honesty. "I'd get blind drunk. It was the only way I could go through with half the jobs I did. They call it 'liquid courage' for a reason, ya know."

"Wish I had some of that kind of courage about now."

"No you don't," she said, squeezing my arm. "You've got more courage in your little finger than you could ever get out of a fifth of whiskey, Angel. Even though you're scared, you're here. And that takes a lot of guts."

"You're here too, Critter."

That threw her off for a second, and she blinked at me.

Then a slow smile creased her face. "Yeah, I guess I am." Then she straightened and released my arm, touching me briefly on the shoulder. "I'll talk with you in a bit."

Then she left me staring after her in confusion as she blended back into the darkness.

Only until I felt another presence next to me.

But this time, I didn't flinch.

Ice crouched down before me, dressed all in black from the tip of her soft-soled boots to the top of the ski mask, which covered her head and face. Only her vibrant eyes, glittering silver, posed a counterpoint to the monochrome. And even in them there was a darkness swirling that I could feel as well as see.

"You doin' ok?" she asked, voice low and only slightly muffled behind the knit material of the mask. A gloved hand reached out and cupped my cheek and her eyes warmed in concern.

Instead of answering her question right out, I leaned into her palm and took that dark, exciting, dangerous scent of leather deep into my senses. Paradoxically, perhaps, that had a calming effect on me.

I looked at her, examined her, asked her, silently, the same question she asked me.

Was she doing ok?

The answer was an easy one.

She was more than ok. Like a prize thoroughbred prancing at the gate, she was ready.

It had been a week since I'd finally gotten out from under the sickly weight of my bout with pneumonia, and in that week, we had practiced, practiced, practiced for this very thing. Practiced until I could go over every move every one of us was supposed to make in my sleep.

Which I did. Often.

And here we were, at this proverbial "D-day," and if all I could think of was running away, all she could think of was running ahead.

I could see it easily in the dark sparkle of her eyes, in the loose and easy set of her shoulders, in the coiling aura of danger and intensity which swirled around her like a living thing. Not only was she ready. She was able. And willing.

She was born for this, I thought, startling myself with my insight.

Perhaps not for this very thing, no. But so close to it that the syntax made very little difference. "Close enough for jazz," my father might have said.

Ice is a hunter. Pure and simple.

And this time, Cavallo was the prey.

To my great surprise, I found myself sparing a brief second to feel a spark of pity for the man who had no idea who, or what, was coming for him.

That spark extinguished itself quickly beneath the weight of the memories of what that man had done to Ice, to me, to us.

Part of me was sad that she was only going in there to take him out alive. Part of me would have gleefully watched her hold him down as I pulled the trigger of a gun I didn't own.

A very small part, perhaps, but I won't deny it was there. If ever a bastard had it coming to him, Cavallo was that bastard.

"I'm doing ok," I answered finally as her eyes started to show a deeper concern. "A little nervous, but basically alright."

The way those same eyes subtly changed their shape told me she was smiling beneath her mask. "You'll do fine."

"I wish I had your confidence."

She shifted a little, her expression going a bit hard. "Be glad that you don't. Confidence in this type of thing is a wasted art. You're not a murderer, Angel. Never wish for that kind of surety."

Knowing I'd well and truly blown the moment, I reached up and captured her hand before she could pull it away. "Ice, even if you'd never killed so much as a spider in your entire life, you would still have confidence in your ability to do this. It's as much a part of you as the color of your eyes or the pitch of your voice. It was something you were born with, not something you were made into."

"Ya think so, huh?"

I smiled as I felt her body relax. "I know so."

A soft rustling, and Pony squatted down next to us, her expression apologetic. "I thought you'd wanna know. They just changed the guards."

Ice nodded. "Alright. Round the others up. It's showtime."

And with that, my nervousness came back as if it had never left. "Ice...."

Coming to her feet, she brought me easily up with her and then steadied me as my suddenly trembling legs threatened all-out rebellion. A moment later, Pony, Critter, and Rio crowded around us, awaiting last minute instructions. Waiting in the car below, Nia was the only one absent.

For a brief second, I felt a flash of blinding hatred for her, sitting so safely while the rest of us ran down to danger. I pushed that counterproductive emotion down with a savagery Ice would have been surprised to see, had she known of its existence.

"Is everyone sure on what they have to do?"

Nods all around from women with somber, pale faces. The fear was there, palpable, like a sixth member of our group. But there was also something else sharing space with us. A keen sense of anticipation which dulled the fear's sharp edges just enough to prevent panic.

Pale eyes pinned each one of us in place for a long, silent moment, and all around me, spines stiffened, jaws firmed, and shoulders squared.

Ice nodded. "Let's go."

Then she disappeared over the breast of the hill while we, for now, stood watch.

As soon as Ice disappeared into the darkness, Critter drew up the sleeve of her long black coat and illuminated the dial of her watch. The soft light bathed her face in an eerie green glow as she watched the seconds scroll rapidly by.

"She's over the wall," Pony whispered from her position half-behind a thick pine. She was staring through a night-scope attached to her rifle and tracking my lover's every move, together with the movements of the guards who patrolled the grounds.

Though the plan was to leave everyone alive, if perhaps a little worse for wear, that was only if things went according to schedule. One hint that something was going badly and that rifle on Pony's shoulder would be doing a great deal more damage than its current incarnation as a simple spying tool.

"Behind the house now."

My sigh of relief was an audible one. She was now out of sight of any guards, at least temporarily, and only an alarm system and a locked door stood between her and gaining entry into the house.

"Fifty seconds," Critter remarked, checking her chronometer. Ice had requested one full minute before we put phase two of the plan into effect.

As Critter watched the changing numbers on her watch, I stared out over the darkened compound. My heart hammered triple time in my ears, so loudly that I felt as if I'd been somehow transported into the very middle of a Jamaican steel drum competition. My head and stomach swam in queasy syncopation, and the spit in my mouth was sour and hot.

"Twenty seconds."

"Ten."

"Now."

Pony relaxed her grip on the rifle and then shouldered it as she turned to look at Critter and myself. "You guys ready?"

"As we'll ever be," Critter replied for the both of us.

"Alright then. Let's do it."

With a shuddering breath, I forced myself to move and prayed I wouldn't break my neck while trying to navigate my way down the mountain wearing the ridiculous choice of footwear I was. "Come fuck me's", Pony had called them, right before her instep was nearly speared by the heel of one such shoe. The pejoratives got a great deal less pleasant after that.

As if reading my mind, Rio came to stand beside me and offered one well-muscled arm. Smiling up at her, I took the assistance gratefully, and almost laughed out loud as her eyes darted shyly away from my own.

Within moments, we were at the bottom, and Critter and I held our places while Rio and Pony sidled up to the stone wall and eased themselves into position very near the wrought-iron gate.

When Pony gave us the thumbs up, I looked to Critter, who nodded. Together, we removed our long coats and dropped them down to the desert floor.

"God, I feel like a two-dollar whore in this getup," Critter grumped as she painfully adjusted the barely-there top that was cinched so tight across her chest that she could have rested her chin on her breasts if she'd had a mind to. "Could I look any cheaper?"

"Yeah, you could look like me." My face was sweating through enough makeup to send Revlon's stock soaring to stratospheric heights. My clothes, what there were of them, were three sizes too small, and if my breasts were pushed up any higher, I could use them for a pair of fleshy earmuffs.

"Yeah, well if there are any pornographers around, we just might get that one big break we've been looking our whole lives for," Critter joked as she finished adjusting the seam of her stockings. "Now, for the finishing touch." From the sack at her feet, she withdrew a tall bottle of liquor and twisted open the cap. "Just what the doctor ordered."

"But I thought...."

"Not for courage, dear. For veracity. We can't just look the part. We've gotta smell it, too."

"Huh?"

"Watch the Mistress in action."

Tilting her head back, she took a long swallow of liquor and then did an all-over body shiver as she swallowed. "Ahh. That hit the spot. Here, have a belt."

"No thanks," I replied, waving the bottle away, and watching as Pony gave us the "hurry up" sign. "C'mon, we've got to get moving."

"Alright. Just let me...there. *Eau de Cuervo.* What all the trollops in the low-rent district are wearing this year."

"Hey! That stings!" Some of the flying droplets had landed too close to my eyes for comfort's sake, and I felt myself tearing up from the fumes.

"Quit being a baby and let's get a move on. Time's a'wasting."

"Great," I muttered as she slipped an arm through mine and almost pulled me right out of my cheaply made shoes. "You really *are* drunk."

"Nah, just acting the part. C'mon."

One hell of an acting job, Critter, I thought to myself as she yanked her arm away from mine and instead slung it over my shoulder, forcing me to bear most of her weight as she swayed against me. Together, we tottered somewhat unsteadily toward the gate, taking care to make as much bumbling noise as possible so as to announce our presence to anyone who might be listening in.

"Hey Candie, look! There's a light on in there. Our prayers have been answered!"

"Prayers? What prayers?" Critter snorted. "Only prayer I got right now ish for another bottle. This n's ammost empty. Helloooo in there! Anybody home?" Striding up to the gate, she wrapped one hand around the bars and shook, giggling madly all the while. "C'mon, open up! Ish cold out here."

"Shhh," I whispered overloud. "You'll wake up the whole neighborhood."

"I *wanna* wake 'em up! I need more booze, dammit! C'mon, open up!"

Though the racket we were making should have caused an entire army to come down upon our heads, the darkened area beyond the gate remained resolutely silent and still.

"Mebbe they don speak English," I said, giggling a little.

"Course they do! Everybody does! Hey, in there! Como...como...como whatever. Open up, dammit!"

"C'mon, Candie," I said, tugging Critter's arm and beginning to feel a little nervous. "Nobody's home."

"Bullshit," Critter replied, shaking me off. "Course they are. I can see people movin' in there. Yoo hoo! Boys! Open up and I'll show ya why they call me Caaandie."

The brilliant beam of a flashlight suddenly pierced through the darkness, blinding me for one heart-stopping second. "Beat it," came a menacing and heavily accented voice from behind the gate.

"Please, sir," I said, blinking rapidly and trying to see through the afterimages imprinted on my stinging retinas. "It's cold out here and our car broke down a mile or so back. Could we use your phone?"

"I said beat it. We don't got no phones here."

"Bullshit," Critter said, pressing her face against the bars. "Places like this got phones in the *bathrooms*. Jes let us in, willya? Jes a quick phone call and we're gone. Unless ya wan' us ta stick around for a little while and show you how grateful we are." Her purring voice trailed off suggestively. "Big strong man like you must get lonely out here in the middle of nowhere, huh?"

"Heh. Heh. You'll have to excuse my friend here. She's a little tipsy."

"I ain't tipsy. I'm drunk. And horny. C'mon, mister, help a gal out, won't ya? I'll make it worth your while." And with that, she upended the bottle and...well...what she did next to that bottle is something they named a movie after.

If we'd have been anywhere else, I might have been tempted to ask just how she'd come by that particular talent. Especially without triggering her gag reflex.

On second thought, perhaps it's better that I don't know.

I heard some shuffling from the darkness behind the gate, then the low murmur of at least two male voices speaking rapid Spanish. A moment later, keys rattled in the lock, and the gate swung slowly open.

The flashlight was turned off and the face of one of the men came in out of the gloom. "Come on in, ladies. I think we might be able to help you both."

Before we could step through, Rio darted between us. A few muffled thumps later, and two unconscious guards were being dragged outside the gate.

Pony hogtied and gagged them quickly, then slipped her arm through mine while Rio did the same for Critter. In the darkness, they could easily pass for the men they'd just disabled, being of the same height and build. Just two lonely guards escorting a pair of willing women into the compound for an hour or so of fun and debauchery.

"The garage is off to the left," Rio whispered. "You guys head over there while I take care of the other two. I'll come back when I'm done."

Pony grabbed my arm as Rio melted back into the darkness, and the three of us headed in the indicated direction, our pace no quicker than a somewhat leisurely stroll, despite the tension.

By the blueprints we'd been given, I knew the garage was huge and could house each of Cavallo's five cars with room to spare. It was also locked, but the muted tinkle of lock-picks being tossed to Critter let me know that that particular situation would be remedied rather quickly and without much of a fuss.

Sure enough, very little time passed before the click of a lock giving way sounded in the silence of the night. The door opened quietly, and our senses were assailed by the scents of motor oil and rubber. They were smells I was well used to, and having them there gave me a strange sense of comfort in an otherwise terrifying situation.

Once we were inside, Pony closed the door and removed a flashlight from the belt at her hip. Soon, the garage was bathed in a faint, white glow.

I looked into the shadows of the far end of the garage, then stopped, my heart freezing in my throat. "Pony? Shine the light down that way, will you?"

"Why?"

"Just do it, please."

Penetrating the shadows, the beam confirmed my suspicions. A black oil stain marred the pristine white of the garage floor like a spot of decay on an otherwise healthy tooth. "One of the cars is gone."

"Shit."

"What are we gonna do now?" Critter asked from her place

on my right.

"Nothing much we can do," Pony replied, sweeping the flashlight's beam over the remaining four cars. "Except to get on with the plan."

"What if they come back?"

"We'll burn that bridge when we're crossing it. Let's just get this over with. Critter, start with this car here. Bust in and open the hood. Angel and I'll take it from there."

Just as Critter began to jimmy the first lock, the garage door opened. The only thing that kept me from screaming in fright was Pony's hand clamped over my mouth.

"All clear." Rio's voice floated in from the darkness beyond.

"Thanks," Pony replied.

"Everything ok in here?"

"One of the cars is missing."

"Shit. Should we do anything about it?"

"Just stick with the plan. Get outta here. We'll meet you at the rendezvous point."

"You sure?"

"Yeah, I'm sure. Now go."

"Alright. Good luck."

"You too."

After the door closed, Pony released her grip on me just as Critter made her way into the first of the cars and popped the hood from the inside. Turning away from my friend, I made my way over to the exposed engine and began my part of this stage of the plan.

Disabling cars is a quick, easy, and mostly mindless task. So much so, in fact, that I made two of them completely undrivable while Pony was still working on her first. Walking over, I pushed my friend out of the way and quickly finished her task as she looked on with something akin to awe on her face.

"Pretty handy around an engine," she said finally.

"I should be. I've helped Ice often enough." Pulling the last part free, I handed it to Pony, who stuffed it in a sack with the rest of the pieces. "What now?" The fourth car would be left intact for our getaway, since Rio had left with ours.

"We wait."

"Time?" I asked Critter, who was leaning against the only working vehicle of the lot.

"Five minutes."

"Alright. I'm gonna keep watch. You guys be ready."

Without waiting for an answer, I headed for the door and opened it up a crack.

The house and the grounds surrounding it were silent as a graveyard. It was killing me, not knowing what was going on inside, and I gave vent to my frustration by repeatedly pounding my thigh with a clenched fist, heedless of the small amount of pain my actions brought me.

According to the almighty plan—set in stone as if the burning bush itself had delivered it unto us—we were to give Ice ten minutes total to carry out her part, then, in her own words, "get the fuck out of Mexico, with or without me."

I think I surprised her when I didn't immediately protest.

I wonder if she realized that I didn't agree to it either.

Knowing Ice, she probably did.

"Damn you, Ice," I whispered as each second took an hour, and each minute took a century. "Where are you?"

In my hyperaware state, I easily tracked Pony's movements by hearing alone as she left her place by Critter's side and walked slowly toward my position. I whirled on her just as she was about to put a hand on my shoulder. "No," I whispered savagely, "no way. You and Critter can leave if you want. Take the car. I'll fix one of the others. But I'm not going anywhere without Ice so don't even bother opening your mouth, Pony."

Hands upraised in a gesture of placation, my friend took a careful step back. "I...wasn't gonna ask you to leave, Angel," she assured me, her voice even. "I was just gonna ask what you thought we should do now."

Though I should have apologized, I'm afraid I didn't have it within me to do so at that moment in time. As each second passed, I became more and more certain that something had gone horribly wrong. "I don't know about you, but I know exactly what I'm gonna do."

So saying, I stepped forward and grabbed Pony's rifle, which was leaning against the wall nearest the door. "I'm gonna find Ice, and so help me God, nobody better stand in my way."

Like some deranged GI storming a French beach half a century too late, I hefted the rifle and marched off into the night, my eyes staring nowhere save straight ahead at the door centered firmly in my sights.

I could hear Pony's half-whispered epithet behind me and her determined footsteps as she struggled to match my determined stride. "Don't try to stop me, Pony. I'm warning you."

"Wouldn't dream of it, Angel," she grunted. "Just figured I'd give you a hand."

When we got about halfway between the garage and the house, the door opened wide. The interior light silhouetted a tall figure with what looked to be a large sack slung over one shoulder like some hellish underground film's version of Santa Claus.

I came to an abrupt halt, and Pony slammed into me from behind, sending both of us forward for several more steps until I dug my heels in and stopped us both again. If it were possible for hearts to leap for joy, mine did just that.

"That's Ice!"

"How do you know?" she asked, peering over my shoulder.

I spared a brief second to give her a pointed look, which caused a sheepish grin to come to her face.

"Oh. Yeah. Forget I asked."

"Go tell Critter to get the car out here."

"Will do."

As Pony left, I started forward again, this time breaking into a flat-out run. "Ice!"

"Hey, Angel," she replied, her voice and manner as casual as if I'd just met up with her coming out of the grocery store. "Just taking out the trash." She paused. "Nice gun."

I blushed. "Yeah, well, you were supposed to be out of there three minutes ago."

She shrugged her unencumbered shoulder. "One of the guys had a little problem with my bedtime story. He's sleeping like a baby now, though."

I rolled my eyes and shook my head. "Any other problems?"

"Piece of cake. You?"

"Not really. Except one of the cars is missing."

"I figured. There were three fewer guards than I expected inside."

Further conversation was cut off by the arrival of Critter, Pony, and our getaway car.

"Pop the trunk," Ice ordered.

Walking to the rear of the car, I pulled open the compartment and stood aside as Ice dumped Cavallo inside. The small light illuminated his face, where a bloody nose and a rapidly swelling jaw bore mute testament to his meeting with my lover. He was deeply unconscious, though still breathing, and his hands were bound tightly behind him. After a moment, I looked up. "I didn't know you brought handcuffs with you."

Ice smirked. "I didn't."

"Kinky bastard, isn't he?"

As Ice slammed the trunk closed, the courtyard was suddenly lit by the twin beams of approaching headlights.

Grabbing my arm at the elbow, Ice opened the rear driver's side door and pushed me in, then followed quickly. "Go," she ordered Pony, who'd replaced a slightly drunk Critter behind the wheel. "Drive out nice and easy if you can. If they follow us, floor it."

"I'm there."

"You can't think they're just going to let us go by," I said, disbelief plain in my voice.

"Stranger things have happened. But I doubt it."

Three men got out of the car after it had pulled through the gate. Three heads swiveled as we passed by. I resisted the urge to wave. Shouting "we've got your boss in the trunk, suckers!" was out as well, though I must admit I was sorely tempted. Giddiness does that to me, and having Ice alive and whole made me very giddy indeed.

"I don't fucking believe it," Pony muttered as we left through the gate and headed down the dark road without any signs of pursuit. "They just gonna stand there with their thumbs up their asses all night?"

"You sound like you want them to chase us," I accused.

"Let's save the arguments for when we get home, alright? Hit the gas, Pony."

"You got it."

If there was one area where I couldn't find fault with Cavallo, it was his taste in cars. The acceleration was so smooth that, though I could tell we were moving at a high rate of speed by the shadowed scenery blurring by my window, it didn't feel as if we were moving at all. The rich scent of leather wove a seductive cocoon around me, and when Ice reached out and gently cradled my hand in hers, I smiled and sank into the soft-as-butter seat and allowed my eyes to close.

The brief respite was over almost before it started. I felt Ice's hand carefully withdraw from mine and felt her body twist, one broad shoulder brushing against my own. "What is it?" I asked, my eyes coming quickly open.

"Company," my lover returned, peering out the rear window, eyes narrowed to slits.

Squirming in the seat, I turned to look just in time to see the twin beams of headlights breast a small rise a mile or so behind us. "Could just be another traveler."

"If so, he's in a hurry," Critter remarked, eyeing the rear-view mirror. "He's gotta be doing a hundred ten, easy."

"Take that turnoff up ahead, Pony. Let's see if we can lose him in the desert."

Grunting in acknowledgement, Pony jerked the wheel hard and spun us onto the off-ramp with a minimum of fuss, though doubtless if Cavallo was awake, he didn't enjoy the maneuver overmuch. Not that I would be spilling any tears over that particular thought, but it helped keep my mind from harping on the probability that we were being chased through the desert by a group of madmen at speeds humans were never meant to travel.

This close to the ground, anyway.

Twisting back in my seat, I snapped the shoulder harness over me, then checked the latch several times to make sure it was secure. No use tempting Fate any more than I already had, especially since cars and I weren't the best of friends lately.

Next to me, Ice also turned to face forward once again, but not before giving me a grin that was half confidence, half glee.

"You're enjoying this, aren't you?" I groused.

She shrugged, her expression unrepentant. "Beats doing laundry."

I had to laugh at that. If there is anything Ice hates more than doing the laundry, I don't know what it is. While I, on the other hand, absolutely love it. There's just something so satisfying in putting dirty, smelly clothes into a machine and pulling them out wonderfully clean and fresh. It's just another example of the odd nature of our partnership, I guess. And one that I wouldn't change for anything in the world.

"So far, so good," Pony remarked softly, her gaze split between the road and the rearview mirror. "Though with all the damn dust I'm kicking up right now, it's hard to tell for sure. I'm just glad we're doing this in the middle of the night. If it were during daylight, we might as well be sending up fucking flares."

"Just drive, Pony," Critter ordered, thumping her lover solidly on one well-muscled shoulder.

"I'm drivin'! I'm drivin', already!"

"Make that right up ahead, then the second left. There are

some mountains to the right. We might be able to ditch them there."

I looked over at my lover, my eyes opened wide. "Do you have an atlas in your head or something?"

"Or something," she replied, throwing me her best smirk.

"Looks like we lost 'em," Pony replied after several moments without a sign of pursuit.

"Oh, they're around," Ice murmured. "Take the next right you can and let's get back on the highway. Once you're there, run her as fast as you can. We need to get to the rendezvous point while it's still dark."

"I'm on it."

Out on the highway, Pony opened up the throttle and we sped through the desert like the devil was on our tail. An hour passed quietly, and then another, before I felt Ice stiffen once again. "What?"

"They're back."

"Damnit!" Pony shouted. "How in the hell could they find us? We took enough turns to confuse a compass, for Christ's sake!"

"This car's got a tracer on it," Ice replied.

"Like hell it does! Ice, I checked it out myself! It's clean!"

"Tell that to our friends. Floor it, Pony. There's nowhere to turn off for another ten miles. We need to outrun them."

"I say we stand and fight."

"We can't. This area is too exposed and too far from anything if we run into trouble. Just do as I say and drive. We'll make our stand at the rendezvous point if we need to."

"You're the boss," Pony grumbled, then stomped her foot hard on the accelerator. The car responded, dredging up extra power from somewhere, and we flew down the road at impossible speeds.

Ice gently removed my hand from its white-knuckled grip on my short skirt, and held it gently in her own. "We'll make it, Angel," she said in a comforting tone.

Drawing in a shuddering breath, I nodded, wanting more than anything to believe.

Time passed. It could have been ten minutes; it could have been ten hours. I was too scared to tell the difference, to be truthful.

I knew enough, however, to know when we were finally close to our destination, especially when the headlights of our purloined car lit up a long copse of trees indicating a water source in the near vicinity.

"Left at the crossroads up ahead, right?" Pony asked.

"Yeah. Then go an eighth of a mile. There's a small loop there. Go around it and park. Rio should be waiting for us there."

"Are they still following us?" I asked, not daring to turn around. A shootout was the last thing I wanted to be a part of, though if it came down to that, I'd be right there at my lover's side, doing whatever I could to keep us whole.

"We're clear for the moment," Ice replied. "Get ready to run the minute this car stops, though."

"You don't have to ask me twice."

Following Ice's directions to the letter, Pony turned on a sharp, if ill defined, hairpin curve and pulled off onto an unpaved path, which was surrounded by tall, thick trees on all sides. As soon as the car stopped rolling, the four of us opened our doors and hopped out. Critter and I ran in the direction of Ice's pointing finger, down toward the river, while Pony stayed behind to help Ice with Cavallo and the small amount of possessions we'd managed to accumulate during our stay south of the border. Rio jumped from behind a large tree and brushed by me on her way to help Pony and Ice.

Hearing a rustling in the bushes to my left, I turned that way, to see a white-faced Nia peering out. "Hey," I whispered. "It's just us."

"Oh thank god," she half-sobbed. Standing up, she came out of the bush and wrapped me in a desperate hug. "I never want to go through that again. I've been so scared, waiting for everyone, thinking that the border patrol was coming down the road any minute. And Rio wasn't any help at all."

"It's alright. We're here now," I replied, hugging her tightly to me. "And we're getting ready to go home."

"God, that sounds *so* good to me right now."

Pulling away, I smiled at her. "Yeah. Me too."

Grabbing my hand, she led me down the short path to the river. "C'mon. We got a boat. Not very much of a boat, but as long as it floats, I'm not gonna complain."

The river was wide, black, and silent as death. It also stank of decay, and I was quite glad that I would be crossing it in the dark, because I had absolutely no desire to see what, exactly, was causing such a stench.

"Ta-da!" Nia sang, throwing out her arm in a dramatic gesture. "There it is."

I looked. Then squinted. Then cocked my head. Well, I supposed, technically what I was looking at *could* be called a boat. Course, I'd seen larger beds, but Nia was right. As long as it floated....

"Um...are all of us going to fit in there?"

Was my first question.

"Who's going to row?"

Would have been my second, had I time to ask it. Which I didn't.

Ice led the way down to the shore, and after gesturing Nia and Critter to the very back, she dumped Cavallo's still unconscious bulk in the middle. Pony came behind her and tossed the duffel bag with our gear in it on top of him. "Now what?"

Ice's answer was interrupted by several soft "popping" sounds coming from behind us. "Angel, Pony, get in the boat! Now!" Reaching behind her, Ice pulled her gun from the waistband of her jeans. "I said *now*!"

Before I could even think to move, Pony grabbed my wrist and all but threw me into the boat, which rocked wildly with the action and almost capsized. Then she jumped in, pinning me inside with no chance to escape.

"Get outta here!"

"No!" I screamed. "Not without you!"

"Go!"

Reaching forward, Critter grabbed the oars and began rowing the second Ice kicked the boat away from the shoreline.

"Ice!"

More popping sounds, and Ice turned away and ran up the embankment toward the sounds of shooting.

"Goddamn you, Critter! Stop!" I grabbed for the oars at the same time as Pony grabbed me, and the resulting flailing almost caused the boat to tip once again.

Critter regained her grip on the wooden oars, and we began moving again as I struggled against Pony's tight hold.

"Let me go, goddamnit!"

"Stop struggling, Angel! I'll knock you the fuck out, I swear I will!"

"Try it, you son of a bitch! Ice!"

Two small splashes sounded to our immediate left. It didn't take a genius to know they came from bullets attempting to halt our getaway.

"Critter! Faster! C'mon! *Row*!"

Grunting with effort, Critter put her back into it and I could feel the boat pick up speed beneath me as Pony shielded my body with her own, still taking care to hold me so tightly I feared my ribs would shatter.

"Let. Me. Go!" My teeth were so tightly gritted, I thought sure they'd break off at the gum line.

"I won't warn you again, Angel." Pony's breath was hot on my cheek. "Keep struggling and you'll tip us. Critter can't swim and neither can Nia, so you'd best be still or I'll crack you one. I swear it by any fucking god you wanna name."

"Well throw me overboard, then, because I...."

The rest of my words were cut off as I heard Pony give a soft groan and felt the weight of her body collapse over me, bearing me right off the wooden seat and to the floor of the boat.

"Pony!" I could hear Critter's muffled scream as I tried to struggle from beneath her lover's limp, full weight

"Keep rowing!" Nia's voice was pitched high with terror. "Oh god! Keep rowing!"

"*Pony*!"

I could tell Pony was still alive by the movement of her chest against my back and the soft moan of pain near my ear, but I didn't know how to tell Critter that from my position.

Then I heard splashes, loud ones, and suddenly our boat was moving again, twice as fast as it had before. We hit the river-bank hard, and Pony's weight drove into me, causing my face to slide against the splintered wood of the boat's bottom, the resulting sting bringing tears of pain to my eyes.

Then, like a blessing from on high, the weight was lifted from my chest, hips, and head, and when I looked up, I met the concerned expressions of people I knew.

Like some sort of modern-day cavalry, the Amazons had come over the hill once again.

Montana and Cowgirl quickly, but gently, grabbed Pony, while others hauled Cavallo from the bottom of the boat and onto dry land, none being particularly careful with where or how hard he landed.

I scrambled to a sitting position just as Cheeto stepped forward and offered me a hand. "C'mon, Angel."

"Not a chance," I growled, moving up so that I was sitting on one of the benches and grabbing the oars.

"Angel! Don't!"

"Watch me."

With swift, sure strokes, I pulled away from the bank, determined to make it back to the other side as quickly as I could. Some of the Amazons jumped back into the river in an attempt to halt my progress, but I made sure that their efforts were futile in the extreme.

Nothing, not heaven nor hell nor anything else was going to stop me from getting back to Ice.

Halfway across, I bumped into...something...hard enough to rock the boat. When that something grabbed onto the side with a bloodied hand, I almost tipped it over myself scrabbling to get away.

"It's me!" came a harsh whisper from below.

I froze for a split second and then scrabbled back the way I'd come. "Ice? Ice, is that you?"

"Yeah, it's me."

"Oh, thank you *God*! Wait a second. I'll try and pull you in."

"Can't. Rio got hit. Just row back for shore as fast as you can."

"Where is she?"

"I've got her."

"Where are the others?"

"Taken care of. Just row."

"Ok. Let me turn around on the seat."

It's amazing how fast and how easily you can move when you've a mind to. Switching positions quickly, I grabbed the oars and began rowing. Ice's hand disappeared for one heart-stopping second, before reappearing over the stern.

Then I rowed for all I was worth, the extra weight I was towing slowing me down not at all.

Once again, the Amazons met the boat in the shallows and helped pull it on to shore. Ice lifted Rio and carried her onto the bank before laying her gently down on her back. I scrambled out of the boat and knelt down next to her.

It was bad.

Very bad.

Rio's normally deeply tanned face was white as a newly-laundered sheet, except for the wide streams of blood, which drained from her nose and mouth.

"Ice?" I whispered, looking up into the stone mask she'd

pulled on to hide her emotions.

Ignoring me, she ripped Rio's shirt open to expose a vastly muscled chest and torso that was marred by three tiny holes, no larger than American dimes, if that. The two in her belly were oozing a slow, but steady stream of blood. The third, in her upper right chest, was bubbling with pink froth with every breath she took.

Tearing her own shirt off, Ice quickly folded it and pressed it hard over the chest wound. "C'mon, Rio," she murmured as she reached with her free hand to the side of Rio's neck, searching for a pulse. "C'mon. Fight."

At the touch of Ice's gentle fingers, Rio's dark eyes fluttered open. They were painfully aware, and my heart seized in my chest. "Hey," I whispered, smiling as best I could.

"Aaaaaa...." One hand lifted from her side and hung there, trembling. "Aaaannnn...."

Grasping it, I pulled it up to my cheek and held it there; the tears starting to fall freely down my face. "I'm here, Rio. I'm here."

"Ssssooo." She coughed and dark blood streamed from her mouth, but her eyes never wavered. "Sorrrry."

I choked out a sob. "Don't be sorry, Rio. You saved our lives. You just concentrate on pulling through this, alright?"

"Sorrrry!" she said again, her hand curling to a fist in my own.

Taking in a shuddering breath, I nodded. "I know," I whispered. "I know. I forgive you."

Her hand relaxing in mine, the faintest ghost of a smile twitched her bloodied lips. "Thaaank youu."

Then she turned her head, just slightly. Her other hand lifted, and Ice caught it and held it tight. "Aaam...?" She coughed again and her eyes rolled briefly up in her head, before returning their intense stare to my lover. "Aaamazon?"

Ice's lips pursed, and I knew she was holding back tears by sheer force of her formidable will. Her eyes, though, were bright and shiny. "Yes," she replied, her whisper harsh with unshed tears. "Yes, you're an Amazon."

With those words, Rio relaxed, seeming to fold back into herself. Her chest lifted once more, then fell, and didn't rise again. Her eyes became doll's eyes that stared blankly into the canopy of trees overhead.

"Rio! Rio, no! Oh, no, please!" I turned to my lover in

time to see one single tear roll silently down her cheek. "Ice! Do something!"

Lifting her free hand from the makeshift pressure dressing, Ice reached up and gently closed Rio's eyes. "Goodbye, my friend," she whispered.

"No! No! It's not goodbye! It's not! Damnit, Ice! Do something! Save her like you saved me!"

Soft hands descended on my shoulders. I tried to shake them off, but their grip was iron. "It's over, Angel," Corinne's voice whispered from the darkness surrounding us. "Let her go."

"No! I won't let her go!" Moving quickly forward, I dropped Rio's still hand in an attempt to start some sort of CPR on her.

But Ice was quicker still and stopped me with a forearm to my chest.

I looked up at her, eyes full of fire, but the look in her own stopped me cold.

I collapsed into Rio's unmoving body and sobbed into her chest until Corinne gently gathered me up and pulled me into a firm, gentle embrace.

I sobbed like a child in her mother's arms as the rest of the Amazons surrounded us, their faces somber and grieving.

Behind me, Ice stood, lifted Rio into her arms and headed silently away.

We cremated Rio today. On a large open pyre, as she requested, so that her spirit would be freed and, together with the smoke from the blazing fire, soar to meet her ancestors in a place beyond death.

Ice lit the fire, as we'd all known she would, and with lit torch in hand, she sang. As mournful and melancholy a dirge as I have ever heard, and hope never to hear again in this lifetime.

I think that she was the only one there who didn't cry.

Not that anyone noticed, since they were too busy shedding tears of their own.

As for me, all I can really feel is a pervading sense of numbness. Like being swaddled in cotton from head to toe. They used to call in ennui, I think, once upon a time. Or maybe it was a different word that I'm searching for. At this point, though, I really can't seem to care.

Pony's the only one who didn't make it to the service. One of the Amazons, appropriately named (what else?), Doc, removed the bullet from her shoulder and declared her bedridden for the foreseeable future. But at least she's alive.

I don't know when, or if, I'll ever be able to face her, though.

What do you say to someone who saved your life just as you were doing your level best to end theirs?

"I'm sorry," just doesn't seem adequate enough, somehow. And I don't think "thank you" would be all that well received, at this point. Though Corinne has gone to great pains to assure me otherwise.

It disturbs me greatly that I would willingly put the lives of my friends in danger just so that I could get back to my lover. A lover who most definitely, and for all the right reasons, didn't want me there to begin with.

I look at the woman I am today and realize how very much I've changed. And not all of those changes have been for the better.

I've become quicker to find fault and quicker to anger. Quick to do violence and quick to lash out.

But by far the worst thing of all is that I find myself becoming someone I swore I never even had it within myself to be.

A woman who puts the needs of herself above the needs of others.

It shames me deeply to recognize how very selfish I've become in that regard.

And I have no one to blame but myself.

Every once in awhile, I see Ice looking at me in that way of hers. As if she's not quite sure what's going on with me, but doesn't quite know if I'd be receptive to her attempts at comfort.

She's pretty withdrawn herself, however, and I'm not sure either one of us is ready to talk it out just yet. Rio's death hit her very hard. There's an angry energy swarming around her. An energy that makes everyone keep their distance from her. This is the Ice of legend. The only Ice most of these women have ever known or heard tales about. They watch her in awe as she passes, and whisper behind their hands when they think she's out of hearing range.

Most of the time, their judgment is off, and whatever it is she hears only serves to increase her anger.

We made love last night. A hard-hitting, brutal kind of

love. The kind two souls and bodies share when they're in pain and just need to feel something beyond that. If even for just a moment.

Ice was relentless in her passion, taking me again and again and again. And I wanted it, craved it, begged for it over and over until she'd exhausted us both and we tumbled down into sleep still wrapped around one another.

Our pain was, for the moment, forgotten.

But it came back this morning, as I knew it would, and made itself at home in my soul. I wish I could cry, or scream, or beat my fists bloody on the walls, but it seems all I can do is just sit here with my thoughts and pray for this nightmare of listlessness to be over soon.

Please, God, if you can hear me, just let it be over.

I awoke the next morning to the sounds of screaming.

Masculine screaming.

Tossing back the covers, I hit the ground running, oblivious to my half-naked and sleep-rumpled state.

The hall was crowded with whispering women and I charged through them all, like some sort of half-sized halfback making an end zone run. I turned to the left and headed immediately for the kitchen, where an even larger and more dense crowd awaited me.

The woman who had owned the ranch prior to Montana was a bit of a survivalist, you see. She'd grown up during the Las Vegas nuclear bomb testings, and she'd decided to build her very own bomb shelter and tack it on to the back of the house by way of the kitchen.

Normally, the shelter held canned goods and various and sundry other items needed to feed, shelter and clothe a large community of women.

Now, it held only one thing.

Cavallo.

His continued screaming led me on, and I pressed through the crowd with renewed vigor. Some of the women were hesitant to step aside, but when they saw who it was who was doing the pushing, they gave ground willingly.

When I finally got free of the crowd, I saw Cowgirl and Cheeto in front of the open door, looking inward. Their bodies were pressed tightly together as they barred the door against the press of women behind them.

A hand snaked out, grabbed my arm, and pulled me off to the side. I looked into Montana's grim face, then into the equally grim face of Corinne.

"What's going on?" I asked, though most of me already knew the answer to that question.

As if in answer, the screaming stopped.

It didn't wind down, as screams of pain often do. No, it was cut off completely, leaving a ringing, pregnant silence behind.

A silence shattered by the heavy double-thud of a body hitting first a wall, then the floor.

Then by the sound of a heavy tread moving toward us.

Cowgirl and Cheeto took a step back, and Ice came through the door. The energy around her was black and menacing. Several women gasped upon seeing her, and they quickly looked away, their faces drawn and pale.

Like those of a hunting cougar, my lover's eyes scanned the crowd of women. Any spark of humanity in them seemed absent. They were flashing silver and promised pain.

It was as if she was culling the herd.

As if instinctually recognizing this, the crowd of women parted, giving her a long, wide path down which to walk.

Her eyes met mine for a moment before sliding away. If there was a hint of recognition in them, it was deeply buried.

And then, like a shadow touched by sunlight, she was gone, disappearing into the throng of humanity as if she was never there at all.

I made as if to go after her, but Montana held me fast.

"Let her calm down a bit, Angel."

Calm? She was already calm. Deathly calm, in fact.

I heeded Montana's request, however. Because I needed to help Ice, and I couldn't do that until I knew what had gone on.

Cowgirl disappeared into the shelter, only to reappear a brief moment later, her face set in grim lines. "Get Doc," she ordered her lover.

As Cheeto turned away, I shrugged off Montana's grip and stepped forward. "Is he...?"

"He got the crap beaten out of him, literally I think, but he's alive."

I rounded on Montana. "Tell me what happened."

For a long moment, she looked as if she was going to refuse, but then she sighed and shrugged her shoulders. "He's been cursing up a blue streak pretty much since he finally woke up last night from Ice's little nap. I wanted to feed him some breakfast this morning, and Ice came in with me." She ran a steady hand through her thick, dark hair. "He started ranting and raving, as usual. Called us some pretty uninventive names and demanded we let him out." She shrugged again.

I shook my head, not understanding. Even grief stricken as she was, Ice wouldn't have done that much damage just because a few ugly names were tossed her way.

Doc walked by, medical kit in hand, followed closely by Cheeto, and disappeared into the bunker.

I turned my attention back to Montana. "What else?"

"He started in on Rio," Corinne said, voice soft and grim. "Evidently, he'd heard some of the women talking in the kitchen earlier and decided to use up most of his idiot points in one fell swoop."

I nodded, beginning now to understand my lover's rage.

"And then," Corinne continued, "he began to talk about you. Though perhaps 'talk' isn't the best description one could use in this instance." She shook her head in mock wonder. "How he became such an important piece of property, I'll never know. That man doesn't have enough genuine wit to fill up a thimble."

"And then he took a swing at her," Montana added. "And it was pretty much over from there."

Hearing all that I needed to, I thanked them both and left, heading out of the house and toward the one place I knew she'd be.

The stables were cool and dim, and smelled strongly of hay and horses. Because the day itself was overcast, my eyes adjusted quickly to the poor lighting within.

She was sitting on a hay bale that had been pushed against the furthest wall, legs splayed carelessly. Her hands, dark with blood, fiddled with a piece of straw, and her face was hidden by the long fall of hair, which hung across it.

I didn't bother treading softly as I approached. I knew she knew I was there. If she wanted to stop me, she would. But I didn't think she wanted to.

Reaching down, I snared an old bucket partially filled with

water, and the handful of clean rags piled next to it. Circling her so that she had a clear path to the door, I dropped to one knee, placed the water bucket at my side, and dipped one of the rags into it.

Wordlessly, I grasped her left hand and began to dab at the bleeding cuts her rage had wrought. Most of the blood was Cavallo's, I knew, and I quickly cleaned any traces of him from her skin. Her face was hidden from me, her body tense and coiled, but I expected that, and concentrated on lending her as much support and love through my touch and presence as I possibly could.

"Rough day, huh?" I finally asked, when I could bear the silence no longer.

"Yeah," was her only comment as I traded left hand for right and began my task anew.

I let that go, knowing when to push and when not to.

Her hands now fully clean, I patted each one dry with another soft rag, then laid everything else aside and took her warm flesh into my own hands, raising each one to my lips before lowering them to her thighs and just holding gently on.

It might have been minutes, or hours, or days, but when she finally lifted her head to look at me, her eyes held the woman I knew shining brightly within their clear, bottomless depths. "Thank you," she whispered.

I gave her my first real smile in days. "Anytime." I squeezed her large hands, gratified to feel her return the pressure. "I love you, you know."

Her hair swung free as she nodded. "I know."

Seeing the question in her eyes, I tried to answer it with what little information I had. "Don't think he'll go dancing with Ginger Rogers anytime soon, but I think he'll pull through ok."

She nodded her thanks, her gaze again going far away.

"Do you think he's got some kind of death wish?"

Her eyes focused once more as a perfectly arched brow rose to hide behind the fringe of her bangs.

"I'm serious! I mean, you've already single-handedly taken out a bunch of his guards up in Canada, you take out a bunch more in his own home, and then you beat the snot out of him and bring him here. He's got to know he doesn't stand a chance against you."

She shrugged. "Maybe you're right. Maybe he doesn't want to go back to prison."

"Or maybe he's just an idiot."

She chuckled, a little. "I thought that was a given."

I couldn't help but grin back. "Well, yeah, you're right on that one."

We fell into a more or less comfortable silence, and I felt her thumbs trail slowly back and forth over my knuckles. I could tell she was deep in thought.

"So," I asked after several moments passed, "where do we go from here?"

Taking in a deep breath, she let it out slowly, then released my hands and straightened. "That depends on how bad off Cavallo is. There hasn't been any news from south of the border, but those bodies aren't gonna remain hidden for long."

"Have you heard from Donita?"

"I called her last night to let her know we have him. She's arranging a drop-off location somewhere out of town. Says things have gotten pretty sticky up there lately."

"Sticky how?" A tendril of fear curled deep in my belly and sunk roots there.

"She couldn't say. I'll try to contact her again tonight. We need to get moving as quickly as we can. I don't want the ranch to come under suspicion."

"And you think it will?"

"I can't afford to assume otherwise, Angel. Not with this."

As she stood, I rose with her and noticed for the first time the small deerskin bag, no larger than a quarter, which hung around her neck on a choker-length piece of rawhide.

"Rio's totem," I whispered, blinking back tears, which were threatening to form at the sight of it. A streak of her blood had dried on the hide, creating a dark crimson slash that only served to make the object even more precious and profound.

Ice's hand went up to the hollow of her throat, and she touched the totem briefly, reverently, before drawing her fingers away. Her expression was a curious and heartrending mixture of sadness, loss, and steely, stoic determination.

Like a moth to a flame, I was drawn in to her and circled her waist with my arms even as she closed her own around me.

And there, in the dimness of the stables on that cool winter's day, we finally found the ability to grieve.

❖❖❖❖❖❖❖

We returned to the ranch house, hand in hand. Most of the women were still gathered there, no doubt discussing the morning's festivities. All talk came to a dead stop once we entered, however, and I was struck with a curious sense of déjà vu. The last time I'd found myself the center of attention, I'd just arrived from a blissful evening spent with my lover.

This time, that lover just happened to be with me.

Curious glances darted quickly away, and I knew at once that Ice had given the women a taste of her patented glare. I almost laughed as I realized yet again that most of these women had never met her, and the stories they'd been told were nothing compared to being in her very tangible presence.

A legend come to life, as it were.

Corinne stepped out of the crowd and gestured for us to follow.

Still joined by our clasped hands, we made our way down one dim hallway and into Corinne's bedroom. "I think you should see this," she said, indicating a large television sitting on her bureau. It appeared to have been tuned to a Mexican station, and though the words being spoken by the reporters could have been Greek for all I understood of them, the scene splashed behind the men was clear as crystal.

It was the clearing where Rio had given her life so the rest of us could remain free. Bright yellow tarps dotted the ground close to the river. I knew those tarps hid the bodies of the men she and Ice had killed as the rest of us escaped to the other side of the border.

"What are they saying?" I demanded as Ice and Corinne quietly watched the events unfold. "Do they know who those men are? Do they know what happened? Do they...."

Ice's hand squeeze quieted my ramblings as Corinne turned to me. "No, they haven't identified the bodies. Seems none of them had any identification." This was said with a significant look in Ice's direction.

"Rio's doing," came my lover's short answer.

"Then how...?"

"One of the men wasn't dead yet."

"Oh." She turned back to me. "In any event, they're only speculating on the happenings at this point. Though the chain of events is rather obvious, even to the uninitiated, wouldn't you agree?"

I nodded, my heart in my throat.

"Would any of the survivors, assuming there are any, have cause to recognize you?" Corinne asked Ice.

"She was wearing a ski mask," I supplied.

"They were all locals," Ice answered. "Those men," she gestured to the television, "were Cavallo's."

"Ahh," Corinne replied, nodding sagely. "And dead men tell no tales. Or so they say."

"Is there any chance at all that this can be traced back to you?" I asked Ice.

"Likely that's already been done," she replied. "If not, it will be soon. Those guards I left alive are gonna tell someone sooner or later that their meal ticket got stolen. It won't be long before someone somewhere puts two and two together."

"And likely ends up with seven," Corinne snorted.

"We'll need to move as soon as Cavallo's stable."

"Which should be in seventy-two hours, barring any unforeseen circumstances," Corinne reported.

"Why so long?" I asked.

"Our physician in residence wants to make sure there are no internal injuries waiting to surprise us down the road." She looked at Ice, awe glittering hard in her eyes. "How you were able to inflict so much superficial damage without breaking any of his bones is something I'll never understand. It was a pleasure watching a master in action."

I looked away, slightly sickened. Accepting that Ice had beaten someone bloody in anger was one thing. Having someone else express joy in that was another thing entirely.

"So," I said finally, just to break the uncomfortable silence, "what now?"

Ice straightened and released my hand. "I need to contact Donita." And with that, she left.

I sank slowly to Corinne's narrow bed, my eyes still glued to the images on the television. Corinne stood nearby, her dark eyes darting back and forth as we watched the bodies as they were loaded into ambulances. Though I knew in my very soul that these were the men who had killed Rio, injured Pony, and tried their best to kill us all, deep down, I still felt a sense of sorrow.

Not for them, of course, for they were dead and beyond caring.

But for their families and their loved ones. For their children who would spend days, months, perhaps years wondering when their fathers would be coming home. For parents who would grieve their passing, and for spouses or lovers who would never get used to going to sleep in an empty bed.

It could have been me.

It still might, one day, given the life I've chosen to lead.

And that's what it all comes down to, doesn't it?

Choice.

Those men lived by their choices and died by their choices. As do we all, I suppose, in one way or another.

That's not to say that I was happy that those men were dead, nor that I would have wished their deaths upon them had I the ability to do so.

But as I've come to realize, especially over these last several gut-wrenching days, responsibility is a great deal easier in theory than it is in practice. Everyone bears some responsibility for their actions and for the pain those actions cause in others.

As the meaning behind that thought hit me full force in the guts, I straightened and turned to Corinne. "I have to talk to them."

She smiled. That wise, almost ancient smile she sometimes uses, and nodded, well knowing of whom I was speaking. "They need that, Angel."

I nodded, sucking in a deep, deep breath. "I know. They're my friends. And even if they weren't, they deserve more than silence from me."

Leaning down, Corinne pressed the smooth, cool skin of her cheek against my own. "That's my Angel."

I squeezed her tight and then stood as she backed away. "I don't feel very much like one right now, Corinne, but thanks."

"We all learn from our mistakes. Even Angels," she said quietly and then sent me on my way.

Swallowing back my fear, I walked the few short steps that would take me to the room Pony and Critter shared. The door was closed, as I'd known it would be, and as I lifted my hand to knock, I played what I would say to them over in my mind. Which didn't amount to much more than "I'm sorry, please forgive me," but it was the best I could do at the moment. It seemed I was suddenly out of words.

The door opened before I could knock, and Critter stood there. We both looked at one another, uncertain. Such a large part of me demanded my retreat that I almost gave into it. Another part of me just wanted to break down in tears and hug her to try to take the pain from her eyes. I stood between that proverbial rock and hard place for a long moment before this newly born sense of responsibility kicked me in the hindquarters and made my decision for me.

"I...um...may I come in?"

After a second, she backed away, giving me space to enter. "Sure."

I entered the room, my steps slow and hesitant. There, on the bed and covered to her chin with a sheet, lay Pony. She looked somewhat pale and somewhat drawn, but much better than I'd honestly expected. Her dark eyes caught and held my gaze. There was some pain in them, as well as some uncertainty, but none of the anger or loathing that I'd expected. Or, in truth, deserved.

"Hi, Pony," I said softly, coming to a stop several feet from her bed.

"Hey, Angel." Her voice, though slightly raspy, was strong and sure. "How are you doing?"

That question, of course, only made me feel worse. I wasn't the one shot, after all. "I'm doing ok. How about you?"

She shrugged. "Not bad. Doc says I should be up and around in no time." She leaned forward conspiratorially. "I just wish Nurse Ratchet here would get that through her head."

Though I wanted to laugh, I didn't, still too scared to hope that things between us could ever be the way they were before.

"How's Ice?" she asked.

"A little better. She's still mourning Rio's death, but...." I shrugged, conveying the impossibility of guessing my lover's emotions.

Pony grinned. "I heard she beat the shit outta Cavallo."

I nodded in lieu of answering verbally, and watched as Critter came to sit on the side of the bed. With both sets of eyes on me, it became even more difficult to think, and my words tumbled out of me like water going over a fall. "I know you won't be able to forgive me, I can't even forgive myself, but I just wanted you both to know how sorry I am for what I did the other night to both of you. It was wrong of me. I almost killed you both. You're my friends and I treated you horribly. I was selfish and pig-headed and blind and I acted like a total idiot. I just wanted to tell you that. That I'm sorry for what I did, and I'm sorry for avoiding you these past few days. You don't deserve that. Not from me, not from anyone else. I was an idiot, and I was scared. I'm sorry."

I ground do a halt, my words all used up. I stood there, numb, not daring to read anything into the way they looked back at me.

What happened next I'll leave for Pony and Critter to tell, if they ever get a notion to do such. Suffice it to say that these two women, who most of society would look down upon and speak ill of because of their past mistakes, have more honor and integrity, compassion and caring, love and loyalty than any thousand who claim that to have the handle on getting into heaven first.

They taught me something about friendship that day, and about forgiveness, and the power of love.

I can only hope that one day, I can feel deserving of the honor they've given me by calling me "friend."

That evening, as I lay naked between the cool, crisp sheets of our bed, Ice walked in, her eyes dark and distant.

"What's wrong?" I asked, immediately coming up to my elbows as her expression registered.

She tapped her cell-phone absently against her palm. "I haven't been able to contact Donita."

My belly fluttered. "At all? But I thought you had a hotline to her directly?"

"I do. She's not answering it."

"Did you try any of the other numbers? No, forget I asked. Of course you did." I wriggled until I was sitting up, my legs crossed in front of me. "Do you know of anyone up there who might know where she is? The prosecutor, maybe? Or the judge?"

"The only person I trust is Donita."

I nodded, biting my lower lip. "So...what now? Do we wait until you can get in touch with her somehow?"

Ice shook her head. "We can't afford to. As soon as Cavallo is able to travel, we move."

"Even if we don't know where we're taking him?"

"Even then," she replied, firm resolution coloring her tones. "Did the news give any more details?"

"Not really. They still haven't identified the bodies. The story doesn't seem to have made it up here yet. At least not that we heard."

"Good." Laying the cell phone down on the nightstand, she tiredly stripped off her clothes, then slipped between the sheets and rested her head on my thigh.

Smiling, I sifted my hand through the soft onyx strands of her hair, enjoying, as always, the feel of it against my fingers.

A small contented hum made its way up from her throat as her body relaxed against mine, and the very tips of her fingers drew abstract designs on my legs.

Sensing her exhaustion, I deepened my touches and rubbed along her scalp and forehead, doing my best to ease away the day's tension. Almost before I knew it, her own touches slowed to a stop and her breathing deepened and evened out into true slumber; the first she'd had in days, if not weeks.

And though we were standing on a precipice over a chasm so deep I couldn't see the bottom, I hugged this tiny island of peace around me like a warm sweater and let my doubts and my fears be washed away by the awesome power that was love.

"Oh yes, love," I gasped as a pair of warm, wet lips applied gentle suction to a particularly sensitive area at the back of my neck. That gasp turned into a groan as long fingers danced across my breasts in time with the rapidly quickening beat of my heart. Leaning back into the long body behind me, I felt Ice's hips rock against my towel-covered behind, and the sensation caused a sudden weakening in my knees.

Overcome with a need I knew only too well, I spun within the circle of her loose embrace and crushed our bodies together even as my hands reached up and through the shining raven locks of her hair to pull her head down to meet mine in an incendiary tangle of lips and tongues.

"Bed," I gasped when I pulled away for much needed air. "Now."

Growling deep in her chest, she lifted me easily from my feet as my own hands worked at the towel girding her lower half, courtesy of our shared morning shower.

Before I could blink, I found myself flat on my back as the bedsprings squeaked out their displeasure beneath me. Ice loomed over me, the look on her face the epitome of every fantasy I'd ever dreamed of and a few I hadn't even thought up yet.

Like a lioness she was, all tawny sleekness and barely controlled hunger. Her eyes, passion-dark, swept over my body setting fires wherever her gaze touched down. Her nostrils flared, scenting the air and the passion growing between us. She growled again, long and low, and my body became liquid and burned hotter than the sun.

Taking care to make sure that no part of our bodies was touching, she came in low. White teeth snatched at my lower lip and a strong tongue swirled and tasted its captured prize, then tugged and released and recaptured until I thought I would go mad with this all-encompassing need she was engendering within me.

My hips sent out a plea of their own, and I groaned when their fruitless quest was answered only by the cool air of the room beyond.

My groan of frustration was answered by a wicked chuckle, but she was fair, this mistress of my passions, and used my own desire against me for only a moment longer before ending the sweet torture and melding our bodies together.

Oh, the transcendence of that one exquisite moment when we joined together as two halves of a perfect whole.

Ice's towel had loosened somewhere along the way, and lush heat of her passion as it bathed my flesh sent me spiraling far and away. Lips softer than the finest silk enveloped my breasts, and the air was filled with the sensual sounds of flesh moving against flesh.

A moment later, Ice stiffened above me, but not in passion. My eyes sprung open to catch an intent look on her face.

"What?" I whispered, barely having the breath for it.

And then I heard it, the sounds of a struggle going on in the next room, complete with muffled shouts and angry voices, one of which was undeniably Pony's.

At that particular moment, however, I didn't care why Pony was yelling or who Pony was yelling at. I wanted Ice, and I wanted her *now.*

She returned willingly enough, capturing my lips in another incendiary kiss as her hand began its slow, teasing trek down to where I most desperately needed it. Then she halted again. I groaned in frustration, slapping my hand down on the mattress hard enough to sting.

This time, we both heard the shout simultaneously.

Just one word, but it was as if ice water had been thrown over both of us.

"Police!"

Ice rolled off the bed and stood, all in one fluid motion. She was across the room and had her hand on the door handle before I even had the chance to sit up.

"Ice! Don't forget your...robe," I sighed, talking to nothing but empty air. "Oh boy."

Managing to get my stunned limbs to cooperate, I stood up a great deal less gracefully than did my partner, grabbed my own robe and belted it over my nakedness before grabbing a second and bolting after her.

If the situation hadn't been so serious, I would have fallen to the floor with laughter as I slid into Pony's room. It was as if I'd walked in on a very adult version of the game of "Statues."

Pony was flat on her back in the bed with Critter half-sprawled atop her in a position that could have very definitely been construed as sexual had they both not been fully clothed. Nia was standing in one corner, her eyes so wide that if they hadn't been attached to her skull, I felt sure they'd pop right out and roll around on the floor like marbles. Cheeto was standing next to Nia, the tanned skin of her face flushed a shining red. Cowgirl, standing next to her, didn't have the benefit of a tan, and the flush on her face was tending toward purple.

And, of course, the centerpiece of this tableau was my naked lover, to whom all gazes were affixed.

Gathering myself, I crossed the last, small distance between us and slipped the robe over Ice's shoulders. Though she pulled it on and belted it closed over the vast expanse of her wonderful flesh, those actions did nothing to break the frozen stares of her admirers.

That feat was accomplished by Montana, who stalked into the room with a grim expression on her face. Entering, she took charge effortlessly.

"Cowgirl, Cheeto, get out to the perimeter. I want to know the second they get within sighting distance. Critter, round up the non-Amazons and get them into the house. Move!"

As Critter jumped up, Pony attempted to get out of the bed, only to find herself pushed down by her lover. "Oh no ya don't, hero. You just stay there and let the rest of us grunts take care of the dirty work for ya."

"Like hell I will!" Pony growled, using her greater strength to overpower her thinner lover. "Get the fuck off me, will ya?"

"Pony!"

"Enough."

Though not spoken in a loud tone, that one word had the entire force of Ice's personality behind it, and once again, the entire room froze in place.

"What's going on?" she asked Montana, still in that same smooth, controlled tone.

"Paycheck just called in. Ten or more police cruisers are heading here full bore."

"Cavallo?"

"No. Apparently, Nia's husband has decided to bring in the cavalry."

Nia stepped forward and laid a hand on Pony's shoulder. "Please, stay in bed. I'll handle this."

"But...."

She sighed, and suddenly I saw a new Nia standing in place of the old. A sadder, wiser Nia who'd learned a few life lessons the hardest way possible.

"Rio taught me something the other day," she said as if speaking to herself. "She taught me that it's time I grew up and stood up for something I believed in." Raising her chin proudly, she looked, in turn, at each one of us. "I've decided to start with believing in me."

"Nia," Pony protested, "you can't just...."

"Yes, Pony, I can. And I will. Every one of you has given of yourselves for me. And it's about time I started giving back." She turned beseeching eyes to Montana. "Please, ask Pony to stay here. I don't want anyone else hurt because of me."

"You're not thinking about going back to him," Montana said.

"No. Never again. He's probably got those police convinced that I was kidnapped and brought here against my will. I'll just have to convince them that I'm here because I want to be."

After a long, searching moment, Montana nodded. "Alright, but you're going to have backup, just in case."

"Alright," she softly replied.

"Great!" Pony shouted, renewing her struggle to free herself from Critter's embrace.

"*Not* you, Pony. You stay in bed. We can take care of this without you just this once."

"Damnit! Not you too, Montana! Come on! I'm not an invalid, for Christ's sake!"

"No, but you might just become one if I see you step one foot outside of that bed, Pony. And I mean that."

With a groan worthy of an Emmy or martyrdom, Pony slumped back on the bed and covered her face with one arm.

Then Montana turned to Ice and myself. "You two need to get out of here. Doc's already preparing Cavallo for the journey. Even though the police are here for Nia, we can't afford to have them do a search of the house."

Ice nodded. "We'll be ready in five minutes."

Turning, she took my hand and we headed back to our room to prepare for a journey whose ending was anything but certain.

Chapter 8

We didn't talk as we returned to our room. There really wasn't much to say at that point. Ice had already tried to talk me out of accompanying her, and I'd turned her down flatter than roadkill. My butt was as much on the line as hers was, and whatever happened, I was more determined than ever that we'd see it through together.

Reaching under the bed, she pulled out her black duffel, already packed, then opened a drawer in the bedside stand and removed her gun. Though it was as much a part of Ice as the color of her eyes, I detested that gun, with its pristine, shining finish and malevolent air. I avoided it like the plague, and if I could have made an evil-eye sign to ward off the cold shudders I got whenever I looked at it, I would have.

She didn't even bother looking at me as she opened the clip and then chambered a round before slipping it into the waistband of her jeans at the back. "You ready?"

"In a second," I replied, reaching for my own, mostly-packed, bag. "How long should I plan for?"

"At least two weeks, but don't pack too much. With Cavallo, we're not gonna have too much room to spare."

"What car are we taking, anyway?"

"Montana said she had something to show us, so I suppose we'll know when we see it."

"Alright. How about if I meet you out back?"

"Fine, just hurry up. Those cops are gonna be here any minute."

"Be right there."

Corinne entered as Ice left and came to stand next to me, arms crossed against her ample chest. "I just heard. Leaving already, are you?"

"Yeah," I said as I looked around the room to make sure that I wasn't missing any indispensable item. Spying the carving Ice had made for me for Christmas, I carefully grasped it from its place on the nightstand and rubbed my finger over the exquisitely carved angel's wings as one would a talisman.

"Your things will be safe here," Corinne said.

"Oh, I know that. It's just...."

"Difficult to leave yet another home?"

I sighed. "Something like that, yeah. Especially since we don't really know where we're going."

Corinne's eyebrows raised. "Hasn't Donita told you at least that much?"

"She hasn't told us anything. Ice can't get a hold of her."

"Now that *is* worrisome."

"Yeah. I know." I rubbed the rapidly forming stiffness at the back of my neck and spared a last look around the room. My eyes lit upon my growing stack of journals which, prior to Mexico, had gone everywhere with me. And now it looked like they'd be staying behind once again. I looked to Corinne. "Would you keep these for me in a safe place? I...don't think I'll have room for them in the car."

"I should be insulted that you even felt the need to ask, but that would be a waste of effort, so I suppose I'll just say 'yes' instead." Gathering the books up, she held them close to her chest. "They'll be here for you when you return."

"Thank you," I replied, for far more than babysitting my journals, and we both knew it.

Dropping the journals onto the bed, she reached out and engulfed me in an all-encompassing hug. I inhaled the scent of her sachet and, as always, drew some measure of comfort from it. My love for her burned fierce in my heart and I hugged her with as much strength as I could manage while keeping in mind the frailty of her elderly bones.

She hugged me back, just as tightly, and we both had teary eyes when we pulled apart. "Go, Angel."

Taking in a deep breath, I nodded and then grabbed my duffel. "I love you, Corinne," I said, brushing a kiss against her cheek.

"I love you too, sweet Angel. Be safe."

"I'll do my best."

I hurried down the halls, duffel in hand, and into the back of the house where I had to push upstream against a tide of women being escorted inside to safety. Stepping outside, I saw Ice and Montana standing next to a very large Jeep—the kind that looks like some sort of hybrid cross between a car and a tank. The engine was on and it was loud and rumbling, giving me what I was sure was just a small taste of its power. It was a dark, metallic blue and had heavily tinted windows, better to keep prying eyes away, I gathered.

Seeing me, Ice grabbed my duffel and slipped it into the back seat. A back seat that I was quite positive could comfortably house a family of four and their dog—and perhaps some cats, a bird or two, and an aquarium thrown in for good measure.

I briefly wondered if it came with its own butler before going around to the very back and peering inside. The interior space was huge, and there was a mattress of sorts laid out on the floorboards together with a couple of small pillows and two pairs of shackles locked to the seat supports.

A perfect love nest for the kinky set.

Which, of course, gave me some ideas, none of which can be shared in polite society.

Hearing a noise behind me, I stepped back just in time to avoid being trampled by Cheeto and Cowgirl as they carried a lolling Cavallo between them. His swollen face was a sunset of bruises and scrapes, and he appeared dead to the world.

The two women slung him inside the Jeep, and then Cowgirl entered and began to secure him. Doc supervised, smiling.

"How is he?" I asked.

"Woke up a little feisty this morning, but I sent him off on the *SS Valium* and now he's feeling nooo pain." She handed me a small black bag. "There're more drugs in there. If he starts yowling, just hit him with another dose. They're pre-measured, so you don't have to worry about unintentionally narcing him."

I took the bag just as Cowgirl jumped back out of the Jeep and dusted her hands off on the legs of her jeans. "Packed up and ready to go."

I stepped away further, and Doc closed the door, trapping

Cavallo safely inside.

Ice came to stand next to me. "You ready?"

"As I'll ever be, I guess."

"Let's go, then."

After sharing quick hugs with Cowgirl and Cheeto, and a firm handshake with Montana, I climbed up into the high cab of the Jeep and settled myself in. My belly was a flaming ball of tension, and my head was pounding in time to the beating of my heart. Ice's face was unusually grim as she settled herself in the driver's seat and reached for the gearshift.

"What is it?" I asked, the tension in my body ratcheting up yet another notch.

"I don't like leaving them this way. I've never run from a fight." Her tones were clipped, her voice measured.

"And you're not running from one now," I replied, laying a hand on her wrist. "I have faith in Nia's word. Rio's death has changed her. For the better. And the police will make sure no harm comes to the women. There's a friend or two of Montana's on the force."

An eyebrow raised in clear surprise.

I just managed to bite back a smug grin. Though the chances were one in a million, I'd actually been able to bring my lover up short with information she didn't already know.

If the circumstances were any less grave, I might have taken the time to savor the once-in-a-lifetime event. "Though the cop/con dynamic sounds pretty cheesy, Paycheck's lover is an officer. As long as Nia does her part and tells the truth, Montana and the rest will be safe."

Jaw set, she nodded and slipped the Jeep into gear. The engine roared, and with no more fanfare than that, we were on our way.

To where, I wasn't sure. I don't even think Ice knew at that point. But at least we were moving, and as long as we were moving, I could convince myself that, somewhere on the road ahead, there'd be a light waiting at the end of a tunnel, which had encompassed almost a third of my life.

Even though it was winter, Ice elected to take the northern route back toward Pennsylvania. That involved heading up into the Flagstaff Mountains, which were a beautiful Faerie Wonderland of snow and ice, not to mention treacherous driving conditions. The Jeep was sure-footed and well equipped to brave the storm buffeting us as we drove along, but I kept my white-knuckled grip on the dashboard (a "mother-in law" clutch, my father used to call it) just the same.

Though it seemed like a year, maybe two, in reality only a few short hours passed before we were out of the snow and entering into the unsurpassed beauty of New Mexico's Painted Desert. Not that I got to see most of it, mind you. My neck seemed on a spring, the way I kept looking over my shoulder to try and see if we'd picked up a tail along the way.

Of course, my chances of actually spotting said tail were about as great as seeing Elvis singing "Blue Hawaii" next to a roadside burrito stand, since I wouldn't know a tail unless it was sporting a "we're following you!" sign in the front window, but I had to feel like I was doing something.

Right before I would have spent the rest of my life with a crick in my neck, a cell phone and piece of paper was slipped into my hand. I looked over at Ice.

"See if you can get a hold of Donita at any of these numbers."

Nodding, I picked up the phone and started dialing. I soon realized that this task would be as fruitless as trying to spot a tail. Each attempt resulted in an infinite number of empty rings echoing back at me, like some sort of discordant curse.

With a sigh of frustration, I flipped the phone closed and laid it on my lap. "No luck," I said, though it wasn't necessary.

"Try again in a little while." Though Ice's voice was the epitome of calm, I could see her jaw muscles tense and bulge.

"Yeah, no problem. We'll get through this, right?" I gave her a sick little smile.

Her eyes, when she looked back at me, showed nothing but confidence. "Sure we will."

I laughed. "After all, what's driving around aimlessly with a kidnapped fugitive everyone seems to want dead compared with the things we've been through already, huh?"

There really should be a vaccine for "Foot-in-Mouth" disease. And if one ever becomes available, I'll be the first in line.

"I'm sorry," I said softly, laying a hand on her thigh.

"So am I," she whispered and then lapsed into a silence which went unbroken until our first rest stop. It was an angry silence, but it was directed at herself and not at me. So I squeezed her thigh and loved her as best I could until I could think up something better to do.

Rest stops themselves, as I came to quickly find, were an exercise in creativity. Since ushering a bruised and battered Cavallo into the men's room at gunpoint seemed to be out as an option, only Ice and I availed ourselves of the conveniences of modern plumbing. Cavallo got to use the bushes by the side of more or less deserted roads.

Since Ice was much more adept at subduing a dangerous fugitive who wanted us both dead than I, I happily let her do the honors, all the while hoping that she would stuff him into a particularly virulent patch of poison sumac or something equally nasty.

He was actually quite complacent that first day. I think it was the combination of the Valium he'd been given and the fact that the woman who was escorting him to and from said bushes could, and had, beaten the living tar out of him, and wouldn't need much provocation to show off that particular skill again, should he wish a replay.

Rest stops aside, we continued to drive well into the night. The fiftieth attempt to contact Donita fared no better than the first, but I was able to reach Montana, which eased my mind considerably. It seemed that all had gone very well at the ranch. Nia had come through with shining colors, surprising everyone from the Amazons, to the police, to, especially, her husband. A husband who, apparently, came within a hair of going to the bighouse for a *very* long time when the police heard the true tale of why Nia was where she was.

Montana had passed me off to Corinne, who, like me, hadn't been able to get in touch with Donita or anyone else who might know where she was. We commiserated for a while, then hung up as Ice pulled into yet another in a long line of nondescript rest areas. This one was long and narrow, with a few parking spaces, a few picnic tables abutting a small evergreen wood, and a tiny clapboard building with a sign in front announcing that it held restrooms and vending machines within.

Aside from a sleeping trucker or two, the place was utterly deserted. A fact, I guess, which caused Ice to pull in there in the first place.

Knowing well my pea-sized bladder, Ice handed me a flashlight almost as long as my arm and grinned. "Go on and take care of business. I'll get Mr. Personality here settled for the evening."

Which, of course, told me that there was to be no hotel bed in my near future. That made sense, really. Being trapped in a motel room with no chance of escape while the police or whomever else came swarming in like locusts wasn't exactly the brightest plan in the world. And Ice was known for being bright.

Still, after twelve straight hours, the last place I wanted to be right then was that Jeep, nice though it was.

Knowing well that beggars didn't really have choices, I accepted the flashlight gamely and returned her smile with one of my own.

At least her mood seemed to have brightened.

A definite plus, in my book.

Turning on the flashlight's powerful beam, I followed a narrow, trash-strewn path up to the building and hunted for the little silhouette that announced to all but the most criminally idiotic that a ladies' room was lingering about. Opening the splintered and graffiti-laden door, I was immediately assailed by the sickly sweet odor of faux strawberry barely covering the baser scent of stale urine and god only knew what else.

After turning my head to take in a deep breath of fresher air, I stepped inside, tried my best to ignore the way the soles of my hiking boots were sticking to the floor, and made my way to the first stall that didn't have five entire rolls of toilet paper stuffed into the toilet bowl.

"God, this is so disgusting." I could feel my whole face screw up as I relieved the pressure in my bladder while trying my best to stay as far off the toilet seat as I could. If I could envy men for one thing, it would be the ability to pee standing up. My mother's ageless warnings about the correlation between "diseases" and toilet seats rang through my head, and for the first time in my life, I believed there to be some small truth to her tales.

Task completed, I rinsed my hand (there wasn't any soap, of course) and didn't even bother trying to give myself the old "once-over" in the cracked and stained mirror which hung gamely over the sink on one loosening bolt.

Then I made my way back outside, breathing in the fresh, pine-scented air with a distinct feeling of relief. Walking down the trail with the beam of my flashlight leading the way, I caught the movement of Ice as she led Cavallo back to the Jeep.

His gaze met mine in what I assumed he meant to be a

vengeful stare full of venom. However, since the eyes doing the staring were mere slits surrounded by swollen, blackened flesh and sitting atop and to either side of a squashed flat lump of flesh which might once have resembled a nose, I'm afraid all the emotion I could come up with was a mild revulsion. Certainly not the white-faced terror he no doubt was seeking from me.

Catching the look, Ice smirked and basically tossed Cavallo into the rear of the truck, then followed him inside. I finished my trek and slipped into the back seat.

Though Ice and I had stopped at a McHeartAttack's for food, there was almost nothing on the menu to feed a man who couldn't open his jaw wider than a half inch, so we settled on a vanilla milkshake. When I handed the shake over the seat, the man glared at me as if I was handing him dog vomit in a cup. Shrugging, I made as if to pour it out, until a resigned grunt made me smile inside.

Using his cuffed hands, he took the cup, caught hold of the straw, and sucked that shake down in two seconds flat.

I guess even dog vomit tastes pretty good to the hungry.

When he was done, Ice eased him back down and chained him up. Then she unbuckled his pants, over his vehement, if badly garbled, protests, took out a syringe from the black bag I handed her, and sent him back into slumberland, courtesy of some really good drugs.

Dusting off her hands, she leapt out of the back of the truck and slid back into the driver's seat. "What're ya doin'?" she asked, eyeing me over the headrest.

"I figured I'd put some pillows and blankets down," I said, shrugging. "It'll probably be better for you to sleep back here, since you're gonna need the extra space."

"Nah," she countered with a faint shake of her head. "I don't want either one of us that close to him. C'mon up here. We'll have plenty of room."

I looked at her doubtfully, but her smile was, as always, engaging, and whatever questions I might have had melted beneath the sweetness of it.

She was still grinning as I heaved myself back into the front seat. Reaching behind her, she grabbed one of the pillows and stuffed it into the well between the two seats to make the area more or less flat. Then she lifted the steering wheel to its highest, most out of the way point, reclined her own seat back, and patted her lap invitingly.

Though I knew that she meant for me to lie down and put my head in her lap, I just couldn't help myself. It took a good deal of wiggling, but the effort was well worth the pain when my lover found herself with a lapful of me, and I found myself the most comfortable seat known to man. Or woman, for that matter.

Grinning at her slightly stunned look, I planted a cheeky kiss on her nose, then snuggled in and rested my head atop one broad shoulder, nestling into the crook of her neck and inhaling her wonderful scent. "Mmm. You always smell so good."

Wrapping her arms around me, she hugged me tight and rested her cheek on my hair. "So do you."

I touched my lips against the pulse point in her neck, then felt the slow, steady beat pick up a little as my tongue took a little taste of her skin. Really, I couldn't help myself. She tasted so good, I took another sample, and then another, and smiled as her cheek lifted from my head, exposing the long, delectable length of her throat to me.

That was all the invitation I needed, of course.

As my lips explored the strong column of her neck, my hands certainly weren't idle. She'd worn a half-shirt, which was incredibly easy to push up, even from my somewhat awkward position, and in virtually no time at all, I held the soft, warm, firm weight of her breast in my hand.

With that, her head lowered, and mine raised, and our lips met in gentle passion.

Having much easier access, her own hand found its way beneath my shirt, and soon my breasts were being deliciously loved, responding to her touch in a way that sent trails of fire to every point in my body capable of feeling.

Which was pretty damn much everywhere.

I tried to move with her caresses, but I was trapped against the glorious length her body to one side, the damnable steering wheel to the other, and the door behind. The entrapment, however, added a subtle erotic underpinning, which helped further fuel my desire, as if that had ever needed any help where the fabulous woman who was my lover was concerned.

Knowing that the man sharing the Jeep with us was sleeping by the sound of his healthy snores, I relaxed further, and when her lips pressed more insistently against mine, I responded with everything in me, opening myself up to her all the way down to my soul.

The moans on her breath tasted sweet as honey, and I drank

deeply of them while I loved her breasts and the searing heat of her skin with hands tingling from the blood surging through my veins.

Her own hands, so large and so relentless, made their way down my belly and quickly undid the button and zipper of my jeans.

I pulled back from our kiss as her hands reached their goal and began to stroke a raging fire into an all-consuming inferno. "God, yes," I gasped, leaning my head against the cool, moisture-condensed window. "Please...keep...oh...like that, love...yes...just...like that."

"God, I want you," she groaned in reply. Her long fingers delved deep, then retreated, then returned, filling me oh so wonderfully full of her. My hips moved and swayed to the tempo of her thrusts and I had to bite my lip to keep from screaming out my pleasure.

Moving her head forward, she buried it in the crook of my neck and then latched onto my flesh with her lips and teeth as her fingers kept up their never-ending dance within and without. The feel of her teeth hard against my flesh released a flood of passion within me so great that I thought we must both surely drown in it.

I could feel myself opening ever wider to her, my body greedy and hungry for her touch, my need for her almost insurmountable.

Her thighs splayed open and I slipped down between them to rest on the seat. Her hips rocked against the outside of my thigh and her low, guttural moans became grunts of both effort and sublime pleasure as she matched the tempo of her own body to mine in a rapturous dance surely composed by the heavens, so great was its beauty.

I almost yelled aloud when I felt her fingers withdraw, and my eyes popped open, dazed with bliss and shock. "Noooo...."

"I need to taste you, Angel."

"But...."

"Now," she growled, somehow managing to slide herself out from beneath me and position me so that my entire back was pressed flat against the door. My knees were pressed up at the same time my jeans were taken, with no small force, from my hips and down my legs.

It might have almost seemed comical, watching as she somehow fit the long length of her body crosswise against the cramped front seat, but any thought of inappropriate laughter flew right out of my mind when her mouth descended upon me and her ravenous hunger followed. I could feel her lips vibrate against me as she hummed her delight. Her tongue, first silky soft, then firm and insistent, twirled and swirled through my wet heat, before sharp teeth latched on and she suckled lovingly.

I felt as if I'd been turned inside out. Though my eyes screamed out their need to close so that all I would know was the feeling of her loving me, I couldn't keep myself from staring at that glossy black head as she feasted. As if sensing my white-hot stare, she looked up, and her eyes were silver and glittering and completely enraptured.

My fingers twined in her hair and she returned to her task with a fervor only seen in the most devout of worshippers. My body was her altar, my wetness her font, and her mouth paid tribute in the most passionate of ways.

My hips ground against her and she pressed back, pinning me and taking me and loving me beyond measure until my eyes, finally, slipped closed, trapping me inside a body that could do nothing but feel, and pant, and pray.

When her fingers sheathed within me once again, I imploded until there was nothing left of me but a small pinpoint of brilliantly colored light, which grew larger and larger until I became that light and found the freedom to soar among the heavens for one brief, aching, transcendent moment.

And in that brief span of time, I truly knew what it was like to be immortal.

Tears flowed, and I let them, too weak and overcome with emotion to do anything else.

Somehow, I was eased, and turned, and wound back up within the warmth and safety of her arms. Her lips gently dried my tears and landed, like butterflies, on each closed lid, until my eyes fluttered open and I looked at her wonderful face through a filmy haze of tears. "I love you," I said, my voice thick with the tears I'd shed. "So much. Sometimes, the feelings, they...."

"Shhhh," she whispered, holding me close and resting her cheek atop my head. "It's alright, sweet Angel. I understand. Shhh."

She began to hum, softly, beautifully, and as her hand drew soft, lazy circles against my back, I felt my eyes drift closed once again. And though I fought against it for a moment, sleep won out, as it always did, and I felt myself relax by slow degrees, save within the circle of my lover's arms.

The second day started out much like the first, though both Ice and myself were a bit stiffer for the experience of the night before. Not that I minded, of course. Nor did she, if the grin on her face upon seeing me awake was any indication.

After quickly attending to our own needs and those of our rather reluctant guest, we started out again, traveling in a rather vague northeasterly direction with no definite sense of purpose. It was as if we were, like a circling jet awaiting permission to land, in some sort of holding pattern. But unlike such a jet, we didn't have the comfort of a control tower watching out for us.

As we journeyed, I stared out of the window at the passing scenery, and began to notice when the jagged edges of mountains gradually gave way to the more rolling plains that characterized the Midwest. It was a homecoming, of sorts, and one that was by no means happy. Even if the circumstances had been different, my return to the general area of my birth would not have been met with welcome emotions.

I've come to realize, during the course of my adult life, that home isn't necessarily the place where you were born or where you lived as you were growing up. It isn't necessarily the place you settle down into after you've gotten married and think to raise a family. It isn't necessarily the place where you go when you become old, a place where the bright sun leeches the pain from your bones and joints.

No, home is, like it says in countless needlepoint masterworks hanging above countless kitchen sinks, truly where the heart is.

A prison cell. A lakeside cabin. A sprawling ranch. A Mexican hovel. A borrowed Jeep traveling miles from nowhere to nowhere.

My heart was in each and every one of these places far more than it ever was in the house I shared with my parents.

Pretty simple mathematics when you get down to it, really. My home is wherever Ice is. She has my heart, and therefore, she is my home. Think of it as Angel's Theorem, if you like.

In any event, as the afternoon wore on, my "home" decided that it was time to take another bathroom break, for which my kidneys swore their eternal devotion.

I went first, then switched off with Ice, who handed me her gun to use on Cavallo, if needed. I handed it right back to her as if it were a poisonous snake ready to bite my hand off. She handed it back, pretty as you please. "I'm not buying his good little boy act," she whispered, lips brushing close to my ear. "Just do me this favor and keep it on you. I'll take it off your hands in two minutes."

"Oh, alright," I sighed, though as soon as she left, I dropped it on her seat and covered it with an overshirt she'd donned that morning.

A bare second later, I heard the sounds of chains jangling, and the jeep began to rock slightly on its springs as a result of the force Cavallo was using to try and yank himself free from his metal bonds. The interior rang loudly with the noise of his curses.

"Stop it!" I shouted above the din. "You're only going to hurt yourself!"

"I'm gonna hurt you and that fucking bulldyke lover of yours a lot more once I get free," he snarled, though with his still-swollen jaw, it came out as more of a mumble than a clearly voiced threat.

"I don't think that's gonna happen anytime soon," I replied.

"Fuck you!"

"No thanks. You're not my type."

Not the smartest thing in the world to say, I'll agree, but I couldn't seem to help myself. The opening was just too wide not to go on and step through.

He bellowed again, and the jeep shook even more violently as a result of his redoubled efforts to break free. "Why are you doing this to me? Why the *fuck* are you doing this to me?" After a long moment, he half sobbed in frustration and gave up his attempts at escape. Sitting up as much as he was able, he peered over the back seat and pinned me with his angry gaze. "Tell me. I have a right to know."

I shook my head very slowly. "You lost that right the day you set Ice up for a murder you committed, you bastard."

He laughed bitterly. "Screw you, blondie. That was all just part of the game. That bitch Steele knew it. If she wasn't so fucking stupid, she'd have realized she was taking the fall."

"She wasn't stupid."

"Yeah? Then why'd she wind up in jail, huh?" His jaw thrust out in challenge.

"Guess that makes you just as stupid, now, doesn't it?"

His eyes widened and his face purpled. "Fuck no. You ain't takin' me to the cops, are ya? That's fuckin' nuts! Do you know what they'll do to me?"

I might have cared. Once. Now, I only shrugged with studied nonchalance.

"You can't do that to me! You might as well just shoot me now, then! I'm fucking dead! Dead!"

"Maybe you should have thought of that before you shot my lover, hmm? Or before you sent that goon squad of yours after her in Canada?"

"Come on! I fuckin' told ya! It's just part of the game!"

I felt my eyes narrow. "It's not a game to me, Mr. Cavallo. Not at all."

He tried to grin, but the expression looked quite macabre on his swollen and bruised face. "Maybe you should stop playin' with the big dogs then, huh?"

"I'm not the one chained to the doghouse, Mr. Cavallo."

"Fuck you, bitch. Fuck. You."

"Interesting command of the English language you have there. Here's a little tip for you, though. Since I've got the key *and* the gun, you might try lightening up a little on the expletives. They're not winning you very many points."

For a long moment, I thought sure that his head was quite simply going to pop off his neck like a rocket. Then, as if an interior steam valve had suddenly opened, he relaxed against his bonds as the redness drained from his face. "Listen. Whatever they're offering you, I'll double it. Triple it, even. I got money, lots of it."

"All the money in the world wouldn't make me let you go."

"What then? You don't want no one sniffin' up your ass no more? Fine. I can do that. I know people. Lots of people. In high places. They'll make it so no-one's ever heard of ya. You'll be free and clear. Just like that. You want a nice house? A nice car? Jewelry? Gals like jewelry. Whatever you want, name it. It's yours."

"I don't think so."

"Goddamnit, woman! I'm offering you shit on a platter here!"

"That's exactly what you're offering me, Mr. Cavallo. Shit. No matter how nice and gussied up it is, it's still shit. And it stinks."

Once again, his face reddened in anger, but just as quickly, the color drained from it. "Listen, lady, just tell me what you want. Anything you want, anything at all, name it and it's yours. Just let me go, huh?"

It had been a very long time, if ever, that I'd seen a grown man about to cry. Where I once might have felt pity, all I could feel was a faint sense of revulsion, which curled the corners of my lips downward.

Fortunately, I was spared from having to answer him by Ice opening the rear door and climbing inside. Cavallo turned and fought her with everything he was worth, but really, what chance did he have against her?

To her credit, Ice was almost gentle with him, and before even two minutes had passed, he was once again slumbering peacefully, all desire to escape drained out with the drug she'd given him.

"Well, that was fun," she casually remarked as she slid once again into the driver's seat.

"You don't know the half of it," I replied, handing her back her gun. "You know, I stood the chance of becoming a very rich woman in return for just a tiny, little favor."

"Ya did, huh?"

I couldn't hide my grin. "Yup. With all the stuff he was offering up I could have been a queen."

"What stopped ya?"

"I didn't have the heart to tell him I already was one."

Grinning at me, she shook her head and started up the jeep.

"Drive on, footman," I ordered, with an imperious wave of my hand. "My public awaits."

Receiving a gentle pinch to my royal cheek (one of the ones on my face), I burst into laughter as we drove away.

As afternoon bled into evening with the setting of the sun, the cell phone rang, startling me out of the comfortable half-doze I'd fallen into. For two full rings, I stared at it as if a viper had come to life in my lap, before finally picking it up and answering. "Hello?"

"Angel, thank goodness. Where are you?" Donita's voice sounded tinny and far away.

I gulped, caught between extreme relief and niggling

unease. "Donita!" I said, cutting me eyes over to Ice, who gestured with her hand toward a small, nearly deserted strip mall.

Nodding, I returned my attention to the phone. "Are you alright? We've been trying to get a hold of you for the past four days! What happened?"

"Long story," Donita replied. "Are *you* alright?"

"Yes, we're fine."

"That's good to hear." She paused a moment. "Remember how I just asked you where you were? On second thought, don't tell me. It's probably better right now if I don't know."

The unease in my gut grew. "Donita, what's going on?"

A longer pause.

"Are you somewhere you can speak freely?"

I looked over at Ice, and though she couldn't hear the conversation, she divined the meaning of my look, and nodded. I paused myself as I watched her drive us through the strip mall until she came to the end, which housed a rather large 24-hour supermarket, which was quite crowded. Finding a spot near the middle between two smaller cars, she pulled in and parked, then eased herself back in the seat and looked at me expectantly.

"Yeah," I said finally to Donita. "We can talk."

"Alright." She took a deep breath and then let it out slowly. The line went to static for a moment and then cleared. "The reason why you haven't been able to contact me was that I was given three days tax free housing courtesy of a couple of very large, very intimidating FBI agents."

I went very still for a moment as my mind attempted to process what she had just told me. "Are you trying to tell me that you've just spent the past three days in *jail*?" From the periphery of my vision, I could see my lover's jaw tighten.

"Got it in one, Angel."

"But how...why...who?"

"Like I said, it was the FBI. They paid me a little visit and tried to talk me into telling them where you were."

"But...you didn't know!"

"That's what I tried to tell them. They didn't like that answer. The one about attorney-client privilege went over real well, lemme tell ya."

My head whirled in confusion. "I...don't understand. Could you start from the beginning, please?"

Donita laughed slightly. I could picture her holding up one beautifully manicured hand. "Alright. I know I kind of caught you unaware here." She cleared her throat briefly and then began speaking. "It's like this. Someone somewhere's found out that Cavallo has gone missing."

"But how is that linked to us? I mean, you told us this plea agreement was made under the strictest secrecy. How could anyone outside of that meeting room know about it?"

"That's the part I haven't been able to figure out yet. The FBI guys weren't spilling any information. They just wanted mine. Which I didn't have."

"Damn." As I sighed, I felt a warm hand reach out and grasp mine. Despite the gravity of the situation, I couldn't help but smile. Ice looked back, her face shadowed, but her eyes full of concern. Not for what I was being told, but for how I was handling it. I gave her a nod to show her I was ok, but she held onto my hand just the same. I laced our fingers so she wouldn't be pulling away anytime soon. "Ok," I said after digesting her words, "what else?"

"Well, when I wouldn't tell them what they wanted to know, not being blessed with superhuman abilities, they threw an 'obstruction of justice' charge at me and tossed me in the pokey to cool my heels. Couldn't make it stick, though, since they don't have any proof at all that my clients, and that would be you, are in any way involved with anything even remotely illegal. So they let me out without too much of a fuss, but I picked up a couple of tails along the way." She laughed softly. "Managed to give 'em the slip though. For now."

"Where does that leave us?" I asked softly, afraid of the answer.

"Safe. Again, for now. They're spreading a dragnet out around the Pittsburgh area. They're convinced you've kidnapped Cavallo and are gonna use him as a bargaining chip to get the charges against both of you dropped. Which is pretty close to the truth, when you think about it. And, obviously, they do *not* want that to happen."

I paused for a moment, ordering my thoughts and trying to figure the questions that Ice would most want answered. I was actually a little bit surprised that she was so willing to let me take the lead on this, but I figured that if she had that much trust in me, I wasn't going to let her down. "How far out does this dragnet extend?"

"Last I heard, it reached west to Dayton, east to Trenton, and south to DC. There aren't that many agents involved so far, though, so it's pretty much a hit and miss affair."

Inwardly, I breathed a sigh of relief. We were still perhaps a hundred miles to the southwest of St. Louis, well out of the boundaries of the net. At least so far. Another question popped into my mind, and I gave voice to it. "Can you tell me why the FBI is involved? They're federal and the last I heard this was a state matter." I could see Ice nod in satisfaction from the corner of my eye. I smiled again.

"It still is, yes, but someone in the upper echelons of state politics, and no one is saying who, managed to convince the FBI to enter under an interstate kidnapping investigation. Like I said, they're sure you've bagged Cavallo and are traveling somewhere with him. Didn't take much to push the right buttons, and presto, enter the FBI."

"Jesus," I blew out, resting my head against the cool window. "What a mess."

"You said it, Angel."

"So, what do we do now?"

"Best thing is to sit tight. I know that's difficult, since I gather you've left the ranch already. But coming anywhere near Pittsburgh is a very, *very* bad idea. Those men want Cavallo, and they don't much care how they get him. He's government enemy number one around here."

I choked out a laugh. "And we're pretty much in there at two and three, aren't we?"

"With a bullet, I'm afraid."

"Your choice of similes leaves a lot to be desired, Donita."

She hissed through her teeth. "Sorry."

"It's alright," I replied, feeling a headache gather behind my eyes. The queasy kind that makes your guts roll and your head spin. "So, we're just supposed to what...drive around in circles until somebody either catches us or figures out what to do with us? Is there *anybody* in the government on our side anymore?"

I knew I was whining, but I couldn't seem to help it.

"Yes, Angel, there are. The good guys want Cavallo just as bad as the bad guys. And they're doing their best to make that happen, but it's a very uphill battle, I'm afraid. They're fighting against an entire mountain of state politics and a good ol' boy network the size of China. And you know how quickly the wheels of bureaucracy turn."

"Like maple syrup in a Vermont winter."

"Just about." It was her turn to sigh. "I'm sorry. I'm supposed to be your lawyer and your friend, and I'm doing a piss poor job at both."

"No you're not, Donita. We're all just in a bad spot here. We'll just keep...um...driving around till you let us know what's going on, ok?"

"Yeah, ok." She sounded dejected, but then her voice brightened. "One somewhat bright spot, though. If this all continues to turn sour, just dump Cavallo off in the nearest trash-bin and head west. I have a few friends there who will keep you safe. They used to do work for the Witness Protection Program, and believe me when I tell you, they're in the habit of making some very famous people disappear."

"Not permanently, I hope."

She laughed. "Well, not in the way you're thinking, no. So, just sit tight, and I'll get back to you as soon as I know anything. I'm just about to wake the Lieutenant Governor out of his date with the blonde-who-isn't-his-wife he had dinner with this evening. Wish me luck."

"Good luck."

"You too, Angel. Tell Ice I said 'hi,' ok?"

"I will."

"Night, Angel."

"Night, Donita."

As I closed the phone with a dejected snap, Ice removed her hand from mine and took it from me. Laying it down in the space between the seats, she then gathered me into her arms as best she could, and rested my head against her shoulder. "It'll be alright, Angel," she whispered, kissing my temple. "I promise."

And because it was Ice, and because I love her and trust her more than I ever thought it was possible to love and trust another person, I did what my heart told me to do.

I believed.

Whoever said that life is just one big series of giant circles was right on the money.

There's nothing else I can think of that comes close to explaining why, nearly three years to the day later, I'm sitting in a hotel room very much like the one I went to with Ice on the day of my release from prison, writing on a pad of paper cheap and grainy enough to be from the same tree, and waiting to dash off somewhere yet again just one step ahead of the police.

It's almost as if the intervening three years between that event and this were just some hallucinogenic or fever inspired dream I couldn't wake up from.

But the difference in my body and the new lines on my face tell a story all their own and, personally, I'm glad it wasn't all just a dream, since there were definitely huge parts of it I'm glad I was there to experience in the flesh, as it were.

It's been twenty-four hours since the conversation with Donita that I related here. Twenty-four hours of mostly bad news.

It didn't start off that way, of course. It never does.

Donita had managed to get a hold of the Lieutenant Governor, apparently our one powerful ally in all this. He didn't seem to mind overmuch getting yanked out of his tête-à-tête with his latest blonde du jour and agreed to help as best he could.

Things moved swiftly throughout the morning, and I could feel an expectant hope bubble up within me. Even Ice seemed to pick up the mood of the day, and her eyes held a sparkle I hadn't seen in a long while.

But the eleventh hour, in this case noon, changed all that when the Lieutenant Governor ran up against a group of men with much bigger axes to grind, and so quickly lost the will to fight.

Like Cinderella's ball gown, our hopes for a peaceful resolution faded away into nothingness and left tattered rags in its place.

Ice happened to field that particular call, and needless to say, our cell phone is now history, may it rest in pieces.

It was then that she decided to take matters into her own hands.

And so we wound up here, on the outskirts of a large, midwestern metropolitan airport, in a small, seedy hotel run by some friends of hers. Friends with heavy beards, crooked noses, and bodies that looked like they could stop a speeding train without breaking into a sweat. Friends who took the description "shady character" and made it into somewhat of an art form. And friends that Ice could, and did, trust with her life. And mine as well.

Cavallo's here too, kept in a separate room, and being watched over constantly by the largest of the bunch. A true bully, our captive turned belly up the very second he set his eyes on his new keeper. I haven't heard a peep from him since, which is just as well, since I have a headache that could drop a raging bull.

We argued bitterly today. For hours, it seemed. So bitterly that I must confess to a tiny thrill of fear seeping into my soul as I watched her eyes, silver and glittering with rage, set upon me. It was only for an instant, but in that instant, I felt what her victims must have felt when staring into those same glowing eyes. And it frightened me. Then she walked away and left me all but trembling in her wake.

We were arguing about her plan, of course, and my part in it. Which was to say, none.

She wanted me far away from here, from her. From danger. The city was large, she said, and her friends would help me blend into it. We had money, lots of it thanks to Corinne, and I could set myself up nicely as the events around us unfolded. I'd be safe, she said. And free.

And, of course, I bought none of it.

We got into this together, and we are going to get out of it together, or not at all.

I can be as stubborn as a two-headed mule when I put my mind to it. And this time, my mind was very much "to" it. I wasn't about to be swayed. Not by her pleas. Not by her rage.

It is my right to stand by her side. I've earned it. And I'm not about to give it up.

In the end, as I've said, she walked away, her anger following her like a roiling thundercloud. She returned an hour or two ago, and though her anger was still there, her mood had mellowed to one of quiet resignation.

She sleeps now, but it isn't a peaceful one. She tosses and turns, and at times, reaches out for me.

And though every fiber of my being aches to join her on that narrow bed, I don't. Because I know, sure as the sun rises in the east, that if I give into my impulses, I'll wake up alone in the morning and she'll be far, far away.

And I'm not about to let that happen.

And so here I sit, drinking cup after cup of wretched coffee, and wile away the hours writing and watching my lover in her fitful sleep, and pray that this plan brings us the peace we both so desperately need.

Her friends have leant us a car. A car so bland that it could blend in with vanilla pudding and no one would be the wiser.

That car will be our means of escape.

Cavallo will be transported by another friend, trussed up and drugged in the back of the jeep, to a spot in the airport's long-term parking area. When the time is right, that friend will place a call to Donita with Cavallo's location, and the chase will be on.

If there's any justice in the world, Donita and the good guys will find him first.

I doubt that will happen, though.

As for us, we'll be on our way to Donita's safe house in our bland little car.

I just hope to God we make it.

It's rather amusing; the things that people say when they think you can't hear them. I've often thought of explaining to the women around me that just because I choose not to speak doesn't mean that I can't hear, or listen, or feel.

I've never followed through on that, however. After all, what would be the point? Would it lessen the pity in their eyes when they look at me? Would it turn their thoughts and words to more pleasant things?

I don't bear them any ill will, in any event. They're young and filled with life. Grief, for them, burns fast and hot, like a flash fire, and is quickly gone, forgotten beneath the exciting weight of the life they're busy living.

My grief lingers, an old enemy come home to roost. It has been with me so long that some days it seems more cherished friend than bitter adversary.

My true friends have all gone, and like the strangers they've left in their places, I bear them no ill will. They have jobs to do and people who need them. The world continues to turn, after all, no matter how much we sometimes wish it wouldn't.

They asked, one might even say "begged" me to accompany them, but the thought of spending the coming winter in a place so desolate and so cold outweighs my desire to have them close around me.

Only Nia has remained behind. She's blossomed into a kind, compassionate woman whose beauty shines brightly from the inside, as it was meant to. She endures my long, morose silences with nary a complaint and helps tend to the few needs I have. Sometimes I despair of what I perceive to be her wasted and wasting life, but she is quick to smile and reassure me that, right now, there's no place she'd rather be.

Perhaps it's a time and a place of healing for us both.

They say that the young live for the future, and the old live for the past. And while once I might have fought anyone with the temerity to actually spout that drivel to me, now I see those words for truth and accept that truth as my own.

While I might have more things to live for, if you can truly call this living, memories seem to be the only things I want to live for.

And memories I have, both in my head where they play constantly like a film I don't have to pay money to see, and in the stacks of journals and scrapbooks which take up constant and reassuring residence at my side. Though I've left the prison library far behind me, it appears my affinity for all things readable has followed me patiently, simply waiting for a time that I was still and quiet enough to realize it.

The journals I've read and reread and reread until the words themselves have taken up residence in my brain. I've memorized them all, I think, several times over. But if there's one good thing to be had by living as long as I have, memory isn't exactly what it used to be. At least short term.

Which means that every time I open one of those precious books, I see the words before me again, as fresh and as exciting and as new as when I first set eyes on them, a little more than a year ago. A small joy perhaps, but in a life filled with anything but, it's a joy I take and hold to me with all the selfishness of a young child asked to share his toys with a stranger.

The scrapbooks I've read and reread as well, but they bring me no joy, and in that I am very thankful that my mind tends to lose hold of the images presented within rather quickly.

For the scrapbooks pick up where the journals leave off, chronicling the last journey of the two women I love most in the world, the women who took my heart and spirit with them when they left, and have never returned it.

They almost made it, you see. Almost, being the operative word. And deep within this rotting blackness I sometimes call a heart, there lives a tiny glimmer of hope that they did, in fact, make it, despite the overwhelming evidence to the contrary.

The others don't share that hope, and I'm hardly in the position to case aspersions upon them for that. It's not as if I don't sound crazy, even to my own mind.

But the elderly have some immunity when it comes to off-the-norm thoughts. It's expected of us, so rather than a shot of Thorazine and lovely men in pristine white coats, I only need suffer the slight indignity of pitied glances and thoughtless words.

I suppose, for one to get the full effect, I should start at the beginning, or at least as close to the beginning as I am able to get. Donita has been kind enough to fill in some of the massive holes left behind, but most of what I know is spread out before me in lines of newspaper ink much too small for my aging eyes to easily comprehend, even with the benefit of the glasses I've been cursed to wear since I was much younger and more sprightly of form and face.

The drop was made as planned, and Donita received her phone call. There was a jet, fueled and ready, and a freshly minted court order she'd managed to pull out of her bag of tricks, along with the state prosecutor who'd originally penned the deal (and hadn't been one lick of help since) as well as two sworn officers of the court who were charged with taking Cavallo into custody.

Somewhere along the way, however, a leak developed, and the FBI jumped in on the case before Donita's plane had even left the runway. Because they have agents in almost every state, the FBI had a tremendous advantage over Donita.

The only information they didn't possess, it seemed, was the make of the car Cavallo was held in. That was one thing Donita had sense enough to keep all to herself, and it quite probably saved his life.

The FBI was already searching the lot when Donita's cavalry came over the hill, so to speak, and I imagine the scene at that time somewhat resembled one of those horrid game shows where the contestants debase themselves by rushing up and down supermarket aisles in search of a certain, big money, product.

The payoff in this case, however, would either make or break the fools in the statehouse who call themselves a government.

I'm told that Donita and the FBI arrived at the holding spot at very much the same time. And perhaps the fight for custody of one simple, if inherently evil, man would have been much fiercer if not for one very large Ace the lawyer held up her sleeve.

The press.

In my scrapbook, there is a picture in grainy news ink that shows Donita holding up her court order for all to see. A triumphant grin is plastered all over her lovely features. She really is quite fetching in her guise of Avenging Angel, and I've told her so, once or twice over the years. Off to the side in the same picture stand several very angry looking men, the bulges in their coats a testament to the heavy firepower they are carrying.

The copy below tells the story very briefly and very succinctly. Donita got her man. The FBI was left empty-handed.

And that should have been the conclusion to this sordid little tale. But it wasn't.

Government agents detest being played for fools, and if they can't take their frustrations out on the guilty, the innocent will do nicely in their stead.

With Cavallo caught and hauled away, there was no reason to continue to chase after Ice and Angel. But continue they did, determined to exact their pound of flesh in whatever way they deemed necessary. That it had stopped being necessary the minute Cavallo was arrested may well have entered into their minds, but it never stayed their hands. Off they went on another chase, one they determined would not end without bearing fruit.

Donita knew none of this, but I don't have it within my heart to blame her for her uncustomary lapse of judgment, though not a day goes by when she doesn't lay that blame upon herself.

The court order had called off the hounds. As is sometimes the way with curs, they turned a deaf ear to their master and continued on the chase, unabated.

No one will ever know with certainty whether or not Ice felt the loop of the dragnet begin to close about her neck. I believe that she did. For it is my steadfast tenet that Ice is, at heart, a feral, wild creature who lives bound to instincts most of us who embrace the so-called civilizing influences cannot begin to comprehend. Such a creature seems, with preternatural senses, to know when danger is closing in.

Perhaps it was that sense of unseen danger, or perhaps it was just a desire to travel a less beaten path, but something made her choose to turn off of a well-traveled highway and onto an almost deserted forest road.

Several witnesses, for there were witnesses, stated that the driver of the log truck coming in the opposite direction had been driving erratically for miles. One of the men who had passed him earlier stated that he saw the driver red-faced and clutching at his chest. Based upon this one report, the coroner concluded that the driver's cause of death was a heart attack. Not enough of the man has ever been found to challenge that diagnosis.

By far the best witness was a young woman, fresh out of college, who had stopped by the side of the road in an attempt to change a flat tire. She never saw the truck coming straight for her, she reported. Never even knew of the imminent danger until an off-white car on her side of the road came, as she says, "charging forward", and a young blonde woman fitting Angel's description exactly screamed at her to run.

She was only able to jump a short distance away before the log truck collided with the front left of the white car, dragging them both down a long, grassy hill. The rear bumper of the car hit the young woman's leg, breaking it, but doubtless saving her life in the process. As she rolled from the impact, she was able to see the very tops of both car and truck as they teetered for a long moment at the edge of a ravine. Then they toppled over and dropped, I'm told, more than fifty feet to the bolder-strewn ground below.

Both vehicles exploded on impact, which started a small forest fire that took several hours to contain.

There wasn't much of anything left when the police came to look for survivors.

We didn't hear of the news until three days later, and the memory of that phone call sits etched indelibly within this capricious brain of mine. Though my descriptive abilities certainly pale in comparison to Angel's aptitude with words, I can only state that if Stonehenge had been given form and face, it would resemble almost exactly the tableau in the living room as Montana ended the call from Donita.

After the shock came disbelief. Which was in no way surprising, in that Ice had by that time attained immortal status among the Amazons. More logical minds pointed out that there simply wasn't enough evidence to conclude anything, no matter what the FBI and the local police were stating with such surety.

Critter, Pony, Cowgirl, and Cheeto made the immediate decision to investigate the matter themselves. They left without packing. The rest of us remained behind, too shocked to speak, even among ourselves.

What they found wasn't revealed to me until well after the

fact. My last clear memory of that night was drifting off into a somewhat fitful sleep.

That sleep was indeed a long one, for when I awakened next, it was fully two weeks later, and I found myself staring at a vast, if rather bewildering, array of medical equipment which surrounded me. I had, apparently, had another stroke, my recovery from which was compounded by what the doctors said was a "rather massive" heart attack. I was told that I was lucky to have survived it.

One look in Critter's eyes told me that such "luck" was a cursed, wretched thing indeed.

I heard the story in tiny increments, in between shots of Morphine to keep me calm and tests that caused far more agony than my life, such that it is, is worth.

The Amazons managed to track down what few witness to the accident there were, including, most importantly, the young woman whose life had been saved by the timely and heroic intervention of two strangers in a white car.

Her description of the woman who had encouraged her to flee was unwavering. Attractive, short blonde hair and brilliant green eyes. As that description also fit a rather large number of women, Pony and the others weren't unduly concerned.

They had brought with them some pictures; some of Angel, some of other women of similar description.

It had all happened so fast, the witness related, though she pointed out the pictures of Angel as bearing the most resemblance to the woman in the car. She couldn't be positive, she warned. She hoped they understood.

But then she saw another picture, and I'm told she stiffened and the color drained from her face.

"That's her," she said. "That's the driver of the car. Those eyes. I've never seen a color of blue like that before, and they were so *angry*! I still have nightmares about them."

After that, Pony reported, the woman became closed-mouthed and wouldn't utter another word, no matter how much they pleaded with her.

Armed with no further information, they left and drove to the scene of what was euphemistically being touted as an "accident."

"There's no way they could have survived it, Corinne," Pony told me after she returned, much against doctor's orders, and with tears streaming down her face. "No way. And even if they did, they couldn't have outrun the fire. It's just impossible. They're gone. Both of them. For good."

I'm afraid I underwent a moment of insanity then, though I don't remember very much of it, except for the memory of a brilliant rage which consumed me, rendering me, even in my weakened state, insensate and all but impervious to the pain I knew I must have been feeling. I hated them all in that moment. Hated Pony for giving up, hated Ice and Angel for dying, and hated myself most of all, for living.

It matters little, however, for that brief lapse into insanity garnered me nothing but the need to be restrained against the possibility of "hurting myself" again.

If it is true that the human species can die simply by willing it so, that fact must have been left out of my genetic make-up, for I believe no person ever willed themselves away from life as strongly as I did during that time.

Yet my traitorous body ignored my wishes and became stronger, until the time came when I was well enough to be released from the hospital.

And the world continued to turn on, uncaring.

As my body continued to heal, I withdrew into myself and refused to speak, even to those closest to me. I remained, however, acutely aware of life going on around me. And, in particular, the events transpiring in Pennsylvania.

The wheels of justice do indeed turn slowly, but eventually, the inevitable occurred. Cavallo was given his day in court, and a government crumbled as a result. Several high-ranking officials went to prison for an entire laundry list of crimes, and others resigned in disgrace, preferring such ignominy to facing the prospect of a long prison term, or worse.

And, thanks to Donita, both Ice and Angel were remembered for their part in lending aid. With firm political pressure aided by the ever-present news media, the Governor was finally pressured into honoring the plea agreement and issuing posthumous pardons to both women as well as ordering their criminal records expunged.

Ice had finally made full restitution for her crimes.

If only she were alive to know of it.

Donita sent me those pardons two weeks ago. They now hang, framed, on the living room wall for all to see. I never pass by without stopping to look at them and run my fingers against the bold, floridly written names of the two women I love. Those scraps of paper, so insignificant to most, are the only memorial I have, save for the journals and the scrapbooks and my own fading memories.

Montana, Critter, Pony, and the rest keep in contact with me, and the weekly phone calls are the only time I consent to speak, aside from brief conversations with Nia. They are all doing as well as can be expected.

The world turns and the living move on.

Only the old and the sick seemed trapped by time's immovable weight, maudlin a thought as that is.

Donita keeps in contact as well, though her busy life limits the number of phone calls she has time to make. We communicate mostly by letters, which I find comforting, in some ways. Letter writing is a lost art, and I was sad to see its passing.

She often tries to brighten my mood with various and sundry bits of nonsense, and constantly chastises me for allowing myself to give up on life. Her threats, of course, hold little sway over me, though I do appreciate that she has taken the time to voice them. I sometimes regret the stony front I put up, but I believe that she understands.

We are bound by our love and respect for two extraordinary women, and a bond of that nature forgives flaws.

I received another such letter—a small packet, really—from her just today, and the contents, though by no means exceptional, caused this entire sojourn into memories past and painful. And though my hand is stiff and aching, perhaps this solitary journey into the past has helped somewhat to ease the demons of pain and guilt which plague me still.

The envelope contained a photograph of the sun setting over some tropical paradise or other. I suppose the setting could be considered beautiful if you enjoy that sort of thing. The photograph was wrapped within a small sheet of unlined paper, which contained a plane ticket and two words.

Small words. Simple ones, really. Insignificant, when taken apart, but when put together, containing enough power to rekindle the flame of hope dancing weakly in a heart weary of living.

Perhaps I'm nothing but a fool for believing in them. But if I am, I shall bear the title of "fool" proudly and damn all who would hope to think otherwise.

The ticket is to an island called Bonaire, someplace in the Southern Caribbean. I imagine that that island is the one shown in the picture in my hand.

And the words?

Simple enough to write, even with an aching hand.

But wondrous enough that I would break my long vow of silence and shout them at the very top of my lungs.

Come home.

EPILOGUE

I sit in the warm, dry sand, the trunk of a tall, stately palm doing double duty as an uncomplaining backrest as I write out my thoughts on a simple pad of paper. The brim of my floppy straw hat helps to shade my eyes from the low, setting sun whose heat warms my mostly bare body in the most wonderful of ways.

The breeze is likewise warm and brings with it the ever-present scent of the sea. Overhead, seabirds whirl and dive for their dinners against the brilliant backdrop of a sky bursting with a kaleidoscope of colors as the sun plays out its last over the open ocean, gilding it in rose and gold.

Thoroughly content in a way I have never before been, I stretch complacent muscles, pleased when they respond quickly and without pain. My broken arm, courtesy of our unfortunate encounter with a runaway truck, is fully healed, and I'm near to being ecstatic that I can write again.

I hear a sound off to my left and turn my head to see Corinne heading my way with a glass pitcher of iced tea and two large tumblers. Her colorful caftan flutters in the breeze and I don't even bother holding in my laughter as her hat, nearly identical to my own, flies off of her head like some new species of wingless bird.

She scowls at me but can't hold the expression for long before the grin, which has become a nearly permanent fixture, reappears on her face.

Gone is the gray, sickly pallor that colored her skin when she first arrived. Gone too is the stiffness of a body grown weak with age and infirmity. She almost glows now and appears nearly half her age, as if Bonaire housed the mythical Fountain of Youth and she has drunk her fill from it.

The guilt, heartache, and tears that plagued our first meeting are things of the past as well. She understands why events played out as they did, and accepts the need we had to continue the charade of our deaths until the final pardons came through. She also says that she understands why we have chosen a place so far away to call our home, and I have no reason to disbelieve her.

"I don't suppose you'd be willing to do an old woman a favor and chase down my hat, would you?"

I laugh again, shaking my head as I accept the chilled glass of tea, which she hands me. "We'll get another one tomorrow."

"I could well be dead by then, you know," she replies, lowering her body to the sand next to me.

"Well, then you won't need it anymore, now will you?" I reply cheekily.

"The youth these days are so very rude," she tsks in the tone of a true martyr.

"Yeah, but you wouldn't trade me for the world," I reply, taking my own hat off and plunking it down on her head.

She adjusts the hat primly before clinking her glass with mine. We sit together in a comfortable silence as the sun continues its final journey to the west.

I look up, and my eyes track the ungainly flight of a flamingo as it moves to the south toward the fresh water lake not far from our home. If there is a god, he or she certainly must be blessed with a wicked sense of humor to create such a creature.

"Mother Mary, have mercy on the soul of this poor sinner."

Corinne's nearly breathless whisper distracts me and I turn to see her, wide-eyed and clutching at her chest.

"Corinne?" I ask, alarmed. "What's wrong?"

She doesn't answer, just continues staring out to sea.

I turn my head slowly, and am then struck with the same affliction.

Out from the water my lover comes as if birthed from the sea itself.

A mask and snorkel are clasped loosely in one hand, swim fins in the other, and the only covering on her body is her deep tan and the sheets of seawater which glide down her magnificent form in iridescent droplets of shimmering fire. Backlit by the setting sun, she is beauty incarnate. Wild, and untamed, and as free as the sea behind her.

I jump to my feet before my mind even realizes my body's intentions, and fly across the sand faster than I have ever run before.

She drops her gear and opens her arms just as I jump into them. With a joyful shout, she twirls me around and around. The sound of our laughter mingles with the sound of the sea.

Then she sets me down, and I am breathless as I look into eyes the exact color of the water behind me. So beautiful they are, so clear and unfettered and filled with the joy of living. No black shadows mar their pristine depths; no guilt mutes their brilliant hue.

I can see right down to her very soul, and what I see is peace and love and joy, and it is so *very* beautiful.

Her teeth are uncommonly white against the deep, burnished tan of her face as she smiles openly at me, looking very much like the young girl in the picture I so treasure, radiating an innocence once so cruelly stripped away from her. Her body is warm and pliant and taut with muscle, and we glide together on the beads of water still dotting her skin.

Our lips come together without pretext or warning. She tastes of the sea, and of passion, and of promise.

I respond, melding my body to hers. My heart and soul follow effortlessly.

The kiss leaves us both breathless as we finally break apart, and we stare at one another, the smiles threatening to shatter our faces.

"I love you, Morgan Steele."

"And I love you, Tyler Moore." A damp hand tenderly cups my cheek as a strong thumb brushes across my lips. "My Angel."

Still embracing, we turn slightly so that we both face the sea, and I lay my head on her chest as the last crescent of the sun dips below the gilded ocean, setting it aflame.

Our journey has been a long one, filled with danger and heartache and angst. But at the end of it, we have both come to find what it was we were searching for all along.

Love.

Peace.

Freedom.

Joy.

And standing on the precipice of this new life we've won, I find that despite the hardships and despite the grief, I am, and always have been, the luckiest woman in the world.

Angel

Be sure to read Susanne M. Beck's

Retribution

Retribution is a story with action, drama, suspense...and too many emotions to list. Told by Angel herself, it will let you see into her very soul.

This sequel to *Redemption* details the lives of Ice and Angel as they cross over the border and try to make new lives in a small vacation town in Canada. They meet both friends and enemies along the way and their love for one another grows and deepens. But obviously, as a fugitive from justice, danger is always only one step away from Ice. The man who fixed it so she was sent to jail for a crime he committed is out to get her again. Several of his cronies manage to find her, and she trades her life for Angel's and is dragged away. Can she save herself and find her way back to Angel and happiness?

Available now at booksellers everywhere

(ISBN 1-930928-24-6)

Other titles from
RENAISSANCE ALLIANCE

Darkness Before the Dawn
By Belle Reily

Chasing Shadows
By C Paradee

Forces of Evil
By Trish Kocialski

Out of Darkness
By Mary A. Draganis

Glass Houses
By Ciarán Llachlan Leavitt

Storm Front
By Belle Reilly

Coming Home
By Lois Cloarec Hart

And Those Who Trespass Against Us
By H. M. Macpherson

Available at booksellers everywhere.

Sue is an RN who has been writing stories for about 20 years now. She lives in Atlanta with her computer, some books, a bunch of Xena stuff, and two dogs.

9 781930 928657